Reckless

Reckless

Cydney Rax
Niobia Bryant
Grace Octavia

KENSINGTON BOOKS
http://www.kensingtonbooks.com

CONTENTS

Desperate Housewife

Cydney Rax

Part 1

This Is a Man's World

1

A heavy rain steadily pours from a cloud-filled sky. Even though it's seven in the morning in late August, the sun is hiding above the clouds. It looks pure ugly outside. And my day isn't starting out very well.

I'm sitting in the passenger seat of my beautiful red candy Lincoln MKT. I feel paranoid. Can everyone see the worry on my face as I'm driving to meet my husband, Forrest, for breakfast? The roads are slick. Dangerously wet. One false move and my SUV could veer off the road. Crash headfirst into an eighteen-wheeler. What if I die? Would death feel better than how I feel right now?

Confronting Forrest Foster is something I dread with everything inside me. Arguing is so draining. Pointless at times. I love peace. Harmony. There's nothing better than when I feel strongly connected to my husband, when we're joking, laughing, sharing a loving smile, and just bonding. Conflict doesn't allow for the good things that I adore.

But I have to go to him. And meeting my husband in a public place is the best way to handle this. I dread confronting him in the privacy of our home. At home it would be just the two of us, hidden behind high walls and closed venetian blinds. After hearing what I'm about to ask him, my husband may get angry and scream at the top of his lungs, sounding and looking as mean as Joe Jackson. The last time Forrest got angry, he screeched so loud it caused such a commotion that the neighbors heard him. My face reddened with shame. I never want to repeat that scene.

It takes another twenty minutes of driving before I arrive at Dot Coffee Shop. Dot's is a popular Houston eatery that serves home-style cooking. They bake some of the best hot buttered rolls within miles. We've eaten here many times; times when things were great between us.

When I enter through the front entrance, I immediately see my husband. I wave and slide into a booth right across from Forrest. I'm calmly staring at him with my hands resting on the wooden table. I silently peer at the man whom I've trusted with my heart for more than seven years. His handsome face consists of a square chin, thick brows above deep-set brown eyes, full lips, neat mustache, and eyelashes so long any vain woman would kill to have them. His broad shoulders, muscular thighs, and long legs make him look like a strong, foreboding type of man.

Forrest Foster is my sexy red-bone soul mate.

Mine.

"Heyyy baby," he greets me. When he's happy, his talking voice sounds like he's singing. "So wassup? You never wake up this early when you don't have the girls." He closely scrutinizes the oversized menu even though he orders the same thing every time we come here. Silly man.

I take a nervous glance around the restaurant. We're seated in a tiny corner and out of view of many of the other talkative patrons. It's busy this morning. The drone of the ringing cash register adds to the energy of the restaurant.

Even so, I lower my voice. "Well, um. I wanted to talk."

"I don't know why you didn't just wait till I got home. I would've been there right after work."

"Oh really?" I ask, sounding doubtful.

Forrest carefully sets his menu on the table. He grabs my hands and pulls them in his. His hands feel soft and welcoming, one more thing I love about him.

"Where's your gold band?" I whisper, nodding at his left hand.

"Huh? It's probably at home . . . in the bathroom . . . on the counter."

"Probably?"

"Look, Carmen, I'm sensing this weird vibe from you." He releases my hands. "Why don't you just tell me why we're meeting here instead of talking at the crib?"

"To be blunt, I wasn't sure you'd come straight home."

"Where else would I be?"

I take a deep breath. "Toni called the house at five this morning."

"So what?"

"She called private, Forrest. I don't like when people call private."

"How'd you know it was her?"

"Don't you remember we can check who phones our landline even if they call private?"

"Oh, you on some bullshit, huh? You're some type of female James Bond now?"

Forrest sounds very disappointed. God, I hate this.

He sneers at me, looking deeply in my eyes. I'm sure he sees the coldness. The lifelessness. I don't want to feel this way, or appear so distressed. Not until I hear his explanation.

But every time I bring up Toni, my husband gets in a funky mood.

"Okay. Big deal. Toni called. That's not unusual. It's probably about Dante."

"But why wouldn't she just call your cell?"

"Maybe it was turned off at the time. Shittttt. I don't know." He barks at me. My insides stiffen with dread. I pray he can control the volume of his voice.

"Forrest, just tell me one thing. Are you fucking Toni?"

"What?"

"Answer. The. Question. Yes or no."

"No!" he shouts. "She's my baby mama. That's all she ever was. All she'll ever be."

"Okay, okay." I nervously back down when I notice two wrinkly faced women staring.

But I can't help but feel skeptical of his claim of not messing around with his ex. The IMs I recently found on his computer screen won't allow me to believe him. The tender words he wrote her convict him.

I miss that. LOL. When we gonna do it again?

And Toni's words in response to his:

bAby u know u can have me anytime, anyplace. xOxo.

Guilty until proven innocent.

"Carmen." He speaks in a more gentle voice. "I've worked hard all night. We had two close calls with my train, plus some of my cargo was missing."

Forrest works as a railroad conductor and has many important responsibilities.

"So these assholes are watching me like a hawk, like I'm incompetent or not on top of my game. That's why I hate working third shift. Always something going down."

"I know, babe. I know," I reply, trying to match his calmness so we won't cause a scene.

"Then why are you starting BS this early in the morning over stupid-ass Toni?"

Forrest calling his baby mama "stupid" doesn't impress me. Not anymore. The fact that he met Toni before he knew me and had a baby with her before we dated used to bother me. But when he married me instead of Toni, I felt like our love was secure. He wasn't going to let any baby mama drama seep into our relationship. And back then, to prove his love, Forrest presented me with a beautiful diamond solitaire, gave me his last name, and solidified his commitment.

"Look," I say and whip out my iPhone. I show him three tiny photos that I'd snapped of the IMs that were on his desktop computer screen. Disturbing messages between my husband and Toni, the mother of their fourteen-year old son, Dante.

"What's that," he asks, squinting.

"That's what I'm trying to find out."

"Woman, I can't see that. It's all blurry. Why are you playing games?" His voice is getting louder. I have no appetite. But Forrest, who quickly shifts gears and begins smiling at the homely waitress who approaches our table, asks her to bring him a plate of French toast, two scrambled eggs, grits, hash browns, sausage, and a big glass of orange juice.

When the waitress leaves, I ask, "You act like you're eating for two. Are you?"

"Shut up, Carmen. Just be quiet."

"Forrest, all I want is the truth. These photos, they're IMs of conversations between you and that, that—" I scowl like I'm sucking lemons.

"Watch it, now. She's Dante's mother."

"And I'm your wife. I deserve the utmost respect. If you flirt with that woman and cross boundaries with her, no wonder she's treating me like I'm the jump-off."

"Don't be silly. Toni knows how to stay in her lane."

I loudly sigh and expel a frustrated breath. I can't believe my husband is so willing to eat a king's meal while I'm sitting up here ready to bite off all my fingernails. An expensive manicure that he paid for. What's his problem?

"I just want to know how long have y'all been fucking? Don't lie. Because you're cold busted," I say, waving my phone at him.

"You don't know what you're talking about."

"Oh right. With some men, unless they get caught in the act, they've done nothing wrong, is that how it goes?"

"Shhhh, Carmen. You're making a fool of yourself."

Now men, women, and even cute little babies are gaping at us.

I hop up from the table. "I'll be back." I can't stand to sit across from Forrest any longer. I feel so frustrated. I hate fighting. And I despise the invisible wall sandwiched between us. Why is he acting so cold? He's in denial. I guess I am, too. When something seems too damn perfect it usually is. For the past seven years I've been pretending like I have the most perfect husband, the most wonderful life.

I'm sick of pretending.

Like Toni said when she called this morning, she likes to keep it "one hunnert."

It's time I start living in the real world, and keep it one hundred myself.

2

I'm barricaded in the ladies' room of the restaurant and examining my face in the mirror. I've been blessed with perfect oil-free skin, strong high cheekbones, wide black eyes that sparkle when I smile, and thick dark hair braided from the front to the crown; the back of my head is filled with lush curls that cascade to my shoulders. I look fabulous, chic, and friendly from the outside, but inside Carmen Foster feels miserable. It's like my brain is about to explode and that's not how I want to feel.

I reflect on the words Toni and I exchanged in the wee hours of the morning when she decided to pick up her phone and call ours.

"Forrest there?"

The call came in as private. But I know Toni's breathy voice even when she's trying to disguise it. "Toni, why are you calling here asking for my husband? Don't you know he's at work?"

"Last night Forrest told me he might not go to work. That he was feeling sick and may call in. I'm checking on him and trying to find out what happened."

He never told me he was feeling sick, although I did hear him sneezing a couple of times before he left for work.

"Well, he's not here so . . ."

"Poor baby. So dedicated. Be a sweetheart and ask him to call me."

I bristle with anger.

"Toni, may I ask you something?"

"It's a free country."

"Why do I sense that you're fucking with me?"

"Oh, it's not you who I'm fucking, honey."

"And what's that supposed to mean?"

"If you had been doing your job as a woman, you wouldn't be going through this."

"Going through what?" I ask in breathless anger.

"Humph, I'm wasting my time talking to you. If he's over here with me does he really belong to you? Even if you do have his so-called ring and last name? Ask him where *his* ring is. Humph. Ask him that."

"Toni, what's this really about?"

"I'm keeping it one hunnert. And I recommend you start doing the same."

That heffa hung up even when I tried to respond. I flung the iPhone onto the bed. I wondered what the hell was going on. Was this woman still bitter over the fact that Forrest and I got married even after she rejected his engagement? Back then she told Forrest she loved him. But the tramp wasn't sure if the baby was his or someone other poor clueless sucker's. So she wouldn't marry him. But later on, after the baby was born, she found out Dante *was* Forrest's and she begged him to marry her. But by that time Forrest had moved on. We were in love. He proposed to me. I said *sí, ja, oui.* And now Toni's claim to fame is being Forrest Foster's baby mama. And all she can do is instigate. Be jealous. Act out.

Because Forrest Foster and I have what Toni wishes she had: a husband with a good job that pays excellent benefits and enough income to take care of his wife plus two adorable daughters: Briana, six, and Jazmin, three. These two kids are the joy of our lives. As far as I'm concerned, our life is complete, content, and lacks nothing. Moreover, Forrest and I are the proud owners of a luxurious two-story brick home located on a cul-de-sac. It features a first-floor master suite complete with master bath, Jacuzzi tub, separate shower, his-and-her closets, and a sitting room. We've got a bad-ass kitchen with top-of-the-line Viking appliances, gas fireplace in the family room, a large library, a spiral staircase in the two-story foyer, and three more bedrooms upstairs.

A house to die for.

When Forrest's amazing father died a year after we got married, the widowed man left his only child a six-figure insurance policy, enough for us to place a hefty down payment on our house, plus tastefully furnish the entire place, travel every year, and allocate funds for future emergencies.

Sometimes when I think about how blessed I am, I can almost sympathize with Toni. But not for long. Women like her make me sick. They chase after knuckleheads that treat 'em worse than murderers, but mess over a decent-hearted man who has goals and wants a better life. But when she realizes she made a mistake, she wants to backpedal. Toni had her chance but blew it. If she hadn't let so many disgusting men get between her legs while she was dating Forrest maybe she would be more than what she is. A used-up jealous whore. But she can't totally complain. Toni may not have the man, but she gets plenty of child support; besides, Dante is on my husband's health and dental insurance. She has me to thank for all of that. Although I hate that he got involved with this skank prior to meeting me, I insist he do right by his child. But just because Forrest acts honorably with Dante doesn't mean I'm willing to put up with Toni's crap. Not when she is pretty much insinuating that she's fucking Forrest.

If there's any truth to what she's suggesting, I will want to bust this home-wrecking heffa upside her head, then pull a Jackie Chan on my husband. I'll jump from the staircase onto his big ole head and fatally injure that fool.

Hold up; let me get a grip on myself.

In reality, I've come too far to let craziness destroy the best relationship I've ever had. In the past, I've dated some scrubs, a couple addicts, and a few unmotivated guys that didn't know where they were going in life. But Forrest was different. I wasn't blinded by a million red flags when we dated. Instead, I recognized his admirable qualities.

Paying the bills on time is a priority with Forrest, so he has excellent credit and is always getting credit card offers in the mail. He takes good care of the house, knows how to repair broken electronic devices, and doesn't mind mowing, pulling weeds, and watering the lawn. He never complains about doing dirty work, like taking out trash or killing roaches and spiders, things I'm not about to touch. In other words, I don't have much to complain about. All I know is that I love Forrest Foster and the splendid life we've built together.

But when I think about all the good and try to be more realistic about our life, everything isn't totally perfect every single day. We squabble now and then like all married couples. We say things we don't mean and act stubborn and petty. And there were a couple of times when Forrest got so angry that I noticed another side of him. A side that scared the dog crap out of me.

A side that made me question things.

A side that brought me here to Dot Coffee Shop.

A side that compels me to keep it one hundred with Forrest and to see if he'll do the same for me.

I say a quick prayer and depart from the ladies' room. But a tall, deliciously handsome man whose head is covered in dark dreadlocks is forced to share the tiny hallway with me. We are in close proximity as we try to pass one another.

"Good morning, beautiful. How are you today?"

I smile back, shocked at his attention. "Fine, and you?"

"You're more than fine. You're incredibly gorgeous. Sexy just like Kim Kardashian, only prettier."

I blush. "Thanks. That's so kind."

"Are you spoken for?"

"Yes, she is," Forrest says with a stern voice, appearing out of nowhere. He taps my arm several times: the classic "she's mine" signal. Forrest grabs my elbow so aggressively a sharp pain shoots through it. He rushes me back to our booth.

"Don't do that," I angrily tell him and sit down. "I feel embarrassed. That was so unnecessary."

"You should feel embarrassed. How can you give that random man some play?"

"He was just giving me a compliment. No big deal."

"Men don't just give compliments, Carmen. They usually want something."

"Oh really?" I say sarcastically.

"Whatever. I'm almost done eating. You want anything?"

"Yes. I do. I want to know what's really going on between you and Toni. I want to know where you were last Saturday morning. I've never known you to be late like that."

"Huh?" he asks like he's hard of hearing.

"Forrest, don't play dumb. Why didn't you come straight home from work? Remember, you promised to take the MKT to the detailer? But you showed up two hours later with no explanation. You had a big grin on your face. Your clothes were wrinkled. And you smelled funny."

"You must be joking."

"Do I look like Chris Tucker?"

"Somewhat."

"Forrest!"

"Carmen."

"Look, be serious, because I'm not joking. Don't forget, details come easily for me. I remember everything."

"What were you doing yesterday afternoon at 4:33 and a half?" he says laughingly.

"Forrest, you know what? I'm starting to get impatient."

"I am, too," he says seriously. "Baby, you just don't understand. I hate being blindsided. We could have discussed this at home. And now you're out of the house early in the morning flirting with some Jamaican-looking punk when I'm a few yards away."

"Forrest, Forrest, listen up. This isn't about me."

His eyes glaze over. He's not hearing me. Disconnect makes me nervous.

When Forrest and I first started dating, I noted everything about him that stood out. How he dressed conservative yet sharp; the colognes he wore always turned me on. I noticed how cute he looked when he rolled his tongue across his bottom lip. I knew he was happiest when I agreed with him and did whatever he said. And when I made him happy, he always made me happy. We were so connected I knew I never wanted to be with any other man for the rest of my life. I loved me some Forrest Raymond Foster. I still love him.

And in spite of what's going on right now, I know this man loves me.

"Baby, I need to tell you something." His voice is shaking. He sounds weird. He wipes his sweaty forehead with a white napkin.

"Carmen, darling," he continues. "You see it's like this. I-I never meant to hurt you. It was just . . . it was stupid really. Something men do but it means nothing. It meant nothing. Trust me. You don't have to worry. . . ." He mutters in a hoarse voice I've never heard before.

My knees knock together underneath the table. It's difficult to breathe, as if all oxygen has left my body.

"W-what did you say?" I whisper. "It's true? You did it? With Toni?"

He sighs heavily, looks at me, then at his empty plate. He tosses a twenty on the table and barks, "Let's go."

I sit in stunned silence for ten minutes.

I managed to recover and am now following him, driving behind my husband's Ford F-150, dark green, sparkly, and shiny just how he prefers our vehicles to look. As usual, Forrest is in "I'm the Boss" mode. Him directing. Me following. Him deciding what we do and when. Me agreeing and going along with the program. All throughout our marital union, his way of doing things has worked. An intelligent hardworking African American male who still embraces traditional albeit chauvinistic values: The head of the house works, provides, pays the major bills, and protects his family.

In Forrest's mind, the wife must be beautiful, groomed, and dignified at all times. He also couldn't wait to get me pregnant. In the early years, he yearned for Dante to have a little brother. As fate would have it, he had to settle for two girls.

And I love being a mom, most of the time, but I'm eight years younger than Forrest. He's thirty-eight. Sometimes I want to do things that young women want to do. But he always reminds me how lucky I was to nab a catch like him.

Many chicks would trade places with you in a minute. How many women your age have a five-thousand-square-foot house with a three-car garage? How many own half a dozen authentic Coach bags? Possess NBA season tickets three years in a row? Shop at Neiman Marcus for every special occasion? Take a two-week vacation in California's wine country in the spring and go skiing in Aspen during winter break? Or fly to Manhattan just to go shopping for the kids' summer wardrobe?

Forrest likes the good things in life and wants to share them with me. He knows I didn't come from a wealthy family and had never been outside the state of Texas when I was growing up. He knew my first car was a hooptie that I loved, but he told me that nothing beats driving a brand-new car straight off the lot. There were many things he wanted to give me. He wanted to make me happier than I'd ever been in my life.

Whenever Forrest reminds me of all he's done for me and how he's given me a dream life, I shut up. I wonder how I can be so ungrateful. How can I take my amazing blessings for granted? I clear my head. I pretend like I'm starting from the beginning, a time when all I desired was pure love with a strong black man who had my back.

My dream got fulfilled through Forrest. But now, as I'm driving directly behind my man, I need to connect the dots of our beginning to what's going on these days. What's with this confession he just revealed? Why would he betray me with Toni of all people? And can I ever forgive him? What is really going on in my so-called perfect marriage?

3

When Forrest and I met, the first place he took me was As-
troWorld. Back then it was such a fun-filled romantic place for
two people in love. The park was packed to the brim with the
sounds of carnival music, laughing children, and rowdy teens.
We'd strolled every inch of the amusement park holding
hands. We'd gotten totally wet on the Bamboo Shoot, hopped
on Batman: the Escape, crashed into one another's bumper
boats, and yelled our heads off on the Texas Cyclone and the
Greezed Lightnin' roller coaster. I loved how even though he
was much bigger than me, he didn't care if I heard him
screaming like a kid.

"You're so pretty. And you're all mine. I'm going to make
you my wife. My baby mama." I'd smile and blush at the same
time. Forrest had a way of making me feel so special. Even
though he was the oldest guy I'd ever dated, the way he made
me feel made up for any age-related concerns. He'd wrap his
arm tightly around my shoulder, especially when he noticed
other men openly staring at me.

Why you wear shirts that expose those tits? he'd ask. *Those are
my titties.* I thought his display of jealousy sounded so cute. So
did my friends. My best girlfriend, Shalita Dixon, was like,

"Heyyy now, you got yourself a keeper, girlllll. Ask Forrest if he got any friends? Or a clone? Humph, if you don't know you better ask somebody."

My girlfriend would make these statements and I'd burst out laughing. But I knew she was genuinely ecstatic for me. A victory for me gave her hope. And Shalita, of course, was my maid of honor at our wedding. She grinned when I walked down the aisle blowing kisses at my guests. And tears streamed down my friend's face when Forrest and I were pronounced husband and wife. Since then, she loves teasing me about "where is your fine-ass husband?"

I settled into my role as Mrs. Forrest Foster. And I had to pinch myself when Forrest showed me the dream house he wanted to buy me two years into our marriage. We'd previously gone house-hunting together, but I hated all of the ones the Realtor showed us. I wanted something really special. Forrest said he'd look on his own. Then one Saturday afternoon he drove me to this gorgeous house in Missouri City, a burgeoning suburb southwest of Houston.

Who needs all this space? I asked.

We do. Us and our kids. My baby that you're having.

What you talkin' about, Forrest? I said.

Forrest was so tuned into me that he knew I was pregnant even before I did. And our family expanded with the birth of Briana. She was underweight but a fighter who was released from the hospital three weeks after she was born. Forrest has doted on her (and her little sister Jazmin) ever since.

Our house is located in Lake Olympia, a master planned community in Fort Bend County, considered one of the fastest growing and most prosperous counties in the United States. Some of the most notable Houstonians live in my neighborhood, including Beyoncé's parents, some NFL players, and various black businessmen and politicians. But the fact that you live around the corner from Destiny's Child doesn't matter when you have drama in the house. What, are they going to stop singing just to run down the street and help me? I think not.

Forrest and I make a left turn onto our street, the one with the man-made lake surrounding the small island. We both click and point our automatic garage-door openers and drive into our respective sides of the three-vehicle garage. I always take the middle port. Forrest takes the left. His motorcycle, golf clubs, skiing equipment, and all our bicycles are stored in the right side.

This morning our impeccably decorated home is as still as a Sunday morning. Normally our daughters would be here, but they spent the night with my mom, Miriam, my sweet angel in disguise, who insists on taking the girls off my hands twice a week. My brother lives with her and I appreciate both Mommy's and his help more than they realize.

Especially today.

I place my leather Coach satchel on the island kitchen lit up by bright fluorescent lights.

"Baby, let's start from the beginning," I say to Forrest, who immediately powers up the coffee maker and grabs my favorite mug. It's lavender and is taller than the average mug, its texture smooth to the touch. He knows Starbucks' French roast coffee quiets my nerves. Plus, the aroma permeates the house, making the first level smell strong and soothing.

"I know it sounds unfair, Carmen, but I said what I had to say. I'm not in the mood to go deep into this."

"But I have a right to know what happened. How did it happen? How many times did you see her?"

"Not many."

"How many?"

"It was, um, two times, Carmen. That's all."

"Twice?"

"Okay, three times, I swear."

Ugh. A butcher knife in my stomach would be great compared to how I feel right now.

"Forrest," I cry in a tiny voice.

"You gotta believe me."

"What I can't believe is that you actually did it. Why? Why her?" I walk in a circle and return to face him. He looks way too calm, something I don't understand.

"I'm sorry, Carmen. It wasn't planned; just happened."

"How? Tell me everything."

"Baby, you don't want to do this. It's just sex."

"Just sex? *Just* sex?"

"Yeah, I don't love her. You know that."

"Then why do it?"

"That's why I don't want to talk about this. You can't handle this. Just let my apology be enough. I just don't want to hurt you any more with the details."

"But I-I-I must know, Forrest. I want to know how this could've happened . . . without me even sensing it. I don't get it."

"It just did." It's amazing how that feeble voice is coming out of his big body.

"How do I know if you caught something?"

"I used condoms. Everything is cool."

"Oh Forrest. Everything isn't cool." I moan. How can he be so laid back? I want to scratch out his eyeballs. "I trusted you. Do you know that?" Using great force, I push in his forehead with my fingers till he stumbles backward. "Do you know that?" I scream.

"Yes, baby, I know."

"Like hell you do. Trust is a big issue with me. Do you know what it feels like to tell anyone who listens, my family, my girlfriends, what a great husband I have? That the father of my kids is my real-life duke, my royalty."

"Now c'mon, Carmen. You tend to exaggerate—."

"No, because see, in my eyes, you were my prince."

"For real? Aw damn. Now I feel worse."

"You ought to feel worse. Because I just can't believe this is happening. You know good and well Toni despises me. She will never stop rubbing the affair in my face. I can't deal with that. Why didn't you think about all this beforehand? Why would you put me in this position?"

"Hell, I don't know," he shouts. "I told you I'm sorry!"

Why is he yelling at me? I can't take this anymore.

I double over and grab my belly, trying to calm the butterflies that have taken flight inside of me. My tear ducts are completely dry. It must be the shock; the pure humiliation that riddles my entire being.

"Carmen, baby. You gotta understand. I love you, girl. Always have. Always will. It's you that I love. I just made a dumb mistake. Forgive me."

I don't respond to him for a long time. It's hard to wrap your head around things that will never ever make sense.

"Carmen," he says softly. "I love youuuu."

"How would I know that?"

"Look around." He knows our home is amazing and he works hard to maintain it.

Whoopty doo!

"Spare me, Forrest. I-I . . ."

I'm left with no more words. Does true love feel like a swift kick that hollows out the gut? Does he really think material things cover up moral failure?

"It'll never happen again, Carmen. I swear. And I am sorry. It meant nothing. Nothing."

I think about the recent pitiful state of our sex life. Dry-ass kisses. Quickies with limp dickies.

I can get a better orgasm masturbating.

I glare at him. "Is your affair the reason why we haven't

made love like we used to? Huh? Your stamina reminds me of your cell-phone battery. You quickly run out of juice."

The more I imagine my husband plugging his "battery" into that woman, the more I feel like the Incredible Hulk. And before I know it, I grab my empty coffee mug and pitch it toward Forrest's big ole head.

4

Time stops.

My all-time favorite coffee mug zips through the air like a football. It makes a whishing noise and heads straight at husband's forehead. He instinctively ducks. The ceramic cup slams against the metal refrigerator door. It makes a horrible whacking sound and smashes into numerous pieces. A tiny dent is now visible on the refrigerator door, a horrible reminder of what shouldn't be.

"Forrest, I'm so sorry, I'm sorry. I'm sorry. I don't like this, I hate this. This has to stop. I'm freaking. What's wrong with me?"

Forrest nods like he concurs. We're out of control. He grabs me and pulls me close to his chest. He plants tender kisses on my forehead, whispering his apologies.

"It's not you. It's me. Baby, forgive me, please. I messed up. You don't deserve this drama. If you hate me I understand, but I hope you don't. I still need and want your love, Carmen. That's all I've ever wanted."

I feel so upset, so torn in half. Even though I don't agree and instantly accept everything Forrest is saying, I am so mentally drained that I slowly allow myself to let the immediate pain go. I'm past the point of screaming. I calm down and recall lessons experienced women taught me over the years. Things like "As long as your man brings home the bacon and is responsible, he's doing way more than what some men are. And if he is discreet, he really does love you because only an asshole would blatantly show off his affairs. If he acts like he's sorry he probably is so forgive him and move on. Because if you divorce him, some other skank will pick up where you left off, and with the way the law works these days, wifey number two may end up with this beautiful house and that's not right."

I listen and think and nod and say to myself, yes, I love my husband and I can't imagine not being with him. We've never had any major blips in our marriage. This is major blip number one.

I reason that as long as Forrest remembers to stick to his vows from now on and never betrays me again, and never gives that freaking tenacious woman any reason to think she's something special, then I'll be okay. I can forgive.

Hell, I think about the time that I totaled the first car Forrest bought me. Hadn't had the damn Mustang convertible two days when I wasn't paying attention and I slammed into a concrete wall of a major highway. Thank God I wasn't badly hurt. But that little car. Forget it. My husband wanted to kill me. He yelled and hot tears poured like buckets of water all over my cheeks and clothes. I let him chew me out big time. Eventually he got over his anger. He began smiling again. Loving me again.

Can I do the same?

We clean up the mess from the broken coffee mug. He talks and tries to smooth things over. After sweeping the floor, Forrest kisses me and holds me a long time. Once he's certain I'm okay, I decide to delete the photos of the IMs from my phone. I ask Forrest to tell Toni to never call our house again. Forrest calls Toni right in front of me and orders her to chill. Reminds her that Dante is his only concern.

The next day he pulls a Kobe and buys me an exquisite sapphire diamond ring. It sparkles at every angle. I feel guilty for accepting his guilt gift. Last time he got on my nerves and bought me a vase of beautiful roses, I dumped them in the garbage and told him to go to hell. But Lord knows I'm a sucker for fine jewelry. And when I call Shalita to tell her about it, she assures me I deserve that gift and I'd be a big fool to reject it.

Shalita and I meet a week later. I have to unload. It takes courage to admit to my best friend that everything that glitters isn't gold. I've never wanted anyone to think that my marriage is less than ideal. That we're actually human and not role models.

We meet at Panera Bread on Highway 6 and the Southwest Freeway. I can't wait to stuff my mouth with something packed with sugar and they bake the best pastries.

I calmly tell Shalita what happened.

"W-w-what?" she says.

"I couldn't believe it myself, Shalita. I felt like I didn't know this man. Felt so stupid."

"You're not stupid, Carmen. It happens to the best of us. We all play the fool at least one time in life." She pokes her lips way out and rolls her eyes. She laughs. I do, too. Shalita is notorious for selecting men that want to date three to five women at a time but swear they're into monogamy.

"At least I know I'm in good company."

"How has Forrest been since then?"

"Like the man I thought I knew. His actions have been perfect, Shalita. I'm still pissed at him, yet I don't want him to stop acting like he has some sense."

"What's he doing?"

"Very attentive. Comes straight home after work. Draws me a hot bubble bath and bathes me himself. And he rubs my feet with lotion and gently kneads them with his fingers. I end up falling asleep on the sofa. He hasn't raised his voice; no arguing whatsoever. He has even helped more around the house, doing stuff I've been asking him to do for a month. This is what I want. It's what I love."

"Hmmm, I heard that. Hope he keeps it up. Hope it's coming from his heart."

"What do you mean by that?"

"Some guys do things as if they're just going through the motions, very robotic like with no sincerity. One time, I dated Hershel Warfield. Remember him? With his Chinese eyes and Louisiana accent. Oooo, I loved that nigga to death. But he'd grow from hot to cold all the time. He'd be there in the moment, then he'd suddenly spaz out. I'd feel like I was all alone even when both of us were in the same room."

"He just wasn't that into you, huh?"

"He was more into dope, that's what it was. I caught him freebasing in my living room with some strange guy and I kicked his cute self to the curb. I will not take second place to drugs. Just say no."

"Yeah, I guess most men have to say no to something if they want to make their relationship work. I'm just happy that Forrest is manning up. He admitted his error. But you know, he did blame it on being a man, like stepping out is what some men are expected to do."

"I don't buy that. It's a weak excuse. It's such a cliché, to hook up with the rough and tumble baby mama."

"Yep, that's what I was thinking. Why can't women pull together and support one another instead of stabbing each other in the back as if that shit isn't going to come back on them?"

"Bitch-ass hos like Toni don't care. She just wants what she wants."

"And it's so hard because I love Dante, too. He's like my own. He's so helpful with the girls. I don't want to take out my hatred for Toni on him. So Forrest and I decided to chill. But I can admit that I've wanted to call Toni and give her a piece of my mind."

"The best way to win this war is to act like she doesn't exist. Have you noticed she only is happy when she's making you miserable?"

"Yes. I have. Sad. So sad. And she only has four fingers on her left hand. Ewww. How could he hook up with that?"

Shalita shrugs and rolls her eyes. "You heard that people who snitch are cowards? People that do bitch-ass moves like Toni and snitch on themselves are cowards, too. Her heart isn't right, you know what I mean? She's evil, Carmen. You better watch yourself around her."

"She's dead to me. And that's that. Forrest and I are making our union stronger. I won't be as trusting anymore, because I can't. I still have a ways to go but I must start somewhere. Anyway, girl, he planned a very romantic weekend for next week. He's keeping the details a secret, but I'm looking forward to that. Forget baby mamas who can't get their own man and always try to push up on your man."

"I'll drink to that."

"You mean you'll eat to that?"

We laugh. Pick up our huge cookies. Raise them in the air. And take big bites until the crumbling pastry melts in our mouths and makes us feel warm and privileged.

When Forrest arrives home one morning after working all night, he comes straight to our bedroom. I'm resting against four pillows and watching CNN. His joyous smile greets me. He reaches over the bed and lightly kisses my forehead, making silly smacking noises. Instead of taking a hot shower like he normally does, he leaves the room. Soon I hear clattering from the kitchen. The sounds of pots, pans, and slamming cupboard doors. I blush and sink deeper into the comfort of my bed.

Forty minutes later he's balancing a tall glass of orange juice swirling with ice cubes, and a large metal tray filled with goodies: hot Southern grits seeping with real butter and lemon pepper; salmon croquettes; French toast topped with bananas, cinnamon, and almonds; a bowl of freshly cut fruit (strawberries, cantaloupe, and honeydew melon); baguette toast; and scrambled cheesy eggs made from farm-fresh eggs. All my favorites.

"You're really going all out for me, huh?"

"This is just the beginning, baby."

I love watching Forrest do his thing. Is this the same man? In a way I believe it is the same guy: Forrest the chef, Forrest the considerate one, Forrest the nice guy. All of these are my husband at his best. And when he's like this, I adore this man to pieces. After we eat, we take a steaming hot shower. I squeeze a handful of unisex citrus shower gel on his back and massage it in using a long-handled wooden shower scrubber. He washes my back, too, and sticks his fingers between my legs, a real turn-on.

It takes me a minute to get totally in the mood, but somehow the romance returns to our sex life. We end up making love in the shower like newlyweds who can only see brightness in their future.

Life can't be better.

That Sunday, Forrest nudges me while I'm knocked out in bed. I open my eyes to see his smiling face.

"We're going to service today."

"Okay." I yawn and cover my mouth with my hands. I need to brush my teeth ASAP.

"When you are fully awake, go in that ridiculous closet of yours and bring out the sharpest dresses you own. Make sure they're something that make you feel like a princess when you wear them."

"Forrest, what's going on?"

"Just do as I say, please."

I let out a loud groan, but nod at him.

Later that morning, Forrest, Briana, Jazmin, and I emerge from our bedrooms dressed to the nines. The girls are wearing lovely matching off-white lace dresses with satin bows. Forrest whistles when he sees us. He rushes us out to the SUV beaming with pride. The man is so excited he even makes a trip to Toni's to pick up Dante so he can join us for church at Solomon's Temple. After we enjoy hearing a heartwarming service and several new songs from the mass choir, Forrest drives us to a park near the Galleria. Williams Waterwall is a popular and romantic tourist destination. The sixty-four-feet-tall semicircle fountain provides a mesmerizing display of falling water. I've seen many a bride and her bridal party pose for photos outside this picturesque location off Post Oak Boulevard.

When I begin to take in my surroundings, I'm shocked to see my mom, brother Varnell, and other aunts and cousins standing in a circle. Even Shalita is there.

"Why is all my family here?" I ask Forrest.

He flashes a genuine smile.

My insides churn with anxiety. I don't like this type of surprise. Temptation urges me to run to the car and wait for Forrest.

But when I see Minister Tillman standing next to the brick arches, I can't move.

Dante jogs up to me, his eyes bouncing with excitement. "My father told me he wants to marry you again, Mama Carmen."

I told this crazy boy a million times not to call me that. It makes me sound like someone's grandmother. I'm only thirty.

I shake my head no, but Forrest pulls me to the side and tries to convince me this is the right thing to do. Ten minutes later, Forrest and I stand next to the minister with a blast of water bubbling in the background. We renew our vows in front of an intimate crowd filled with family and dear friends. My voice is shaking. My joy is full. I rapidly fall in love with Mr. Foster all over again. His actions move me. He's genuine. He's reaching far to touch my heart.

My nightmare is over. True love conquers all.

5

Weeks fly by. Marriage feels strong. Better.

No more weird calls from baby mama.

Routinely, Forrest gets home from work around seven-thirty. He putters around the house for an hour, then sleeps till it's time for him to get up in the afternoon.

My normal day is tending to Briana and Jazmin. I wake up the girls and get Briana ready for first grade. She loves to read, engage herself with her Squinkies' toy collection, comb her dolls' hair, play with her dollhouse, and climb into her daddy's lap after she comes home from school so she can tell him about her day. All around she's a sensitive and curious little girl and is excited to learn French.

While Briana is gone, Jazzy and I hang out. I fix our breakfast, wash and fold clothes, read to her, and take her on play dates or outings like the Children's Museum or Downtown Aquarium. I try to get home by two or three so I can fix my family's dinner. The fact that my hubby doesn't mind that I only know how to cook six or seven fundamental entrées makes me love him even more. My specialties are turkey spaghetti, steak and potatoes, deli deluxe club sandwiches, baked tilapia, smothered chicken, chili, and oven-baked ribs. I'm not ashamed to admit Forrest is the true chef of our house and I can't wait for him to make his way around the kitchen every Sunday.

Life has been going great.

But then things happen.

They always start small, but not small enough to not be noticed.

"Baby," I say to Forrest on the phone one morning in mid-October. It's a little past ten. He still hasn't made it home from the railroad company. "What's up? Where are you?"

"My brother needed a favor. I drove him to Austin."

"Austin? Why? You need to sleep so you can work tonight."

"Well, this was an emergency so . . ."

"You don't sound like you're in the car."

"I am in the car. I'm waiting on him. He had some business to take care of."

I don't know what to say. Don't know if I should believe him. One thing about cell phones is you really don't know if people are where they claim they are. You just gotta take them at their word.

"What kind of business?"

"That's *his* business."

"Oh."

It could be true. Phil, Forrest's younger half brother, is trifling like that. Needy. Clingy. Pathetic. Phil wishes he had a daddy who died and left him a good chunk of change, but that isn't the case. And instead of working to obtain the material things Forrest owns, little brother sticks out his hand. Like someone owes him. Phil makes me sick.

"You sure are good to him. Why is that?"

"Don't start," Forrest laughs. I hear his phone click. "Another call is coming in. Gotta go." He hangs up. I don't like that. I am torn between calling him back and tearing a new one in his ass or chilling out and not making a big deal over small stuff. But small stuff turns into big stuff. That's what Shalita always says.

Later Shalita stops by my house for dinner. I make a huge pot of Texas chili. The thick aroma of sirloin steak, kidney beans, garlic, onion, bell pepper, cilantro, and chunky salsa permeate the entire house.

We sit at my breakfast room table in front of the bay window. She listens intently while I tell her that, for the most part, Forrest has continued acting decently, but it's the little things that grind my gears. I hate when he rushes off the phone with me and barely says "Good-bye."

"And on the seventh day, woman gets sick of man's BS, and dumps him."

"I'm not ready to dump him. I need to first know why he's acting different."

"What do you plan to do?"

"I know what I want to do, but I'm scared. Don't ask if you really don't want to know the truth. Yet if Forrest proves to me that he's on the up-and-up and not back to his old ways, I will throw my hands up and admit I've been tripping."

"How's the sex?"

I squirm in my seat. "It's all right."

"You haven't had any good loving in a while, have you?"

"Girl, salt is the engine of flavor. And salt is what's been missing from my bedroom the last two weeks. I'm horny as hell."

"You feel like a virgin again?" Shalita laughs. But I can't.

"Sorry, girl," she apologizes. "You might want to try seducing your man. Put that creamy coochie right up in his face. When he's well rested and in a good mood. No man can resist a clean-smelling vajayjay covered in lace."

I stand up. Grin. "Shalita, you're right. Forrest loves lace panties. They're like an aphrodisiac. So I'm stepping up my game. But it'll have to be on Saturday afternoon when I know he doesn't have to work that night."

"You need me to pick up the girls?"

"Nope, they'll be with my mom." I wink. "And I'll be with my man."

When a woman's gotta have it, she will pull out all the stops. And it has been a minute since I've really enjoyed a nice, nasty lovemaking session with my baby. I get sick of him whining about he's too tired. What? That's the line women use to death, right?

So Saturday evening, I ask Forrest to go on a beer run. He loves Dos Equis. I love Smirnoff Ice. I tell him to take his time. He laughs.

Thirteen minutes later, Forrest comes back home. Note cards stuffed in envelopes with his name scratched on the front are sitting on the breakfast bar.

I am wearing a lavender bustier with lace panties and some white glossy five-inch pumps.

Forrest moans the second he sees me. He practically throws the six-pack and the beer carton on the counter.

"What's—."

"Shhh," I tell him. "Pick a card. Whatever it says is what we're going to do to each other."

"Um, wow. Woman, I don't know what to do with you."

"If you don't know, then we have a problem, Mr. Foster."

I swear I see the front of his gym shorts rise slightly. That's a good thing. What I'm doing works. All I want to do is get my marriage straight. Our love life has to be on fire and I won't accept anything less.

"Go on, silly. Don't just stand there."

He shakes his head and goes to select one of the envelopes.

"Here. I hope I did well."

"All of them are good. And we're going to do all of them before tomorrow night."

"W-what? All of 'em?" he scowls. That hurts.

"Why don't you open it?"

Right then his cell rings. He glances at the screen but doesn't answer. Good.

He rips open the envelope and reads out loud. "Have sex anywhere as long as it's outside the house."

He actually blushes, something that I love.

"Carmen."

"Yes, baby." I go and hug him tight around the waist. This man smells so good I can eat him. I love the big muscles that ripple underneath his shirt. He was born to be held and squeezed tight.

"I love you, girl, you know that?"

"I do, too—."

Then the house phone rings loudly. Talking caller ID says, "Call from Williams Toni."

"Forrest, I told Toni not to call my house anymore. Why is she so contrary? What does she want?"

"Calm down."

"I will not. She's being messy on purpose."

"That sounds crazy," Forrest says and places the envelope on the counter. He looks upset. My feet are starting to hurt. I want to thump Toni across her head so bad. She leaves a message that loudly crackles on our home answering machine.

"Hey, it's your first wife calling. Come fuck with me when you get a chance." She snickers, makes a kissing noise. And hangs up.

"Woo, that beyotch crazy," he cackles.

"What's really going on, Forrest?"

He turns around and makes a mad dash upstairs. I kick off my high heels and sprint after him. I find him in our home theater rummaging through a large assortment of DVDs. This is where we enjoy spending Saturday night. He'll extend an invitation to his brother Phil plus a couple of his male friends. "Safe men," he calls them. I'll invite Shalita and another non-horny girlfriend who's bored out of her mind. We pop popcorn, drink cold beer, and recline in theater seats to watch classics like *Love Jones*, *Independence Day*, *Raiders of the Lost Ark*, and *The Color Purple*. Sometimes we check out bootleg movies. But now?

"Carmen, look. I appreciate what you tried to do. But I really am tired. My job has been laying off people left and right. Those left behind gotta put up with the BS. It's unreal how they coming down on a brotha."

"That's cool, but when did work stop you from wanting to fuck?"

"Huh? What are you talking about? You just don't get it. You just don't."

"I'm tired too, Forrest, of your attitude. Can't you understand?"

He makes a lot of noise fumbling through all the movies.

"I'm talking to you."

"I know. Hold up a sec."

"How can a stupid movie be more important than me? Than our relationship?"

As he's bending over, his cell phone slides out his pocket. He doesn't notice. The plastic containers are making too much noise. He's too busy avoiding me. Fine.

I hastily snatch his phone from the carpet.

"If you want to talk later let me know. I'll be waiting."

My bare feet fly down the stairs. I go directly to the first floor powder room, which is right next to the kitchen and breakfast room. I twist the lock and flick on the lights.

Forrest's phone is locked. Not surprising. Why does he employ a pass code? I don't have one. I have nothing to hide. Apparently there's something he doesn't want me to see. Just like those IMs that were on his screen. The only reason I saw them is because he forgot to log off and the screen had frozen.

I punch in a four digit code. Our home address. The iPhone buzzes. "Wrong pass code," it says. "Try again."

"Damn."

Another four digits are punched in: 0-4-2-2. My husband's date of birth.

More buzzing.

His phone begins to chime. A ringtone. *There Goes My Baby* by Usher.

I smile and my heart beats like a drum.

The caller ID says "Only on Tuesdays."

"What the hell?" As badly as I want to answer, I don't.

I hear him back downstairs. I'm not ready to confront him yet about who's calling him and why he's putting code names in his phone. There will be plenty more opportunities for me to find out what's really going on with my husband and any other woman. And once I find out all hell will break loose.

6

That night I stand outside in the driveway and wave at Forrest when he tells me he was unexpectedly called to work. Next I go upstairs to make sure Briana and Jazzy are occupied. They are crazy about Pet Pals 2, the LeapFrog app that's used on the LeapPad. The talking interactive game allows children to design pets that make all kinds of noises.

When I feel certain the girls are thoroughly engaged, I carry my laptop to the guest bedroom, which is right next to both girls' invidual rooms. I flop onto the bed and power up.

After clicking a few buttons on my keyboard, the Web page to Forrest's e-mail account loads.

It asks for an e-mail address, which I quickly enter. Easy.

Password?

Taking a wild guess, I hold my breath as I enter Briana's full birthday.

No go. I try Jazzy's. No luck.

But when I input Dante's birth date, bingo. I'm in. My adrenaline surges through my body. It feels so wrong to look, but that's the only way I'll know for sure what's going on.

When the page loads there's mostly junk mail. Mystery shopping solicitations. Fake PayPal notices. Tax refund messages. And so on. But my eyes fall to a previously read e-mail.

From Daphne Cox to Forrest Foster. Two days ago. Late at night while he was at work.

I left something for you at ur job yesterday. Hope u liked it.

That was from Forrest.

The insides of my mouth crumble into dryness. Who the hell is Daphne? Why is he giving her anything?

She writes back:

LOVED THOSE ICE CREAM CONE EARRINGS. Ur 2 sweet, Raymond. The good ONES r always taken. :-(.

He got her earrings? That's not innocent at all. And I hate that she calls him by his middle name. Is that what he told her to call him? I'm livid. My eyes fill up. My heart loads with depression. One part of me wants to call Forrest. Or e-mail this tramp. But I can't. I want more ammunition.

I see other e-mails. Not just from Daphne.

From Forrest to Aristacia:

I'm a TAURUS. What's ur sign?

That's so high school.

Then he writes:

Let's hook up. Saturday afternoon good 4 u?

Aristacia sent him six photos. Fat white chick. Dirty blonde. Cleavage popping out her tank top like floating beach balls. Her face suggests she'll suck anything of any size for any amount of money. And she's younger than me. But much uglier. What's up with that? Shalita is right. A husband brags about his beautiful wife and hides his ugly street whores.

Why would Forrest leave such a paper trail? Some men are so stupid.

My mind is a machine gun. Tat tat tat. Tat tat tat. I'm thinking, fretting, wondering what the hell I can do.

My phone rings and I nearly jump out my skin. It's Forrest. Fuck him. I don't want to talk to him. But I change my mind and try to answer him a few seconds later. The ringing stops. Missed call.

I try dialing him back.

The call goes straight into voice mail.

On a whim, I push a key.

The phone prompts for a password.

"Damn," I mumble. I type 0422, Forrest's birthdate.

"Invalid password. Please reenter."

I try other combinations. Our address. The girls' birthdates, even Dante's. None work.

Dammit.

The doorbell rings.

I hang up.

"Wonder who that could be?"

I walk up to the front door and peer out the window. Toni's beat-up-looking Honda is idling at the curb. What does she want now?

I open the door. Dante looks sheepish and apologetic. He's clutching a couple of textbooks under one arm. His iPod buds are stuck in his ears. Backpack slung over a shoulder.

I hold the door open for him and he offers me a thankful grin. I pat him gently on the shoulder. I try to be nice and wave at Toni, who's sneering at us while she's standing next to her car with the motor running. She gives me the finger.

Toni's bone-straight long hair is dyed purple this week. Two weeks ago it was red. She oughta be ashamed of herself.

I shake my head and slam the front door.

"To what do we owe this pleasant surprise, son?" I say to Dante. Toni hates when I call Dante "son."

"Moms and I kinda got into it. So she said I should hang out over at my dad's and study. You don't mind, do you, Mama Carmen?"

He shrugs and grins at me with his beautiful deep-set eyes. The Forrest DNA of this young man is awesome. Dante's destined to be a heartbreaker one day. He's tall enough, laid back, and athletic.

"You're welcome at any time and for any reason. And if you don't stop calling me Mama Carmen, I'm going to beat you."

"For real?"

"Yes," I insist, trying to look irate.

"For real, for real?"

I giggle and gently punch him in the gut with my elbow. "If you promise to call me Carmen, I promise not to beat you. Oops, don't tell Toni I said that."

Dante chuckles and goes to set his belongings on the breakfast room table. I follow him.

"I want you to be okay. I want all of us to be just fine, so never think you're intruding. You're family."

"I appreciate that."

"Anyway, enough of that. How are your classes?"

"They're all right."

"What are you taking?"

"Oh, the same old stuff," he says. He's too busy scoping out the fridge. He grabs a gallon of milk. I automatically go to the walk-in pantry and retrieve the Nesquik.

"You know what I like, huh? That's sweet. I wish I could meet a girl like you," he shyly says. "Carmen."

"Oh, so you like older women, huh?" I reach for two big black mugs and set them on the counter. We both make ourselves cold cups of chocolate milk. I open up a new pack of Oreos and hand them over to Dante.

I feel a little guilty while sitting and chatting with Dante. He's such a good boy. I don't want him to know what's going on between me and his dad. What would he do if he knew I snoop in his dad's e-mail account?

I excuse myself and hop up. I gotta go to the guest bedroom and make sure to log off from that e-mail page.

When I get to the screen I can't believe my eyes.

More freaking e-mails.

From Daphne. I jot down her e-mail address and log off the computer.

"What are you doing?" Dante asks. I jump and swirl around.

"Boy, you scared me. I'm going to have to buy a cowbell or something and place it around your neck."

"Oooohhh, you must be checking out porn, huh?"

"What do you know about that, young man?"

"I know a lot. Moms lets me know about a lot of stuff, but not porn."

"Well, she and I finally agree on one thing. A boy your age shouldn't be looking at porn. Online or magazines."

He starts to say something, but simply mutters, "Yes, ma'am."

"Don't study too hard," I tell him and wave good-bye. His presence makes me a little bit nervous. I decide to relax by heading for the home theater to watch *Soul Food* for the millionth time.

Forrest claimed that his condom didn't work that one fateful day when he had sex with Toni. He said that "if the stupid thing did what latex was invented to do," Briana would've been his firstborn.

"But fate kicked my ass and played a cruel trick on me," Forrest explained early in our marriage.

"Forrest, get real. Fate gave you Dante. God doesn't make mistakes even when men do," I reasoned. He blankly stared at me. Then his face lit up. He kissed me. Then started whistling and walking around like he was happy. Happy he met and married me. That's when he felt I was the one. Although we'd already been married and had Briana, he liked that I convinced him that Dante wasn't a mistake. Toni was, but Dante wasn't.

"You're forever my lady," he sang to me. I didn't appreciate that he realized my worth so late, but I didn't hold it against him.

So now, these days, with me finding out things about Forrest that I don't like and can barely believe, I wonder if I should apply my logic about fate to what's happening in our marriage.

I'm nearly driving myself crazy being in the house near Forrest's computer. So, right after Toni picks up Dante, I invite Shalita over that evening. I can use the company.

We're curled up in our theater seats, this time watching *Knocked Up*.

"When you think about it"—Shalita gulps a bottle of raspberry sparkling water—"no one has a say-so about who gets pregnant."

"Shalita, yes, they do. If you don't have sex with anyone, then you can't get knocked up. Simple as that."

"It's not as simple as you put it."

"There's cause. There's effect. That's as easy as things can get. If you have sex with the wrong person, someone will get screwed."

"Why are we talking about this anyway? Dante is a done deal."

"Yeah, but I don't know if Forrest is working on any new acts of fate," I say sarcastically. I tell her about the flirty e-mails. I admit my anxiety about my suspicions and how I'm getting angry all over again. "I don't know if Forrest is practicing safe sex. Even though he said he used condoms with the four-fingered heffa. I hate him all over again every time I imagine him putting his penis in her. Just talking about this makes me sick to my stomach."

"Then don't talk about it."

"Not talking about it won't make it go away."

"I know one thing that might."

"What?"

"Don't get mad. Get even. Take a walk on the wild side. Put yourself in Forrest's shoes."

"Think like a man?"

"Don't just think like one."

"Act like one," we both say at the same time.

My landline rings. There's no caller ID in this room so I pick up.

"Foster residence."

Silence. Then laughter. "Bitch, please."

I frown and put the caller on speaker. Shalita starts throwing punches in the air.

"Now, what were you saying, Man Stealer?"

"Ooh, I like that. But it ain't accurate. 'Cause if a man is yours in the first place, he can't be stolen."

"I guess that's why Forrest didn't stay with you, huh, Toni?"

"What you say, bitch?"

"Toni, your little words don't scare me at all. All you are is entertainment to me."

"Dude, you wish you was me. Anytime Forrest is at my place, his hands are all over me. And from what I heard ya'll barely fucking."

"And how would you know that?"

"Trust me. In that big ole mansion you got, your walls have eyes. Betta recognize."

"Toni, why do you always start mess with me, huh? Let it go. Find your own man."

"I have no reason to look any farther. Because far as I'm concerned, Forrest is my man. He wanted to marry *me*, you saditty-ass fake dumb bitch," she yells.

"He wanted to marry you, but he *married* me!" I shout back. "Don't you get it? Leave us the hell alone. I hate women like you."

"Oh, this nucca finally trying to keep it one hunnert."

"Hang up on that ho," Shalita screams.

Toni continues, "If you think I've started some shit before, keep living. You gonna regret fucking with a bitch like me." And the bitch hangs up.

7

I never mention to Forrest anything about Toni or the e-mails I saw. But today, when he tells me he's leaving for work an hour early because he has some errands to run, I tell him okay.

I drive over to Shalita's. We exchange cars. She is thrilled to have use of my MKT and I have to make do with her white Chevy Equinox. It's so bland it looks like every other crossover driving on Houston freeways.

I get on the road with two things in mind. Sometimes with men you gotta catch them in action. Because some are known to deny every shred of evidence that you present to them.

If the glove doesn't fit . . .

I'm trying to make sure the glove fits in this case. Why? I don't know. I feel I need something solid before I get in Forrest's face again.

Approximately thirty minutes before Forrest's start time, I quietly pull up and park on the main street across from his company's parking lot. At this angle, I can easily view him once he arrives.

I know my man. He told me he likes to get to the job about fifteen minutes before check-in. When it's five minutes to seven, and he still hasn't shown up, I call OnStar from my cell phone. I let the nice-sounding lady know that when I went shopping a little while ago, I parked my F-150 in a big old parking lot and I just can't seem to find it.

"It's so embarrassing," I tell her and provide her with the account number. "It's so dark out here I can't see. Can you tell me where my car is?"

"Sure, no problem. One moment."

My forehead feels sticky with wetness. I roll down the window.

"Um, it's not parked at all. It is currently driving down a major street."

"What street is that?"

She mentions the very street of my husband's work address.

"Do you want me to call the police for you?"

I hang up on her. And right then I see Forrest's green pickup fly past me. I know it's his vehicle because he installed those annoying LED undercar lights on the bottom. They make him stand out like a throbbing sore thumb.

Forrest makes a right turn into the employee parking lot.

"Damn."

I don't know if I should feel good that he seems to be running late, or if I should question why he's late.

Another thought for another time.

"The things you attain in life are based on the opportunities you make or the opportunities presented to you."

That's something my father would tell me while I was growing up as the daughter of an electrician; my mother taught middle school English and modeled in local fashion shows.

We didn't have tons of money, but I never went hungry. And Briana's and Jazzy's bedrooms would make my childhood room look like I was on welfare. Yet Mommy made sure I participated in Girl Scouts, soccer, and performing arts. If there was ever a school production that involved wearing fancy clothes, she would always sacrifice and buy them. My father would fuss. "You'd better find you a rich man to marry when you get of age." He'd laugh. But I never forgot his advice.

By the time I met and got engaged to Forrest, my brother Varnell nudged me with a snicker. "I see you're making a life out of the opportunity that was presented to you."

Varnell liked Forrest from the start. Thought he was exactly what I needed. My brother proudly said I looked like a beautiful princess on my wedding day. I felt like one, too.

Every woman deserves to be a fairy princess at least once in her life.

My job is to maintain that storybook feeling. To preserve the fantastic blessing that God gave me. I must fight and hang onto it, because if I lose it another woman will surely find it.

That can't happen at all.

The next afternoon I rinse off several huge white potatoes and peel them in the kitchen sink. I grab carrots, onions, and bell peppers from the refrigerator. The vegetables feel natural in my hands. The carrots get peeled and sliced, onions and peppers cut into small chunks, and all the contents dumped into a large roasting pan.

I open a large can of mushroom soup. Sprinkle some steak sauce and onion mix over the meat.

After I slide the pan of meat and vegetables into the oven, I quickly clean up the mess that's scattered all over the island kitchen.

Two hours later, my handsome husband stumbles into the kitchen.

He starts sniffing. "Mmmm. That smell woke me up."

I smile when he kisses my cheek.

"What's the occasion?

"I dunno," I lie. "I just wanted to do something different."

"I didn't know you knew how to cook pot roast."

"I didn't know either."

"Woman, you're full of surprises."

"So are you."

He raises an eyebrow but refocuses. "I'll be in the library checking e-mails till you're done. Okay, my love? You sure are looking pretty today." He winks and leaves.

Insecurity makes me want to run after him. I stay in the kitchen tending to what a good wife is supposed to tend to. Wiping down the counter. Putting away the spices. Tying up the smelly garbage. And getting out the bag of rice and a medium size pan. Butter. Water. Salt.

Just because you pretend like nothing is wrong doesn't mean it's true.

I measure one cup of wild rice and set it aside.

Your walls have eyes.

"Have you been in the library lately?" Forrest has returned to the kitchen. He looks confused.

"Um, no, I lost my library card." I turn on the water faucet and place a measuring cup underneath.

"I'm not talking about the real library, smarty."

"Why? Anything wrong?"

"Um, it's just—Never mind."

"Say what you have to say."

"I noticed that some of the e-mails look like they've been tampered with. You know, the subject line isn't bold like normal."

I shut off the faucet and dump the water into the pan.

"Hmmm. Maybe you should place a call to Dell Technical Services."

"And maybe you should stay out of my library."

"Huh?"

"Carmen, I'm not half as dumb as you think I am. You're

cooking this grand meal. I know you. You don't do shit like this without a motive."

"Forrest, that's not fair. I'm just doing something different and proactive for a change. Like I said before."

"Next time you want to go snooping in my stuff, you may want to do it when my son isn't here."

I stiffen. No way Dante would tell. That's my buddy. Not my enemy.

I guess you can't trust anybody these days.

"Hold on, now. Wait just a minute. You mean to tell me that I'm wrong for being curious, but the crap you're doing, isn't that worse?"

"Are you admitting that you looked at my e-mails? How'd you manage that? You a hacker and didn't tell me?"

I throw two oven mitts at Forrest's head. This time they make contact.

"Stop snooping, Carmen." He picks up the mitts and calmly hands them to me. "Because you can't handle or under-stand the truth."

"I hate when men say that."

"This isn't about men. It's about me. I like my privacy."

"I only did it one time. Wait, make that no more than three," I say. My voice drips with sarcasm. Some men love to give women hell, but they can't take it themselves.

"Carmen, how many times have you called OnStar?"

Is someone following me while I'm following Forrest?

"OnStar followed up with me after that phone call you made to check up on me. Thanks a lot."

He storms away.

I feel so convicted. "Hold on, Forrest. What about dinner?"

"I'm eating out tonight."

"I don't like how that sounds."

"I don't like how you're looking right now."

"You told me I look pretty."

"Pretty desperate. 'Bye, Carmen. I'll see you tomorrow. By the way, I changed the e-mail password. Knock yourself out trying to guess this time."

It's only five o'clock. Forrest doesn't usually leave for work till 6:15. I hate this. I feel so miserable and depressed, like I'm the one that's screwing up our marriage and creating a horrible wedge. But wait. Isn't this all his fault? If he knew how to keep his penis safely in its cage, we wouldn't be arguing and butting heads like never before.

He hurts me with his actions, but the love I have for Forrest is so strong. Normally when we get into it, I swear at him. Threaten him. We make up within twelve hours. We're sorry. We laugh. Tease each other. Ask for forgiveness. Make-up sex is real nice. Sweaty. Painful. Good loving. We cuddle. Reconnect. Gratefulness settles back in. Love churns back up. It's our cycle. A cycle that should never be penetrated by outsiders.

But this time I must say Forrest has gone too far. He's only thinking of himself.

Feeling more pissed, I dial his cell number. It goes straight into voice mail. He's pissed, too. I press the star sign. Punch in his work address.

You have five saved messages.

Bingo.

"Forrest, this is Daphne. I waited for you. I don't like to be kept waiting. Hit me back."

I slowly sit down on the family room sectional.

Next message. Received two days ago.

"Hey, Sexy Man. It's me. I'm just returning your phone call. You just called me and now you're it. Smooches. Love you." Who the hell was that? Her call came in at two a.m.

Listening to these sultry female voices is driving me crazy. The rest of the messages are from Phil. Begging for something. A ride. A loan. To borrow my car. *My* car? What? Brother-in-

law has a lot of nerve. I guess because Forrest pays for my pos-
sessions Phil thinks that they're really my husband's. That's
going to have to change.

But for now, I gotta step up my game. The days of being
naïve and trusting are officially kaput.

8

I'm at home with my girls the next day.

"Mommy, I don't want this réchauffé."

"Okay, Briana. What does that mean, sweetie?"

"It means warmed leftover food. Ewww."

Briana is such a picky eater. She prefers freshly prepared food. No dog scraps for her, ever. Jazzy will eat whatever we put in front of her, just like her dad.

With Briana's prissy attitude, this little girl is destined to create her own opportunities in life.

"I'm so proud of you, darling."

"*Merci*, Mommy."

I giggle and squeeze her little body in my arms. "You're actually teaching me something. Keep up the good work. I love to hear you use French in a sentence—"

Briana cuts me off. "Will you make me a peanut butter and jelly sandwich, please?"

"Hmm. Ask your brother."

Dante has just come over again. His presence keeps me from having to directly talk to Forrest. Not that we're talking. When my husband came home from work this morning he barely said hello. He took a quick shower and fell into bed like a chopped-down tree. He turned over in bed and faced the wall. I had an unfriendly view of his back. I waited a few minutes and gently kicked his leg, but he grunted and started snoring.

Fake. No one falls asleep that fast.

The girls and I make a plateful of PB and J sandwiches and check out the *Shrek Forever After* DVD.

A few hours later, Forrest wakes up. I catch him in the hallway and try to block him before he can get away.

"Hey, hi, now move," he tells me.

"Where are you going so fast?"

"Laundry room."

"Whatcha looking for?"

"Why you wanna know?" His consciousness of guilt is all over his nervous-looking face.

"Why are you so testy?"

"I'm tired. That's all. I think I left something in my pants pocket. I–I don't want it to get wet."

"Wash away the evidence, huh," I say half-jokingly as I duck out of his way.

He appears frantic. When I see the frightened look on his face, the room starts spinning. I feel weak with fear.

"Forrest, who or what are you trying to hide from me?"

"Carmen, please don't start that again. You talk what you don't know."

He bounds downstairs, his big feet making thundering noises.

I race after him. How dare he accuse me of not knowing?

All the kids are settled in the family room, which is in direct view of the kitchen. The washer and dryer are situated in a tiny but functional room also near the kitchen.

Forrest stands next to the center countertop glaring at me. "Carmen, I'm getting sick of your paranoia. Stop taking the crazy pills, you hear me?"

"W-what? I'm not the one who's crazy. You need to stop acting like you're doing nothing wrong."

"I'm not."

I shoot him an enraged look.

"Okay," he says, "then what do you think I'm doing?"

"I know that you're hooking up with random chicks on the side."

"Huh? No, you do not."

I can't help myself. Against my better judgment, I pick up my iPhone. Put it on speaker. Dial his cell number.

"Don't answer," I order.

I push buttons that access his voice mail.

All the kids race to the kitchen looking scared.

"Hey, sweetie," the voice mail loudly crackles. "It's Daphne. I miss youuuuuuuuuuuuuuu. Call me."

Forrest's eyes grow round. "Carmen, you must be out your mind." He storms toward me. Raises his hand, something he's never done before.

"Daddy, don't," Dante yells. He runs up to his father and grabs his arm.

The girls cry and clutch my leg.

Forrest screams, "You have no right to listen to my messages. I can't help it if these women say these things. They want to know me, want to be my friend."

"You don't need friends. You're *married*." My insides hurt so deeply that nothing can hold back a flood of tears that starts to drench my face.

"You don't have to worry about them. They mean nothing to me. You're my number one, Carmen."

I gasp. "You did it again, didn't you?" I sniff. "Forrest, how could you?" I try to beat his chest with my fist.

Briana yells, "*Vous arrêtez*. Stop."

Jazzy screams and runs around in circles.

Father and son tussle for a few seconds. Forrest gently pushes Dante off him. Dante paces back and forth, looking distressed.

The frenetic energy of my house must cease.

I gather my senses, scoop my three-year-old into my arms, and set her firmly on my hip. Jazzy presses her cheek against my lips so I can give her a kiss.

Loud knocks on the front door shatter the moment and lessen the hostility.

Dante races to open the door. I can hear my neighbor, Gloria Stone, a fiftyish married woman, in her booming, no-nonsense voice. "I will call the constable just like last time. Tell your father to lower his voice and leave the house if necessary. I don't play that."

"Yes, ma'am."

Dante walks slowly into the kitchen. Bewildered eyes. Mouth withdrawn.

"Daddy, please, *please* don't treat Mama Carmen this way. I have nowhere else to go. Don't know what else to do."

For once I don't care if Dante calls me that name.

"Stay married. There's nothing out there." My brother Varnell always keeps it real with me.

When I stop by my mother's on Friday to drop off the girls for a sleepover, Varnell is outside her house watering the front lawn. Beads of sweat soak through his maroon cotton T-shirt. Aggie alum. I'm shocked he'd let his precious TAMU shirt merge with his body fluid.

"Why'd you say that to me?" I grin at him.

"I know you, sis. You have that look."

"What look is that?" I wait for Briana and Jazzy to go into my mother's house. The smell of baked chocolate chip walnut cookies greets them before they slide inside the screen door. Mommy waves. I wave back.

"You look like you've been through hell. You getting any sleep?"

"Okay, so I have insomnia. That doesn't mean I need to stay married, as you say."

"Yeah, but there's a reason you can't sleep."

"I hate that Forrest works this shift. It doesn't feel right, him not being there with us. Anything can happen."

"Has it?"

"Varnell, now," I say and take a step toward Mommy's front door.

"All it takes is one call and I will lay aside my salvation and beat the black off that boy."

"Thanks," I whisper and nod. "It'll be okay. We're fine."

"You're lying. He better not put his hands on you either."

"Oh no. Nothing like that. We can work it out. But I'm glad you have my best interests at heart."

"Just call me anytime, sis."

"No need. We're good. Stay blessed."

"Always."

I love the fact that Varnell is there. Especially since Daddy has been dead for two years. A brother is not a father, but his support means just as much.

I go inside to chitchat with my mother, then kiss the girls bye-bye.

I decide to go grocery shopping at the biggest H-E-B in the area. The sounds, sights, colors, and textures of the merchandise inspire and transport me to another place.

I grab a big silver shopping cart and begin pushing it around the produce section. These cucumbers are the greenest vegetables I've ever seen. I caress the hardness of a coconut, sniff a carton of strawberries, and pop an organic white grape into my mouth.

"Hey there, how you doing?" A man with his red, blue, and orange shirt partially unbuttoned greets me. He's standing next to an arrangement of lemons. He's offering me a warm smile. I smile back. He accidentally bumps his hip into the corner of the display. One by one, a dozen lemons spill to the floor, reminding me of tennis balls.

"Oh my God." I laugh. I stoop down and pick up as many lemons as possible.

"Thank you," he replies, his cheeks turning red.

"No problem."

He starts restocking the fruit. "That was nice of you. Most people would have just walked on by. I'm Alfred, by the way. I'm single. And I'm looking. You?"

"I-I am, um . . ."

He throws back his head and laughs. "You don't sound so sure."

"I guess it's because I'm not."

"Well, how about I give you my number? Once you know what's up with your situation, give me a call. It's refreshing to run into a gorgeous, smiling, conscientious young woman." Alfred hands me his card.

I whisper, "Thanks."

He turns around and I watch him head toward the bakery.

I shove his card into my purse and hurriedly leave H-E-B.

9

By the time Saturday arrives, I'm in a different state of mind.

The air is fresh and crisp, void of Houston's normal humidity. The sun sparkles brightly. I feel happy. More relaxed. But I want and need love. Will do whatever to get it.

The kids and I are taking a leisurely stroll toward the neighborhood park. Dante bounces his basketball on the sidewalk and pretends to shoot through an invisible hoop.

"All right, now, you future Rocket," I call out to him.

"No. Future *Laker*."

"Beat LA. Beat LA," I tease.

"Thanks for getting out the house and coming down to the park; you haven't been here in so long." Dante smiles.

"Well, if you hadn't begged me a hundred times, I'd still be doing housework."

He laughs and scampers off when he notices a pickup game has already started.

It feels good to escape the house. I tremble when I think about the last big fight I had with Forrest and am happy to be doing something positive with Dante and the girls.

Briana and Jazzy begin shouting with joy when they spot playground equipment. Other neighborhood kids wildly slide down the sliding board.

The girls yelp and play for ten minutes. The soft breeze that caresses my cheek feels wonderful.

A stray basketball rolls till it lands near my feet. I bend over and scoop the orange ball into my hand.

"Over here," a man yells.

I squint.

"Hey, is that Carmen Foster?"

"Oh my God." I break into a broad smile at the man's acknowledgment. "Long time no see." We walk toward each other.

"Jordan Harris," I say in surprise. Back in the day, I was crazy about Jordan. He was sexy, fun-loving, intriguing, intelligent, sensitive. Jordan and Forrest were good friends. But I ended up with Forrest.

Today Jordan is wearing long black gym shorts, a crisp red T-shirt, and a fitted cap perched backward; the hat barely covers his full head of dark curly hair. He is one of those light-skinned brothas with gray-green eyes that see right through you. I notice he's grown a beard. It looks good. Two diamond studs sparkle, one in each ear.

I haven't seen Jordan in about four years.

"My my my, you got it going on, Carmen. Still sexy as ever." He actually holds my hand, politely kisses it, then asks me to turn in a circle so he may inspect me from every angle. My cheeks flush. I'm so surprised but happy to see him.

"This must be my lucky day," he winks and does a silly little two-step.

"I see you haven't changed," I giggle.

"But you have in all the ways that are good. Woman, your body bangin'."

"Jordan, you're still so crazy."

"Still crazy about you, Carmen. I hate that we lost touch. Never again," he vows.

"Hey, fool. Throw the damn ball."

Jordan absentmindedly tosses the basketball back onto the

court. He turns back to me and wraps his arms around me and pulls me close. My nose is pressed against his neck. He smells good.

I am touched by his display of affection, but I soon ease away from his hug. "Jordan, are you okay?"

"Forgive me. I just can't believe I'm seeing you. I know it sounds crazy, but you've been in my dreams all this time."

"Don't lie." I smile.

"I wouldn't lie to you."

"Oh really? What makes you different than some other men?"

"Baby girl, baby girl." He examines my ring finger. Only thing he sees is a tan line. "Oh, it's like that, huh? Forrest couldn't hang?"

"Jordan, I don't want to talk about that right now. Why don't you tell me what's been going on with you?"

He excitedly informs me about his travels all over the country to work at various chemical refineries: Corpus Christi, Port Lavaca, Texas, Louisiana, Kentucky, Minnesota.

"And you're going to be settled in Houston for a while? Or are you leaving again?"

"All depends. Only one thing can make me stay here long term," he says giving me a sly grin.

"Don't even try it."

Jordan starts playing with the back of my hair, something he used to do years ago. Electricity races through me. His touch feels so strong, sincere. I like that.

"Carmen, you're so pretty you make Eva Longoria look like Shrek." Jordan stands closer and gently raises my chin toward his lips.

Years ago, I may have eaten up his compliments and be really feeling this. But now?

"Stop that. My kids . . ."

"Oh all right. Maybe some other time. What's your number? We need to catch up."

I think about Forrest and all his little side chicks. He downplays those relationships and calls them "nothing." *Nothing wrong with having "friends"* is what he says.

I still consider Jordan a friend. And it's true that the guys you used to love always hold a special place in your heart.

I recite my cell number. Jordan gives me his and I enter his into my iPhone as "Good Ole Dayz."

"Close your eyes," he says. "You got some type of gooey-looking stuff stuck in the corner."

I close both my eyes.

I feel his lips press against mine. Really soft. Really quick. And as warm as a buttered biscuit.

My eyes fly open.

"Please don't—"

"I'm sorry. But I wanted to show you how much I've missed you. At least now I know how it feels to kiss you instead of just dreaming about it."

He always knew how to say things that touch my heart.

"I'm sorry if I've scared you, Carmen. Forgive me?"

"Of course."

"I'll let you go. Good to see you again. I'm gonna hit you up soon." He pounds his chest with one fist then runs back to the basketball court.

On the way home, I'm amazed that Good Ole Dayz already texts me twice.

LET'S CATCH UP.

I giggle and try to deal with my mixed feelings. I ponder Forrest and his casual attitude toward other females as if extra women in his life are natural and nothing to worry about. I remember the horrible hurt I've felt since discovering my husband's philandering ways. And I recall how, even after the recent major blowup, I try to do the right thing.

For example, just last night I managed to calm down and attempt to communicate with Forrest. Acknowledged we need professional help. Suggested counseling.

He groaned out loud and his eyes rolled to the back of his head. He shot down everything I said. Wanted nothing to do with counseling. Told me to look at the bigger picture. Thought I should open up my eyes and see all the good things he's provided for me and our kids. Forgive him, move on. The end.

Move on to what? More deception? A living room full of new furniture? Another Coach bag? I went to bed feeling discouraged and insecure.

So when I'm thinking about all of this and Good Ole Dayz texts me again, I quickly respond:

WHAT HARM CAN IT DO? WHEN? WHERE? WHAT TIME?

I delete all his messages after we agree to meet.

I place a call to my mother. "Mommy, would you like to spend time with your granddaughters this evening?"

"Sure. Bring them over anytime. You got something planned?"

"Yes, an unexpected but nice emergency."

"Have fun, sweetie."

"I hope so." I laugh.

Two hours later it feels so weird to be in public at a sports bar with a man who isn't my husband. We're at Christian's Tailgate, Jordan's suggestion. In my head, Jordan and I might as well be spread out on top of a table having sex in broad daylight, that's how strange this is. But we settle in and play catchup. We nibble on hot wings and salted fries, and sip non-alcoholic beverages. And although this spot is clear across town, I can't help but scrutinize my surroundings every few minutes.

"Hey, relax. We're old friends. We have a right to reconnect. You're grown."

"True that," I respond, but inside I'm thinking if I don't want Forrest to know I'm here, is it okay to do this?

And does Forrest think like me when he's out with his so-called friends?

"I'm glad we're meeting," I tell Jordan and give him a reassuring smile. "I just want to be cautious."

"Baby girl, I promise I won't hurt you. I'm not like Forrest." He laughs. "Man, dude was tripping back in the day."

"Yeah, he was so possessive it turned into a problem. That's why I had to change my number so abruptly. I regret we lost touch." Long ago Jordan and Forrest were tight even after I got married. And back then, Jordan was one of the crew that came over to the house for our famous movie nights. But after a while, especially after too many innocent touchy-feely moments between Jordan and me, Forrest cut him off. "So sorry. I didn't need Forrest to constantly falsely accuse me even though we weren't doing anything wrong."

"I guess he was threatened by me. We used to work out together all the time, you remember that?"

"Yes, you two used to meet up at the gym every other day." Forrest wasn't in shape like he is these days.

"I guess old boy got bothered by what he saw." Jordan flexes his bulging muscles, tosses back his head, and laughs. Then he quickly changes the subject. He asks dozens of questions. How is life treating me? How do I enjoy being a mother these days? What are my favorite movies, music CDs, and places to go? Am I happy? It feels like an interview, yet I detect a rare sincerity.

"You could have been my woman, you know that, don't you?" Jordan has a serious look on his face. "It was all a matter of timing. And luck."

"You think?" By now we've ordered red wine. Two glasses of Pinot Noir for me. I'm feeling good, sexy, and no longer care about who's coming in the front door of Christian's Tailgate. Plus there're mostly white folks in here anyway so . . . I need to chill.

"Carmen, you were my dream girl. But I was still trying to get it together back then. I wasn't quite ready for you, but I always wanted you."

"That makes me feel good, Jordan. You know I was crazy about you, too . . . years ago." What difference does that make now?

"And a man never forgets the woman he almost hooked up with."

It feels so hot in here all of a sudden.

"I always imagined what you looked like without those cute T-shirts and tight jeans you loved to wear."

"Jordan, please—"

"I've always wanted to do just that."

Jordan was always very direct. In the past, his candor intimidated me. Now it intrigues me. I like feeling wanted, attractive. Jordan's chasing after me turns me on in a way I haven't felt in a long time.

Before I know it, I'm following this man back to his place. I'm pleased to find out that Jordan lives in a luxury town house near downtown. He insists that I pull my MKT inside his one-car garage while he parks right at his front door. We walk upstairs to the living area right above the garage. It's a decent-sized and impeccable contemporary place with a homey feel. He gives me the classic tour. Living room with white walls, dining room with chandelier, medium-size kitchen with black appliances, and a cute powder room on the first floor. His huge master bedroom with full bath and spacious closet are located upstairs.

"Nice pad," I say when we return to the living room. Based upon Jordan's pimped-out entertainment center, I can tell he's crazy about electronic gadgets. He has iPhone, iPad2, iPods, DVR, DVD, underwater digital cameras, you name it.

"Whenever I'm home, this room is where I like to chill, get my drink on, and listen to my music."

"Who do you like?"

"Kanye, Drake, B.o.B., Babyface, Trey Songz, Ben Tankard, and the King of Pop, to name just a few."

"No females?"

"Ooops, yeah. Alicia Keys is *bad*. She's a great musician."

I notice a full set of Casio keyboards set against the far wall of his dining room.

"Speaking of musicians, I assume you still play, huh?"

"You remember?" His tender look makes my heart skip a beat.

"Some things you never forget."

We lock eyes.

Jordan pours me some Chardonnay. I relax on his sofa. He takes a seat in front of his keyboards and starts playing a beautiful version of Pachelbel's *Canon*. I remember this song as a child. The music relaxes me. I get lost in the dreamy melody and feel shocked and impressed. There aren't too many men I know who can play classical pieces. He's captured my complete attention.

Once Jordan's done, he plops down next to me and we chitchat. He shares stories of his travels across the country and describes his life as an adventure. He tells me how it's hard for him to maintain a long-term relationship with a woman but how he needs one nevertheless.

"Everyone has needs," I reply.

"I'm glad we agree on that."

He scoots closer to me and, after a while, picks up my hand and threads his fingers in between mine. I sense that he's staring at me as he talks. It feels good to have his attention.

I feed Jordan's ego by telling him how wonderful he looks and how great he smells.

"What cologne is that?"

"Usher for Men, of course."

"That is definitely your signature fragrance. You smell irresistible."

I pretend like I'm Forrest, trying to envision how he connected with all his jump-offs. Gradually, I release self-consciousness and sweep away thoughts of my husband.

This is nothing. No big deal.

A little later, Forrest begins affectionately touching my face and running his fingers through my hair. I love this and I let him. Not long afterward he unbuttons my blouse and caresses my breasts. He strokes my nipple with his fingertip. I shiver and moan. He leans next to my mouth and begins teasing me by kissing my cheeks, my nose, my chin. His tactics work because I grab his face between my hands and forcefully press his lips against mine. We kiss and explore each other's tongues for a good half hour. Forrest's face flashes in my head. I squeeze out the vision of my husband until he disappears. French kissing is not a felony. But when Jordan reaches in my panties and starts groping me, I clear my throat.

"Mmm-mmm," I say breathlessly, coming up for air. "That's enough."

"Why?" he complains. "I want you."

"Don't worry," I tell him as I stand up and button my blouse. "This is just the appetizer."

10

When I get home that night, thankfully Forrest is in the front yard retrieving our empty garbage cans from the curb. So when I park in my side of the garage, I simply wave at him. I'm appreciative of the fact that he's focused on trash outside our house while I'm left to deal with my trashy thoughts.

I rush upstairs and get undressed so I can shower. It feels odd to admit that I enjoyed secretly meeting up with a sexy, attentive man who I know likes me. Scrubbing Jordan's scent off me isn't easy. But it's a must. I engage in a mental war. *I'm not a slut. I'm just doing what some men do. It's just sex. But it wasn't even that. So I haven't a thing to worry about and no reason to feel guilty.*

By the time the evening is over, the only thought I entertain is *act like a man, think like a man.*

I convince myself that I've done nothing wrong. Besides, I know my limitations and I'll never do anything to truly hurt Forrest. Plus, if he ever finds out, what can he say?

I spend Sunday afternoon getting my nails and hair done. While I am at the salon, Jordan texts me to ask if we can meet tomorrow for lunch. His treat. I tell him "sure."

So on Monday, I walk Briana to her first-grade class. Ms. Collette, her beautiful young teacher, stops to chitchat with me for a minute. When we're done, she wishes me well, takes Briana's hand into hers, and escorts her into the classroom.

I rush back home to make sure Forrest is sound asleep. Then I spend time getting Jazzy dressed and we take a trip to the Sugar Land Ice & Sports Center. Even though Briana is the one who's in the beginner's class, Jazzy gets mesmerized watching the other kids glide and spin on the ice. I park the car, and we enter the facility and find one of the few available seats remaining in a section designated for spectators. I place Jazzy in my lap and she excitedly claps her hands while watching several skaters practice some moves from *The Nutcracker on Ice*. Before long, my little girl falls asleep. That's when I decide to call Shalita.

"Girl, this is getting so tricky. I made plans to meet with J for a late lunch, but it'll feel weird to ask Forrest to watch Jazzy."

"You're doing the damn thing, huh," Shalita says.

"It's nice to reconnect with an old friend."

I tell her how he played the keyboards for me at his town house while I sipped wine. And I mention how he acted like he wanted to hear anything I had to say. But I leave out the freaky deaky parts.

"It all made me feel very, very special, something that I desperately need. You know how long it's been since I've actually made true headway with Forrest. Seeing J is a nice little release."

"I heard that, but are you absolutely sure about this?"

"Oh, now you want me to be cautious, yet you encouraged me to go for it. What happened to the chick that was angry for me?"

"Girl, I still have your back. I'm just saying. You have little ones to think about."

"I've always had little ones to think about, Shalita." For the first time, a small twinge of regret occupies my heart. But hell,

Forrest is a parent, too. The fact that he has three kids hasn't stopped him from making new friends and whooping it up on the slick. Of course, rules are different and more advantageous for some men.

"Well, hell, now I don't know what to do."

"Cancel." Shalita sounds more serious than usual. "Tell him you got rained out and Elvis has left the building."

"Shalita, girl, you sound like I'm treating this like a game. But I assure you, I'm not playing games."

"And that's what I'm scared of. Who knows how this can end up? I don't want you to get caught up and hurt."

"It isn't even about all that. I can handle myself." Inside I feel resentful. So Forrest can get away with engaging in casual sex, but I can't even be around a male friend because I wasn't born with testosterone?

"Don't leave your baby with your hubby to go fuck your man."

"We aren't doing that."

"Not yet."

"Oh Shalita, chill, I got this."

"All jokes aside, Jordan may be a nice, former friend, but I just think that's a dangerous hole to crawl into."

"I still need to climb in."

"Okay, I give up. You're stubborn, girl."

"I'm determined."

"Then go head on witcha bad self."

Shalita and I talk some more. I have to make sure she isn't angry with me for my male-driven decisions. She argues I can think like a man, but I mustn't forget that I'm still a woman. Soon, I hang up from my best friend feeling anxious. Is Shalita right? Am I too feminine to try and safely accomplish what some men do?

Jordan texts me:

WE STILL ON?

I reply:

How about dinner?
Kewl. What time? Everything ok?
7. Babysitter issues.
Gotcha. TTYL.

On impulse, I text Dante and tell him he'll be paid fifteen bucks to watch the kids.

He quickly replies:

NO PROB.

Right before twilight, I stand in front of my house chatting it up with my neighbor. After a while, Toni's Honda slowly pulls up. She turns off the ignition. Dante exits the car. Then Toni gets out and slams her door. Today her hair is burgundy.

I say good-bye to my neighbor and walk up to Toni. "I thought Halloween was over."

"Carmen, you can only hope you look this good." She smirks, then stares me up and down. "You're sure dressed mighty fancy tonight. You don't look like you're about to go to Bible study."

"Don't worry about where I'm going."

"I will too worry when you call my son at the last minute on a school night asking him to babysit while you go to church. That's sounds so fake. *You* and *church*? Bitch, please."

"Toni, like I said before, I don't pay you any attention."

"I'll bet if Forrest knew what you're doing you'd pay attention."

"He already knows," I lie.

"Then it won't be a problem when I bring it up to him next time we talk."

"I can't stand you." I break down. More than anything it feels disturbing to see Dante gape openmouthed at me and

Toni. And why shouldn't he? We're further perpetuating the myth that some women just can't get along. Do I really want to be viewed in this manner? Why can't I just let her comments slide off my back?

"Toni," I reply, trying to calm down. "If you'd just remember your role and let me play mine, everything would be okay."

"I'll try to remember that next time your husband eats my coochie while he's on the phone lying to you. Bye, bitch."

I watch horrified as Dante runs into the house. What must he think of his mother's words and actions? And is Forrest actually still sexually involved with his baby mama?

The stress of my encounter with Toni makes me even more eager to see Jordan. Damn Forrest. Damn Toni. Damn everybody and everything.

Desperation is driving me to a place I never knew I could go.

Endless traffic laws are broken as I try to get to Jordan's. He meets me outside the town house and lets me park in his garage again. I follow him upstairs. It's only my second time in his place, but it feels like my home away from home. I slide my shoes off my aching feet and get settled. He hands me a glass of wine, then sits on the far corner of the sofa and pats his lap. I hesitate but scoot closer to him and take a gulp from my glass.

"You look stressed. How was your day?" Jordan asks.

I talk. Jordan listens. I tell him about how I cleaned the entire house until it was spotless. And I let him know that I successfully completed the *People* magazine crossword puzzle. He laughs out loud, then says he is proud of me. I like that. I feel myself begin to loosen up. He cracks a couple of jokes and does a mean impression of President Obama.

"God bless you and uhhh, God bless the United States of America." I scream with laughter. He's so dead on. He tickles me under my arms until I beg him to stop.

"You look so beautiful when you're happy."

"Do I? I-I don't know what I am sometimes." It's an honest answer.

"Well, what do you ask for when you pray?"

"To be honest, I just want to have true joy in my heart, peace in my soul. I want my family to be happy, safe, and secure."

"That sounds reasonable."

"I hope so."

"Well, young lady. My prayer is for you to be happy and feel safe, especially when you're with me."

"That's hard to achieve considering what we're doing."

"Well, don't think about it too much. Enjoy the moment. I love you to pieces and love having you around. And your body is just irresistible."

I scowl, a little perturbed. "How would you know that, since we've never had sex?"

"Don't get me wrong. I respect you immensely, but I must tell you how I feel about you. Is that fair? Can I help it that my attraction to you hasn't wavered over the years?"

What can I say? I am flattered.

"I guess I can't fault you for being honest about what you want."

"See there. That's all I'm trying to tell you, Carmen."

I love the way Jordan's voice sounds when he's talking to me. I detect sincerity. And I like the way he keeps it one hundred with me.

Minutes later I wonder how my head ended up resting in his lap with my face looking up at him. Several fireless candles are lit and reek with the scent of apple cider. The mood feels so romantic and cozy. I'm touched by his attention to detail.

And when we both relocate to his bedroom a half hour later, I feel tipsy as I get undressed.

"You got a condom? I don't want to get pregnant."

"Don't worry. We're good."

We lock eyes as he smoothly slips on a condom and, satisfied, I turn around in his bed and crawl on my knees with my back facing him. Jordan starts out placing sweet kisses on my neck, shoulders, and the center of my back. All my weak spots. Waves of pleasure flow through my body and I can't believe how good it feels. He moves his juicy lips across my ass. He flicks his long tongue across my vagina over and over again. I want to open up my mouth and scream. But I let him keep doing his thing. When he has me wet and ready, he enters me from behind. I let out a yell so loud I bury my face in the pillows. As he pounds and thrusts against me, I release all my frustration from the past six months. I scream, growl, weep, and moan, and start speaking in tongues.

Sex with Jordan is better than I'd ever imagined. I feel liberated, powerful, and desired.

"C'mon, now your turn," he says. I get on top of him and start pumping into a sexy rhythm that makes his toes curl.

"Woo baby, you're a tigress," Jordan says, exhausted from his orgasm.

"I'm glad someone thinks so," I pant. I feel totally content.

11

After that first night with Jordan, I can't bring myself to sleep in bed next to Forrest. Sleeping next to him would feel too odd, like he's an enemy whom I wouldn't want watching me from close range. Every weekend when Forrest doesn't have to work, instead of lying in bed next to him like we usually do, I quietly retreat to the upstairs guest room, the bed where Dante sleeps whenever he spends the night.

Of course, Forrest notices my pattern change right away and corners me with a barrage of questions.

"You're on your period?"

"No."

"I smell funky or something? I snore too loud?"

"Stop asking me. You already know why," I say in a biting tone. But of course, Forrest hasn't a clue.

The next time my mom has the girls overnight, I go and spend time with Jordan. I actually stay with him from early evening until the next morning. We make love and cuddle afterward. One thing I crave is engaging pillow talk. So I love it when Jordan lets me rest my head on his chest and listens to me chatter about whatever I want. He happily holds me in his arms and I have to fight images of Forrest flashing in my head.

When I begin to cry, Jordan thinks it's because he's pleased me so well.

It feels weird to quietly slip into the house right before Forrest returns from work. I lay my Coach bag on the kitchen counter, then retreat to the library. The light from the computer screen gives the room a spooky glow. Of course he forgot to log off from yesterday. So when I see more unread e-mails from Daphne and Big Titty Blonde Woman, I don't feel guilty. In fact, it feels amazing to keep a dirty secret from my husband. And when condemnation lashes at me later that day, I shut out the voices until they turn into a whimper.

The third time I sleep with Jordan, I come home in the middle of the night, take a shower, and retreat to our guest room. Forrest practically gets on his knees and begs me to come back.

"I told you I'm sorry," he pleads when he enters the guest room looking for me. "I'm not doing anything."

"Not according to your definition, huh?"

"Baby, please don't do this. You don't understand."

"Oh, I understand all right. Trust me."

"What you mean by that?"

I turn away from him and walk out the room, leaving him alone. Is this how it feels to act like a man, think like a man? Do hurtful things and freeze out any emotional feeling associated with my actions?

Two days later, when I go visit at my mom's, I slyly ask Varnell about the psychology of men.

"I'm sorry, but it seems that some men lack emotions and can act uncaring and I don't like it."

Varnell disagrees.

"Sis, men are very emotional. Just because Forrest acts uncaring doesn't mean a thing. He has feelings and they're deep just like yours. He just has a different way of expressing them."

"Hmm, oh really," I say as if I don't care at all. "Then why is it when I used to ask Forrest about the issues we're having, he blew me off? I'm trying to get to the root of our problems. He will talk two to three minutes and after that, it's time to change the subject."

"He feels bad about the topic. That's it. He wants you to move on at his pace, not at yours."

"That's bull," I say angrily. "It can take him six months to do his dirt but he wants me to get over it in two days. Not gonna happen."

"I see your point, Carmen, but if he said he's sorry, believe him. You gotta move on at some point. Can't punish the man forever."

"Are you taking his side? You don't know what he's done to me."

"I can pretty much figure it out and it's not that I like it one bit. I will put my foot up his butt if he hurts you, but if y'all ever get to the point that you can really talk and he is remorseful, that's different." Varnell looks at me with kindness. "Forgive the man wholeheartedly and you may see the change that you desperately want."

Listening to Varnell only makes me angrier. Why can some men do wrong and don't want to be reminded of their faults? Was the world really made to accommodate the wants and desires of men, and women were conveniently left out?

I try to go about my day and wonder if Forrest and I can ever recommence a normal relationship. Memories of our good old days make me smile: the silliness, teasing, closeness, and being down for each other. Once you have experienced beautiful things in a relationship, you never ever want to let them go.

When I depart from Mommy's, I'm occupied throughout the afternoon with light grocery shopping, getting an oil change, and going to the mall to pay my Dillard's and Macy's bills. But when I look up and see that Good Ole Dayz has texted me ten times and left three voice mails, I wonder what the hell is going on. I dial his number.

"Hey there."

"Are you okay?" He sounds worried. "I called you a long time ago."

"I know," I say, slightly put off. "I was pretty busy this morning running errands."

"Oh okay. Cool. Well, um, are we going to hook up tonight?"

"No, I need to help Briana with her homework. And Jazzy has been battling a slight cold so I want to be there for her."

"How about tomorrow?"

"I'll have to let you know."

"As long as we see each other this week."

"Hmm," I say, barely listening to him.

"I-I miss you, my little Carmen Foster."

I don't say anything. It feels awkward to divide my heart between Jordan versus what's going on at home. I'm distracted and ready to get off the phone. I tell him good-bye and promise we will meet up as soon as I get a chance.

Insanity reigns the entire week. My daughter's cold turns into the full-blown flu. I spend many hours attending to her, monitoring her temperature, giving her over-the-counter meds, and trying to make sure the rest of the household stays healthy. It's only after her temperature stabilizes that I can feel relaxed.

Saturday mid-morning, Dante pops by unexpectedly.

"Oh hey," I tell him in surprise when I open the front door.

I look past his head at the scene in front of our house. Toni actually gets out the car, smiles, and waves. I stare openmouthed at her.

Dante says, "The fellas are getting together today for b-ball. Sorry I forgot to call you before I came."

"Don't be silly, son. I told you before you're always welcome."

Dante struggles to maintain eye contact and he keeps shifting from one foot to the other.

"Are you okay? You want me to fix you something to eat?" I ask. He quietly follows me to his favorite room in the house.

"I'm cool." He rummages through the cupboards. "I can use a bowl of cereal. Then I'll head to the court." He turns to face me. "You're coming, right? Is my baby sister better?"

"Actually, she is." I beam at him.

"Then ya'll have to be there to watch me play. Jazzy needs some fresh air."

"Sounds like a plan because we are sick of having cabin fever. Tell you what, give me time to fix the girls' hair and we'll join you in a bit."

This morning I'm feeling significantly better than I have in the past few days. Jazzy scared all of us. Her fever got so high I rushed her to the emergency room two days ago as a precaution. The ER physician assured me my baby would be fine in no time; just a nasty bug going around.

When I brought Jazzy home from ER, both Forrest and I kissed her so much she got mad at us. I loved how my husband and I pulled together and collectively handled the care of our precious daughter. At one point, Forrest even broke down and cried. It felt so awkward and I didn't know how to comfort him. Yet his rare display of emotion cemented my belief that Forrest does care about his family.

Thinking about how grateful I am, I happily pour Dante a big bowl of Rice Krispies. I laugh when he insists I make him a mug of chocolate milk, too. He hastily eats and waits for me to get the girls ready.

I carefully bundle the girls in jackets and hats so they're warm and snug. As a precaution, I also wear my thick wool coat, tie a knit scarf around my neck, and pull a matching oversized hat over my hair.

Soon we walk down to the neighborhood park. The crisp November air that sweeps across my cheeks makes me feel good and alive. The brilliance of the sun makes it a beautiful Saturday morning. We feed the squirrels and enjoy being outdoors.

After a good ten minutes, I feel someone standing behind me. Two warm hands cover my eyes.

"Guess who?"

"I don't know."

"Who do you want to see more than anyone else on earth?"

"Hmmm, my husband?"

Suddenly I see sunlight again and I turn around. Even though Jordan is scowling, he still looks very handsome. "No wonder you haven't returned my calls."

"Please, not here," I tell him, feeling slightly uneasy. "My baby got sick. I told you that."

"No, you didn't."

"Well, I could have sworn I texted you."

"Check your phone."

"What? I'm not doing that. I couldn't make it and that's that."

He actually gives me a steely look and walks away.

Although his actions hurt me, I simply concentrate on the girls while they play. I try hard to ignore the guys as they shoot hoops. The blazing sun provides a little warmth on this cool day. I remove my hat and scarf and stuff them into my satchel.

Later on, Dante races up to me out of breath. "The fellas are all going to meet at Cici's Pizza for a bite to eat. You wanna come? You and my sisters?"

"Yayyyyyyyyyyyyyy," Briana screams. Jazzy screams, too, even though she hasn't a clue what's going on.

I reluctantly agree. We practically run home, pile up into my MKT, and head over to the pizza parlor.

In the restaurant, I ease through the buffet line and load our trays with mouthwatering zesty pepperoni, ham, and pineapple slices, some fresh tossed salad, pasta, and dipping sticks. We settle into a nearby booth next to a big window adjacent to the parking lot. Briana occupies the seat across from me. Little Jazzy is stationed between me and the window.

It doesn't take long for Jordan to join us.

"May I sit down?" He squeezes in next to me before I can respond.

"I'm sorry for running up on you at the park. I was just happy to see you. Forgive me?"

"Of course."

Then Jordan pretends he's Obama and starts cracking jokes as if he's headlining a comedy show. The goofy expression he makes causes me and the girls to shriek with laughter. I realize how much I've missed his company. When he isn't pressuring me he can be a lot of fun.

"Man, you're too much," I tell him. Jordan smiles at me like he's grateful to be in my presence.

"You look amazing even in a lot of clothes."

"Jordan, stop it," I giggle.

He leans against me and places his arm around me. He presses his lips against my ear and starts nibbling on it. "I can't wait to make love to you again," he whispers.

Several bright lights flash.

I look up. Toni is aiming her digital camera at us. She takes two more shots, then runs from the restaurant.

Forrest is gone with Phil when we finally get home from Cici's, a trip that was delayed because the girls insisted on finishing their pizza.

Once I step inside my house, I am shaking like I'm in sub-zero weather.

I don't even get a chance to undress and think about what just happened when my doorbell rings.

I answer. Purple-haired Toni is standing on the landing. Her face is stony. It's clear she hates my guts.

"You gonna let me in?"

Normally the answer is hell no, but I widen the door and step aside.

She struts around like she owns the place, inspecting all our family photos, admiring the furniture, the African-American artwork that graces the walls, and our top-of-the-line kitchen appliances.

"Mmm, mmm. Must be nice."

She's salivating like she knows everything I have will be hers one day.

"Toni, what do you want?"

"You know what I want."

"No, I do not."

"Well, it appears you're living your best life."

"I'm not. You don't know what you're talking about."

"I know what I saw." She laughs. "I know that damn much."

"So what are you saying?"

"I'm saying that I will keep your secret safe and I promise not to release these photos if you don't make a big scene when I hook back up with Forrest. I miss feeling his lips on me. Both of my lips."

She makes my skin crawl. "What? Are you trying to black-mail me?"

"Bitch, I can destroy your marriage. But actually it's you who's destroyed it. If you hadn't whined about Forrest getting a little bit of sex on the side—"

"I beg your pardon."

"Look, you need to keep it one hunnert. If I had a nice ass pad like this and drove around in a late-model whip like you, I'd keep my stupid little mouth shut and let my fine rich hus-band do whatever he wanted. You can't find men like him on every corner, sweetie."

"First of all, we're not rich."

"Do you live in a roach-infested apartment? Is your neighborhood known for muggings and constant breakins where you fear for your life and you're scared to come out after dark? Does your car constantly break down on the highway?"

"Well, no."

"Point is, compared to me you're Oprah, or even Stedman. You're living large. Y'all got a whole lot more than—"

"I ain't no damn Oprah and you know it. Poor excuses." I try to reason with her. "Toni, I happen to know there are plenty of well-off good men out there if you'd just take the time to find them."

"I don't have time for all of that."

"Oh, but you make time to interfere with my relationship and be all up in my business?"

"I have business with Forrest, too, and there's nothing you can do to change that."

I look at her in disbelief. "I get it now. You still can't get over this sick fairy tale you have where you think Forrest would have married you. And you'd have all this, right, Toni?"

"You damn straight."

"But don't you know that Forrest's father wasn't going to leave him a cent as long as he was dating you? Daddy Foster breathed easier about that sizable insurance policy only after you broke it off with Forrest. He felt like I was the better woman for his son. You were never going to have all this."

She looks like I just slapped the taste out her mouth.

"Look, bitch. For all I know you're telling lies on a dead man. I'm getting what's mine whether you like it or not. And if you give me any trouble, guess who's going to see these pictures? Then what's mine will really be mine. 'Cause Forrest will flip out if he knows what you're up to: that you're fucking a man that's the worst frenemy he's ever had. You know it would mess him up and you still too damn selfish to care about your own husband."

Part 2

A Woman's Worth

12

I believe that some people were born just to squeeze out all the joy from other people's lives.

Overnight Toni starts calling the house like she's lost her mind. Talking caller ID announces her. I pick up and say hello and she asks to speak to Forrest. I want to slam down the phone so badly. Instead, I hand the phone over to him. I want to walk away, but I can't. I hang around and can hear her cackling over the line. I really despise this woman.

When Forrest gets off the phone with Toni, he looks at me like he's expecting a war. But he doesn't even get a small battle.

"Are you okay?" he asks.

"I don't know what I am." I walk away and leave him confused.

Sometimes I blame myself. I did a pretty good job of getting myself into this situation. But if he hadn't cheated on me, I wouldn't be cheating on him. Previously I've never been unfaithful in a relationship. Always despised cheaters. Now it's undeniable that I am one.

My nerves are so shaken that I have started sipping on wine in the evenings when Forrest goes to work. And if he comes home two hours late the next morning, my lips are sealed together as tight as super glue.

I want to explode.

I want my old life back.

But a thief has infiltrated my house and I don't know how to get her out.

Not long afterward, I decide to go spend Saturday night at Shalita's. And since Forrest doesn't have to work, I conveniently leave the girls with their father.

He agrees to watch them, but asks me where I'm going.

"I need to get away. But I'll be back."

"Have fun."

His casual attitude irritates me.

When I arrive at Shalita's, I feel so anxious. Restless. And like I'm getting farther away from the things that I really cherish.

Why can't I have a simple, happy family life with a loving husband? What happened to the man I thought I married? Who is this woman I'm becoming?

I walk into Shalita's place loaded with questions. She gives me a nice hug and invites me in. We retreat to her tiny but comfortable living room, where the music of Mary J. Blige is softly playing in the background.

"And what's been happening in your world, young lady?" Shalita asks. She has a wicked gleam in her eye. I guess she thinks I've turned into a wild and crazy housewife.

"Shalita, nothing's going on. Trust me."

"And your fine-ass hubby been on his best behavior?"

"As good as can be expected."

"What does that mean?"

"It means absolutely nothing."

"Girl, you're scaring me."

"You don't know what being scared is."

We end up having an awful time, even though she tries to cheer me up by making homemade Margaritas.

"I've been drinking way too much lately," I tell her after one glass.

"That means you're either very happy or very sad."

"Well, all I can tell you is one of those answers is correct."

We talk some more until I feel so drowsy that I want to pass out. She lets me sleep in and doesn't harass me with more probing questions. I leave her house mid-morning the next day and I drag myself home.

When I first enter my house, it sounds eerily quiet.

The first person I see is Briana in the kitchen. She's struggling to hold a gallon of milk and is trying to pour some over a bowl of cereal.

"Negligee. Negligee," she quietly says to herself.

"Good morning, love. I see you're practicing a new word." I beam at her and playfully tug at her hair. "What's that mean, sweetie?"

"A negligee is a sexy nightgown a woman wears when she wants to be with her man. It also means 'neglected.' "

"I know you didn't learn that from Miss Collette."

"No, Mommy. I didn't get that from school—"

My purse makes a thud when it drops on the floor. All the contents spill out. I bend down and start picking up my wallet, lipsticks, ink pens, packs of gum, Kleenex, pens, and my checkbook.

"Briana, baby. Has anyone been in our house?" I say in a gentle but shaking voice.

"I dunno," she shrugs. "Daddy made us go to bed early. I didn't even get to play first."

"Oh my God."

Briana's still talking as I leave her to run to the master bedroom.

The door is closed.

I twist the handle.

The lock won't budge.

"Oh Jesus," I utter. I frantically knock, bracing myself in

case I hear animal noises. But I hear nothing. I envision Forrest's head between Toni's legs. I can't stand thinking about it.

"Briana, bring me the phone."

I can barely think straight when I call Forrest. My call goes straight into voice mail. I am tempted to dial his voice mail, but I just can't do it. I'm so tired of all this.

I'm still standing at the bedroom door staring into space.

A finger taps my shoulder.

"Looking for someone?"

I spin around. It's Toni. She's smiling. Her bone-straight hair is dark orange. She looks like a fool. I feel like one.

"What? How?"

"I came to y'all's door ringing the doorbell and knocking for the longest. It took a while for Briana to open it."

"So you're just now getting here?"

"Yes! What is your problem? I'm dropping off Dante. I saw Forrest in the backyard when I walked around to see if anyone was home."

Relief washes over me.

"Now, sweetie, I'm going to need to borrow him in a few nights. There's a big production being put on at Dante's school and I don't want to roll up there without his daddy. So . . ." She looks at me like I'd better not disagree with her.

"I don't think that's a good idea."

"What did you say?"

"I said I'm sure he'll be happy to adjust his schedule for the play."

"Much better. Ciao."

Several times that week, Forrest comes home late. He doesn't say a word to me. I pretend like I don't see him. The tension feels unbearable.

Jordan continues to blow up my cell phone. I ignore his calls. I'm not ready to talk to him.

On Sunday, we're all eating breakfast in the kitchen. Forrest has made his fabulous banana pancakes, crispy fried bacon, cheesy eggs, and hot grits. I'm standing next to the island counter pouring everyone small glasses of apple juice. The doorbell rings. It's ten o'clock in the morning.

Forrests volunteers to answer the door. Toni bustles into the kitchen with her heels loudly clicking across the floor. She's wearing a dark brown suit and her hair is black and tied into a neat ponytail.

"She said you wouldn't mind." Forrest shrugs and resumes fixing our meal.

"Toni, what do you think you're doing?"

"I know you're not talking to me in that tone."

I stare at this chick like she's lost her mind. Here I am in front of my family, the people I love and care about, and she's acting as if I'm the one barging into her home.

"Forrest, will you excuse us?" I ask. I nod at Toni and she follows me into the family room.

"Toni, let me be frank. You either have a lot of damn nerve or a lot of confidence."

"Thanks for the compliment."

"What?" I say, exasperated. "This is not a compliment. You're crazy, not confident. And I'm sick of your taking all this a little too far."

"You haven't seen far, sweetie." I hate when people threaten me.

"Toni, c'mon, this is ridiculous. What are you trying to do?"

"I'm trying to keep you out of trouble."

"Oh okay. When I really think about it, those photos don't mean anything. And I'm getting to the point where I don't care anymore."

"Is that right?" She reaches inside her tote. "Hey Forrest, come here. I wanna show you something—"

"No, please don't. Please." In my heart, I don't want Forrest to know what I've done. He's a man, and men do not play when it comes to cheating wives. The double standard sucks. I know I'd end up with nothing, and as much as I want revenge, losing my husband and my family isn't what I want.

Toni grins satisfactorily at me. "No more of your trying to interfere. 'Cause one thing I know is you don't want anyone messing up your perfect little family. If you ever threaten me again, I will go to Forrest's job. You got that?"

I can't believe her. A woman that colors her hair a different shade every couple of weeks is liable of doing anything. She just doesn't have sense enough to care about herself or anybody else. Hot liquid gathers around my eyelashes and my vision blurs. I feel so broken, so trapped.

I follow Toni back into the kitchen. She convinces Forrest to let all of us attend church together as a family.

"Why would we do that?" he asks.

"Carmen will do anything, and I mean anything, to keep her little family together."

He looks baffled and turns to me for approval. I feel like a woman with heavy chains tied around her feet and legs. All I can do is nod.

What can I do to fix this mess?

13

I walk into the bedroom when I notice Forrest hurriedly getting off the phone. I'm carrying a basket filled with folded laundry that needs to be placed in the dresser drawers.

"Who were you talking to, Forrest?"

"Toni."

"Again?"

"Why? Does it bother you?"

"It depends. Were you talking about Dante?"

"Not really."

"Then . . . yes. It bothers me."

"Oh really? Because lately it's obvious you don't give a damn what I do."

"Oh, but I do."

"Then why are you letting Toni take over?"

"Well, um, it's just that I've been trying to do something different. It's called trying to trust you."

He looks as skeptical as I feel. "Is that what you call it?"

If only you knew.

"Your *trying* to trust me doesn't seem to be working. I've never seen you so miserable. That bothers me."

My thoughts immediately turn to Varnell. Maybe my brother is on to something. If Forrest notices my demeanor and appears concerned about my well-being, is it true he does care and have feelings? Not just about his kids, but me, too?

During the week leading up to Thanksgiving, I am nearly tempted to change my cell number again. The last time I held a conversation with Jordan was nine days ago.

I'm in the kitchen trying to relax with a hot cup of coffee. As I sit at the breakfast table, Jordan continues to contact me via text. He goes from heavy flirting, to pleading, to sending me sexy photos of him wearing no shirt. His chest is firm and tatted up. I'll admit the guy does have a nice body. But so what?

I text him: **PLEASE STOP.**

He responds: **WHAT HAVE I DONE 2 U?**

I text: **NOTHING. IT'S NOT U. IT'S ME.**

Him: **I DON'T UNDERSTAND.**

Me: **AND U NEVER WILL.**

Jordan sends me so many texts that I'm forced to turn off my iPhone.

The emotional struggle of dealing with this man makes me yearn for a change of pace. I venture upstairs and notice Forrest carrying a large Target bag into the home theater.

"What you got there?"

"I stocked up on some DVDs: *Unthinkable*, *Brooklyn's Finest*, *Boondocks*, *Taken*, and a half dozen Disney movies."

"That's cool. Nothing for me?"

"Like what?"

"Well, something a woman would like."

"Oh romance. Toni bought some girl-friendly movies that you might like. I just haven't unpacked them yet."

"What did you say?"

"She told me that you were okay with her going with me to Target and picking up a few things."

"Why would she say that? And why would you believe her?"

"I thought it was kind of strange, but figured this is the new you, you know what I'm saying? The woman who now trusts people including her own husband. Imagine that."

"Forrest, you're not being fair."

"Well, hell, lately you've been acting so strange I don't know what to think anymore."

I reach for my pocket to grab my cell, but realize if I power it up, a bunch of new texts from Jordan will chime as they load up. I really don't want to take that chance right now.

"Say what you want about Toni, at least she's trying to be more civil these days."

"Hmmm," I say absentmindedly, ignoring a comment that would normally make me livid.

"You were okay with Toni getting the movies, right?"

"Hold that thought. Be right back."

I jog down the stairs and head to the library. I'm thinking I can just use a landline. But Forrest's cell phone is sitting on the desk. It's just there. Calling to me like a hundred-dollar bill lying on the street. So, of course, I pick it up. My adrenaline surges. I slide my finger across the phone. What? No pass code like normal? When I nervously scroll through the phone to view the history, all recent calls are from his family. Or friends. No random chicks.

I can't believe that Forrest is suddenly on the straight and narrow. I race back upstairs holding his phone in my hand ready to apologize.

But before I reenter the home theater, I hear his voice. His back is turned to me. It looks like he has a cell phone pressed to his ear. And he's giggling like I've never heard him laugh before.

Who is Forrest talking to and why does he have two cell phones?

When he sees my face, he hangs up immediately.

"I *knew* it was too good to be true."

"What are you whining about now?"

"Forrest, even if I was trying to trust you, I can see it wouldn't do any good. Every time we take one step forward, we go two steps back. I'm tired of regressing!"

"Huh?"

"Stop it. Just stop it. I know you have two cell phones. Why would you deceive me and hurt me like this? What have I ever done to you?"

"Calm down, Carmen. This here is my work cell, not a decoy like you're probably thinking. You really need help."

For the first time, I agree with him. We all need big-time help.

14

The Saturday before Thanksgiving, Forrest decides we should have a movie night. We haven't had one in a while.

"Oh really?" I say to him as we're eating the delicious meal he's prepared. The girls and I are in the breakfast room. Our plates are loaded with hash browns, cheese and mushroom omelets, oatmeal, turkey sausage, oven-fried bacon, and sliced pears and cantaloupe.

"Yes, really. It's getting close to the holidays. We need to kick it with our friends and family. Chillax. You should invite Varnell."

"He wouldn't want to come."

"Why not? You've been poisoning him against me?"

"Forrest, please. I'm just saying that he has other plans and has better things to do than watch DVDs."

"Carmen." He shakes his head in pity. "Lately, you've been a hot mess. You need to loosen up, get out more, and have some fun."

"That's what I keep trying to tell Wife Number Two," says Toni. She's just burst into the kitchen with Dante trailing behind her. She drops a Walmart bag on the counter. "Here are some more movies. We're going to have so much fun tonight."

"She knew about this before I did?" I ask Forrest.

"Is there a problem, sweetie? Don't be mad at Forrest. Blame it all on me."

I swear I could kill this woman.

"It was my idea." She smiles broadly. "He was just nice enough to agree with me."

"W-what?"

"I thought that becoming more involved around here and being a leader would be a great way for me to work on my personality. Set a good example as a woman. You know I told you that, Carmen, now why you fronting?" Toni grins at me. "Keep it one hunnert."

"Um, can I have a word with you?" I grab Toni by the arm and yank her into the family room.

"Toni, I'm not sure what you're trying to do, but whatever it is, I've had enough of it. I want you to get the fuck out my house, out my life, and leave us the hell alone."

"Um, Forrest," she yells and reaches for her camera. "Come here. Right now."

Folding my arms over my chest, all I can do is leer at her. Forrest bumbles into the room looking aggravated.

"Yeah, what's up?" he barks. I hate when he is angry. I don't want his wrath to fall on me. Not today.

I plead at Toni with my eyes.

"Um, hey Forrest. I was wondering if you want me to play photographer tonight. You know, for, um, movie night. If so, I'll have to buy a new battery for my camera."

"It's cool. As long as Carmen doesn't mind."

"It's fine," I say in a feeble voice and sadly leave the room.

That night we have a packed house. Shalita comes over to give me moral support. Even Phil shows up.

"Hey, sister-in-law," he says and actually tries to kiss me on my cheek.

"What up? How's life treating you?"

"Oh well, I'm okay. My blood pressure has been bothering

me and I can't afford all the medicine and follow-up doctor appointments. Can you give me a payday loan?"

"Phil, I don't even have a job."

"Oh snap, my bad."

I shake my head and go sit next to Shalita, who is eating from a huge bowl of freshly popped popcorn.

At the front of the room, Forrest stoops before the DVD player and pops in a bootleg but decent copy of *Rise of the Planet of the Apes.*

"Welcome," he says. "Please, make yourselves at home and enjoy the first film of the evening."

"Yeah, about time," Shalita shouts, trying to be funny. "Hey you. Move out the way. I can't see."

"You talking to me?" Toni asks. Ever since the party started she's been scrambling all over the place acting like she's the happy little host. She seats all the guests as soon as they enter the theater and hands them drinks and everything. And when I approach her with that look, she smiles sweetly at me as if to say, "I wouldn't do that if I were you."

I don't want to make a scene in front of company, so I retreat to my seat and contemplate my next move.

Fifteen minutes into the ape flick, someone enters our darkened room. I sniff and smell the musky scent of Usher cologne.

I squint and clearly see Jordan's silhouette as he takes several steps in the dark.

When Toni seats him next to me, I whisper, "Who invited you?" Jordan points at Toni.

"I've missed you," he whispers back.

"Toni invited you? H-how long have you been in touch with her?"

"Long enough," he replies.

I start trembling like I have Parkinson's.

And when Forrest walks over to us and sees Jordan, I want to die.

15

I can't stand it. I begin to hyperventilate and feel like I cannot breathe. Shalita notices me right away and runs to cut the lights on before returning to my side.

"Everyone stand back and give the girl room to breathe. Someone please go get her a glass of water."

Shalita takes over and fans my face with her hands.

"Are you okay, Carmen?" she asks.

"No. No."

I freeze up when Forrest kneels next to me. His brows are raised and he clutches my hand firmly. "Why is he here? Who invited him?"

I glance at Toni. She shrugs and walks away.

"Did you ask him to come over here, Carmen?"

"No, I-I—"

"You sound like you're lying."

"Look, man," Jordan speaks up. "Just chill. I'm here because I was told you and I could squash our beef."

"Whoever told you that doesn't know me!" Forrest hops to his feet and begins pacing. The movie is on pause. And all our guests are giving us perplexed looks.

"Bottom line? I do not care for you, man. And I thought I

told you a long time ago to never come around my wife again. Do you remember that?"

"And do you remember I told you that you need to chill? Because the more you act insecure, the more those things will manifest themselves in your relationship. And even when nothing is happening, you'll think it is. But you're paranoid more than anything."

"Oh really. And how would you know all this?"

"Just value what you have, my man. Don't take her for granted. You got a good thing here. Real good."

I gasp. I can't believe Jordan is telling Forrest all this needless information. Why won't he shut up?

"And you know all this because . . ."

"Carmen is a sweet, kind, loving woman as long as you don't get on her bad side. She comes from a good family, that's all I'm saying."

"Jordan, don't tell me about her. I know her better than you. And from what I can recall, you've wanted to get with my girl since way back."

"Yes, Carmen and I go way back, man, that's no big secret."

Jordan looks so emotional, like he's seconds away from reaching over and gently stroking my cheek, a gesture he did four years ago that started all this mess between the three of us. Thankfully he thinks twice and keeps his hands to himself.

It feels like two men are fighting over me. And I realize that maybe hooking up with someone I actually know, rather than a casual stranger, may have complicated things more than I wished.

"Look, Jordan, I don't want to hear anything you have to say. The way I felt four years ago is how I feel today and how I'll feel tomorrow and the day after that. So catch a clue, get the fuck out my house, and I better not ever see you again."

Jordan gives me a frantic look like he wants me to defend

him. I feel so torn, so bad inside that it's hard to make heads or tails of anything right now.

"Baby, why don't you tell him?" Jordan asks.

I start wheezing heavily. My chest rises and falls, and everything grows silent and fades to black.

I never thought I'd see the day that I wake up in a hospital room with an IV attached to my arm. The room feels so cold. The curtains are drawn and I'm lying in the dark. I want to go home. I want to see my children. Where is my husband?

Shalita's face suddenly appears. She smiles brightly at me. Then Varnell whispers, "Thank you Jesus," and steps closer to my bed.

"Visiting hours are almost over," Varnell says. "But we've been here since six."

"What time is it?"

"Almost eight-thirty," Shalita says. "The nurse brought you some dinner, but you barely ate."

"I don't even remember eating. I feel drowsy and sick to my stomach."

Shalita brings me up to speed. She said that I passed out and was rushed to the hospital. I've been here two days. The doctors determined I had an anxiety attack, but I'll be okay. Forrest and the kids have visited as well as my mom. When Forrest caught Jordan entering my room, by the time it was over with, security had to escort both men from the hospital.

"Oh my God."

"Yeah, girl. It's been bad. And the worst part is Toni has been spending big time at your house."

"Don't tell my sister things like that."

I wince and try to sit up in bed.

"Get better soon. Get the hell out of here and go get your husband," Shalita tells me.

16

I get released from the hospital at noon that Tuesday. Shalita agrees to pick me up since Forrest told me he'd still be sleep. I hold my breath when I get into the house. The girls are with my mom. She feels I need my energy before I reconnect with them. So Varnell will bring them home tonight.

I go to my room and open the door. The bed is unmade. And empty. Where's Forrest? This homecoming falls drastically short of what I envisioned.

"Hey, if you don't need anything else, I'll be on my way. Glad to see you back where you belong," Shalita says.

"I'm not feeling the love right now, Shalita." I gasp. "It hurts so bad."

"Oh baby girl," she utters and gives me a warm embrace. "Despite me talking smack, I really do want everything to work out for you. You have that right. It may be a long struggle, but what's yours is yours."

"Oh great, now you tell me."

"I've always believed that. I just never appreciated seeing how Forrest treated you when he wasn't giving you his best. Your happiness is my main concern."

"I gotcha. I know. I feel you. I love you. Pray for me," I yell to her as she leaves the house.

I decide to go lie in my bed since I'm a little too exhausted to be climbing all those steps to rest in the guest room. It feels good to settle into my own bed and I am truly grateful to be out the hospital.

God knows there's no place like home.

But when I slide my feet around near the foot of the bed and hit something silky, the color drains from my face; the warm fuzzy feelings turn to disgust.

I dive headfirst under the covers and keep digging until my hand reaches a piece of clothing. I slide back out from underneath the comforter holding a red silk nightgown that I know I don't own.

"Oh God, why, why?" I wail and weep so long that my body and my mind surrender to the comfort of a deep sleep.

Later I call Varnell and ask if the girls can stay with Mommy one more night. I explain I need more time. He says no problem.

Satisfied that the girls are okay, I take a deep breath and pick up my phone and dial a number.

"Hey there. What's up? Are you okay?"

"Yes, I'm good," I say, pleased to hear the sound of concern in his voice. I like knowing he still cares.

"How's everything?"

"Well, I need you. Right now. Get to me."

"I'm on my way."

I tell him I'll be waiting and I text him exactly where to meet me. He responds:

YES MA'AM.

I take off the clothing that I wore to the hospital. And I search through my drawers, but nothing seems appropriate.

That's when I grab the red silk nightgown and slide it over my body.

When I hear a light tapping on my bedroom door, I say, "Come in."

Jordan looks around as if he's verifying it's safe to be in my home. Alone. Just me and him.

"I told you he's not here. It's cool. I wanted you to visit me here since you weren't allowed to see me at the hospital."

"Just making sure."

"Well, the fact that you're brave enough to show your face around here means a lot. You either care about me or have more confidence than anyone I know." Inside I'm rolling my eyes at the words I'm feeding to Jordan. Does he really love me or is he a nut bag? I don't care. I'm so tired. If this is a man's game, then I need to play it one hundred percent.

"Come over here." I open the covers for him.

"Carmen, you're crazy."

"I'm crazy about you."

"You're crazy, all right."

He bends over and I wrap my arms around him, squeeze tightly, and pull him on top of me. The fact that I can feel him throbbing makes this so much easier.

Yet I can't help think about what if Forrest walks in?

Lying there in bed with my arms wrapped around another man, I'm Elin Nordegren, Sandra Bullock, and Elizabeth Edwards all rolled up in one. These women are not black, but pain is colorless.

Revenge has no face.

Payback is merciless, doesn't care about gender, and each victim is at pain's mercy.

"Take off your clothes," I growl at Jordan.

He hesitates, but removes enough clothing to get the job done.

I smother his face with kisses. He shivers in my arms when I climb on top.

I lean over and press my lips against his, kissing him so fiercely he probably thinks I'm in love.

"I don't want nobody—nobody kissing you but me," I sing to him.

I'm too exhausted to stay on top. So when I ask Jordan to take over, he doesn't argue. When I let Jordan make love to me in Forrest's bed, I finally understand how it feels to act like a man.

17

The hardest thing in the world is to be married to someone who has become a stranger. The last few days—hell, the past several weeks—have been so trying. Many detrimental things are happening in our lives, but Forrest and I haven't been able to hold a real conversation in a long time. We got through the holidays, but the tension in our household was thick and nearly unbearable. Something's got to give.

Midweek, I go pick up Briana from school.

Miss Collette greets me at the driveway circle where kids safely play as they wait for buses or parents.

"How was your Thanksgiving?" she sweetly asks.

"Fine. Wonderful."

"Are you sure?"

"Why would you ask me that?" I look around to make sure my daughter can't hear us.

"Briana is an absolute doll. She's a joy to be around, but—"

"But what?"

"She recently asked me how to say something in French."

"Yes, I've noticed she's started to introduce even more French words around the house."

"Have you heard her say, '*Ma mère est triste*'?"

"As a matter of fact I have, and when I ask her what it means, she gives me a strange look, then runs away. After a while I just forgot about it." I pause and sigh heavily. "Miss Collette, what exactly is she saying?"

"My mother is sad."

"What?"

"Yes, ma'am. I've wanted to probe, but felt it wasn't my place. Yet when one of my most adorable ones is hurting, I've got to speak up."

"Oh Lord. My poor baby. I just had no idea. She's always smiling. Always playing."

"Mrs. Foster, I'm sure you know that children are very sensitive. And little Briana sees and feels everything that's going on in your home. She's your *daughter*, for God's sake! I just want to make sure everything is really okay."

"It hasn't been," I tell Miss Collette with honesty. "But it will be."

I go grab Briana's little hand and clutch it in mine. We get in the car and I buckle her seat belt. I lean over and hug her so long and hard she tells me to back off and complains that I'm hurting her.

"I know, baby girl. And I promise to never do that again."

I'm at home on Saturday evening taking a break after mopping and cleaning the oven and refrigerator. All the kids are gathered in the family room. They are sitting at the table hovering over Trouble, a fun game Varnell and I also played when we were younger. I'm so happy that Dante is completely taken with his little sisters. Both of them seem to bask in his presence and that makes me feel better. I quietly stand underneath the archway and observe my kids.

"Hey, now, no cheating," Dante playfully fusses at Briana.

"*Taisez-vous*," she says back.

"Are you telling me to shut up?"

"How'd you know?" she squeals.

"You think you're the only one who knows French?"

She claps her hands over her mouth.

"I'm watching you, little girl," he says sternly.

Briana bursts into tears and runs to me when she hears me chuckling at the exchange between her and Dante.

"Mommy, Te is acting mean to me."

"Me, too," Jazzy chimes in, although he's done nothing to her.

"Okay, 'Te,' " I tease him. "Leave us girls alone." Briana walks back to the game table.

Dante scoops both girls in his arms and gives them big fat kisses. "I'd never do anything to harm my little sisters. I love you, ya hear me? Even if you girls *do* cheat."

Forrest stumbles into the family room. His hand grips the neck of a whiskey bottle. That alarms me. He and whiskey have never been a good mix.

"Lying bastards, I'mma fuck y'all up." Forrest's slurred speech causes the color to drain from my face.

"Forrest, hush up. The kids can hear you. What are you doing?" I ask when I see him take a long swallow from his bottle.

"Leave me alone. Go find boyfriend number two since that's who you like laying with these days."

"Excuse me," I say and immediately gesture for the kids to leave. Briana starts crying and runs out the room, Jazzy following her.

Dante refuses to budge. He stands protectively by my side.

"I have a mind to whip your ass," Forrest slurs.

"What's wrong with you? What happened?" I'm scared to death.

"You and Michael fucking Jordan."

"What? That doesn't make sense."

"Stop lying. I saw what you've done. I have the proof you got with my boy. I can't believe you."

"Forrest, slow down. Tell me what you're talking about." I

wish I had my purse and phone with me. I'm so ready to escape this house.

"If you hadn't been so sloppy and left a condom in our toilet for every damn body to see." He stops talking, cries for a few seconds, and takes another swig. "I hope you're happy now."

"I don't know what to say. It's not what you think."

"I don't have to think shit coz I know what I see. I've seen the texts."

"How?"

"I cracked the code. I saw the photos. Him wearing no shirt. Bird chest bastard. I know it all."

I just stand there numb, staring into space. I curse myself for not remembering to delete the last few texts exchanged between me and Jordan. And the condom thing? For all I know Jordan didn't flush the toilet on purpose. I'm through with him.

Forrest stares at me, at the rings on my fingers, all around our huge family room with the tall ceilings, expensive furniture, and family photos in every corner. He takes one long look at me, then lunges at me and shoves me so hard I stumble backward, fall down. The back of my head hits a wall. I'm more startled than hurt, yet I feel afraid and so regretful.

"Daddy, don't. It's not her fault."

"What you talking about, boy? I'll beat your ass, too, like I'm about to beat hers."

"Forrest, you've never hit me," I cry out, rubbing my head. "Please don't start now. Give me a chance to explain."

"Nothing to explain. Your ass is mine."

He hovers over me looking like a monster and raises his hand.

"Noo, please don't," I scream. Dante tackles his dad and pins him to the floor.

"Daddy, listen. All this is my mother's fault. It's a setup. I feel like it's my fault, too. This whole Jordan stuff, I made it happen, but I didn't want to."

"Have you been drinking, too, boy?" Forrest asks.

"No, Daddy. It's the truth. For real, for real. Ma wants to marry you, Daddy. She wants you back. And she wanted you to have an affair. And she got Mama Carmen to hook up with Jordan so you'd find out and divorce her."

Tears slide down Dante's scrunched-up face. He gets off his dad and turns to me. I tremble while he holds me and hugs me tight around my waist.

"I'm sorry, Mama Carmen. I didn't mean to do it. I love my family. I do."

"I know you do, baby, I know. I-I'm sorry, too."

The girls are shrieking, Dante is crying, and Forrest looks completely devastated.

What have I done?

I'm so bewildered I unloose myself from Dante and run out the house.

18

I rush through the front door and step outside, my heart thrashing wildly inside of me. I've heard that man's biggest fear is that a scorned woman will flip out and pay him back. But woman's biggest fear is that a man will kill her.

Just as I'm standing there uncertain about what to do, I see Phil waiting in the passenger side of a car I've never seen before. I race down to the curb and motion at him to roll down the window. He rolls it down and smiles at me, his eyes glassy.

"Whassup, sister-in-law?"

The putrid smell of pot hits my nose.

"Phil, I need you. Can I get a ride?"

"Where's your car?"

"I can't find my car keys." I glance at the guy behind the wheel. He looks so out of it I'm shocked that the two were able to find our house.

"Please, if you let me drive your car I will pay both of you twenty dollars. But I don't have the money on me." My purse, cell phone, and keys are stuck in the house. "I'm good for the money. But we have to leave right now."

I run over to the driver's side and plead with Phil's friend.

Phil says, "Hey, I can use that money. Please let her do her thing. Get in the back."

I thank the guys for doing me this last-minute favor and we take off. I don't have my driver's license but simply do not care.

"Carmen, this is Doug. Doug, Carmen."

"Heyyy," I say, but I'm in no mood to meet any of Phil's friends.

"I just cannot believe this, I just can't."

"Who you talking to?" Phil asks. "What you talking about?"

"Don't mind me, Phil. I've got an issue that I need to handle and I'm sorry to put you in the middle of all this."

"It has to do with Forrest, huh? Girl, that man loves you to death. You're all he talks about."

"Are you serious?" I'm wondering if Phil is being frank, talking trash, or completely making it up.

"I'm telling you, sister-in-law, you're the truth to Forrest."

I want to scream. Phil's words tear through me like a pain I've never known. But it makes what I'm about to do even more critical.

When I stand in front of Toni's apartment door fifteen minutes later I feel like I'm in a nightmare. This type of drama has never been a part of my life. I'm barefoot, no phone, no money, nothing. But my heart and everything important to me are on the line.

As soon as Toni opens the door, I race straight for her neck. I grab her forcefully and push her up against a wall.

"Let me tell you something and you listen to me good. Stay away from my husband, my family, my house. If I ever see you near my house again, I will personally see to it that you'll live to regret it. You hear me?"

"Carmen, let me go. What the hell's wrong? What is your problem?"

"All this stuff going on. I just feel like a crazy person."

"Oh, in other words, it's a normal day for you."

"Toni, you know what? You're one sick-ass bitch."

"Oh no, you are not going to roll up in my house threatening me and calling me out my good name. But I'm glad you did because maybe now Forrest will finally see what type of bitch you really are. What does he see in you anyway? I'm about to call his ass right now."

"Call him. And while you're at it let him know that you used your own teenage son to break up his marriage."

She stops dead in her tracks. "What you say?"

"You heard me. What kind of mother does that? Dante told me everything. How you put him up to Jordan meeting me at the park. How you got your little girlfriends to 'accidentally' meet Forrest so they can seduce him. It's all a plot to build your case against me. To get me out the picture so you can have my husband."

"Bitch, please. Dante's lying and he's crazy."

"He's not lying, Toni, and you know it. You're the crazy one. I feel sorry that he has you for a mother."

Forrest walks in. Dante sheepishly follows behind him.

"My wife is right. Toni, you are crazy. And you're wrong. You're wrong to think I'd ever choose you over Carmen. And you're wrong to manipulate my son—my *son!*—in your dumb-ass scheme."

"I did all this because I love you. I've never stopped loving you."

"That's not love. That's manipulation. You know damn well I haven't slept with you in months, but you've done everything you can to make her think I did. And that red gown you planted in my bed? Do you really think that little stunt was big enough to get me to stop loving Carmen?"

Toni stood openmouthed. Shaking. Wordless.

I am openmouthed because Forrest finally backs me up, something I've wanted him to do for so long.

All I can do is shake my head at Toni and ask her, "How's that for keeping it one hunnert?"

19

Forrest and I are sitting on the small couch of a therapist's office. It took a miracle to get him to come here. He complained he didn't have time to go to the appointments. He didn't see what good it'd do. He wasn't into baring his soul to strangers.

But I told him if he wouldn't come, then our marriage could never be healed. Our children wouldn't have a full-time father in the home, and their firm foundation and sense of security would be ruined.

"If our marriage is worth anything, we need to do something to save it."

"Okay," he told me. He insisted on a male therapist. I didn't care one way or another as long as we began the journey of healing our marriage.

And so here we are at our first session.

The therapist starts out asking us about ourselves, childhood, family relations. He wants to know our versions of what happened the day we met. And he's curious about what attracted me and Forrest to one another.

"Look at her. She's a head-turner. She had my attention from day one. We met while standing in line at the grocery store. It was around Christmas time. I was pissed off 'cause the lines were so long. She heard me grumbling and told me I looked mean. It shocked me. I calmed down. She offered to let me put my things in her shopping cart. I paid for her stuff to prove to her I was a nice guy. And we started dating shortly after that."

I pretty much concur with what Forrest says; however, I know the exact day, date, and time we met.

"Once we hooked up for good, I knew she was the best girlfriend. I had a few other bad relationships and she was like sunshine."

"Then what happened?"

"She became my wife and everything was perfect."

Listening to him talk, I'm amazed. For someone who claimed he didn't want or need therapy he sure is talking a lot.

"If I was so wonderful, why did you stray?"

"That's the problem. You were my dream woman, perfect in every way, except for cooking—"

"What?"

"You do well enough, but the rest of our life was great. So great that it was boring."

"You think that I'm . . . boring?"

"Carmen, don't take it the wrong way. But sometimes I couldn't imagine you throwing back a few forties, smoking some Kush—"

"I didn't even know you like doing all that."

"Parts of me do. Especially when you started calling me old and outdated. I tried to prove I still had it going on."

"Are you serious?"

"Yes! Sounds stupid, but I had to prove something to myself. I knew you would never betray me with another man even if I didn't trust any of the guys that admired you."

"Forrest, this is so bizarre. If only I would have known."

"I can't count the number of times I've wanted us to go to a sex store. But I was like no, she's not like that. She's reserved, pure, untainted."

All I can do is shrug.

We discuss more aspects of our lives, then the therapist gives Forrest a thoughtful look.

"Tell me about your father."

"That man passed away years ago. I don't remember what year, though."

"When you attended the funeral, how did it make you feel?"

"I didn't go."

"Speak up, I can't hear you."

"I said I didn't go to that man's funeral."

I stare at Forrest. "I never knew that." He looks down at his hands.

I continue, "I thought your father's death was so hard on you that you didn't want to talk about the details."

He just shrugs then looks up and stares me dead in the eye. "I hated that man."

I gasp. "What?"

"I hated the way that man did my mother. I would hear her screaming. Phil and I would try to help her, but my father told us to stay out of grown folks' business. I promised myself I would never end up like him. Staying out all night. Sneaking around. Humiliating my dear mother."

"But . . ." I stare at him in amazement. "The money he left you?"

"Blood money. He felt guilty for how he treated her. That's the least he could have done. And I didn't want the money at first, but Toni convinced me it would only be right to honor my father by accepting it. So I did. I learned to just spend that money on my wife, my family, and make ya'll happier than my dad ever made me."

"Oh Forrest. I had no idea. I always assumed you two had a strong relationship. And that you had those fatherly talks that you have with Dante."

"Nope, not true. My dad would whip my ass over stupid shit, and when I tried to explain that I didn't do anything wrong he yelled at me to shut up. He didn't want to hear what I had to say."

The therapist spoke up. "How has this affected you? Your dad not allowing you to speak?"

Forrest shrugs and sighs. "It's one reason why I kind of shut down Carmen's conversation. And why I don't always listen to her."

"Forrest," the therapist gently advises. "Tell your wife everything you want to say."

Forrest stares deeply into my eyes in a way that moves me to my soul. "Baby, I want to hate you, but I can't. I take the blame. It's all on me. I'm the head of this household and the buck starts and stops with me—"

"No, Forrest, I knew what I was doing, too. I'm equally wrong."

"I can't allow you to think that. Put that on me." He chokes out a sob. "Put it all on me, Carmen."

I hold my husband in my arms as he makes animal-like noises, releasing years of pain, sorrow, heartbreak, and frustration.

Finally his whimpers turn to silence.

"I'm sorry," he finally tells me. "I shouldn't have broken down like that. You shouldn't see that."

"No, you're wrong. That's exactly what I want to see. I want to know who you are, Forrest. Your joys, your pains, your sorrows. I want to share them all with you. That's what a wife does."

He nods and places his head in his hands. I reach out and caress his shoulder. Then I embrace him. He embraces me back. I feel his trembles. I kiss his cheek and tell him I love him. Then I lean my head against the strength of his big but vulnerable body. I close my eyes, squeeze his hand, and know deep inside, with time and professional help, Forrest, me, and my family are going to be all right.

Perfection will be ours again.

I'll spend the rest of my life making sure of that.

Within one month, right after Christmas, Dante signs legal papers that indicate his decision to stay full-time with his father, two sisters, and stepmother.

Eventually, Toni loses custody, is forced to pay child support, and threatens to quit her job and leave the state.

My reply?

"No matter what you do, Toni, you will never take away my joy or my life again."

Sinful

Niobia Bryant

Prologue

"Tell me I'm the best."

Bree Bailey closed her eyes and wished like hell that the sound of his voice didn't float around her head. She couldn't remember his name, she couldn't place his face, and she wished she could scrub the memory of his sex from her life—but those words she remembered. Maybe it was because his bravado was so ironic or because, in her search for the ultimate sexual experience, finding "the best" was harder than most dicks she came across.

And there had been plenty.

Bree shifted her eyes up and locked them on her reflection in the mirror. Her eyes glazed as the hundred different faces of the men she vaguely remembered fucking flashed before her.

Black. White. Asian. Latino. Tall. Short. Fat.

And the dicks to go along with them.

Large and small. Straight and curved. Decent and completely laughable.

The number of her lovers numbered in the hundreds and she was only thirty years into her life. Bree's own mother always bragged that she was a woman of fifty who could count all of her lovers on one hand and still have fingers left over. That was something they would never have in common.

But she had never been one to try and fill her mother's shoes; she was too busy still trying to find a way to live on her own terms. To be happy with herself. To not be detested because of her compulsion.

She closed her eyes, swallowed hard, and released a hum, trying to soothe herself as she recalled going to her local Chinese restaurant to pick up a lonely-girl special that had led to a flirtation with a tall light-skinned brother who smelled of warm musk. She couldn't recall how the flirtation turned into a sweaty fuck session in the back of his SUV just twenty minutes later.

Bree shook her head as she felt the contents of her stomach churn. She had barely bent over the commode before she threw up every bit of shrimp lo mein, and her lack of self-respect nearly choked her. The shame, regret, and loathing never came until after she found herself wiping the scent and juices of some stranger from between her thighs.

She wiped her mouth with the back of her hand as she unbent her body and chanced another look in the mirror. Bree didn't see her fair complexion, the light freckles across her nose, her full lips, or the frame of fine auburn curls surrounding her heart-shaped face. She saw nothing but her shame. And the thing was, she *knew* better to be able to *do* better.

It was really a damn shame.

"God, give me strength," she prayed.

1

Bree sat up straight in the middle of the bed at the first sound of her alarm clock going off. As she did every morning that she spent alone, she kicked away the sheets, pulled her knees to her chest, and wrapped her arms around her legs as she purred like a cat being stroked. She breathed deeply with her wide-set eyes closed and her forehead lightly resting in the seam between her knees, doing a silent count to one hundred as she inhaled and exhaled slowly.

Brrrnnnggg . . . brrnnnggg . . .

"Incoming call from 9-7-3-5-5-5-1-2-6-0."

She ignored the ringing of her house phone until she was completely done counting. It was her mother. The phone had stopped ringing before she stopped counting. She didn't care.

"Ninety-eight, ninety-nine, one hundred," Bree said softly, her voice a husky timbre that made you think of either the vocal melody of a jazz singer or the beginning effects of a lifetime of smoking. The latter was more true than anything.

She slid her thick, pear-shaped frame off of the cool, crisp sheets of her queen-sized bed. She grabbed her soft pack of Newport Lights and a lighter. Not wanting to get the smell of smoke inside her house or clothes, she padded barefoot across the polished hardwood floors to the French doors leading out to her small balcony with the intricate wrought-iron railings. She lit the cigarette quickly and inhaled deeply for just a few seconds.

Bree had quit her pack-a-day smoking habit last year, but as part of her morning ritual she allowed herself half a cig before she showered and got dressed. Sometimes she didn't even inhale the smoke into her lungs.

She pressed the cigarette out in the dirt surrounding one of the two ivy-ball topiaries flanking the French doors. She didn't leave the butt sticking in the dirt, though, and instead carried it into the house to flush it down the toilet.

Bree's home and the landscaping outside of it was immaculate. Her mother was no domestic goddess and Bree knew she herself rebelled against the kind of house she'd grown up in, with its constant stack of dishes in the sink and dirty clothes in various corners of the house that never seemed to make it into the washing machine fast enough.

In fact, most things about her adult life were so very different from her childhood; she made sure of that.

She breezed through her remaining morning rituals: brush her teeth for two minutes, give herself a facial using only a clockwise motion of her fingertips against her smooth shortbread complexion, and take a steaming hot shower that lasted exactly fifteen minutes as she methodically washed her body in counterclockwise circles from her neck to her feet.

Bree wrapped a plush towel around her thick and curvy frame as she exited the octagon shower stall and stood before the pedestal sink again to run lavender-scented olive oil through her auburn curls with her fingers until they were glossy and soft. Next she did her makeup: just bronzer, blush, lip gloss, and light eye shadow and mascara. After she dropped the towel, she smoothed her honey-and-almond-scented lotion over every inch of her body.

And then she released a sigh that was filled with her sense

of peace and contentment. If anything disturbed her morning rituals she felt like the rest of her day was screwed.

In her line of work, Bree needed every moment of peace and balance she could get.

She breezed through her bedroom to one of her two walk-in closets. Her print wrap dress in soft muted pastels already hung on the door of one of the closets with a pair of nude platform heels sitting on the floor. She was easing her all-in-one Spanx onto her body when her phone rang.

"Call from 9-7-3-5-5-5-1-2-6-0."

She shifted her eyes over to the digital clock on her bedside: 7:30 a.m. The morning phone call from her mother was one ritual she could do without. Again she just let it ring. There had been many a morning she'd gotten trapped into a long diatribe about one of her crazy neighbors and had her tight schedule completely wrecked. For the rest of the day she'd felt like she was playing catch-up and that made her anxious. So the ringing continued as she pulled the wrap dress onto her body, tied it, and then smoothed it over her curves.

Bree turned and looked in the mirror as she put on her medium-sized diamond hoops, diamond locket pendant, and two-toned diamond Rolex watch. Her eyes dipped down to her exposed cleavage and she pulled the edges of the top of the dress together.

Let me nut on your titties.

She shifted her eyes up to lock on her face in the mirror's reflection. She shook her head slightly as she licked her lips and fought to push the memory of the demand from her thoughts. Bree ignored the unease she felt at the memory . . . at her behavior.

Clearing her throat, she moved from her reflection and picked up her crocodile briefcase and opened it to slide in the files she'd brought from her office yesterday. She hadn't even gotten a chance to review them.

Make me come. Please . . .

Unfortunately she'd blown off a night of necessary work to be disappointed . . . again.

Snapping her briefcase shut, she gathered her keys and her designer handbag before leaving her bedroom. Her heels clicked against the hardwood floors of her spacious, professionally decorated town house. Her stomach grumbled a little, but she decided to bypass any treats in her kitchen for the cappuccino and muffins she knew her office manager had waiting for her.

She smiled a little as she climbed behind the wheel of her convertible BMW. She worked hard to have her own business with her own small staff, to own her own home, and to enjoy luxuries in her life. And the thing that excited her the most was the fact that her career was "still on the rise" and so the best of it *all* was yet to come.

According to most standards, she had the perfect life . . . except for her single status. But that was just the way she liked it. For her, love and relationships led to misery and heartache. Believing she was hopelessly in love with "the one" would make her lose so much. Her focus. Her determination. Herself.

Time. After time. After time.

As Bree pulled the vehicle to a smooth stop at a red light, she cut her eyes to the rearview mirror. There was only so much heartache, lies, and deception anyone's plate could hold. *Thank God I put a stop to the bullshit,* she thought as she accelerated forward, wishing she could leave the memories behind as well.

Derrick, her first boyfriend—and lover—got caught when their two a.m. phone call was interrupted by the operator saying he had an emergency break-through from "Derrick's girlfriend Tahira." That was in the days before call waiting and Tahira definitely wanted to make sure whoever "her boyfriend" was on the phone with knew she was laying claim.

After all his stuttering and inability to come up with a decent lie, Bree gladly let her have him.

And then there was Jeorge, who admitted to her with a face wet with tears that he'd gotten another girl pregnant. She loved Jeorge more than she even thought about loving Derrick and that shit had crushed her. Bree gave him credit for telling her the truth, and although he begged her to stay . . . she couldn't.

Charlie she'd caught in his dorm room getting blown by a pair of redheaded, big-busted twins, who didn't even stop when they spotted Bree standing in the doorway shocked as hell. That was a total mindfuck, but it took just two seconds for her to shake off the shock and rush into the room to beat all three of their asses.

And then Eric, her fiancé, whom she met in grad school and had been with for close to ten years. He had the audacity to bring their next-door neighbor's wife into the apartment they shared to bang her so loudly that everyone in the four-family building knew when they were at it . . . everyone except Bree and the husband, that is.

Eric was the final straw.

No more heartache and drama. It wasn't worth it.

Men are good for only two things: their dicks and their money. Well, Bree had her own cash flow and it was very possible to have the dicks (real or fake) without all the emotional baggage.

Bree pulled her car into the parking lot of the medium-sized brick building of her office. Glancing at the clock, she grabbed her briefcase and tote and climbed out of the vehicle to cross the brick paved walkway into the building that was as comfortably decorated as her home.

"Good morning, Dr. Bailey."

Bree removed her oversized shades and smiled at Nola Oliver, her middle-aged office manager sitting behind her antique desk in the front office. Bree didn't want the office to have that generic medical-office feel. "Morning, Nola," she said, moving across the waiting area that was more like a cozy den.

She continued down the long hall to her private office, passing the door leading into the smaller office she used for her appointments and the door leading to a larger conference room that she used for group sessions.

Bailey Counseling Services was a one-woman show . . . and she loved the sound of her professional name: *Doctor* Bree Bailey, Psychologist, PhD.

Bree unlocked the door to her private office and paused in the doorway, enjoying the subtle leftover scents from her giant aromatic candles and essential oils. When she first leased the property, the office had more of a feel of a masculine study with lots of dark woods with the floors, paneling, and book-shelves. New carpet, lots of soft lighting, accessories, and femi-nine furnishings now gave the office a French country feel that she adored.

Before Bree could settle into the chair behind her glass-topped mahogany desk, Nola walked in with her glass cup of cappuccino and apple walnut muffin on a saucer. "What would I do without you, Nola?" Bree asked, as her stomach grumbled loudly enough to echo in the quiet of her office.

"Issue me unemployment and hire someone younger," Nola drawled.

Bree just chuckled as she peeled the paper from the base of the oversized muffin. They both knew it would never go down that easily.

Nola also set a stack of messages on Bree's desk. Bree knew most of them were transcribed from voice mail.

"Your mother wants to know why you have a cell phone if it's never on," Nola said. "Your six o' clock appointment rescheduled and you have your eight a.m. group session this morning."

Group therapy was just a small part of her practice. She specialized in depression, anxiety disorders, and compulsions, but this particular session was a group of males in therapy for their sexual addictions.

Hypocrite.

Bree cleared her throat and nodded as she quickly went through the messages, and then set them aside as Nola quietly left her office. Bree shook her head and sipped her coffee. She knew each case and all of the facts inside the files by heart, but it was her custom to review last week's entries before the next group session.

Make me come . . . please.

Closing her eyes, she took a deep breath and counted to ten. When she reopened them they fell on the oversized glass apothecary jar filled with her beloved gourmet jelly beans. She fought the urge to remove the lid and grab a handful. Instead, she reached into her briefcase for the files she'd never gotten to last night.

There were six. All male. All with issues. Stories complete with sordid details. Graphic details. Serial cheaters. Exhibitionists. Voyeurism. Sexual perversions. Hours upon hours of watching cyber sex. Masturbating numerous times a day. Interruption of work and healthy relationships.

It was her job to guide them to recovery. To make them better. Make them accountable. To use every bit of her education and training in psychotherapy to help them understand, relate, and make better choices in their lives. To control their impulses and compulsions. To have a healthy, normal life. Recovery. The dynamics of each group member could at times make the treatment therapy all the more challenging or encouraging. It was her job to moderate just which way the wind blew during the two hours.

If that ain't the blind leading the blind . . .

Bree slapped the top file closed, wishing her own conscience and "inner voice" didn't hound her so much. The faces of a dozen men flashed before her with the speed of a moving train. Some she knew well, many she didn't know at all. She'd given in to her own compulsions.

Her clients didn't know—and didn't need to know—that she understood them very well. Too well.

Bree stood and smoothed her dress over her hips as she picked up the iPad she used just to document therapy sessions. She left her office and walked up the hall. *I got this*, she encouraged herself, as she opened the door and stepped into the spacious room. All six group members were present and gathered around the table Nola had prepared, complete with coffee and breakfast pastries. Nola swore it was too early in the morning to not feed grown men. She said if Bree handled the mind, she'd take care of the stomach.

Bree's eyes landed on the tall and deeply dark-skinned man who glanced quickly at her over the Styrofoam rim of his cup of his coffee. Carter Steven. She smiled politely at them as they moved toward the padded seats gathered in a circle. "Good morning. Good morning," she said, taking her normal seat, crossing her legs, and smoothing the hem of her dress over her knees.

Carter bent his tall frame into the seat across from her. The young jazz musician had been arrested for solicitation. He liked wild and kinky sex but felt ashamed to admit his true desires to his long-term girlfriend and paid for a whore who passed no judgment when he asked her to slip a greased finger in his ass while giving him head. A condition of his probation was attending therapy. After her first one-on-one session with Carter she considered him to be Mr. Shameful.

Bree looked up from her iPad just as his eyes shifted from her. "When we ended our session last week, we were discussing some of the ways to deal with the anxiety you may feel from fighting off the urges," she began, turning to lock her eyes on the tall and solid man sitting to her right. "Reverend Teel, you were saying that for you it was important to refocus on your connection with God," she said, in a steady tone meant to lead him to finish the conversation.

"Rev," as he liked to be called, nodded his shiny bald head. "Yes, I got caught up in the attention and the power of the pulpit . . ."

Reverend Brenton Teel's extramarital exploits with his female parishioners were discovered by his wife when an anonymous and concerned member of the church e-mailed her a link to an online sex tape of her husband and the president of the Usher Board getting it on in the same front-row church pew where Sister Teel faithfully sat every Sunday during service. To hold onto his position in the church—and his two-year marriage—Rev had sought help.

Using my stylus, I scribbled:

Still not confident the Reverend has an actual sexual addiction. I think he's going through the motions to prove his adulterous actions were "not really his fault."

Like many men—and some women—caught cheating, Rev seemed to be seeking forgiveness from others more than treatment for himself.

"I have been meditating and fasting," Rev was saying.

"Is it working?" Bree asked, glancing over at him.

"No."

That made her look back over at him and she had to fight in that millisecond to keep the shock from her face. Rev always said the right things, gave the right answers. He usually breezed through the sessions.

She noticed the rest of the group's faces showed the surprise she felt. That made her swallow back any questions or comments.

"Did something happen, Rev?" one of the men asked.

Rev crossed his thick fingers in the space between his knees and looked down at the floor. "One of the . . . women that I slept with texted me nude photos."

"Did you respond?" Bree asked.

Rev shook his head. "But I started thinking about it. I wanted to get over to her house. I wanted to go over and give her what she said she was missing," he said with intensity.

Some of the men in the group stirred in their seats. Bree nodded in understanding. "But you didn't go. You didn't give in to the impulse."

"But he wants to."

Bree turned to look at the slender man of mixed heritage sitting to her right. Deon Cochran. His reddish-brown complexion and short curly hair spoke to a mix of African American with Native American or Latino. He was good looking. Fine. Eye candy.

And he knew it.

He knew and he used it to his advantage to have slept with more than two hundred women in the past year. And he liked to brag about it. Unfortunately he had proof: more than a thousand different sex videos. Deon was "the conqueror." He cared nothing about a woman's pleasure outside of making her come and then sending her on her way with nothing but the memory of his fucking. The man was in his midthirties and had never been in a relationship or had sex with a woman more than once. He was here to find help so that he could settle down and fall in love.

"Of course he does," Bree said, fixing her eyes on Deon. "Life is about temptations for everyone every single day of their life—whether it's food, sex, drugs, or anything else. But one of the issues in sexual addiction is the difficulty ignoring that immediate rush to have sex, to expose oneself, to participate in risky behavior. And then having to deal with the shame, the regret, the denial. The aftereffects."

"But what to do when the desire is distracting?" Deon asked.

"Yes," Carter chimed in.

"It seems like being celibate is making me want to have sex even more. It's like the pressure is building up and I could explode," Deon said, his voice husky. "Sex is about more than just stroking inside a woman. I miss touching a woman's body. I miss kissing and licking her skin. I miss hearing her moan because I am pleasing her. I am using every bit of my focus and my skills to give her what she needs the most in that moment."

Bree cleared her throat and pretended to jot down a note. "Is it possible that the reaction from the woman is helping to feed your addiction?" she asked, her voice calm even as she felt a thrill race across her swelling clit.

Deon shrugged as he purposefully eyed her legs and then shifted in his seat like he was looking for comfort.

As she had many times in the past month, Bree felt her body flush even as she pretended to remain nonchalant. Her heartbeat sped up as an image of Deon tearing open her dress and then sucking her nipples and the warm moisture between her thighs.

"For me, I love my wife, but the sex ain't satisfying," Rev agreed. "She won't even let me . . . she won't . . . I mean . . . I can't even perform oral, you know?"

Bree looked up at Rev and hated that her eyes fell on his mouth. "Did you take my advice and have a serious conversation with her about your sexual needs, Rev?"

He held his hands out in exasperation. "I told her I love to eat pussy—"

Bree held up her hand. "Language, Rev," she said sternly.

"I apologize," he said instantly.

She thought about Rev burying his head between her thighs as she spreads her legs over the arms of her chair. *Was his wife crazy? Shiiit. . . .*

Bree knew she had to get it together, and sitting there imagining the men of the group all catering to her sexual needs at once wasn't going to do it. "Okay, fellow, let's go over some of your triggers and things you can do mentally and physically to not relapse," she said.

"Can I get your number?"

As she pulled her skirt down over her hips, Bree looked over her shoulder at the lucky busboy she had invited into the ladies' room of the Mexican restaurant, hoping he could curb the sexual edge she'd walked ever since the end of her session earlier that day. He was handsome enough. More than available enough. Dick was big enough.

Still, he had no clue and no finesse on how to make a woman come.

And she felt as frustrated as before.

"Definitely not," she told him in no uncertain terms, shoving her Spanx deep into her bag as he stood there with his condom-covered dick still limp above the ashy knees and pants down around his thin ankles.

Sighing in frustration, Bree grabbed her pocketbook and flew out the bathroom and then the restaurant to her car. She rushed back to her office.

"How was lunch?" Nola asked.

Bree smiled stiffly. "Not so good," she said honestly, quickly making her way to her office. She locked the door behind her before she dropped her purse to the floor and scrambled over to her desk to unlock the bottom drawer. She removed the bright pink vibrator as she dropped into her seat, spread her legs, and pulled her panties to the side to expose her clit.

Bzzzzzzzzzzzzzzzzzzzzzzzzzz. . . .

Bree felt an urgency deep in her bones that she knew wasn't a bit healthy as she pressed the vibrator to her clit and let thoughts of Carter licking her clit while Deon suckled her nipples fuel her desire.

The tiny pulsations against her clit soon had her arching her hips up off the chair as heat infused her core and she cried out harshly with each white-hot explosion as she came. She brought one hand up to rub her nipple between her fingers as she bit down hard on her bottom lip to stifle her sounds and keep Nola from intruding.

Long after, she lay slumped back against the chair. Heart pounding, clit still pounding, pulse throbbing, she closed her eyes as she felt tears well up in her eyes. It was in those fleeting seconds right after her release that she felt the most shame about her desires, her compulsions, her needs.

For the life of her she couldn't fight it.

Hypocrite.

She swiveled in her chair and dropped her head to her desk.

2

Bree had cancelled last week's group session, feeling she needed some space to get her perspective back . . . and to get over how their session had sent her spiraling into a sexual tizzy that led to a quickie with a stranger and then an erotic interlude filled with visions of two of her clients sexing her as she fulfilled herself with her vibrator.

"Damn it," Bree sighed, making herself take a deep cleansing breath as she silently counted to a hundred.

She had to get her shit together and quick.

Bree looked up after a quick double-knock on her office door. Nola. "Come in," she called out, reaching for her iPad as she rose to her feet.

Nola opened the door and poked her head inside. "You're running late for your group," she reminded Bree gently.

Coming around the desk, Bree tucked the iPad under her arm and eased her hand down over the hips of the wide-leg denim trousers she wore with a crisp white cotton shirt. She followed Nola out the office and then made her way to the group therapy room.

Six sets of eyes shifted to her as she entered and took her seat in the circle. "Hello, everyone. I apologize for running late," Bree said. "And I thank you all for understanding about not having group last week."

They all greeted her with waves, head nods, or "good mornings."

"Since we didn't have group I would like to check in with everyone about the last week," Bree said. "Who would like to begin? Anyone face any challenges or setbacks?"

"I did."

Bree tensed for a second at the sound of Deon's voice. Putting her most professionally blank look on her face, Bree looked over at him. He was sitting to her immediate left. "What happened?"

Deon looked down at his folded hands. "This new woman moved into my apartment building and she was just too fine to resist . . . and plus I was *ready* to get some and to give some."

"Did you attempt any of the techniques that we discussed in group?" Bree asked, jotting down:

Deon had a relapse last week. Shows no remorse.

"She put me in a corner . . . and I came out," he said.

Bree looked up at him and his eyes were on hers boldly. "You seem proud of . . . yet another conquest," she said.

Deon continued to hold her gaze.

Bree forced herself not to look away, feeling an unspoken challenge from him.

"At what point do you think sex will have meaning for you?" she asked.

"That's why I'm here, Doc, for you to help me," he countered.

Eyes were still locked.

Bree nodded. "A part of it, though, is accepting the help and also helping yourself . . . to more than sex."

"But I've been watching her watching me," he said. "I'm

not crazy. I know when a woman wants me. *Any* woman. I know it. It's like I can smell it."

Bree arched a brow as she pressed her back against the chair. "Perhaps in your mind, as a part of your addiction, you believe that no woman can resist you. Do you think it's possible for a woman to *not* find you desirable, Deon?"

He smiled suddenly and his eyes seemed to glimmer. "I didn't say every woman wants me, but I am saying—again— that I know the ones who do."

"You would think someone with that much intuition would know early enough how to avoid a sudden impulse," she said, knowing her tone was slightly sarcastic.

"Easier said then done. Right?"

That comment and the slight sarcasm in his tone did make Bree finally shift her eyes down to her iPad. She felt like her own dirty little secrets had been exposed for his eyes to see. "I don't know—"

"It was late at night and I was in the pool enjoying a skinny-dip—"

Bree looked up. "Deon, were you in a community pool naked?" she asked, her voice filled with disbelief.

"I don't own a bathing suit."

Carlos, the voyeur who liked to masturbate on his front porch, chuckled.

Bree gave him a stern look more suited for a teacher to an unruly student than a therapist to her client.

"She got into the pool with me and took her bathing suit off. She was up on me, touching me, pressing her body against mine before I could even think about getting out of there," Deon said, continuing his tale. "Once I pressed my lips to her body I couldn't turn back."

Bree hated that a vision of the scene played out in her mind . . . except it was *her* nude and ready who swam to Deon and pressed his body against the wall of the pool with her softness. She shivered slightly as she imagined the feel of his hands easing up her thighs to grasp her buttocks as his words came back to her: *"I miss touching a woman's body. I miss kissing and licking her skin. I miss hearing her moan because I am pleasing her. I am using every bit of my focus and my skills to give her what she needs the most in that moment."*

Uhm, uhm, uhm.

"You should have told her to get off you," Carter said. "If you trying to get off drugs and somebody sit a bag of dope in your lap you brush it off and get out of there. This is the same thing, man."

"Dope and pussy ain't the same thing," Deon countered.

"Language, Deon, man," someone admonished him.

Bree blinked, causing the image to disappear as she focused on her group. She was losing control of herself. The Group. Every damn thing.

"Gentleman," she said, sitting up. "Listen, relapse is a part of recovery. It doesn't mean that Deon cannot get back on track with his recovery. I do think having this sexy neighbor in your building is going to present a challenge for you."

Deon nodded his head in understanding. "Especially since she was pretty good."

Bree couldn't avoid looking exasperated.

"Good sex is hard to come by," Rev muttered under his breath.

Bree turned to him. "So you and your wife are still having difficulties in that area?" she asked.

"Yes," Rev stressed.

Wow he really wants to eat some pussy, huh? Bree flushed with warmth. She couldn't deny that she absolutely loved when a man could navigate his way around a clit with his tongue.

"Perhaps you can talk to your wife about attending a couple's session with me or someone else and that's an issue that someone can referee for you. It may be that oral sex is important to you, but there's a reason she's so averse to it . . . and if that's the case you have to respect that and work with her to overcome the issue. You understand?"

Rev looked disbelieving.

"What's that look about right now?" she asked, biting the gloss from her bottom lip.

Rev held his hands up. "I'm asking her to let me eat her—not a rim shot or golden shower or something like that. What woman doesn't want her—"

Bree held up her hand to stop his words. "Talk to her about the counseling and let's see how that goes," she said, before turning back to Deon. "I would like for you to avoid the friendly neighbor and if she does approach you again, maybe be honest with her about the struggle."

"So I should tell this stranger—"

"That you had sex with," Bree inserted calmly.

Deon paused and looked to the ceiling. "I should tell this one-night stand that I'm a sex addict."

Branton, the lone white man of the group, held up his hand. "It's like being alcoholic and going to a party and someone offers you a drink more than once. You finally have to say to some people that you're an alcoholic and hope they respect your recovery," he added.

Carlos nodded in agreement. "Some people will even test you harder because they know you're struggling with it. You gotta be prepared to fight hard for yourself against your inner demons . . . and the outer ones."

The men in the group agreed as Deon listened.

And that was the dynamic that Bree liked most about group therapy sessions, especially for men: they were willing to relate to someone who was going through the same struggles, rather than some educated therapist who they might feel was judging them.

"When you first started the group, Deon, you said you

wanted to have a real relationship. You wanted to step into your manhood," Bree said, stepping into a lull in the group's conversation. "If you continue to follow the urges and have these one-night stands and then immediately put the woman into that category, then you are closing the door to someone who could be a real candidate for a relationship."

Deon shrugged. "I look at it like no chick I would take serious would let me blow her back out on the first date anyway."

Bree thought of the countless one-night stands she had had over the years since her last breakup. She bristled a little at the double standard. It was odd for a man-whore like Deon to be so judgmental. "And you have to remember, as you move toward your goal of finding a good woman, many of them won't take you seriously for the amount of times you've gladly 'blown a woman's back' on the first date."

Translation: Negro, a ho is a ho is a ho. Male *or* female.

But she couldn't *say* that.

"Okay, so, let's check in with the rest of the group," Bree said, using her fingertip to open the file on Carlos, her client that got a thrill off of masturbating on his front porch . . . until his next-door neighbor had looked out her window and down at him flinging his lengthy erection back inside his shorts when a car rode by.

"How did your week go, Carlos?" she asked, making her tone light.

"Very good. I haven't jacked off in weeks and my wife is considering moving back home," he said, looking happy at the thought of reuniting his family.

"Very good, Carlos, I'm glad things are working out for you and your family," she said, jotting down notes.

She glanced over in Deon's direction and did a double take at the calculating look in his eye as he watched her silently.

Clearing her throat, she focused on listening to her clients and not wondering just what the hell was on his mind.

After the session, Bree made her way to her office and released a heavy breath as she set her iPad on her desk and made her way over to the minibar by the fireplace. She let her hand skim past the bottle of white wine and grab a mini bottle of water instead. She was enjoying a deep sip and thanking God that she wasn't in the same sexual tizzy she had been after the last group session. *I was just horny, that's all. . . .*

Bzzzz.

Still carrying the water bottle, she walked over to her desk to answer the intercom. "Yes, Nola."

"Reverend Teel was making an appointment and then he asked if he could speak to you really quickly before he left."

Bree raised her brow in curiosity. "Did he say what it was about?" she asked, still frowning a little bit.

"Nope, sure didn't."

"Uhm . . . okay. Send him back," she said, setting her water bottle on the corner of her desk before she moved around it to take her seat.

Bree didn't usually have sessions in her office, but she assumed Rev just had a quick question for her. He knocked softly twice. "Come in," she called out.

He stepped into the office, his tall and broad figure seeming to swallow up most of its space. "Sorry to bother you, Dr. Bailey," he said, folding his tall figure into one of the leather armless chairs in front of her desk.

"Did you have a question, Rev?" she asked politely, folding her hands atop the desk as she met his gaze.

Rev nodded his square shaped head. "I . . . uhm . . . made the appointment for us to come for a session, but I don't know if she will."

"All you can do is ask," Bree offered. "I actually look forward to speaking with both of you."

"But my wife thinks oral sex, anal sex, anything out of the norm, anything not missionary is sinful. The affairs I had with the women in the church opened up a lot of doors in me that I don't want closed."

Bree set her chin in her hands. "These are issues that we can discuss within the boundaries of the therapy session," she said.

"But I can't admit to her how badly I want to taste her, to have her moan and scream as I suck her. Sometimes I don't even want to make love, I just want to eat her."

Bree eyed him as he licked his mouth, his tongue wet and glistening. Her clit throbbed and her nipples tingled behind her lace brassiere. She imagined Rev turning her desk over with one strong thrust of his hands and pressing her legs up to her shoulders and snatching her tiny underwear away to bury his tongue deep inside her. *He loves it too much not to be good*, she thought with a little lick of her lips as she forced herself to look out the bay windows.

There was a skill to using the tongue to trace the lips of a woman's pussy, to circle her clit gently and then more firmly before flicking the tip against the bud until tiny shivers filled her core and she came into his mouth. Over and over and over again.

I want to come over and over and over again until I fall straight to sleep with my pussy still throbbing. . . .

"Dr. Bailey . . . Dr. Bailey . . ."

Her eyes refocused as she gave him a quick smile. "Sorry about that," Bree said, becoming fully present again as she rose to her feet. She had to get him the hell out of her office that felt as spacious as a sardine can, with him—and unspoken promises of sexual bliss—in it. *Good sex was hard to come by.*

"Are you okay, Dr. Bailey?" he asked, rising to follow her to the door.

Bree nodded. He lightly touched her back. She turned and jumped back from him, her back almost pressed to the door.

"I'm sorry. I didn't mean to scare you," Rev said, looking concerned.

Bree was afraid of herself. That familiar rush she felt was swirling around her like a tornado, wrecking havoc on her sense and sensibilities. Pressing her hands to the door behind her, she took a deep cleansing breath as Rev watched her closely. She didn't miss when his eyes opened up slightly in awareness.

The awareness swiftly changed to desire.

No, Bree. You can't.

She sidestepped him and moved quickly back around to reclaim her seat. "Have a good day, Rev," she said firmly, pretending to focus her attention on some file open on her desk.

Thankfully, he said nothing else and quietly closed the door behind himself.

As soon as the door closed, Bree allowed her body to go lax as she slumped back into her chair. Her practice was important to her. Her lifestyle was even more important. One was necessary for the other. She couldn't risk it all behind a good pussy lick.

Feeling on edge and tense and wild, like she could crawl out of her own skin, Bree pressed her knees open wide and slid her hand down into her lacy underwear to press her fingers against her moist, warm, and throbbing clit.

She had to get off and get back to her workday.

Bree took a sip of her oversized goblet of red wine as she settled back against her chair and looked across the candlelit table at her date for the evening, Marc Hamlin. He smiled back at her and she wondered just what in the hell she was doing there. Everything about the attractive banker screamed "boyfriend/

exclusive man/long-term relationship/husband material"—things she wasn't looking for.

So why did I exchange business cards, answer his call a few days later, and then accept his eventual offer for a date?

"You're very quiet," he said, leaning forward and placing his arms on the table to look at her with his round, boyishly cut face. "You're not analyzing me, are you?"

Bree fought the urge to roll her eyes. "No. My going rate is more than dinner," she said. "Now . . . if you feel the need to be analyzed we can end the date and you can just call and make an appointment for a session on Monday."

"I'd rather have the date," he assured her smoothly as he took a sip of his cognac and soda.

"I'll be honest with you. I'm not really in the market for a relationship," she told him.

He looked reflective for a bit before asking, "Why not?"

The question caught Bree off guard. "I thought I was the therapist," she countered lightly.

He shrugged as he worked his wrist to send the ice in his drink in a circle inside the glass. "Just curious. Which is it?"

Bree let her eyes skim over his face. "Which is what?"

"Which cliché. No good black men? Ms. Independent?"

Both, asshole, Bree thought as she raised a brow along with her wine goblet. "I don't deal in clichés," she said, before another sip. Translation: *Back up out of my business!*

He just chuckled lightly as their waiter brought their entrees to the table.

Bree used the slight distraction at their table to really eye the man sitting across from her. He wasn't over-the-top gorgeous like Deon and wasn't built tall and solid like Rev, but he wasn't bad on the eye. He had boyish good looks, average height, and a nice athletic shape.

Still, he did absolutely nothing to peak sexual interest in her. Nada.

She absolutely refused to waste another second on her

back or her knees or pressed up against a wall trying to enjoy bad sex. Fuck faking it 'til she made it. Hell to the no.

Bree wasn't looking for love, but she needed a good lover. A great lay. One. Someone who wanted no more ties than she did but was more than willing to meet up to sexually satisfy each other. No sleepovers. No phone conversation or even sexting. No dinners. No dates. Simply: "I'm in the mood to fuck. You game?"

Bree shifted her eyes across the table. This man sitting across from her didn't fit her needs at all. Bree wanted her pussy stroked, not her heart.

"Have you ever had a one-night stand?" she asked him suddenly, but very seriously.

He looked put off by the question as he paused with his fork and knife frozen above his steak. "Have you?"

"I asked you first," she countered smoothly, her eyes on him as she enjoyed his discomfort.

"That's not appropriate conversation for a first date," Marc said, refocusing on cutting his steak.

It is when the first date is the last date.

Bree opened her gloss-covered mouth to come back with a witty quip, but her eyes widened slightly to see Deon cuddled up with a dark-skinned beauty with long hair and a short dress. Bree wondered if she was his sexy neighbor or a new conquest. Either way, there was no chance of him not "blowing her back out," the way he was pressing his lips to her neck and his hands to her thighs under the table.

Bree couldn't take her eyes off of them as she watched Deon in action. His date giggled. Her body swayed. Her smile was sultry. He was pouring it on her and she was eating it all up.

For sure they were having a damn better time than she was on her date.

A part of Bree willed Deon to look up and see her. But she was his therapist and not his mother. He wasn't exactly *caught,* but she would love to see his face as she toasted him from across the room.

"Do you know them?" Marc asked.

Bree shifted her attention back to him just as he turned from looking across the room, following her line of vision.

Bree shook her head and kept her focus on her dinner, wondering just what dessert Deon was offering up for his date.

3

One Week Later

Bree was already sitting in the smaller of the rooms that she used just for private sessions when Rev walked in. She looked past him, but he was alone.

"She's not coming," he offered without Bree having a chance to ask.

Bree crossed her legs at the ankles as he sat across from her on the brown leather sofa. "I know the purpose of the session was to try and mediate a conversation about sex for you and your wife. Did you want to reschedule the appointment?" she asked, nervously running her fingers through her curls as she tapped her fingernails against the screen of her iPad.

"No, maybe a one-on-one session will help me more than the group does," Rev said with his knees spread wide like he was trying to make room for a big dick.

The innocent-enough L.L. Cool J–like lick of the lips intrigued her more. "You don't think the group therapy is effective?" she asked, trying not to think of wrapping her thighs around his neck.

He shrugged his broad shoulders. "I haven't cheated on my wife since group started, but the urges haven't stopped . . . especially when I began to feel like my wife is just as in love with my position as minister as the rest of the women."

"Why do you think that?" Bree asked, making a note.

"It's like it's all a front. She wants to be the first lady of the church more than she wants to be my wife," he said, furrowing his brows. "I think I always thought that and maybe that was a small piece of the cheating, but I think it even more now."

Bree nodded in understanding. "So sex isn't the only issue in your marriage?"

Rev shook his head. "No."

"Are you still communicating with the young lady from your church?"

Rev shifted his eyes away before shifting them back to lock on her. "Yes."

"Have you cheated again?" Bree asked. Her question was blunt, but the tone of her voice remained neutral.

"No."

"But?" Bree asked softly.

"I miss the attention of the women. I miss feeling wanted. I miss feeling desired," Rev admitted.

Bree wrote down:

Explore Rev's own issues beyond the sexual cravings for the affairs.

"Why did you jump away from me when we were in your office last week?" he asked.

Bree's heart pounded hard as she looked up from the iPad. "Excuse me?" she asked politely.

Rev bit his bottom lip as he shifted forward on the sofa to sit on the edge. "Do I make you nervous, Dr. Bailey?"

Bree frowned. "No," she answered him quickly. Maybe too quickly.

"Can I be honest?" he asked, his voice soft and his eyes intense as he looked at her.

Bree said nothing as she closed her iPad.

"I've been dreaming about what it would feel like to taste your cum."

Shit. Bree shook her head. "This is inappropriate—"

"I swear I wanna eat you so bad . . . and I think you're curious," Rev said. "Is he as good as he says? Can this country preacher boy make me come? Can he make me squirt?"

Bree stood even as her clit throbbed between her heated thighs. "I want you to leave, *Reverend* Teel," she stressed. "I'm also going to recommend that you find a new therapist."

"I bet I can make you come in less than . . . twenty seconds," he said, daring her as he dropped to his knees before her and clasped his big and wide hands on the back of her thighs in the navy pencil skirt she wore.

Bree gasped, pushing her free hand against his forehead as he pressed his face against the vee of her thighs.

"Ah man. I can smell your pussy," he moaned in pleasure.

Bree closed her eyes and let her head fall back. *I can't. I can't do this. I can't do this.*

She saved her sexual exploits for after hours. She didn't cross the line in her work. She couldn't. Even her curiosity over the last few weeks was unethical. But giving in to the strong desire to see if he was just as good as he claimed? She couldn't cross that line.

Bree looked down at him. *It's been so long. . . .*

Rev moved his hands to the hem of her skirt, and began to push it up over her knees . . . and then her thighs . . . and hips. He moaned in the back of his throat, his dick hard and standing up, straining against the zipper of his pants. "Damn, you got it bald," he said in wonder, before looking up at her like a puppy dog begging for a meaty bone. "Please, please. Let me eat your pussy. I don't want sex. I just want to eat you."

Bree's clit was throbbing so hard that it felt numb. She wanted to come. She needed to come. Right then. She felt all the nervous anxiety of a head trying to avoid a crack pipe and several rocks sitting with a lighter. She felt like she had to get the edge off. The vibrator wasn't gonna cut it. Chancing her pussy and her needs on a random fuck was a no-no. *Just this once. . . .*

She dropped the iPad to the chair and pressed her hands to the back of his head. He tore her lace panties away with his teeth and she gasped hotly, biting her bottom lip before he'd even lifted her leg over his shoulder to drag his tongue across the split of her moist lips. "Yessss," she moaned, loving the rush. It was forbidden. It was wrong. It was beyond reason.

But it was so good.

Rev pushed her back into the chair and used his strong hands to push her legs up on the arms of the chair, spreading her pussy wide in front of him.

Bree's heart pounded in anticipation as she watched him through half-closed eyes as he stared down at her bald pussy like he'd never seen anything like it. That turned her on even more and she worked her walls with a soft laugh that was taunting.

"Oh damn," he moaned as he pressed one of his beefy fingers inside her to circle against her walls before he pulled out the finger and suckled her juices like he was thirsty.

"Good, ain't it?" she asked in the small distance between them.

"Uhm hmm," he moaned around his finger.

She placed her hands to the back of his head and guided his mouth to her pussy. "Eat me," she ordered him, needing her fix.

Bree refused to let herself think about anything or anyone outside that room as Rev uncurled his long tongue and licked a path from the split of her ass and up to flick the pointed tip against her clit.

Bree arched her back and had to bite her mouth to keep

from hollering out in pleasure. She circled her hips against his mouth as he sucked her clit with a smooth and steady motion, slid one finger deep in her pussy, and then eased his thumb into her ass, moving both in small circular motions that made Bree's entire body shiver with heat. *Oh shit!*

She brought her hands up to tease and massage her aching nipples through her shirt and bra as he alternated between easing his tongue inside her to sucking her clit to putting pressure on it with the flicking tip of his tongue.

Lick. Suck. Flick. Lick. Suck. Flip. Over and over again.

All the while he worked his fingers.

Bree cried out, not giving a damn, as she arched her hips. "I'm gonna come. Don't stop. Don't stop. Suck that pussy good. Make me come," she moaned between clenched teeth as a fine sheet of sweat caused her shirt to cling to her body as her heart pounded wildly. She felt every bit of the white-hot pleasure over her entire body like she'd placed a wet finger in a socket. *Yessssssss.*

Tears formed and she gasped deeply as she came with such force that she thought her heart would explode.

Didn't matter. In that moment she felt ready to see the pearly gates.

Rev moaned as he kissed her clit and sucked all of the juices drizzling from her. When he finally freed her from his spell and rose to his feet, Bree was a wreck. She lay slumped against the chair, her legs still swinging over the arms of the chair, her heart pounding, her clit sensitive as hell, her hair surrounding her face like a wild and bushy halo.

Damn.

"Told you," he bragged, stepping back from her. "Shit was good for me, too. Look?"

Bree shifted her sleepy eyes down to where he pointed to his crotch. The front of his pants was damp. "You came, too?" she asked.

The Rev just smiled and winked at her before he turned and walked out the room like he didn't leave her shivering like a junkie in his wake.

When Bree finally emerged from the room she barely moved on steady feet. She quickly made her way down the hall to her private office, glad to close the door behind herself. She kicked off her platform heels and made her way to her en suite bathroom. She quickly rinsed her face and then removed her skirt to wash up at the sink. She tossed her torn panties into the wastepaper basket.

The entire time she was in there she avoided looking in the mirror, knowing she couldn't take the sight of herself. In the moments right after Rev left, her moods swung between remorse and exhilaration. It had been so long since a man had brought her pleasure. She thought she would have to kill another vibrator to keep getting pleased the way she wanted.

But . . .

He was a married man. A married minister. Her client. Her client that came to her for help for his sexual addiction . . . and she had just let him eat her.

Weak ass.

She closed her eyes and stomped her bare foot on the tiled floor before finally turning and facing the mirror . . . and herself. But the shame she thought she would feel wasn't in the depths of her eyes. She wrinkled her brows a bit as she leaned forward to study her reflection.

Her face was flushed. Her eyes were bright. And there at the corners of her mouth was an ever so slight hint of a smile. A naughty smile. A naughty smile that hid a secret.

Bree felt a rush as she thought of how just eating her pussy had made Rev come in his pants like a horny teenaged boy. That felt powerful.

The hint of a smile soon was replaced with a full-on grin

and then laughter that bubbled up from deep within her to echo around her.

"Good night, Dr. Bailey," Nola said, coming to stand in the door.

Bree looked up from transcribing her notes from the day's session. She genuinely smiled at the woman. "You, too, Nola," she said.

"You sure you not ready to leave?" Nola asked.

"No, I'm gonna get these notes printed and filed away tonight before I get behind." Because of patient-client privilege Bree always handled the notes personally. She didn't even trust them with Nola.

"Okay, then," Nola said.

Bree turned back to the computer, transcribing her written notes into typed pages.

"Oh, Dr. Bailey," Nola called out, eventually walking back to Bree's office door.

Bree looked up.

"Please call your mother. She said it's an emergency and she blew up the phone lines all day." Nola gave a chastising look. "Maybe something really is wrong this time. Just check. Okay?"

Bree nodded, even as she knew she was lying to Nola. "Okay. Thanks."

Her mother's idea of an emergency was asking Bree to drive the hour-long trip to her house to help look for her Chihuahua Tiny or to tell Bree to turn to one of her reality TV shows to see something real quick. Her mama would have to wait. Bree was determined to finish up her task for the night.

She turned up the volume on the Ledisi CD she was playing on her computer as she settled into her chair, crossing her legs under the spacious desk. It was well after nine by the time she finished and placed the last transcribed notes into the folder of a couple who were coming to her to deal with their communication issues.

Bree actually felt she was on the cusp of a breakthrough with the young couple. The thought of that gave her a thrill that almost topped . . .

She shook her head, not allowing herself to remember what had happened earlier. It could never happen again and she knew that.

She had to go forward with her plan to find a no-strings-attached lover and Rev wasn't it. She had no desire to kiss or even touch the man. She couldn't care less if his dick was as big as a prizewinning cucumber.

Sighing, she left her office, secured the alarm, and locked the building after she stepped out onto the porch. Turning, she gasped at the sight of Deon leaning against her car. Her heart pounded. It was a mix of surprise, fear, and pleasure.

"Late night?" he asked, crossing his arms over his chest.

"What are you doing here, Deon?" Bree asked, her feet locked in the same spot on the small stoop as she watched him.

"I wanted to talk to you," he said.

Bree's heart pounded. "We have group tomorrow."

Deon shook his head and pushed off the car to walk over to her. "It's not about that," he said dismissively, coming to stand before her. His height made them eye level even though she was on the stoop and he was on the ground.

Bree jammed her car key between her index and middle finger, readying herself to gouge his eyes out if he made a wrong move to hurt her.

"I think you're more like us than you want to admit," he began with the hint of a wolfish smile on his mouth.

"Oh really?" she asked slowly, still trying to grasp just what was going down.

Deon nodded. "I told you I can tell when a woman wants me," he told her, his eyes taking her in under the illumination from the streetlamp.

"Listen, Deon, I really need to head home. We can have this conversation tomorrow during group," she said, motioning with her hand for him to move out of her path.

"I can tell that *you* want me," he stressed, sliding his hands into the back pocket of the denims he wore with a V-neck T-shirt.

Bree arched a brow. "Your ego is astounding."

Deon chuckled. "You know I'm right. Don't be embarrassed by it."

Bree laughed. "How can you stand to look at the greatness of yourself in the mirror? It must be overwhelming," she said sarcastically.

"I want you, too," he said. Cocky. Bold. Taunting.

"Is there any woman with an available pussy that you *don't* want?" she snapped before she could catch herself. She knew this little interlude between them was wrong on so many levels, but she couldn't walk away from him. She was intrigued and excited by his boldness.

"My dick is selective, believe it or not."

Bree leaned back and opened her eyes wide as she pressed a hand to her full bosom. "So I should feel honored that you want me to be your next one-night stand. I should fall to my feet, risk my practice, profession, and reputation to be blessed with a poke from you."

"What if I told you it was worth the risk?" he asked.

Bree flung her head back and laughed, hoping to break the mood between them. She felt as if she were being offered a deal with the devil. It was in the same vein as the spider asking the fly to walk into its parlor.

"It's not just what I'm able to do to you or for you," Deon said, reaching up to lightly grasp her chin, to pull her head down so that they looked into each other's eyes under the subtle glow of the streetlamp.

Bree felt her pulse pound and she felt breathless. An energy shimmied around them that made her feel more alive than she had in a long time.

"I think it's what we would do for and to each other," he said, his deep and masculine voice sort of husky as he tried to draw her into him.

This is wrong, Bree, she warned herself as his hand came up to cup the side of her face. She shivered as she licked her lips. His touch made her feel like her entire body was on fire.

"I can promise you the best sex of your life . . . and you need it, don't you?" he asked in a low whisper.

Bree closed her eyes and pressed her face into his hand. His touch. She released a shaky breath.

Her eyes opened in surprise when she felt his mouth land on hers. She stiffened as he traced the fullness of her lips with the tip of his tongue before she opened her mouth and welcomed it in with a sigh. Her knees almost gave out as he moaned deeply and touched his tongue to hers.

Hypocrite. Shameful, lying, deceitful hypocrite.

Bree jerked her head away, breaking the kiss as she sidestepped Deon's overwhelming presence and stumbled on her heels to her car.

"Bree—"

She rushed inside her car, started the ignition, and pulled away in record time with a squeal of her tires. She couldn't believe she'd just been making out with one her clients in front of her office.

But it had felt good. His lips. His touch. The electricity.

And the fact it was so wrong made it even hotter for her.

I can promise you the best sex of your life . . . and you need it, don't you?

"Yes," Bree whispered as she slowed her car to a stop at a red light. She lowered her head to the cool leather of the steering wheel. *Shit.*

★ ★ ★

As Bree turned her vehicle down the treelined street where she lived, she slammed on her brakes in the middle of the street at the first sight of her parents' pickup truck in her driveway.

"What the fuck is this all about," she muttered out loud as she eased off the brake and pulled behind the truck.

Her front door opened wide and standing there was her mother holding her crazy-looking Chihuahua, Tiny, in her arms.

"Mama, I know you don't have that dog in my house," Bree snapped as she climbed out the car. "As a matter of fact, why are *you* in my house?"

"First, you know I don't let Tiny outside," Bree's mother said, her voice raspy from years of cigarette smoking. "And second, your daddy and I need to bunk with you because our house got damaged from a fire at our neighbors'."

Noooooooooooooooooo! Bree screamed in her mind.

Vera Bailey stood just shy of five feet but she had a big presence and an even bigger mouth. She eyed her daughter as she raised a hand and took a deep drag off her Newport cigarette.

Bree felt tension race from one shoulder to the other before settling at the base of her neck with the intensity of a fighter's punch. She turned back to the car and forced herself to count to a hundred as she breathed slowly.

"Vera! Vera-baby, the fish ready!"

Bree's eyes popped open at the sound of her father yelling through her house.

She had given them an emergency set of keys to her house. Emphasis on emergency at *her* house.

When Bree finally turned around, her mother and the dog had gone back into her house. She grunted and shook her hands, futilely trying to release some of the stress she felt building inside like floodwater.

A dog.

Cigarette smoke.

The smell of fish grease.

Her house, her serenity, and her sanity were under attack.

What the fuck else?

Bree leaned back against her car as she dragged her fingers through her curls and fought the urge to pull out every last strand of hair. There was no way in hell she could make it living with her parents. No way. She released a frustrated sigh and hummed low in her throat hoping to soothe away the anxiety she felt rising.

All of the order of her home and her life would not make it go away.

Biting her lip, she turned and opened the door to grab her briefcase. She grabbed her iPad and unlocked it, pulling up the client files. Grabbing her phone, she reacted on pure impulse. She needed a distraction. A release.

The phone rang just once before he answered.

"Deon, this Dr. Bailey . . . Bree. This is Bree. Meet me at the Hilton in Short Hills. I'll text you the room number," she said.

"You won't regret it," he promised.

Bree ended the call and climbed back into her car to speed away.

4

Knock knock.

Bree looked over her bare shoulder at the door of the hotel room. She closed her eyes and released a breath as she tightened the plush robe around her body. She was still damp from the hot shower she'd taken and she left moist footprints on the carpet as she crossed the room and opened the door.

Deon said nothing as he stepped into the room and wrapped one strong arm around her waist and pressed his face to the base of her neck.

Bree shut her eyes and exhaled through pursed lips as she pushed the door closed. He suckled deeply on her throat as his hands grabbed at the edges of the robe and flung it open to expose her naked body just as she fell back against the bed.

"Damn," he swore, already unbuttoning his shirt as his eyes took her in from her toes, up her solid and shapely legs, her plump bald mound, belly, and soft voluminous breasts. "I knew you were beautiful."

Bree smiled softly as she stretched her body against the cool sheets, causing the dark brown tips of her nipples to point to the ceiling. "Best sex ever, huh?" she asked, lightly licking her lips as the intensity swirled around them.

Deon undid his belt and dropped his pants, releasing the long and hard, curving length of his dick.

Bree let her eyes skim every inch, loving how it was as dark as chocolate even though his skin tone was the complexion of smooth caramel. She bit her bottom lip and pressed her legs open wide before him.

His eyes lit up as he dropped to his feet and grabbed her ankles to roughly jerk her body to the edge. He bent forward to press his nose against her pussy, inhaling deeply. "Aw man, it smells so good," he moaned, unrolling his tongue to lick lightly at her core.

Bree cried out and tightly grabbed the sheets above her head. She used her stomach muscles to lift her plush ass off the bed until all of her was laid out and exposed to him.

Deon blew a warm stream of air from her ass up to her clit before he slipped several fingers deep inside, loving the feel of her rigid walls as he worked the tips against her g-spot with long-practiced skill.

Bree arched her back off the bed so high she resembled a bridge as she worked her hips in small up and down motions that brought her clit against his tongue. *Rev eats better pussy*, she thought. And the thought of thinking of Rev while having Deon eat her made her feel so deliciously naughty that she giggled softly.

Bree used her scarlet-painted toes to push against Deon's head lightly before she flipped over in bed, turned around on her stomach, and inched toward him with her tongue extended. He sat up and she pressed the side of her face against the hard length of his dick with a soft moan before she took the thick and heated tip into her mouth.

Deon cried out loudly as Bree closed her eyes and circled his tip with her tongue, being sure to keep her mouth good and wet as she made his tip glisten before she sucked it so deeply that her cheeks caved in.

"Awww shit!" he whimpered with a hiss, bending over to dig his fingers into the flesh of her ass as his entire body went stiff.

Bree loved it. She loved turning her head to the side as she sucked more of his hard inches into her mouth until the tip reached the back of her tongue. She spread her legs wide on the bed and tooted up her buttocks.

Deon drizzled some of his spit down between the split of her full ass before he slipped his finger deep inside of her ass.

"Yes!" Bree moaned around his dick in her mouth.

Deon knew exactly what she had wanted and she felt ready to come from him being so on point. He used one hand to massage and stroke her ass cheeks as she began to work her hips, sending his finger in and out of her as she continued to suck the length of him.

Suddenly he jerked back, sliding his dick out of her mouth with a loud slurp. "You 'bout to make this dick come," he told her, slapping her ass. "Roll over."

Bree wiped at the corners of her mouth as she rolled over onto her back. She looked up and smiled at his erection hanging over her face. She lifted her face to lick at his balls with a wink.

Deon pursed his lips. "You fuck around and this gonna be over before it even begins," he told her, wrapping his strong hand around the thick base of his dark dick as he walked around the bed down by her feet.

"You said the best sex I ever had," Bree reminded him as she watched him climb onto the bed on his knees between her legs.

Deon locked his eyes fiercely on her flushed face as he picked up one of her legs and kissed her ankle before he began to massage her calf.

Bree's eyebrows dipped as she released a little grunt of pleasure. "This is the touching part you love so much, huh?" she asked, enjoying the feel of his hands on her body.

"There's nothing better than the feel of a woman's body," Deon admitted, as he began to massage both of her thick thighs. "Not silk. Not satin. Nothing."

Bree allowed her body to relax with a sigh as she enjoyed the feel of his hands. It was a mix of pressure and tenderness all at once as he moved up her thighs to the vee of her legs. "Oooh, that feels good," she said.

"It's a tender spot," Deon said, tracing his thumbs along the length of the crease between the top of her thighs and her plump mound.

Bree's clit swelled with renewed life.

She felt his movement on the bed and soon his breath shimmied across her clit before he pressed his mouth to the crease and sucked it softly. She brought her leg up to caress his strong back with her smooth knee as he moved across her mound to bless it with a moist kiss before he suckled the other crease.

Bree moved her hands up to massage the back of his head as he shifted up to lick a hot trail from her navel and up to the valley of her breasts as he scooped his hands beneath her to massage the fullness of her ass.

This slow and tender and sensual attention he paid her body was just what she needed. It was just what she was searching for. A man who set out to please. And not just with his dick and some hard pounding of the pussy that avoided any spot that would make her come. He wanted to feel and experience every inch of her like he was recording it in memory. Like he never wanted to forget.

Like he never wanted her to forget.

Bree shivered as Deon slowly took one of her hard brown nipples into his mouth. The feel of his tongue skirting over her bud sent a jolt through her body. She pressed her fingertips into his broad shoulders and massaged him, loving the moan of pleasure and appreciation she evoked from him.

He pursed his lips and suckled all of the brown areola into his mouth deeply as he flicked his tongue against her nipple.

Bree released a cry of pleasure that floated up to the ceiling as she tilted her head back against the plush bed. "Yes. Oh God yes."

He worked his way across the valley and gave her other nipple his attention as his fingers continued a rhythmic circular motion against her buttocks.

He shifted his hands up to her back and the massage continued against the small of her back as he rubbed his face back and forth against her breasts, his skin teasing her plump nipples. "A woman's body was made to touch . . . and taste," he whispered against her skin.

"Touch me," Bree commanded softly. "Taste me."

He held her body closely, wrapping her in his embrace and enclosing her legs with his. Bree felt like she was in a sensual cocoon as she lightly bit a trail from his shoulder to the base of his neck and held him just as tightly.

"What do you want me to do?" he asked against her ear before suckling the lobe.

She tilted her head back and looked up at him through half-closed lids. "Fuck me, Deon."

She felt his dick press against her stomach. "You want that dick, don't you?" he asked, dipping his head down to lick hotly at her chin and then her bottom lip.

Bree nodded, lifting her head to suck at the tip of his tongue.

"Tell me."

"Give me that dick. Now," she told him into the heated air between their open mouths.

Deon raised his hips and probed the moist lips of her pussy with the tip of his dick before he made the connection and swiftly thrust deep inside of her.

They both cried out.

Bree bit her bottom lip as her core adjusted to the width of his dick pressing against her walls and making its presence known.

Deon buried his face against her neck as he strained not to fill her with his seed from the heat and the tightness of her surrounding him like a vise. "Oh, I knew your pussy was gonna be good," he moaned.

Bree kissed his cheek as she buried her feet into the softness of the bed and began working her hips so that she slid up and down the hard length of him.

He leaned up to look down at her as he shook his head. "Let me handle this," he told her with a smile, reaching to put one of her legs up on his shoulder.

Bree's lips shaped to form an "O" as he pressed one knee into the bed and lifted up to began working his dick inside of her. "That's n–n–n–n-ice," she stuttered, feeling energy brewing from their connection.

Deon turned his face to press against her leg before he licked it hotly and then suckled her calf as he pumped away inside of her, sending the base of his dick against her clit.

"Can you make me come?" she asked him, thinking of the countless times that very question had been answered with lies and false bravado.

"What you think?" he asked, as he looked down at her with determination, his jaw tight as he fought not to come himself.

Bree brought her hands up to lightly tease his nipples.

"Look," he told her thickly, reaching down to pull his dick out of her just as some of his nut dripped from the tip.

Bree released her tongue and he shifted his body forward to press his dick into her open mouth.

"Agggh!" he cried out as another shot of his release filled her mouth before he pulled out.

Bree licked her lips as she looked up at him rolling over

onto his back, his dick standing up to the ceiling. She straddled his body and reached out to grasp his dick tightly as she slid down onto it. "Ooh, it's hard," she moaned as she pressed her hands on his chest.

Deon grabbed both of her wrists as he sat up, leaning back against the pillows. He put her hands on the headboard and Bree leaned back as she rode him with a slow and deliberate back and forth motion that slid her clit against the hard base of his dick. Deon suckled one of her hard nipples into his mouth and he pressed his hand around her body to ease a finger into her ass she rode him.

Bree was gone.

The feel of him in her and against her . . . his mouth tasting her nipples . . . his finger making tiny circles in her ass . . . their bodies pressed close together . . . all pushed her over the edge. And she fell with cries. White-hot spasms exploded inside of her as an electricity surrounded her body. She cried out as he pressed his arm across her back and his face into her breasts as he worked his hips up off the bed with hard thrusts that intensified her climax.

"Oh God, I'm coming," she moaned, sweat coating her body. Tears formed in her eyes. Her heart pounded. Her clit throbbed. Her juices echoed in the space around.

She was way gone.

Deon grunted. "Shit," he roared.

Bree grabbed the headboard tighter as she jumped up to her feet and squatted as she worked hard to draw every bit of his nut from him as his face contorted and twisted in pleasure. She didn't stop riding him until his dick went slack inside of her.

Deon looked up at her in wonder. "Damn," he swore.

Bree released a sigh filled with satisfaction before she rolled off his body to lie on the bed. Her heart and clit were still racing, but she felt completely exhausted. "Best sex ever?" he asked near her ear.

Bree nodded with a smile as she buried her face deep into the softness of the pillow and allowed her body to drift to sleep.

Bree awakened the next morning to an empty bed. She was grateful Deon had taken his leave sometime during the early morning. She wasn't looking for spooning or lies in the morning about calling.

They had both gotten what they wanted and that was all there was to it.

She glanced at the digital clock on the bedside table. She was going to be late getting to the office . . . and Bree couldn't care less.

When she went home she knew she was going to find her parents had taken over her house and swept any chance of tranquility out the door. And in that moment, as she lay there still a little sore from really good sex she couldn't care less.

She stretched her body across the bed with a little yawn, feeling like she could roll over and go back to sleep for the rest of the day. The last twenty-four hours had been filled with new things. Both Rev and Deon had lived up to their word. First Rev and the spectacular oral sex and then Deon truly giving her the best sex she ever had—bar none.

Bree fanned herself as she forced herself out of bed and into a quick shower. She could zip home, dress, and get to her office in about an hour. She couldn't cancel another group session and she was curious to see if Rev and Deon would even show.

As she stood under the steaming spray of the shower and lathered the curves of her body, she allowed herself to visualize Rev kneeling before her with his head buried between her thighs as Deon massaged her breasts, stomach, and buttocks from behind. A steamy ménage à trois that made her body tingle at the very thought of it.

She had to end things with both men and suggest they

turn to new therapists—maybe male. Bree knew she had already crossed so many ethical lines that there was no way she could continue to treat them . . . or see them.

She felt a moment of regret at that, but what could she do? They had come to her for treatment, not pussy. Period. Point blank. And hindsight being twenty-twenty and all that.

Bree quickly dried the dampness from her body and dressed in the skirt and blouse she had worn yesterday. Her torn panties from Rev's oral seduction were still in the trash bin in her office's bathroom. She could imagine what the cleaning lady thought when she saw them.

Bree left the room with one quick glance at the bed over her shoulder.

She slid on her shades as she stepped onto the empty elevator. She paced the elevator a bit, ready to get to work. She was looking forward to a full day of sessions. The challenge of helping people sort out underlying issues to eventually become fully self-actualized individuals intrigued her.

Hypocrite.

She looked up and saw her reflection in the metal of the elevator doors. She was glad when the door slid open and the reflection was gone.

5

Two Weeks Later

Bree smiled politely at the men as she entered the room and closed the door behind her before taking her usual seat. "Good morning," she said, avoiding the eyes of Deon and Rev.

The men all greeted her in return.

"So, I thought this week we should focus a little bit on support systems. It's very important when struggling with any addiction to have someone whom you can turn to for support, but not to enable you as you recover." Bree set her iPad in her lap as she crossed her legs in the navy pinstriped skirt she wore.

It was hard to miss the way Carter's eyes stayed locked on her legs. She quickly jotted:

Carter's attention toward to me is increasing with each session and becoming more noticeable and inappropriate. Possible transference of affection. May necessitate additional session to get to the root of the transference.

It wasn't the first time Bree had experienced a client—particularly male clients—transferring their emotions toward her and actually believing they had true love for her. Her experience had taught her to recognize the signs, and although she preferred not to alienate Carter by bringing it to his attention, she didn't want his feelings to develop further as she waited for him to bring the subject up to her.

"Carter, do you feel you have a support system in your life?" she asked him without judgment or reproach.

The handsome jazz musician shook his head. "My girlfriend and I are still together and I can tell she appreciates me coming for therapy, but I'm still afraid to talk to her about certain things."

"What's the fear you feel?" Bree asked.

"That he will be judged."

Bree tensed at the sound of Rev's voice. Just yesterday, during their one-on-one session, he had stripped her naked and lifted her body up onto his shoulders as he pressed her back to the wall and ate her pussy like he was starved for it. When he was done, he'd left her a shivering, sweaty naked mess on the top of her desk.

"Do you think she will judge you, Carter?"

"Yes," he stressed. "I don't like to be rejected and that's why I would turn to prostitutes and tricks because I knew they wouldn't make me feel like a pervert or some shit."

"Sometimes you have to take a risk and just ask for what you want, man," Deon said, looking at Carter before he turned his eyes on Bree. "Ain't that right, Doc?"

Their eyes locked for just a second, but in that flash, Bree saw a heated image of Deon gliding his dick in and out of both of her openings as she tooted her ass to him in the shower.

"Yes, Deon, sometimes you do," she agreed, not letting him or their sneaky fuck sessions fluster her.

Bree sat back in her chair as one of the men discussed taking a chance on being honest with his mate. She let the group have at it as she looked back and forth between Rev and Deon's faces. Two handsome men with sexual appetites to equal her own. One to eat her pussy and the other to "blow her back out"—as he liked to say.

She had never felt so satisfied *in her life*. And the sexual satisfaction took the edge off of other aspects of her life. She felt more levelheaded, more balanced. She was carefree and loving it. Her complexion was even better. The addition of her lovers to her life was ideal for her and she wasn't ready to give it up. Not yet.

And so Bree knew she had to stay in total control of their situations. If they switched to a new therapist and revealed their sexual encounters with her, they could be encouraged to report her to the state board. A therapist having sex with his or her clients was a definite no-no and could lead to civil or even criminal repercussions that would destroy her practice and the lifestyle she treasured. She could not let a fuckfest with two men who had begged for it ruin her life.

Still, that extra restriction on her affairs with these men made it all the more exciting and titillating for her. And so she decided to have it all. Her lifestyle. Her practice. Her sexual boys willing to ask how high when she said to jump for the pussy.

Bree felt she knew these men inside and out. They were hers to do with as she pleased when she pleased. Love was not a factor. This was all about sex.

And she was giving as good as she was getting.

She bit down on the tip of her stylus and smiled. When Rev and Deon looked over at her, she felt her desire for them stir. No, she wasn't done with them yet. Not by a long shot.

Bree sat on her small terrace clad only in a short satin robe as she sipped wine and enjoyed a cigarette. After a deep inhale she flicked the ashes into the night wind before she tilted her head back and released small smoke rings. She was glad that her bedroom overlooked her spacious backyard that was shielded by plenty of trees. It almost felt like being in the middle of a forest, and when Bree wanted to escape from the real world there was nothing better to her than relaxing on her balcony. Sometimes when it was really late at night she would even venture out there nude and let the wind blow across her body.

"Bree!"

She flinched at the sound of her mother screeching her name. Moments later she heard her bedroom door open and her mother's slippers sliding across the wood floor.

"Your Aunt Reeda is downstairs and we want to play whist." she said. "We need one more player."

Bree turned her head to look over her shoulder at her mother, seeing a shorter and older version of herself dressed head to toe in animal print. Various animal prints. "I don't feel like playing cards, Mama," Bree told her. "And y'all having company over, did you straighten up the house?"

Vera Bailey scrunched up her face as she reached down and took a cigarette from Bree's pack. "There is nothing wrong with the house."

Dirty dishes were stacked on the counter. Her father's shoes were in random spots, wherever he kicked them off, all over the house. Old newspapers and books were scattered all over her living room. There were overflowing ashtrays. The smell of whatever greasy food her Mama cooked was heavy in the air.

And Bree just hated to think of the fuckery that was going on beyond their closed guest-room door.

"When did the contractor say the repairs to the house would be done?" Bree asked, reaching for her cell phone sitting on the table beside her.

"Another two weeks . . . tops," Vera said, eyeing her daughter. "We can go to a hotel if we're in the way of your oh-so-fabulous and oh-so-lonely life," she snapped.

Bree's shoulders dropped because she knew she had hurt her mother's feelings. "You're more than welcome here, Mama. I just was asking," she said, pulling up the camera feature on her phone.

"Well, come on down if you change your mind about playing cards," Vera said, before turning and leaving.

Bree had a lot to escape from in her home. As soon as the bedroom door closed behind her Mom, Bree spread her legs wide and took an up-close shot of her pussy. She attached the photo to a text and typed:

WANT SOME?

She sent the text off and then propped her leg up on the railing to lightly play in the slick folds of her pussy as she waited for an answer.

Bzzz.

Her heart pounded as she opened the text. It was from Rev.

I SUCKED THE SCREEN.

Bree lit another cigarette before she texted him back:

I NEED IT LICKED RIGHT NOW.

And she did. Rev's tongue game had a way of making every stress in her life disappear in those moments he made her come in his mouth.

Bzzz.

She looked down at the phone vibrating in her hand. The image of a glistening wet and hard dick filled the screen. Deon. She had sent the pussy shot to both of them.

I ALWAYS WANT IT. ON A DATE. L8TER??

"On a date?" Bree said, biting her bottom lip as she dialed his number.

She laughed when he didn't answer but called her back a few minutes later. "Where are you?" she asked, already rising to walk into her bedroom. She let her robe slip from her body and onto the floor.

"I told you I'm on a date, Bree," he said.

"Where?" she asked, reaching in her closet for a black wrap dress and heels. She didn't bother with any underwear and her nipples pressed against the thin material like they were ready to rip through.

"We're at Yoni's on Riverdale. Why?"

"I'm taking my parents out to eat and I didn't want to run into you," she lied. "Well, you enjoy your date and call me when you're done."

Beep.

As soon as she ended the call her phone vibrated with a text from Rev, but Bree didn't even bother to open it. She left her bedroom and came down the stairs, not even caring about the chaotic combination of loud voices, a blaring television, and a yapping dog coming from her living room. She left the house and climbed into her car, making it to Yoni's Restaurant in twenty minutes flat. During the entire ride she had driven with one hand and lightly teased her clit with the other.

Bzzz.

Bree looked down at her phone. Rev again. "Not tonight, Mr. Preacher Man," she said, parking her BMW at the rear of the parking lot in a dark corner.

She called Deon instead. Again she smirked when he didn't answer her but called her back after a few minutes.

"Bree—"

"Come outside. I'm parked in the back," Bree said, exiting the car to get into the rear seat.

The line stayed quiet for a few seconds.

"*Now*, Deon . . . or I'm coming in," she said, loving the thrill she got.

Beep.

She felt high. The rush was better than a shot of adrenaline.

It was just a few minutes later that she saw Deon's tall, muscular figure come around the restaurant and make his way toward her car. Bree's entire body tingled as she opened the wrap dress and spread her legs wide.

The interior light came on when he opened the door and Deon's mouth fell open at the sight of her. She slid two fingers deep inside her core and then offered them to him. "Think your date's pussy tastes like that?" she asked him as he dipped his head to suck her fingers with a moan.

He closed the driver's door and opened the rear door to climb into the back with her. "What, you're jealous that I'm on a date?" he taunted as he scrambled to undo his belt and zipper before lifting his hips to jerk his denims down to his knees.

Bree climbed onto his lap and guided his head to one of her throbbing nipples in the cool darkness of her car. "I couldn't care less about you being on a date," she told him truthfully. "I wanted dick. I wanted *your* dick. And I get what I want when I want it. Now when *I'm* done she can have you."

Deon licked wildly at her nipples as she felt his dick harden and grow against her stomach. He dug his fingers into her hips and raised her up to lower her pussy onto his hardness. "Oh shit. It's wet," he moaned against her breasts.

Bree gasped hotly at the feel of him against her walls as she leaned back against the rear of the front seat and began working her hips in slow circles.

Deon massaged the tops of her thighs, her soft belly, and then her full, brown pendulous breasts as he watched her work his dick. "You the best," he said, his voice shaky. "I swear to God you the best."

Bree leaned forward and raised up on her knees to make his dick stand up as she slid back and forth on him like she was racing a horse to the finish line. When his mouth closed around one of her nipples again she felt her core pulse as her juices drizzled on him. "*Mmmmmmmm*, dick good, daddy," she whispered to him hotly, as he twisted his fingers in her hair and jerked her head back.

Bree cried out hoarsely as she quickened her pace until her heart was racing just as fast, and her sweat dripped down onto his body as she felt the first hard jolt of her nut squirt from her. She closed her eyes and allowed herself to get lost in the explosion as she came and came in wave upon wave.

Deon grabbed her hips tightly and arched his hips, sending the base of his dick against her moist lips as he filled her with his nut, and round after round of his seed exploded from his dick until he cried out in a feminine-sounding high-pitched tone that he would regret later.

With one last tortured cry, they both felt their bodies go slack even as their hearts pounded. Bree fell over onto the seat next to him as she wiped the sweat from her face back into her hair. She watched Deon through half-closed eyes as his chest rose and fell as he struggled to reclaim his breath.

Smiling, she opened the car door and stumbled out, not caring that her sweat-soaked dress was open and exposed her naked body to whoever could see. "Enjoy the rest of the dinner," she told him, licking her parched lips before she closed the door and stumbled around the front of her car to open the driver's-side door.

Once Bree was in the seat and behind the wheel she cranked the car. "You want me to drop you off in the front on my way out?" she asked, looking over her shoulder.

Deon looked at her like she was crazy before he pulled up his pants and tried his best to tuck in his shirt before he left the car. He opened the driver's-side door and bent down to kiss Bree deeply as he cupped the back of her head with his hand.

"Drive safe," he whispered against her mouth, before rising to his feet, closing the door, and walking away on unsteady feet.

Bree focused her attention on arranging her hair in the rearview mirror and closing her dress before she finally cruised out of the parking lot without another thought to Deon or his date. She had gotten exactly what she wanted.

The next morning, Bree was sipping chilled green tea and going through e-mails when Nola walked into her office carrying the day's mail and one of the huge muffins she knew Bree loved. Bree smiled up at her before turning her attention back to an update from the New Jersey Psychological Association.

"It's a rainy day out today," Nola said, separating the professional journals and magazines from the day's newspaper. She knew Bree always read the paper first, then devoured the journals, and left the brainless entertainment mags for later.

"I know we're going to get some cancellations of appointments," Bree said. "You know how people act when a little rain falls."

"Already got two," Nola said with a chuckle.

Bree yawned behind her hand as she picked up the newspaper. She frowned at the sight of a colleague's picture on the front page. South Orange was a small city and there wasn't press to fill the pages, but front page . . . *Probably a symposium or something*, Bree thought.

"Can you believe what they're saying about Dr. Hammerstein?" Nola asked, shaking her head.

Bree remained quiet as she read, but her body became tense with each word exposing the therapist for engaging in a sexual affair with the wife of a couple he was treating. The wife had attempted suicide when Dr. Hammerstein ended the affair after nearly six months. Both the wife and husband were suing him civilly and were calling for his license to practice to be revoked.

Bree couldn't deny that the story made her heart race.

"Isn't that just sinful?" Nola asked.

Bree nodded as she swallowed over a lump in her throat.

The phone rang in the outer office and Bree was glad for something—anything—to draw Nola out of her office. Although it really didn't matter because her words of condemnation remained heavy in the air.

Isn't that just sinful?

6

Three Weeks Later

Bree set her iPad on the table by her chair and rose to her feet as the door to the room she used for private sessions opened. She gave Carter a polite smile as she extended her hand to him. "Hello, Carter," she said as he took her hands in his.

"This is a little different, huh?" he said, before releasing her hand and folding his frame onto the sofa.

"A little," Bree agreed, taking her seat and picking up her iPad.

He wiped his hand over his mouth and settled back against the chair.

"Okay, so I want to thank you for agreeing to a one-on-one session," Bree began. "I like to check in with members of group therapy just to make sure that they are on track and getting the best possible experience from the group sessions."

He nodded.

"So how is everything going for you, Carter?"

"Honestly?" he asked, locking his eyes on her.

"Absolutely," she stressed, swinging her leg back and forth.

Carter inched forward on the edge of the chair and looked pointedly down at her leg. "You turn me the fuck on."

Bree stopped the movement of her leg and fought the urge to throw her hands up in exasperation. *What the hell? Not another client trying to bang me.* She held up her hands. "Language, Carter," she insisted.

"I'm sorry, but it's true," Carter said, shrugging like "And what?"

Bree closed her eyes and allowed herself a fifteen-second countdown. Her life was C-R-A-Z-Y!! "Okay, Carter—"

Her words faltered when she opened her eyes to find him stretched back on the sofa with his hard dick in his hand as he massaged the length of it.

Bree paused long enough to note how it was as thick as a roll of cookie dough before she jumped to her feet. "I need you to leave, Carter. Now!" she stressed, her voice hard.

"Just watch me while I jack off," he asked her thickly as his strokes picked up the pace.

Bree's eyes widened as he began to thrust his hips up off the couch.

She couldn't lie; the man was fine and he certainly *looked* like he packed quite a punch, but Bree wasn't attracted to him or *it*. She made her way to the door and jumped back when he sprang to his feet to block her path. The tip of his penis swung against her arm with a *thump.*

"I'm sorry, I didn't mean to freak you out," Carter said, reaching for her and then snatching his hands away to hold them up.

"Carter, just leave, and . . . and . . ." Bree squeezed her eyes shut as he still stood there with his dick as hard as jail time as it hung from inside his open zipper. "And put your dick away. Please."

"Sorry," he told her.

Bree turned her back on him.

"I hope you can still be my therapist, Dr. Bailey," he said, before she heard the sound of his zipper going up.

Bree turned and faced him, crossing her arms over her chest. "I'll be honest with you, Carter, I was aware that you possibly had feelings of some sort for me. I was hoping we could get to the root of that issue, which is probably you placing the emotions you want to have for your girlfriend onto me. It happens. But this little scenario may be too much to move on from."

Carter nodded. "I don't want to start over with a new therapist. It would feel like going all the way back to step one. I just lost my head and I apologize. It won't ever happen again."

Who am I to judge? she thought, remembering how far her own impulses had pushed her the last few weeks.

Bree's shoulder dropped as she went back and forth with her decision. "Let's take a couple weeks off from group or any one-on-one session and if you feel you can continue your therapy then I will continue to treat you."

Carter opened the door but paused before he stepped out into the hall. "I'm sorry again," he said before he finally left.

Bree released a steadying breath before she massaged the bridge of her nose. Picking up her iPad, she made her way out the room and down the hall to her office. She opened the doorway and paused to find Rev lounging on her sofa that sat in front of the bay windows. "How did you get in here?" she asked, closing—and locking—the door behind her.

Rev set his cell phone on the oversized padded ottoman she used as a coffee table in the sitting area. He slid down to the floor and tilted his head back against the seat of the sofa. "Come and sit on my face," he told her, unrolling his tongue and flicking the tip like that of a snake.

Bree walked over to him. "But I didn't call you and ask for you to eat my pussy," she told him as she crossed her arms over her chest and looked down at him, tapping her foot.

Rev reached out and grabbed her ankle tightly before sliding his hand up to her calf. "So I can only eat your pussy when you say so?" he asked, looking up at her as he moved to sit up.

Bree stepped out of a stiletto and then pressed her foot to his chest. "What a good little pussy licker you are," she said, taunting him and wanting to regain control.

Rev looked affronted, but when Bree hitched her skirt up to her waist he reached up and tore the front of her sheer lace thongs. Smiling, Bree straddled his face, sitting her ass on his chest as she grabbed the back of the sofa tightly. "Suck my clit," she demanded, looking out the window at traffic passing by on the road and a car pulling up in the parking lot outside the building. A tall, fair-skinned woman with bright red hair that flowed to her back climbed out of a Mercedes. Bree smiled, thinking she could be spotted at any moment if the woman just peered closely enough through the trees in front of her office windows.

Rev moaned at he sucked and plucked her clit with his tongue and his lips, using the skill she had come to crave. She drew heated air in between pursed lips as she felt her toes curl up from the nerve he was striking. He released his tongue so that the tip touched his chin and Bree glided her hips back and forth, lightly sending her pulsing clit against it. She grunted softly and arched her back, feeling her climax building from deep within her core. Her ass and thighs shivered in anticipation. She brought her hands up under shirt to lightly tease her nipples as she cried out with each spasm of release.

Rev moaned and sucked her core deeply, not missing one drop.

Bzzzz.

They jumped apart of the sound of the intercom. They both laughed at the shock.

"Shit," Bree swore, her clit still pulsating as she quickly moved to her desk with her skirt around her hips and her shirt askew with one of her breasts freed from its sheer brassiere.

She pressed the button. "Yes, Nola."

"Mrs. Teel is here for her one o'clock appointment with her husband, but I can't seem to find *him*," Nola said, sounding annoyed.

"Actually, he came to my office to talk to me first and you can send her on back," Bree said, thankful that she sounded normal even as she turned to glare at Rev.

"Oh . . . okay. In your office? You're meeting in your office?" Nola asked, sounding surprised.

"Yes, ma'am. Thanks."

"Your wife is here!" Bree snapped, as she jerked down her skirt and tucked in her shirt. She rushed to the door and motioned for Rev to sit on one of the club chairs in front of her desk. As soon as he landed in one, she opened the door wide and then rushed to take her seat behind her desk.

Moments later, the tall redhead from the parking lot walked into the office looking pretty and stylish in her white strapless eyelet dress and a peach sweater tied around her shoulders. Bree felt herself flush with embarrassment as she rose and extended her hand. "Nice to meet you, Mrs. Teel," she said.

Rev held his wife's chair while she shook Bree's hand. "Anana," she offered with a smile.

Bree looked on as, when the woman took her seat, Rev lightly touched her face to turn it so that he could kiss her.

No . . . he . . . didn't! Bree screamed inside her head, knowing the woman was tasting Bree's juices on her husband's mouth. She turned from them and then spotted her panties poking out from under the sofa. *Oh Lawd!*

She turned back to eye them both and then her eyes widened when Rev leaned back in his chair and smiled at her with a wink. His bold and disrespecting move unnerved her and Bree had to shuffle papers on her desk as she struggled to compose herself. *What kind of sick shit is that?*

"Uhm, I'm glad that you are able to attend a session together to try and discuss and hopefully alleviate stumbling blocks that many couples face," Bree began.

"A lot of couples have a husband who is addicted to sex?" Anana asked, her voice soft, pleasant, and dignified, but her intention was filled with disapproval.

Rev made a face and then motioned with his tongue at Bree. He was taking pleasure in his dalliances with Bree behind his wife's back.

"My husband is a young man, but he is supposed to be a man of God whom people in his church want to look to for guidance and leadership. If he can't control himself, how can he help others control themselves?" Anana said.

Bree pulled her iPad from the top drawer of her desk. "And the image he presents is important to you?" she asked.

Anana nodded. "I believe you have to not only preach the word, but live the word or you're a hypocrite."

Hypocrite.

Bree continued with the session and went through the motions as Rev and Anana volleyed insults and condemnations back and forth, but her mind was focused on the slightly sadistic nature of Rev purposefully eating her out when he knew his wife was coming there and then topping it off by kissing the woman with Bree's pussy juices still damp on his mouth. There was something cruel about it that she couldn't shake.

The only note she jotted on her iPad during their session was:

Refer the Teels to a new counselor.

The last thing Bree wanted was to have his life intruding upon hers. If Rev thought he was going to bring his wife to her for couples counseling and still be allowed to lick her kitty, then he was sadly mistaken. She wasn't gonna smile in the woman's face *and* stab the bitch in her back.

He had just hammered a nail in the coffin of their sexual relationship.

Bree leaned down and opened the bottom drawer where she kept her purse. Reaching down inside her purse, she grabbed her cell phone and quickly texted Rev:

IT'S OVER. SERIOUSLY OVER.

She dropped her cell phone and closed the drawer with her foot as she refocused attention back on Anana, who was discussing her embarrassment over all of his affairs. Bree nodded and gave Anana a sympathetic smile, although she really had no clue what the woman had just said.

She was glad when the fifty-minute session ended and they took their leave.

Five minutes later, Bree was leaving her private bathroom after cleaning up some of the wetness between her thighs when she heard her cell phone vibrating loudly. She reclaimed her seat behind the desk and pulled her cell phone from her purse.

A text.

From Rev.

So I can't eat ur pussy no more???

Bree ignored the text, dropping her cell phone back into her purse before she focused on reading the file in preparation for her next client.

Later that night Bree was at her favorite liquor store buying a bottle of wine to celebrate the news that her parents—and all their chaos—could move back into their own home in the next week or so. It wasn't a definite date, but just the possibility of order reigning in her house again was the first bit of nonsexual bliss she had felt in weeks.

Bree loved her family but . . . *They gots to go!*

She snapped her fingers at her side and sang softly, "They gots to go. See you. Deuces. They gots to go. See you. Deuces."

The sudden laughter of a man behind her caused her to look over her shoulder. Her curiosity changed to awareness as she eyed the man whose skin was as dark as midnight and dreads as long as time. Bree smiled, hoping his dick had the same traits. *We could have some fun*, she thought as she eyed the broadness of his shoulders.

Bree went into full flirt mode, tilting her head to the side and lightly licking her lips as she softened the look in her eyes. "Hi, I'm Suzi," she lied, extending her hand.

Since she had Deon and Rev tag-teaming the pussy it had been a minute since she'd scooped up a one-night stand. But it had been an even longer minute since she'd run across a man who looked like he was built to fuck and be fucked.

"Yuri," he said, reaching out to enclose her hand in his.

Bree felt the familiar nervous energy as she held onto his hand when he moved to extract it. His brows lifted a bit.

"Yuri and Suzi sitting in the backseat. F-u-c-k-i-n-g," she said to him, extending her finger to massage tiny circles on his inner wrist. She missed being naughty and bold and limitless.

She felt his body tense.

"Wow, you just gonna put it out there like that?" he asked, his finger now tracing circles on her inner wrist as well.

"Listen, I'm a grown woman with no time for games and a glove compartment filled with condoms. You down?" she asked softly, loving being the aggressor. The one in control. She already knew she would ride him and make sure they *both* got what they wanted.

And maybe . . . *maybe* if he was good she would slip him right into Rev's spot and train him well to come when *she* called.

Bree didn't even bother with the wine as she took Yuri's

strong hand in hers and led him out the liquor store. As soon as they got to her car he reached for her hips and pressed his body into her until her buttocks and back were against the passenger door. His dick was already hard and she could feel the length of him against her belly as he leaned in to plant a kiss to her neck.

Bree frowned in irritation. His lips? Too wet. His grip on her hips? Too tight. The length of his dick? Too damn short.

I knew this Negro was too good to be true, she thought. *He is not Deon.*

"Whassup, Bree?"

She stiffened and her eyes widened as she looked over Yuri's square shoulder at Deon sitting behind the wheel of his black-on-black Jag.

"Bree?" Yuri asked.

Deon climbed out of the car, dressed in all black, and came over to stand beside them. He shoved his hands into the front pockets of his denims as he looked down at Yuri's hands still on her hips.

"That's Bree and she likes to be fucked . . . by me," Deon said. Smug. Cocky.

And sexy as fuck, Bree thought.

Yuri released her and flexed his shoulders.

"Now Bree, tell this boy to go jack off or find some new pussy because yours belongs to me," Deon said with emphasis, his eyes intense as they stayed locked on her.

Bree felt like the whole scene was breathing new life into her pussy. "Good night, Yuri," she said, keeping her eyes locked on Deon.

Deon reached out and jerked Bree's body to his, bringing his hands up to cup her ass as he licked the outline of her mouth. Bree moaned in pleasure and released her tongue to flick at him before he caught the tip and sucked it into his mouth.

"Ain't this 'bout a bitch. Freaky motherfuckers," Yuri muttered in anger somewhere outside the bubble of chemistry around them.

When Deon led her to his car, brushing past a stunned Yuri, Bree was wet, hot, and ready for the dicking down she knew he could deliver.

7

One Week Later

Bzzzzzz . . . Bzzzzzz . . . Bzzzzzz . . .

Bree forced the sudden tension from her shoulders at the sound of her cell phone going off from where she'd set it on the edge of her desk.

Bzzzzzz . . . Bzzzzzz . . . Bzzzzzz . . .

She ran her fingers through her loose curls as she leaned back in her office chair and eyed the phone like it was a poisonous snake about to bite her and fill her system with its venom.

Bzzzzzz . . . Bzzzzzz . . . Bzzzzzz . . .

Rolling her eyes heavenward, she leaned forward to scoop up the cell phone. It was a text. And like many of the texts she'd received over the past week she didn't recognize the number.

"Humph. What now?" she asked out loud as she used her thumb to open it.

I hate you because you won't LET me love your pussy. I'm sad . . . but I'm getting mad. Real mad . . . Joe Jackson

Bree rolled her eyes again. There was no need to reply or call the number back. Whomever it was never responded to her request for him to "Suck a dick and die" and the phone always went straight to voice mail.

At times the texts were desperate:

Please let me have that pussy.

Or jealous:

Somebody else getting that pussy now, huh?

Or mean:

Fuck that fishy shit anyway.

Or scary:

I'm going to get that pussy . . . 1 way or the other.

Bree was mostly just irritated by the texts . . . especially when they arrived at odd hours of the night.

She had already assumed it was Rev. She assumed—and hoped—he would get tired of being childish and desperate and instead focus on repairing his marriage. She refused to acknowledge him by calling to demand he stop playing on her phone.

Bree released a heavy breath as she rested her chin in her hand and eyed her phone. She had a way to handle the text in a passive-aggressive manner that would get her point across, but did she really want to go that far? Was it worth a new hassle to avoid another?

Moving quickly before she changed her mind, Bree called her cell phone provider and had her number changed.

★　★　★

Bree rose to her feet and took her keys and purse from the top drawer of her desk. She was ready to go home and sip wine as she pampered herself with a lavender-scented bubble bath, listened to some music, and just enjoyed having her home all to her lonesome. Her parents had finally moved their dog and their belongings back into their newly renovated home. She had sent them on their way with an eighteen pack of their beloved Bud Lights.

I might even call my mama tonight, Bree thought as she left the building and turned to lock the door. Nola had left early for the day, leaving Bree behind to take a seven o'clock session with a couple trying to recover from the wife's adultery.

Bree felt like she was being watched. The tiny hairs covering her nape stood on end. Her heart pounded. Her bladder filled. She was alone in the parking lot with no one but the night sky to witness her getting attacked. She rushed to finish locking the door, never turning her back fully. Her heart beat so loudly that it felt like it was pounding in her ears. *What the hell?*

She was struggling to turn the key in the lock.

"Late night?"

Bree shrieked and jumped like a D-list actress in a horror flick. She pressed a hand to her chest as Carter stepped forward under the circle of light created by the streetlamp. "What the hell are you doing here?" she snapped, her heart racing and pounding against her hand as she eyed him.

Carter held up his hand. "I'm sorry. I didn't mean to scare you," he said. "Plus, I wanted to apologize again for what happened—"

Bree looked past him only to confirm they were alone. Knowing his attraction for her, she couldn't deny that he creeped her out. Her eyes darted over the entire small parking lot and then out to the street running outside the office. Cars zoomed by, but there wasn't a person in sight. She wished she had a weapon—or even a can of mace—just to feel more secure in his sudden appearance. *If I have to pull up my hood roots and straight knock him the fuck out . . . I will.*

He stepped closer to her. "And I wanted to tell you that I can't stop thinking about you. I want to—"

Bree held up her hand. "This isn't appropriate, Carter. Now, go home," she said as she moved past him to rush to her car and climb inside, locking the door before she started the car and pulled out of the parking lot. She checked her rearview mirror to make sure Carter wasn't following her, even though she didn't even see another vehicle in the parking lot.

Was that fool on foot?

She felt a nervous anxiety causing her body to tremble. He scared the hell out of her, especially after all the text messages.

The messages, she thought, stopping in the middle of the street. Was Carter behind them?

No. She shook away the thought that it was Carter texting her. True, his sudden appearance after she changed her number was suspect . . . but Carter hadn't had her personal cell number in the first place.

Closing her eyes, she forced herself to calm down as she accelerated forward slowly. Her number was changed and the texts had stopped. Rev was handled. She just had to figure out how to handle Carter. She wanted him to get help, but she now knew the boundaries he crossed in their patient-therapist relationship couldn't be erased or forgotten.

There were statistics proving that a large number of therapists had been attacked by a client. Usually the clients were more disturbed and mentally ill than she believed Carter to be, but she was beyond taking a risk.

Bree hated that when she drove up to her office the next morning and spotted a large black van parked next to Nola's Volvo, she immediately had fears of Carter waiting to snatch her inside as she passed. After she parked, she reached into her purse for the can of mace she'd bought from a Walgreen's on her way home last night. *Just in case.*

Her plan was to find a therapist to refer Carter to, but if he stepped to her again and showed any sign of harming her? *Humph, a quick spray to the eye and then a foot to the balls should fuck any man right on up.*

She kept her hand securely wrapped around the cool can inside her bag as she left her car and made her way to her office. She relaxed when she saw the name Greater Healing of Christ Church painted on the side of the van with a huge cross in gold.

Her focus was so great on Carter that she'd completely forgotten about the connection of the church van to Rev . . . until she walked into the office and spotted him sitting in the waiting room, flipping through a magazine.

Bree paused in the doorway as she eyed him.

"Good morning, Dr. Bailey," Nola called from her desk.

Bree eyed her and Nola made a face showing she was just as surprised by Rev's appearance as she was. "Morning, Nola," she called, finally stepping inside to close the door. "And good morning, Reverend Teel."

He rose to his full height of over six feet, his browns dipping in as she addressed him formally. "Good morning, Dr. Bailey," he said. "I wondered if I could speak to you very quickly before you get started with your day of *appointments.*"

Bree kept her hand on the can as she turned and reopened the door. She waved him out. "Sure, let's talk," she said, keeping her voice neutral even as she felt her nerves on overload.

Rev waved his hand for her to lead him out.

She did, hating the lack of control in her life. She felt like she was spiraling in the center of a flushing toilet without a way to stop it. "What do you want, Rev?" she asked as soon as the door closed behind him.

"You know what I want, Bree," he told her, moving to lean back against the side of the van.

Bree shook her head at the image of the cross flanking his body. "Rev," she began, her mind spinning as she tried to figure out the best way to handle him.

She pulled from her notes on him during their weeks of group sessions. He was insecure and enjoyed the adoration of his female parishioners. He felt rejected by his wife and used by her for his standing in the church. He felt unloved by her.

"Let me get to it, Bree," he said.

She shifted her eyes to him, wondering if it was too late for her to play therapist now.

"I want to eat your pussy one last time and you're going to let me do it," he said calmly, like he was announcing something as simple as the weather.

Bree's back stiffened and her eyes hardened. "Are you here because I changed my number?" she asked.

Rev frowned. "I don't need your number. I don't *want* your number," he said, eyeing her legs in the pencil skirt she wore with four-inch heels. He licked his lips.

"Is this appropriate behavior, Rev?" she asked.

He shrugged as he pushed up off the van and opened the door. "No less appropriate than a therapist using her client to eat her pussy when the mood hits her," he tossed back, looking over his shoulder at her.

Bree's eyes squinted deeply as she watched him. She felt tension across her shoulders and neck. Her stomach fluctuated between gripping tension and a looseness that felt like she could clear her bowels. She reached up to pinch the bridge of her nose and tried her best to breathe and count to find some relaxation, peace, and above all . . . control.

"See, I know that I can report you . . . and even sue you for the way you used our therapist-client relationship to your own advantage," he said, sounding like he quoted a line from one of her journals or something as he pretended to sound wounded before he smiled as big as the Cheshire cat in *Alice in Wonderland*.

Bree wanted to kick every tooth out his head and then kick herself for missing the hint of a vindictive streak in the man . . . and for even crossing the line with him at all.

"So you climb your pretty ass in this van and let me eat you one last time. . . . As a matter of fact, I think you should return the favor this time, too," he said, climbing into the back of the van to take a seat before he unzipped his pants and released his dick to begin massaging it.

Bree felt lightheaded and ill as she stepped back from the scene.

Rev shook his head and released his dick to snap his cell phone from his side. "Who should I call first: my attorney, the police, or the state board?" he asked.

Tears filled Bree's eyes as she felt like she had stepped out of her own body and was a witness to the scene of her slowly walking over to the van to climb inside. She felt numb. And lost.

"Shut the door," he told her, back to massaging the hardness as he let his head fall back against the headrest with the cross stitched into it.

As she did as he told her, Bree felt a scream released inside of her. It never left her lips, though, and she didn't know if it was a mental block or the feel of dick filling her mouth and blocking it.

It took just another day for Bree to realize her nightmare wasn't over.

She was being stalked and she didn't have a soul to tell about it.

The garbage cans were filled with flowers and cards and small stuffed animals. She found them on her car. They were delivered to her at her office. They were accompanied by notes claiming either love or hate for her.

She received endless e-mails fluctuating between compliments and threats. At times she received violent images of a woman mutilated from the waist down. She would block freakytherapist@zmail.com and then nogoodtherapist@zmail.com or hatemytherapist@zmail.com and so many others would replace it. Again it was either compliments or degradation.

The shit had her completely fucked up. She was a wreck. Jumpy. Fearful. Nervous. On edge. Spiraling completely out of control. It was wreaking havoc on her life.

Bree just went through the motions of her day, but she had no clue if she was coming or going. She hated even more that she had no clue just whom her tormentor was.

Rev? Carter? Both had denied it.

Another client out for sick entertainment?

And she couldn't call the police because a good enough investigation would open up a Pandora's box of sins that she couldn't outrace.

"Bree, what is this?"

She quickly wiped at the tears that had filled her eyes as she deleted yet another animated image of a woman being fucked by a horse. She jumped to her feet as Deon stormed into her office and flung his cell phone onto her desk.

"Dr. Bailey, he ran right past me," Nola said, rushing into the office behind him.

Bree held up her hand as she saw the concern on her office manager's mothering face. "It's okay, Nola. Thank you," she said, coming around the desk to steer the older woman out of the office and securely close and lock the door.

Bree let her body slump back against the door as she fought to breathe in air.

"I know we're not a couple or nothing like that, but I don't need some shit like this sent to my phone," Deon was saying, thrusting his hand at his phone perched precariously on the edge of her desk.

What now? Bree wondered, feeling panic rising from deep within her.

The room felt like it was spinning as she stumbled past him

to pick up the phone. She gasped and dropped it at the sight of her naked body riding a man's dick backward.

"All I know is that's you and that ain't my dick," Deon was saying.

Bree ignored him. Who else had her tormenter sent the photo to? Where did they get it from? How did they get Deon's number? Was this not just a client but one of her many lovers over the years?

She started to hyperventilate as she dug her fingers into the arms of her chair. Sweat coated her body. Her heart pounded. She undid the top two buttons of her frilly lace blouse with shaky fingers as she gasped so deeply for air that her back arched with each intake.

Deon came around the desk and bent down in front of her. His hands gripped her face as he forced her to look up at him. "What's wrong with you?" he asked, his deep voice a calm in the middle of the storm.

The act of compassion caused Bree to break and she flung her arms around his strong neck as her body was racked with tears, filled with the spectrum of emotions that she felt.

Deon scooped her up into his arms and carried her over to the sofa to sit and place her in his lap. "Tell me what's wrong?" he asked.

Bree bit her lip so hard her teeth sunk deeply into the flesh. She couldn't dig the hole she was in any deeper by revealing her sinful truths to Deon. That wasn't their relationship. They were basically fuck buddies and the definition of that didn't include confidant or friend.

She said nothing, but she allowed herself to enjoy the strength and comfort of his body as she tried to make sense of the bricks crumbling beneath her feet in a world she once thought she totally controlled.

The next morning, Bree calmly walked out her front door carrying her briefcase, a Styrofoam cup of coffee, her cell phone, and her keys. She tried her very best to bring normalcy back to her life. She forced herself back into her rituals. She assured herself that the foolishness would end soon. Her tormentor would tire of the games. Life would be back to normal.

Soon and very soon, she assured herself, reaching back to close the door.

Everything in her hands dropped to the ground when she turned and spotted the word "bitch" scratched into her driver's-side door with a huge arrow pointing up to the window.

Her heart raced as she looked up and down the street, but she saw nothing other than her neighbors going about their own morning rituals, heading to work or loading up their children to take them to school.

No sign of Rev or Carter or any of her other clients who might be out for misplaced revenge.

She squinted as she noticed the dried flecks on her hood. It looked like dried spittle or cum. Bree knew it was the latter. She gripped her railing as she allowed her knees to give out from under her. She sank down to the top step of her porch.

Whomever her stalker was they knew where she lived. Calling the police meant taking a chance that her dangerous liaisons with her clients would be discovered. But what if the stakes grew and became about more than shaming her or stalking her or unnerving her. What if they wanted to kill her?

She let her eyes race up and down her street again.

Bree had never felt so unsafe.

8

Bree undid the large belt she wore around her V-neck fitted dress as she kicked off her shoes. She reached behind her and unzipped the dress, releasing a sigh of pleasure as she finally stepped out of it. Dressed only in a soft peach lace teddy, she pressed a hand to her stomach, trying to steady her nerves.

She'd closed her practice for two weeks and given Nola paid time off. She'd already put the home she treasured up for sale and moved in with her parents until she found somewhere to rent. Never did she think she would find some safety and solace back at the home and the life she'd fought so desperately to escape.

But the close quarters had replaced her fear of being stalked with the irritation of trying to readjust to her mother's ways of living.

She needed a fix.

She needed to forget.

She needed someone to help her forget.

Knock knock.

Deon.

Her body instantly reacted to the very thought of him as Bree rushed across their favorite suite and flung the door open wide. Her eyes widened at seeing Carter standing there with a bouquet of red roses in his hand. Bree gasped as she quickly tried to push the door closed.

He pushed back . . . and won.

Bree stumbled back from the force of him pushing the door open wide. She turned and flew to the phone, but again he won the race and snatched it from her grip using one strong arm to push her against the bed as he calmly unplugged the phone and tossed it onto one of the chairs.

Bree scrambled off the bed, her eyes searching the room for a weapon. She saw nothing and turned to the only weapon she knew she had against him. Her smarts.

"Carter, its not too late to stop this," she said, forcing calm into her voice as she held her hand out to him.

He walked over to the door and closed it, picking up the flowers he'd dropped.

"If you just leave now and swear to leave me alone, I will not call the police," she told him.

Carter walked over to her and handed her the roses. "Take them," he said simply, his eyes devoid of emotion as he looked at her thickness in the clinging teddy.

Bree crossed her arms over her breasts.

He flung the roses at her face and Bree cried out as thorns scratched her cheek. He grabbed her arms and forced them back to her sides. "Don't hide from me," he said, sounding like he ground the words out from clenched teeth. "I'm not good enough to get all this pussy you giving out?"

Bree tried to break free of his strong hold on her arms. "Carter, don't," she begged.

He released one arm to reach down and palm her pussy into his fist.

Bree cried out in pain. "This isn't right. This is not you. Not the Carter I know. This is *wrong*, Carter," she said, trying to draw on his feelings of shame. "You are *better* than this."

For a second, his eyes filled with compassion, but then moments later they hardened and he laughed at her bitterly. "Shut the fuck up," he said, sounding irritated.

He grabbed her shoulders and shoved her down into a chair. Bree straightened her body in the seat and brought her feet up and wrapped her arms around her knees as she eyed him warily.

Carter paced in front of her. "Tell me why I couldn't get the pussy. You 'round here giving it out like free cheese. I ain't good enough? Huh? My dick ain't big enough?" he asked, unzipping his pants to pull it out.

Bree leaned back when he stepped in front of her and thrust his hips forward and slapped her across the cheek with his dick.

"All those men you fucking and you got a nerve to be picky with me?" he said, his voice angry as he reached out and grabbed a fistful of her hair to jerk her head forward to smash his dick against her lips. "Huh? A dick is a dick for a ho like you. Ain't it?"

Bree pressed her lips together as the smell of his crotch assailed her. Thankfully it was a mix of sweat and soap. *How long has Carter been watching me? What all does he know about me? What all has he seen?*

Bree winced as he gripped her hair so tightly that she thought he would snatch her bald. "Carter, this will get you in a lot of trouble. You don't want to do this," she said, looking up at him and trying to connect with some sense of decency inside him.

Knock knock.

Bree's eyes widened and she felt hope spring to life in her chest. "Help!" she screamed at the top of her lungs. "Help me!"

Carter grabbed her up and turned her, placing a hand against her mouth, lifting her up with an arm around her neck as he walked over to the door. She fought against his strength, bringing her hands up to claw at his hand as she kicked wildly. Tears of frustration and fear filled her wide eyes.

When he calmly looked out the peephole and then opened the door, her fears turned to confusion as she watched Rev walk into the room and close the door behind himself. He reached out and used one strong grip to tear the front of her teddy from her body.

Bree kicked out as he tried to slip his hand between her thighs. His fingers stroked and probed her pussy as he just laughed and smelled his fingers before sucking the moistness with his lips.

What the fuck? she wondered as Carter released her and roughly pushed her across the room from him.

Bree tried her best to cover her voluminous breasts with her arms as she looked from one man to the other. They looked at each other and laughed. "You two in this together? What kind of sick game are you playing?" she asked, feeling a moment of bravado.

Rev waved his hand at her dismissively. "No sicker than you thinking you better than us when nobody in our group sessions was getting more sex than you, Miss *Perfect*," he sneered, with a twist of his lips.

Bree reached behind herself and roughly snatched down a curtain to wrap around her nudity.

Carter stormed across the room and snatched it from her body. "You're not running *this* session, Dr. Bailey," he told her, picking her up around her waist and flinging her onto the made bed.

Bree rushed to correct her body and pull her knees up against her chest as she pressed her body against the headboard attached to the wall. Tears filled her eyes when they both began to undress. For a second, she closed her eyes, wishing herself somewhere else. Anywhere else.

She let her head fall to her knees as she felt like the room was spinning around her. For a second she allowed herself to visualize the bed rising like a flying carpet to spin its way through the walls and out to freedom.

And in the next instant she wondered if she had truly lost her mind.

One of the men grabbed her legs and roughly jerked her body down to the edge of the bed.

"Aaagh," she cried out, opening her eyes to see two hard dicks parallel over her face.

"Don't do this," she begged them, looking from one to the other with harried eyes filled with tears.

Rev climbed onto the bed, straddling her head with his knees. His balls swung above her nose and again Bree was assailed by the scent of a man's crotch. "I just want to eat her before you hit it," Rev said to Carter.

"No problem," Carter said, massaging the length of his dick with one hand as he reached down to split her pussy lips with his other hand.

Rev bent down the length of her, causing his dick to press against the side of her face as he licked at her clit and Carter still held her lips open.

Bree felt a wave of revulsion as she tried to close her legs.

Carter moved to stand between her legs and pressed his hands against her knees to open her legs wide.

Tears overflowed from Bree's eyes as she tried to block out what they were doing to her. She tried her best to go completely numb. She wanted to pretend that two of her clients hadn't conspired against her and now held her captive and at their sadistic will. To pretend she had never let her own impulses—her own sexual addictions—lead her to this. To pretend that she hadn't risked it all for sex and now she didn't even know if she would leave this ordeal and be the same—or if she would leave alive at all.

There was no pleasure where she had once found bliss. Now Rev's actions felt like an intrusion into her body, her soul, and well-being. The tears that raced from her eyes were filled with her torture. Her shame. Her helplessness.

God forgive me, she prayed silently.

"Oh, you don't like it now?" Rev asked.

Bree barely heard him. She had found a zone where she knew what was happening to her body, but she allowed no emotions to be evoked. She couldn't control what they did to her body, but she had to control what happened to her mind.

God help me, she prayed again.

Rev spat against her core with cruelty before he rolled off the bed. "You used to beg me to eat your pussy," he said, obviously angry that she hadn't reacted to him. He reached down and slapped her face.

"You brought condoms?" Carter asked. "I ain't fucking this ho without a condom. Fuck that shit. Ain't no pussy that good."

Bree kept her eyes closed.

"I don't need condoms to eat her pussy," Rev snapped.

"Shee-it, you can catch shit eating pussy, too, you know," Carter told him.

"Man, shut up," Rev countered in irritation.

Click.

Bree's eyes popped open at the sound of the door opening. She raised her head off the bed to see Deon close the door to the hotel room with the card key she had left at the desk for him still in his hand. She sat up and ran over to him.

"Look at that ho, she happy as fuck Deon here now," Carter said, sounding disgruntled.

She stopped halfway to Deon.

He wasn't acting shocked to find two of the group members naked in the suite she'd purchased for them to use. He continued forward with a smile and reached out to stroke one of her nipples. "Surprised?" he asked.

Bree shook her head in denial as she backed away from him. The bubble she'd created for herself popped and all of the emotions flooded her in waves overwhelming her. One of the men grabbed her arms from behind and she turned her head to eye them all.

Rev.

Carter.

Deon.

They're in this together?

Rev. Carter. Deon.

The texts. The cards. Flowers. Threats.

"Which one of you been stalking me?" she asked. "Or was it all three? Or are there more of you in on this? Is someone else coming through the door next?"

Deon laughed as he stepped forward and wrapped a hand around her waist, bringing his hands down to massage her ass softly. "No, it's just the three of us that were tired of you playing God when you were dancing with the devil, too."

Bree flushed in shame and tried to step back out of his embrace. His face flashed to total coldness as he deepened his grip until her flesh stung.

Deon brought one hand up and grabbed her hair hard, jerking her head back until she could only look up at the ceiling. "Still feel like playing your games, Bree? Huh? Still getting your kicks off?" he asked her, his voice low and angry. "Still think you so fucking smart? Huh?"

Bree shook her head as her eyes stung from the tears and from staring directly into the ceiling light. She closed her lids. She had to admit Deon's involvement weakened her. She'd never suspected him. Never.

God save me, she prayed.

Deon pushed her roughly from him and her body spiraled out of control. She fell to the floor in a heap, crying as the carpet burned the flesh from her knees as she slid. She looked up as all three stood over her, their shadows bringing her body some ironic coolness in the heat of the situation.

"Rev and I were surprised as hell when Carter told us he was following you and saw you having all kinds of sex with strange men," Deon said, with his hands pushed into the pockets of his pants.

Rev glared down at her, his dick now soft and swinging across his balls as he leaned down to spit. "You sat in those group sessions and judged us when you wasn't no better. We were paying you for help and you was running a big con game."

"But we fixed your no-good ass," Carter said, sounding satisfied as he still stood there massaging his erection like he wasn't in the room with two other men.

Bree looked up and eyed them all, wondering if there was a bit of sanity between the three of them. Her heart pounded as she wondered just what they had planned for her.

"You liked fucking the hell out of me and Rev, didn't you?" Deon asked, his eyes filled with a fiery anger.

Bree's eyes shifted to Deon. She knew his issues with women were flaming inside of him.

"I knew she couldn't get enough of me eating that pussy," Rev added.

Bree looked over at Rev and quickly recognized his need to be wanted.

"I wasn't good enough," Carter said, kicking her leg with his bare foot. "You couldn't fuck or suck me, right? You couldn't let me stick a finger in your ass, right?"

She locked her eyes on Carter and honestly had no clue what all issues lay within him. The only thing she knew for sure was his unbridled anger for not being chosen by her.

And that participation, that claim to her, had been a part of their own con game. They had bragged to each other on their conquest and Carter had nothing to contribute.

"You thought you were the puppet master and the whole time we pulled the strings," Deon bragged, mocking her with his words and his eyes.

Even among the madness it all made sense. Three clients approaching her, offering the sex they knew she desired and craved. The info they shared with each other—likes, dislikes, cell phone numbers, etc. The tag team they pulled to pay her back for what they considered her con game.

"You brought condoms?" Carter asked, licking his lips as he eyed her breasts and thighs where she lay on the floor.

Deon reached into his pocket and pulled out plenty of the gold-foil Magnums. One by one he dashed them at her like darts.

Bree cried out and covered her face as the foil corner of some of them lightly scraped her skin or dug into her flesh from the force of his throws.

"You're going to fuck all three of us and then you're going to carry your ass home and forget it ever happened," Deon told her.

"She don't want us to report her ass," Rev added smugly.

"Yes!" Carter exclaimed. "I'm getting some of that pussy . . . today. Let me see if it's as good as y'all say."

"The pussy good," Rev assured him.

"You only ate her," Carter said. "You don't know."

"I know more than your dry-dick self know," Rev countered, taunting him.

"Man, shut up," Carter snapped, squeezing his dick so hard that the skin stretched until it was two shades lighter.

"Both of y'all shut the fuck up," Deon said, his voice hard.

Deon was obviously the leader. Bree saw that clearly. And in the midst of her fear she grasped at some control of the madness so that she could escape to her freedom.

Bree sat up and stretched her legs out slowly, forcing herself to swallow her fears as she smiled up at them. "Y'all know me, right. We can all have fun," she said, rising to reach forward to stroke Deon's face before she suckled his bottom lip into her mouth.

She turned and smiled as she pressed a kiss to Rev's lips as well.

And then she turned to Carter, stroking the side of his face before she swallowed hard and kissed him.

Carter deepened the kiss and pressed her back down to the floor, grinding his dick against her belly as he forced her hands to his ass.

"Let me eat her first. That's all I want," Rev said, bending down to try to move Carter off her.

Bree closed her eyes, trying not to show how repulsed she felt. "Only Rev can eat me. He's the *best* at it," she said, cutting her eyes just as Deon frowned so deeply that his eyebrows damn near caved in to a deep vee.

Rev flexed his shoulders in bravado.

"And then Carter, I'll give you some, but Deon goes last because he's the best at blowing my back out," she said, patting Carter like a mother comforting a sad child. That pat was just as good as saying, "Poor Carter."

He jumped off her to his feet. "Don't feel sorry for me," he roared.

"What the hell you mean, Rev eat better pussy than me?" Deon asked, his face angry.

"He do," Bree said, rising to her feet. "But your dick is bigger."

"What?" Rev snapped behind her.

Bree looked down at Carter's dick. "It's bigger than yours, too . . . but it's okay. I can try and work with it," she said consolingly as she walked past them.

Men hated a pissing game because none of them wanted to lose it.

Bree was in survival mode. Regardless of what schemes they came up with, some of the images and text she'd received were violent, and she wasn't sure if one or all of them would flip and hurt her.

God strengthen me, she prayed again.

Deon laughed.

Rev shoved him. "What you laughing at?"

Deon flexed and shoved him back, sending Rev flailing back against the nightstand.

Carter turned Deon by his shoulder and swung on him, sending Deon flying back to land in the middle of the bed.

Bree rushed over to her bag in the chair and grabbed it and her dress from the floor as the men's voices escalated and the sound of objects crashing echoed around her. Her heart raced as she unlocked the door and flung it open wide, not caring that she was as naked as the day she was born. The smell of freedom was sweet as she hurried to the elevator.

She kept looking over her shoulder as she waited for it, rushing to jerk the dress up her body.

"Hey, she's gone," she heard one of them yell just as the doors slid open and she rushed onto the elevator. She damn near broke a thumbnail as she pounded the button to close the door.

God, please . . . please . . . please, she prayed, hearing their feet pounding against the floor as they raced down the hall.

The doors slid closed just seconds before their footsteps got louder.

Bree wrapped her arms around herself, searching for comfort as her shoulders shook with her tears.

Ding.

The elevator slowed to an easy stop on the lobby floor and Bree rushed to swipe the tears from her eyes and run her fingers through her hair. The lack of shoes she couldn't help.

She stepped forward as the door slid open. Bree looked up at Rev, Deon, and Carter standing there with their chests heaving from obviously racing down the stairs to beat her to the lobby.

"Where you going, Dr. Bailey?" Deon asked. "You don't want everybody to know our little secret. Do you?"

They were counting on her wanting to save face. But she was free and there was no turning back.

Bree quickly reached into her bag for the mace and extended her arms to spray all three across the face as she raced off the elevator.

They hollered out and grabbed at their eyes.

Bree pushed through them and rushed over to the front desk as the eyes of the hotel's patrons and personnel eyed her.

"Ma'am, are you okay?" the woman behind the desk asked.

Bree's heart raced as she looked over her shoulder at Carter, Rev, and Deon still trying to control the effects of the mace on their eyes.

She could very well walk out, go home to her parents and fight to reclaim her life. She had some blame in all this. She knew that. But she couldn't risk that one or all of them were more than sexual deviants and truly capable of following through on their threats to hurt her. She knew reporting them meant exposure of her own behavior and the possible loss of her practice. *But I can't lose my practice. I can't . . .*

"Ma'am?" the clerk asked again.

Bree turned to eye her, still struggling with her decision. *Maybe you don't deserve to be a therapist. Hypocrite.*

She took a deep breath and let the tears fall.

Tears for her shame, her regrets, and her loss.

"Yes, I need you to call the police so that I can report a sexual assault," she said.

Bree looked over and saw her three tormentors standing still in the tracks they had been making over to her. They heard her words.

There was no turning back now.

It was time they *all* faced their retribution.

Epilogue

One Month Later

"Dr. Bailey?"

Bree looked up at the white receptionist smiling politely at her from her seat behind the mirror. "Yes?"

"Dr. Pryor will see you now."

Bree set the *Vogue* magazine she'd been reading onto the seat beside her and picked up her tote from the floor as she rose to her feet and walked across the waiting room to enter the door where a tall man with a bald head and glasses stood in the hall outside an open door waiting for her.

Bree smiled politely as she passed him and took a seat on the brown leather loveseat adjacent to a oversized arm chair. "This reminds me of my office," she said.

"So you miss not practicing?" Dr. Pryor asked as he folded his tall frame into the chair and picked up a notepad and pen.

She started to tell him about her iPad and the app she used to document her therapy notes, but she refrained.

"And so these sessions have been ordered as part of a stipulation required by the state board to have the suspension of your licensure lifted," he began, tilting his head to look at her over the rim of his glasses.

He has nice eyes, she thought, letting her eyes dip down to take in the hefty bulge of his crotch as he sat with his legs open. She felt an immediate reaction to him and had to press her thighs together to stop the steady pulsing of the rosy clit buried behind her thick lips.

Bet he can tear a pussy up, she thought, crossing her legs as she looked down to peer at his shoe size.

"Dr. Bailey . . . Dr. Bailey?"

Bree looked up and found his eyes intently on her. The same urges and weakness that controlled her and sent her life spiraling out of control still nipped at her.

She licked her lips and released a heavy breath. "Dr. Pryor. I have to be honest with you," she began, looking down at her hands briefly before she looked up at him. "I am a sex addict and I need your help. I need you to be a better therapist to me than I was to my clients. I miss my practice. I miss my life. I want it back. More than sex. More than the rush. I need you to help me be a better woman and a better therapist."

He nodded and gave her a smile that she found to be fatherly. "The first step is always honesty and we'll get there. Together."

God forgive me, heal me, strengthen and save me, Bree prayed silently.

L. A. Confidential

Grace Octavia

Act I

Here she is. Sitting across from me with eyes as clear as a kitten's. The blond streaks in her hair came straight out of a box from some dusty pharmacy bargain shelf. Between big, gap-toothed smiles, she grins. Her voice stinks of the Deep South. Maybe Mississippi. And I know because I'm from there. I got to Hollywood on a one-way bus ticket—and looking at her scuffed, buy-one-get-one-free plastic shoes, I'm sure she did the same thing. When I first got to Los Angeles, I, too, had soft kitten eyes and hair made blond from a $5.99 bottle of hair dye I'd found on some dusty pharmacy bargain shelf. But that was ten years ago for me. And maybe ten minutes ago for her. The results of the former are amazing. The latter? Not so much.

"I just loves all your work, ma'am—I mean, Silver . . . Mrs. Stone," she says, grinning and laughing a little, covering up her buckteeth with her hand like some bashful schoolgirl. And I'm thinking that her voice sounds like it's 1950 and we're white. But we're black and it's 2011. "Do you mind if I call you Silver?" she asks and I know she must be asking me this because I'm looking at her like she's crazy.

I don't answer. I sit there on ice

She repositions herself in her seat. "OK. . . . Well, Mrs.

Stone, I've been watching you on *The Black and Bourgeois* since I was just a little girl. I've always wanted to meet you and learn everything you know. I know Diamond DeLoach is just a character you play on the show, but she's so smart and so strong. I look up to her . . . you." She leans into me like she's telling me a secret; like any of the other people running around in my dressing room getting ready for tomorrow's taping care anything about what she has to say. "I learned everything I know from her. She's like my . . . *Lady God!*"

"I see," I say dryly, sitting up on my leopard-print chaise lounge and signaling for Oscar to hand me a damp face towel so I can remove my makeup. Oscar's my stylist and the person who's been on my team at *The Black and Bourgeois* for the longest. The rest—assistants, hair and makeup artists, coaches—come and go. Having decided that outpatient treatment for her heroin addiction wasn't working, my last personal assistant recently joined the list of the gone, and Kitten Eyes is sitting before me in a metal folding chair someone set in front of my chaise lounge, trying to convince me that she's the perfect replacement. "Have you ever assisted any other celebrities?" I ask.

"Yes, ma'am—I mean, Mrs. Stone." She straightens up in the metal folding chair and tries to hand me a slip of paper she's pulled from a scruffy bag she probably got at the Salvation Army.

"No." I put my hand up to stop her. "Just tell me."

"Well, I was the first assistant for Ms. Markina King, the head anchor at the news show in my hometown." She nods along at each point to impress. But I'm too tired to nod. We'd just finished shooting for the day and my mind is spinning.

"And where's that?" I ask. "Where's your hometown?"

"Biloxi, Mississippi."

I force a smile and look down at the shoes she's matched with some $7 sheath dress she got on the dark side of Hollywood Boulevard. "Do you know why my last assistant quit? Do you know what this job did to her?" I ask, and everyone in the dressing room—my makeup artist, JimBo; hairstylist, Pria; and Oscar—stops moving, puts down whatever they're doing, and leaves. They say I'm mean, harsh, but when you've paid your dues and done what you had to do to get someplace that'll use you up and spit you out as soon as it's done with you, you learn that simply being pleasant isn't always the best practice.

"No, ma'am. I don't." Kitten Eyes turns and watches the people leave like she wishes they wouldn't.

"She has a heroin addiction. It's all over the blogs. *Bossip. RollingOut.* Do you read?"

"Well, I . . . Dear God. A heroin addiction?" If she was wearing pearls, Kitten would've clutched them. She's all Mississippi right now.

"No, God didn't do it, so don't call his name." I look down and see that my robe has opened, but I let it hang; let my tits sit out and look at Kitten. Welcome her to LA. "Hollywood did it. See, she was so busy here chasing her dream, she didn't know a real-life nightmare was riding her every night. Like you, she came from some two-street town so close up on the Gulf of Mexico she still smelled like shrimp after two showers. She came to Hollywood and she ain't never had alcohol, weed, not even a bump." I wipe my face with the towel Oscar had given me. I can see a question on Kitten's face. "That's cocaine."

"Well, how'd she—"

"I'm not finished," I say. "But like I said, she had a dream, and when she realized that dream was never going to play out exactly how she'd planned, she had to reach out for whatever was reaching back to her. See, this city has a way of breaking you down and showing you who you really are. What you really are."

Kitten is peering at my coal-colored nipples like she's never seen her own. I know she can't hear anything I'm saying. I bend down a little to catch her stare.

She snaps back.

"Oh, I don't worry about that," she says. "I would never do anything like that."

"And that's how I know this isn't the job for you, sweetie," I say, getting up from the chaise and walking over to the mirror. "If we're in a room at the Beverly Hills Hotel with zebra stripes all over the suite table and a cop comes knocking at the door, I expect you to sniff that cocaine up your pretty little nose like you're Scarface. See, in Hollywood, you can't ever say what you won't do. Not if you want to be famous."

"But I don't want to be famous," she protests to my back as I stand in front of the little heart-shaped mirror over my antique vanity. "I just want to be your assistant; to help out behind the scenes."

"Please, darling." I turn around to face her with the robe wide at my hips. "Everyone wants to be famous. Those who say they don't are lying to themselves."

I let the robe fall to the floor and walk to the shower, knowing Kitten will soon get the picture and let herself out.

Silver Stone isn't my real name. I found it on the cover of a coffee-soaked newspaper I'd collected from a table at the Denny's on Sunset Boulevard where I was a waitress for two years before I got my first steady acting gig. I'd finally gotten a decent agent who actually had business cards and didn't double as a pimp when the sun went down. He said if I wanted anyone to even give me a call back, I needed to come up with a name better than Mildred Gibson to put on my headshots. "No one wants to fuck somebody named Mildred," he said, snorting a line of coke from the top of his desk. "Get a name that sounds like sex. Reminds people of sex. It should sound like a mix between a hooker and a senator's wife. Because that's what people want you to be. *Capisce?*" He finished in an awful Italian accent, though his last name and nappy locks were as Jewish as a bagel and lox. He loved the new "Silver Stone." Paid for me to get a boob job and lined up seven auditions. The last was for a bit part on the pilot for an evening black soap opera no one believed would make it past its first season. But I got the part and it did make it. Eight years later and I'm the star of the top-rated black show on television. The second-rated show, period. My husband, Alex Coin, is the show's producer. He was married to someone else when we met—the show's first lead, Antoinette Prowl. But I gave him one hell of an audition. And by the third episode, my character, Diamond DeLoach, had kicked Antoinette off a cliff during a cat fight and she was never heard from again—not on *The Black and Bourgeois* or anywhere else.

"You should've shown yourself the door, sweetheart," I say, walking back into the dressing room with one towel over my hair and one around my torso. Kitten Eyes has her back to me and is looking at my wall of pictures of Diamond DeLoach's many fashion choices over the years. "The job isn't yours. Nothing personal. I just need someone with a little more fight in them to keep up with me. You understand?"

I pull the towel off my head and wring out my wet hair; the one gift my mother's Cherokee father left us was his thick black curls that look so much like weave hair that half of the Hollywood bloggers still argue over whether or not I wear hair extensions.

"I have fight in me," I hear her say, and I look up as she turns around to me—but who I see isn't who I'm expecting. "And I'd prefer to at least have an interview before you tell me I didn't get the job." She pauses. "Mrs. Stone." She extends her hand to shake mine, but I only nod and go sit at the vanity.

"Interviews are finished for today," I say. "Sorry. Not sure who let you in here, but I've seen all I need to see right now."

I look her up and down in the mirror and pull a cigarette from the pack sitting on top of the vanity. The dressing room is draped in crimson and cream fabric. Candelabras and old black and whites of Dorothy Dandridge and Josephine Baker summon the early 1900s, 1940s glamour.

"All I need is five minutes, Mrs. Stone," she says sternly, walking over and lighting my cigarette with an antique silver lighter that seems to come from nowhere. She's long and lanky. Looks more like a model than an actress. Her voice is Northern. Probably New York. The diamonds in her ears are real. The Rolex on her right wrist isn't.

"Five minutes?" I say, taking a deep drag to wipe the day's worries from my mind. When I first started acting, I only did it because I thought it was the fastest way to make a million dollars and prove my parents and everyone in my hometown wrong. But, like Oscar says, this show business is just ho business—without the dirty thongs and STDs. "You know how long five minutes is in Hollywood? It's just long enough to ruin a career. You should be able to prove your point much faster."

"Two, then," she says. "Two minutes."

"You think you can convince me to give you a job in two minutes?" I laugh as I cut the ashes from my cigarette into the ashtray.

"Oscar."

"What about him?"

"That's how I got in here. I paid him all the tips I made dancing this weekend to let me in just to speak to you. To get a shot."

"A shot at what?" I ask. "At being famous? Or are you going to be like all the other girls who come in here and lie and say all they want to do is help out and how they'd never try to take my place?"

"Of course I want to be famous," she says and just then I notice that one of her eyes is half amethyst and sea foam green.

"Everyone wants to be famous. Those who say they don't are lying."

"So, you heard me say that? You were standing outside the door listening to my conversation?"

"No, you said it in an interview with *People* magazine seven years ago. I remember because I was sixteen and I'd just decided I wanted to be famous. And I knew I'd never let anyone stop me. See, the way I see it, this is the fastest way for me to make a million dollars and piss off everyone from my hometown."

She stands still in front of me, watching me so hard I'm sure she's reading my mind, so I don't say anything. Don't think anything. I sit and look into her, too. Something there, right in her cat eye, is hungry.

"You're a stripper—" I pause to catch her name.

"Melanie . . . and yes, I am." She doesn't flinch. "I work at Sam's. Pays the bills. Gives me time to audition."

"You ever work with an actress before?"

"No. And I ain't never shoveled shit neither, but I'd do it if it meant I'd get the chance to work with you."

I squint and sit there to see if she'll break. But she doesn't. She looks right at me.

"Melanie," I say, turning back to my face in the mirror. "I think you got yourself a job."

"Really? Well . . . When can I start?"

"Right now."

She looks around the room.

"What do you need me to do?"

"Send natural blue orchids to Juliette Heart at the Safe Changes Drug Rehabilitation in Encino," I say, taking another long drag from my cigarette. "Tell her she broke rule number three."

"Rule three?" Melanie is writing everything I say down in the palm of her hand in red ink.

"You'll know soon enough."

There are three rules everyone on my staff has to follow:

1. Always answer your phone.
2. Always keep it confidential.
3. Never talk to my husband.

The last rule is more important than the other two. Maybe. Alex Coin has roaming eyes and a penis with a brain larger than the one in his head. That's how I got him to marry me. I spoke to his little brain through his big brain, thinking somehow that would get me to his heart. I'd never met a brother like him; one who moved in powerful circles like he could and did. I fell for him hard and whole and convinced myself that I loved him, and dreamed maybe he could love me, too. But that was when I was young and still willing to lie to myself about his capabilities . . . and even my own. Now, I know that love exists only in scripts in Hollywood. Here, you take what you can get based upon what you have and leave the rest to loyalty. The result is flimsy relationships that build and dwindle between projects. Between what you can and can't offer. Project loyalty. That's what we have here. What Alex and I have. And I know for sure that as soon as he wants to get something else, he'll trade it in for a new promise. A new project. And you can't expect more than that from a man who's made it in a city of failed dreamers, drives a Lamborghini, and has only one black credit card and no ID in his wallet.

"So, you have a new girl," Alex says, leaning down on the side of our infinity pool that seems to spill out over the Hollywood Hills.

I saw him walk out the open sliding glass doors that sit from floor to ceiling on the entire back of our ranch and onto the patio when I was halfway through a lap in the pool. He'd stopped on the side of the pool where he always sits to watch me swim.

The lights at the bottom of the pool sprang up into the

night in a glossy blue glow. From underwater, he looked like a giant staring down at me.

"You say that like you care," I say, bouncing up and down on my tippy-toes in the water, kissing him on the cheek three times as he smiles into my eyes. "What's it to you, boss man?"

Alex isn't exactly a handsome man, but his features are so confident, so hard, he demands a double take. His bald head and almond skin make him look regal. Important. In her first and last visit to our home, my mother said it was the look money makes on a man.

"It's nothing to me, Silver," he says. "Just surprised you moved so fast on this. It usually takes three or four days for someone to rub you the right way." Though it's dusk, he slides the mirrored Aviator shades from the top of his head to his eyes and I can see myself looking at him.

In the last eight years, I've had six assistants. Juliette lasted the longest.

"What's her name?" he asks. "The new girl."

"None of your fucking business," I say and we laugh two more lines into the conversation no one else can understand.

"Oh, I'll find out."

"I'm sure you will." I feel a cool current move down deep in the water. "But you won't get it from me."

"This'll be fun for sure."

I roll my eyes, kick off from the edge of the pool, and turn into a lap. Back and forth I go twenty-one more times to complete my nightly set. Alex watches me, on and off the phone as he gets people in line for tomorrow's shoot.

When I come up on the side of the pool where he's sitting with his legs dangling in the water, he's licking his lips slyly.

He doesn't say anything. He dips his right hand into the water, pushes it down my bikini bottom, and slides his fingers into me. We're quiet and I watch myself moan in the mirror in his sunglasses. I put on. Toss and turn until I climax and float away, my arms extended out in the water like angel wings.

★ ★ ★

I dream of Diamond. Or maybe I should say, in my dreams I am Diamond DeLoach, the oil baroness on *The Black and Bourgeois*, whose worst realities in her pretend world are far more complicated than mine in the real world, but they can usually be solved in one soap season. Sometimes she goes to jail for a murder she didn't commit; sometimes she doesn't go to jail for ones she did commit. Sometimes she steals a baby and tries to raise it as her own. Gets attacked by an angry ex-lover. Stabbed in the heart with a rusty knife. I don't dream of her that way, though.

In my dreams, she leaves Jackson Ridge and jumps on her private jet. It lands in Mississippi. People are lining the streets for her parade. Welcoming her home. Everyone is cheering. Smiling. Grabbing for her. Flowers. So many natural blue orchids make a walkway from the foot of the jet where it's landed and down Main Street. Diamond emerges from the jet waving at everyone. She blows kisses and a breeze whips up the white scarf she's wearing, making it flap like a flag as she walks past her anxious spectators. Her father is waiting at the head of the parade. Her mother and her books of poetry in her arms are behind him. They hold out their hands to her.

I feel sprinkles on my forehead, but I know it's not rain. July is the driest month in Los Angeles. Rain is nearly impossible.

I open my eyes to see Alex standing over me, dropping pool water from his fingertips onto my face. After our moment in the pool, he'd carried me over to the patio lounges and we'd sipped on vodka tonics as the moon took over the sky.

"I fell asleep?" I ask, slapping his hand away.

"Yep. Said some jibberish about throwing money from a jet and nodded off." He sits beside me and slides his shoes on.

"My Diamond dream."

"She always dreams of Diamond," he says. "A true Method

actress. And I never had to pay for acting classes." He pulls his phone out and starts clicking buttons. "You just make sure you tell Diamond to be up and at 'em by call time tomorrow. I need you to be on point."

"Aren't I on point every day?" I ask. I can see Flower, our chef, moving around in the kitchen through the open glass doors. Long leaves of something green dangle from her fists. She calls herself a "Microbiotic Nutrition Engineer." I don't think much of her or the microbiotic diet, but after a viewers' poll said I was looking a little too "Rubenesque" on screen, Alex hired her to cook three meals a day. Twenty pounds later and now the polls say I look too gaunt.

"Of course you are, darling," he says without looking at me. "But tomorrow isn't just *every* day. The station execs are coming."

"The execs?" I reach for Alex's phone and push it away. "What do you mean the execs are coming?" Suddenly, I feel the night air all around me and wish I had my robe. Cold pocks spring up all over my arms. "How didn't I know about this? Why didn't you tell me?"

"Because I just got word." He cuts his eyes at me.

"Well, what do they want?" Station execs almost never visit the sets of successful shows—unless they're considering closing it or making major changes.

"It's the new story line idea again. The Santiagas. They're thinking about bringing in Brinson O'Neal to introduce Maria Santiaga."

"But Brinson is white. She's not Hispanic. If they want a Hispanic story line, why can't they find a Hispanic actress?"

"She's hot. She has a calendar. A major Web site. A following. She looks Latina."

"*Looks* and *is* are two different things." I stop and look at Flower standing over a boiling pot on the stove. "It just doesn't make any sense. Why do we need a Latin story line? We're a black soap. We're the second-rated show on television."

"Well, we're not the first. And you know numbers have been sinking for weeks. They just want us to prove that we can cross over. Get an edge."

"Don't fall for that, Alex. I have more Emmys than we can hold in this house. And they think we need to cross over? And the way to do that is to get a white actress to play a Latina?"

"Her husband is Dominican."

I look at Alex, reach for the box of cigarettes on the glass table between us, and wrangle one out with a shaking hand.

"This is about more than cash and cross over, and you know it. They're trying to get me out."

"Oh, with this again," Alex says, getting up. "No one's trying to get you out or get rid of you. You're the lifeblood of the show . . . of our show." He smiles his smile.

I scramble through the mix of glasses and bottles on the table to find my lighter.

"Look, just get yourself together for tomorrow. Run your lines tonight. Be ready to go in the morning."

"They want me out."

As I watch Alex smooth out his slacks, I remember a line I read on the soap's fan blog site: "I'm so sick of Diamond. They need to throw her ass off a cliff and get it over with. BOR-ING." A bead of cold water trickles from the nape of my neck and down my back.

"What am I going to do?" I ask.

"You're overreacting." Alex moisturizes his hands with a fresh wad of hand lotion from a tube he keeps in his pocket. "Just let me handle it."

He wipes the excess lotion on his cheeks, chin, and neck.

"Where are you going?"

"Back to work," he says and we both know he doesn't mean the studio. "If you want a deal in this town, you make it over drinks—not doughnuts."

His phone starts vibrating.

"Will you be home before sunup?"

He clicks the vibrator off and slides the phone into his pocket. Exhales deeply.

"Don't sweat me, Silver. You know I hate that."

"Guess that's a no."

Alex bends down and kisses me on the forehead.

"I'll be home, darling," he says. "You just be ready for tomorrow."

Flower is sitting in the chair beside me in the dining room talking about the balance of the meal she's arranged in tiny bowls: adzuki beans with barley miso, sesame seeds with rare salmon, fresh spinach.

I try to hear her, but all I see is the execs on their way to the studio in a black limousine. Brinson is with them. My separation notice is in someone's pocket. The last person booted off the show only got a text message.

The blogs are always right. Even when they're wrong, they're eventually proven right.

Flower goes on. She's a white girl with approximately seven blond dreadlocks hanging from her tiny head. While she's thirty-one like me, she looks no older than fifteen, weighs no more than 100 pounds, and smells like marijuana every day.

My phone rings and I get up from the table. I know it's Oscar.

"I need you to get to the studio early tomorrow," I say, leaving Flower and the tiny bowls in the kitchen and walking into the living room.

"Early?" he whines and I hear that he's drunk. There's music playing in the background. People talking.

"Yes. Like seven."

"But I'm out—"

"The execs are coming tomorrow. I need at least three looks for Diamond. Old stuff. Those Erica Kane throwbacks. Seriously."

"But I'm—"

"Did you not hear me? The execs. I need you fresh. Go in and pull the looks. I want it done when I get in."

"But it's my birthday—and I'm out with everyone celebrating." He says something in Spanish.

Someone laughs. It sounds like Pria. She calls his name.

"Your birthday?"

"Yeah. . . . I invited you out to celebrate with us. Didn't you see the cake? Hear people singing to me? Balloons . . ."

"Look, Oscar, if you don't handle this, there won't be any cake next year because there won't be any show. You hear me? Get on it. We can't slip. I want to wow them. Remind them of why Diamond's the star."

"OK." Oscar sulks.

I click the call off and scroll down to Pria's name, but the front door chime stops me.

I look at Flower standing in the kitchen looking at me confused with two bowls in her hands. Alex and I live in a 10,000-square-foot ranch that sits behind two thick rows of birches at the back of a winding street in the Hills. You can't even see it from the street. The metal gate out front has entry only through code or call. Getting to the door to ring the bell is impossible without either one.

The bell chimes again.

"You expecting anyone?" Flower asks.

"No," I say. "Don't worry. It's probably just Alex. He leaves his key sometimes." I turn to walk to the door.

Midway down the hall, Carmen, our maid, meets me, but I wave her off.

"I have it, Carmen," I say. "It's just Alex."

She nods and shuffles her egg-shaped body back down the hallway to her room.

The bell chimes a third time.

"Calm down," I say, pulling hard to open the heavy cut of wood Alex had shipped from a castle that was being destroyed in Italy. "You left your key again. . . . Maybe you should stay your ass—"

I look and standing on the steps is Juliette holding a sloppy fist of blue orchids.

"You got the flowers," I say, stiffening.

She drops them at her feet. Her white sweat suit is stained and smelly. Her hair is everywhere.

"You didn't change the gate code," she says.

"Well, luckily, we changed the locks," I say, looking at the key dangling from a chain on her wrist.

"Where's Alex?"

"The sun's down in LA. You know where he is."

"I need to talk to him."

"No . . . you need to talk to your therapist and a drug counselor."

"I need to talk to Alex!" she screams and I can feel Flower coming up behind me.

Juliette says some things I can't make out. She's shaking. Scratching at her head.

"He told me . . . He promised me . . . He said it would all work out."

"Let me guess," I start. "He promised you that you'd get a big role on the show? One bigger than mine? You'd be the new star? Or was it a new show? One just for you?"

Juliette's sobs get louder. Guttural. She looks down and at her swollen, red arms.

"I warned you. I told you to stay away from him. Now you need to stay away from me!" I step back to close the door, but Juliette pushes back so hard she nearly knocks me over.

"I'm pregnant," she yells with her hands still out to me. "He got me pregnant."

I position myself in the doorway and turn to Flower inside the house to see her standing and holding a butcher knife.

"I'm fine," I say as calmly as I can. "You can go wait inside."

She squints at me and tries to hand off the knife.

"It's OK," I say, holding my hand up. "Just go wait in the kitchen."

Flower backs up slowly and I wait until I'm sure she can't hear me anymore before I turn to face Juliette again.

"How dare you walk your junkie ass up to my fucking house talking about you're looking for my husband and that you need him. Are you high right now?"

"I'm not high. I haven't had anything," she cries, wiping spit from her mouth.

"Well, you must be if you think you're pregnant by Alex." I stop myself. Look over my shoulder.

"But I'm—"

"Just stop it," I burst in. "I've been married to the man for seven years and I haven't gotten pregnant. Neither did his first wife . . . or any of the other hundreds of women like you he's slept with in this godforsaken city. Does that tell you any-thing?"

Juliette rubs her stomach some more and shakes her head at the moon.

"Silver, I never meant for this to happen." She's crying some more. "He tricked me. He tricked me!"

"I'm calling the police!" I hear Carmen holler behind me. "You leave!"

"Juliette, get some help," I say. "This isn't for you. Just go home and get some help."

I close the door and turn to Carmen with the phone in her hand.

"Everything is fine," I say to her. "Don't call the police."

It usually takes two Valium and a glass of wine to get me to sleep at night, but tonight I take three little pills and have a sec-ond glass. My bedroom starts to feel like a prison most nights. The walls close in around the bed and I feel like I can't breathe. But tonight that's not what's keeping me awake.

I try to read over my lines again, to focus and sip my wine. Flower walks in with her tea. She smells like jasmine oil and vanilla and marijuana.

"You need this," she says, sliding the cup and saucer onto my nightstand. She takes the wine. "It'll calm you."

"Thank you," I say. "You can leave when you want."

"I left food in the refrigerator for Mr. Coin."

"Thank you."

She nods deeply and turns to exit.

"Wait a minute, Flower," I call.

She turns back.

"Yes."

"I know you've worked for celebs in LA before, but I need to remind you of something very important—to make sure you know it."

"What's that?"

"It's about what you may have heard today. You know everything you hear in this house is confidential? Right?"

"Yes, of course I do, Mrs. Stone," she says. "It's LA."

Act II

To someone visiting LA, the city might seem like it's still sleepy when the sun first comes up over the back of the Hollywood sign. Slow moving. Much more sedate and sluggish than the traffic and bright lights that clogged every artery of the enclave the night before. The deals have been made. And great whites can no longer be seen swimming just close enough to the SoCal shoreline to bite someone's leg off.

But in the midst of all the tranquil restoration, underneath the silence, someone's up. Someone's moving. Someone's putting her dream for the day into action. And by the time the sun rises, she's run ten miles. Lifted fifty pounds. Written that next scene. Sent that first e-mail with her headshot attached, praying they open it and just read.

If someone stands really still at dawn, he can actually feel the energy of all this going on. The countless desires of a city of dreamers collected in an invisible cloud right under LA's smog that rains down a furious shitstorm of energy.

After running through Runyon Canyon alongside the rising sun, I make it to the studio. Inside, everyone is planning and plotting, seemingly working on borrowed time. It's still early, though, too early to be nervous about a regular taping, so I know they've all heard about the execs coming.

There's so much whispering it sounds like a fan is spinning right next to my ear. And what's not whispering is moving, going this way or that, making me step over and under large sections of set pieces just to go in a straight line to my dressing room.

From costume to design and lighting, every team leader is holding a color-coded copy of the day's script like a Bible, simultaneously arguing with folks on their phones and whispering to their assistants beside them.

Manuel, our new director, whose wedding band and beautiful wife provide odd ornamentation to a man who's obviously gay (per Oscar), is standing to the back of the set beside his assistant Leeda and a few of the writers. Unlike most black shows in Hollywood, our show has mostly black and Latino writers.

Before I can make it through the ruins, I see Melanie, fresh-faced, rushing toward me. She's dressed appropriately in all black. Her long hair is back in a braid and she's smiling pleasantly. I look at my watch to see the time.

"Good morning," she says, extending a cup with a steamy cloud spinning from its brim. It's on my list of likes and dislikes. Morning coffee: Kopi Luwak beans, fresh cream, hot as hell.

"Thank you," I say, taking the coffee, handing Melanie my bag and walking ahead of her. "Next time, I'll expect you to meet me at my car. Didn't Oscar tell you? It's on my list."

"Yes. Well, he said I should, but we were looking at the dresses for today's shoot, so I figured I should be sure to oversee that process for you." She hustles up beside me.

"Listen to Oscar. He knows what I expect," I say dryly, nudging the dressing room door open with my hip.

"OK. Gotcha!" she answers, stopping me with an impulse

in her voice. Her cat eye lingers on me. "And Mrs. Stone, I just wanted to say thank you for giving me this opportunity. I am—"

Half inside and outside of the dressing room, I lean into her over the steamy cup in my hand and whisper, "It's work time. You already impressed me yesterday; don't fuck it up now with pleasantries. And no more 'Mrs. Stone.' "

"OK. I wasn't—" she tries, but I nudge off the door.

"OK, let's go, people!" I announce, walking into the dressing room to see Pria, JimBo, and Oscar standing at our style table in front of the 16x16-foot closet where Oscar keeps only a fraction of Diamond's clothes, shoes, and jewelry. Most people think going on stage is as simple as easing into a spectacular dress and brushing on a little eye shadow. The real pros know better. Style sets mood . . . and mood, well, that sets everything. Today's story is called "Baron's Birthday Surprise." Diamond's archenemy, Red James, her ex-stepsister turned bloodsucking extorter, is throwing a birthday party for Diamond's brother (who's now engaged to Red). Action: Diamond plans to crash the party, project a video of Red demanding money from their sickly grandfather, and break up the engagement. Now, whoever's to pull off all that and still look good has to be dressed to hold her head high and keep her knife low. "What do we have, team?" I say. "Give it up." I ease into the circle around the table where I always stand. Set the hot cup down after a sip. Oscar hands over my dark-rimmed Chanel frames.

"Let's show Silver what we picked," Melanie ad-libs my directions.

JimBo, Pria, and Oscar peek up at her and then at me over their dark-rimmed glasses.

"Yeah, well, thanks, Melanie," Oscar snaps, never looking away from me. "So, *Silver*, I pulled that yummy Simon Duncan gown we used in season one—an oldie but goodie. Second is the dress Tracy Reese made for the Emmys that you didn't wear—we loved that one. Right? And the third dress I pulled is the last one McQueen sent to you." He points at dresses hanging on hooks on the wall as he speaks. One is navy blue with a beaded batik belt; one is red; the last is the McQueen, all golden and dripping sequins to the floor. "I'm leaning toward the Reese, but they're all just divine. Big shoulder pads. Couture. Just what the boys are looking for on Diamond nowadays."

"I'm thinking pin curls in your hair," Pria jumps in. She's half Indian and black and one of the only "hair designers" in all of California who seems to understand how to manipulate my hair without adding a whole bunch of horsehair and glue. "We can mix the '80s' shoulder pads with '30s' flapper. I think we did that in season six for the holiday episodes."

"Yes," Oscar agrees. "That'll go spif with the red dress. I can do black pearls . . . down to the knees." They nod to each other with all of the sincerity of surgeons in surgery. Oscar walks over to the red dress and inspects. He's Mexican. Short. Fat. Dyes his hair blond for some reason.

"Today's a shit-tossing day!" JimBo adds in his gritty Texan drawl. As usual, he's chosen to dress all six feet and five inches of his tawny frame in full cowboy regalia, including a dinky cowboy hat and a holster stacked with makeup supplies. Half white cowboy and Cherokee Indian, he has the cheekbones of a God and an accent right off an old Texas Western. "Heavy eyeliner. Red lips. And I think I'ma try something new with the shadow. Depends on the dress." He walks over to the red dress and inspects with Oscar and Pria.

They nod and soon twist from the hook to me.

I sip some more and see myself in the scene. See my action. I sip. I see.

"McQueen," I say, sliding off the Chanels.

I feel them sigh.

"Why'd she make us come in early if she was going to pick her own look," someone murmurs, and I'm sure it's Pria—though it sounded like a man. I ignore it. Give more directions.

I change the pin curls to a slicked back wet look, à la Diana Ross in Italy in *Mahogany,* and switch JimBo's heavy eyeliner for Egyptian arrows drawn under my eyes only.

After running lines with the rest of the cast and meeting with Manuel, I'm dressed and walking down the hallway behind my team. People run up and whisper things in my ear, but all I can hear is Alex the night before: "I need you to be on point." And I try to focus. To put my walk on real hard. Like how I know everyone's expecting. Hold my head up high for all of them in the hallway, watching me, waiting for something to happen. But I can feel that black car with Brinson and the execs on the way to the studio. The letter in tow. I hear, "I need you to be on point."

"I read over the script," Melanie says, slowing down and walking beside me as we enter the set. She turns to a page. "And I think, well, I know you know better, but when Diamond goes to pull Baron into the ballroom, maybe she should take him by the tie. You know? Not just pull his arm—be aggressive. Take his tie!" She points to a section, tries to hand it to me.

"I've got this, honey," I say tightly. "You"—I turn to find the gaggle of assistants and interns standing by the breakfast setup—"go over there and wait with everyone else. I'll let you know if I need anything."

She bows out, but keeps her eyes on me until I make it to the seat with my name on the back.

The lights go dim. I become someone else for a little while.

The Black and Bourgeois
"Baron's Birthday Surprise"
(EPISODE: 02009)

Scene 5

EXT: BALCONY JACKSON RIDGE COUNTRY CLUB GRAND
BALLROOM - NIGHT
CONTINUED:
DIAMOND and RED are on the balcony watching guests
gather in the ballroom.

DIAMOND

You'll never take my brother from me, Red. You're a liar and
now he'll know it. Everyone in Jackson Ridge will know it.

RED
(Laughing)
Oh, Diamond, you've always been a consummate idealist. I ad-
mire your spunk. Too bad you're all bark and no bite.

DIAMOND

Oh, Little Red, I have your bite. And I'm going for blood.

Baron enters.

BARON

So nice to see my favorite girls getting along at my birthday
party. What more could a man need?

RED

Oh, darling, I'm so happy to see you excited. I was just telling
Diamond about us moving the wedding date up.

BARON
Great news, right, Diamond?

DIAMOND

Yes, Baron. I couldn't be more excited. And when exactly is this little shindig taking off?

RED
(Cuddles up to Baron)

Next weekend. We're flying out to Granddaddy DeLoach's lodge in Sun Valley.

DIAMOND

Oh, wonderful.

BARON

You coming, Diamond?

DIAMOND
(Pulling Baron to her)

I couldn't possibly make it, Baron. What with my fainting spells . . . You wouldn't want me to ruin your perfect day, would you, brother?

RED
(Pulls Baron back)

Well, baby, it's settled. She can't—

BARON
(Pulls away from Red)

Nonsense, Diamond! You're my little sister. I can't get married without you. I insist you come. Granddaddy wouldn't have it any other way. You're coming with your fainting spells and all. (Reaches out to Diamond)

DIAMOND
(Cuddles up to him)

I'll make it my top priority.

(Looks inside the ballroom at the guests gathering around the birthday cake.)
Looks like everyone's getting ready for your birthday toast.

RED
(Annoyed)
Yes. Let's go inside, Baron.

DIAMOND
You go on ahead, Red, and get everyone ready. I wanted to chat with *my* Baron.

RED
But—

BARON
It's fine, Red.

Red exits.

BARON
What's up, Diamond?

DIAMOND
Just wanted to hug my big brother. Wish you a happy birthday on my own . . . without the audience.

BARON
Oh, don't tell me you're still jealous of Red. I thought you all made up after she pushed you into the lake. She said she was sorry.

DIAMOND
Of course I'm over that, Baron. And, hey, she may have thrown you this lavish party, but my gift is on the way.

BARON
What is it? You know I hate surprises.

DIAMOND
You'll see in just a minute. You won't hate this surprise.

Through the balcony doors, lights show a film being projected onto a wall in the ballroom. GUESTS turn surprised, wondering what it is. THE IMAGE reveals Red standing over Granddaddy DeLoach with a pen in her hand. HE'S clearly drugged and out of it. At the party, RED runs from standing beside the cake to find out where the projection is streaming from.

DIAMOND
Looks like my surprise is underway. Let's join the party.

Manuel yells "Cut" as I pull Baron into the party by his tie.

We're through the first half of the taping and I'm finally feeling my rhythm. Finally forgetting. Finally past Alex in my ear.

Darrin Sam, the Shakespearian-trained actor who plays Baron on the show, pinches my side and whispers, "Nice move, pulling my tie," into my ear. After realizing there was no chance he'd be the lead in any other Shakespearian production outside of *Othello* (whom he'd already played three times), Darrin came to Hollywood to make use of his chiseled face and NYU connections. He flirts with me like that's what keeps him on the show.

I sit and listen to Manuel's directions for the next scene, but I'm thinking and looking around, wondering like everyone else about the execs. Alex isn't even on the set. Maybe they decided not to come.

I look past the crafts table to see Melanie standing alone beside the drinks. The other assistants are talking among themselves, but she's looking right at me.

"You go in for her. Charge her at the gut like you're tack-ling her on a football field. High drama," Manuel says to me with Alicia, the actress who plays Red, listening in.

Manuel turns to Alicia and my team comes to repair my messy hair and flawed makeup. Oscar starts fixing something on the train of my dress.

"Thought you might be thirsty." Melanie appears with a bottle of tepid water in her hand and pushes between every-one.

"Thank you," I say, taking it, but before I can steal a sip, Leeda rushes in with her BlackBerry in her hand, walking purposefully toward Manuel. JimBo with his eyeliner straight from his holster, Pria with her comb, Oscar with his needle, me with my water: we all stop and watch.

Leeda whispers into Manuel's ear, but we don't have to read lips or wait to hear the news, because following behind her, the other production assistants come with extra folding chairs they open and place far away from us in the dark on the other side of the cameras.

Suddenly, I hear everything. Footsteps. Talk. Laughs. Alex's laugh. The doors open. In walk men in suits. There seems to be some kind of smoke kicking up behind them, but I know it's just my imagination. I search the crowd for a dress. For Brinson.

"Carry on, everyone," Alex says to us as he ushers the group to the extra seats. They don't even look at us, just go right into the dark. "We're not here to interrupt."

I try to catch his eyes to see if he can tell me anything. Show me anything. But he keeps walking.

At the back of the train of suits, there's another black man.

"Who's that?" Melanie asks.

"I don't know," JimBo says. "Can't tell." He squints, but the chairs are so far in the dark we can hardly see them anymore.

"I think it's King—" Pria says, smoothing out my hair.

"King Colson?" Oscar asks. "No . . . Can't be. Why would he be here?"

"I know that big-ass head anywhere. Had it tacked up all over my bedroom walls until I left for college," Pria says. "It's him."

I lean my head back a little so I can see a bit better without being obvious.

"King Colson from *The Pick-up Boys?*" Melanie squeals in the way someone would who was a teenager when the show King starred in was still on the air. He played a well-off high school football team captain, who's trying to hide his love for a girl from the wrong side of the tracks by dating nearly every other girl in the school.

"Sure is," Pria confirms. "Right, Silver?"

King switches seats with one of the other men and sits beside Alex.

"Places," Manuel calls and everyone starts moving back to the set.

Melanie takes the water from my hand. "Don't worry about them. You'll be great," she says cheerily. "I know it."

All eyes are always on me when we're taping, but now I can feel them. Watching me. Tearing into me. I can't make sense of King being here. He's washed up. A former teen heartthrob who found Buddha and yoga when the LAPD caught him in a hotel room shooting up and his show was canceled. The last I'd heard about him, he was engaged to some French model and selling his own yoga DVD series on the Home Shopping Network.

When the scene starts, I see King stand up and step from the darkness and into the light. He's facing me. His arms are folded.

I hear Alex: *I need you to be on point.*

I exhale and step into the scene. I wipe everything away. Everything I know and think. I become Diamond. Live in her world. There's no set. No cast. This is her reality. Her fight. I remember my agent saying acting isn't a mystery. It isn't a show. It's all reality. The job isn't about convincing. It's about being. Your cast mates, the people watching, even you, shouldn't see anything in your eyes but the scene, the life of your character before and after that moment.

The first time Diamond pushes Red on the dance floor, Red's surprised—Alicia's surprised. I see it in her eyes. I push harder. Diamond pushes harder. Red pushes back. Then Diamond tackles her across the floor and jumps on top of her. She's screaming and swinging; tears and sequins are flying everywhere.

I look into Alicia's eyes and I see Red now. She grabs my hair and we roll along the set of the ballroom so fast the extras scramble and jump over us.

DIAMOND
You can't have my brother!

RED
He's mine!

We roll and roll and Baron tries to pull us apart. The scene is over; we're off script, but Manuel doesn't stop us. I pull a track of weave hair from Red's head and throw it in Baron's face.

"Cut," Manuel yells, but we keep going, fighting like we're in a school yard. "Cut! Cut! Cut!"

Baron and one of the extras get a hold of me around the stomach and someone else pulls Alicia away, but we're still clawing at each other until everyone starts clapping.

I stop and look around and they're all on their feet—the execs, King, even Alex—crowded around the set, clapping wildly. I feel like I've just come back to some place.

"That was amazing." Wendell Morgan, the drama executive for the network, rushes over to shake my hand.

"No problem," I say, wiping my sweaty hand on a towel Oscar's placed on my neck before shaking Morgan's hand. I've met him several times, but each time he looks at me like it's the first and I'm not the star of the highest-rated show on the network. People think studios worship their stars, invite them over for dinner, have them on the list for their sons' bar mitzvahs. But that's not the case. Never has been. No one wants to get too close.

"Just splendid," Steve Turner, another exec standing beside Morgan, says.

"Again, no problem. I'm just happy you all could come to the set to enjoy—" I'm out of breath, still sweating.

"Yes, and enjoy it we did," Alex says, leading King to me. "Silver, have you met King Colson?"

They stand side by side in front of the others, who've started talking to Manuel, and I notice that King's chest is wider than Alex's. He's a little taller, too. He's outgrown his boyish looks that got him tacked to Pria's bedroom wall, but you can still see it there. Maybe it's his eyes.

"I don't believe I have—" I start, but stop when King lowers his head to bow to me.

"Magnificent. Just superb. You have much to teach," he says, sounding like a fortune cookie before he bows and kisses my hand so softly and slowly, you wouldn't think my husband was standing right there.

We all stop at this pregnant pause. Through the corner of my eye, I see Oscar whisper something to Pria, and I know this response is exactly what King planned with his grand introduction. It's so Hollywood.

"Thank you," I say unaffectedly.

"King's visiting from South Dakota," Alex points out, still on business.

"South Dakota?" I repeat.

"Yeah, I have a ranch there. Just some horses. A few cows."

"Excuse me for one second." Alex nods his way out of the conversation.

"Wow. A ranch." I watch Alex walk over to the execs talking to Manuel. "Well, welcome . . . back to Los Angeles." I look back at King. "Will you be here long?"

"If I have business, I will." He winks at me. "Speaking of business, I was wondering if you were free for an early dinner. I was thinking Campanile."

"Dinner? Oh, I don't know. I have—" I look back over at Alex.

"I won't keep you out long. Don't worry. I'm sure Alex won't mind."

"Oh, that's not it." I laugh a little as I watch Alex walk off the set with the execs. "I'll look at my schedule and let you know ASAP. How's that?"

Oscar charges me before I can make it into the dressing room. "What was that, Silver? Why's King here? You keeping secrets from us?"

"Please just get me out of this dress," I say, trailing him to the full mirror beside my vanity.

Melanie, Pria, and JimBo come to help pull me apart with damp towels and combs.

"Is he coming on the show?" Pria asks, sliding bobby pins into her pockets.

"Yeah, is he guest starring?" JimBo asks.

"I don't know. I don't know and I don't know," I say, remembering King's little beady eyes squinting at me when he said he'd be in town if he had "business." What kind of an answer was that? What kind of business?

"Alex told you he was coming?" Oscar helps me step out my dress, and when he doesn't hear me respond, he looks up at me with the others. "Did he?" he asks again when there's a knock at the door.

Melanie comes over and slides my robe over my shoulders as Pria opens the door.

Alex walks in with his jacket closed. His phone at his ear. He's talking loud and laughing grand.

Pria and JimBo walk right out without saying a word. This is on the list.

Oscar grabs Melanie's hand and pulls her to the door with him. "Let's go," he says.

Alex is still on his phone, walking around the dressing room casually, looking at things and laughing, when the door closes again and we're alone.

I sit at the vanity and pull out a cigarette. I take two puffs and turn away from the mirror. I didn't even smoke when I moved to Los Angeles. Now, I'm sure I'll never even try to quit.

"My diamond indeed," Alex says, finally hanging up the phone. "You were amazing." He comes over to the vanity and crouches down in front of me so we're eye to eye. "Guess you showed me."

"Whatever, Alex."

"You were phenomenal. The guys can't stop talking about it. The way you tore into Alicia?" He laughs. "Now, that was drama. Girls gone wild!"

"That's not what I'm talking about. What was King Colson doing here? You didn't say anything about him coming. You said Brinson. What's King about?"

"He's a good guy. Has a following." Alex stands and walks away from me, perusing the room again.

"What? Alex! You said Brinson!"

"And now I'm saying King. You have a problem with that?"

"I have a problem with you saying it's one thing and then it's another. You lied to me."

"I didn't lie. I protected you. If I'd said it was King, you wouldn't have prepared like you did. You would've thought it was a joke."

"Of course it's a joke. King's career is over," I say. "No one's checking for him. He's some washed-up sitcom star. There's no way—" I stop. "Wait . . . Is he the one? The one you're writing into the show?"

"He has a following. Actually a huge one." Alex picks up a *Vogue* and tosses through it.

"What? You're writing King Colson into the show? Into *my* show?"

"That's what it looks like. Today was his walk-through, tonight's his private meeting with the star, and tomorrow's his reading. If we like how things go . . ." Alex smiles his smile.

"Private meeting? I'm not meeting with him. No way." I get up and take a drag from the cigarette. "This is ridiculous. He can't be on the show. It'll look desperate. I'm not meeting with him."

"Yes, you are." Alex laughs, throwing the *Vogue* onto the table in a smack.

"Whatever. Look, I'm not stupid. This is a bad idea and I won't back it. He's a nobody. He sells yoga DVDs!"

"Silver, don't push me. I said you're doing it and you're doing it. That's all," Alex says flatly. "Just trust me."

"Trust you? Oh, that's a joke," I say, taking another drag from the cigarette and holding it out as I speak. "Very rich. So, should I trust you like how you said Brinson was coming to the studio today? Or like how you managed to fuck over yet another one of my assistants?"

Alex walks over and snatches the cigarette. He puts it out on the vanity top.

"Yeah, she came over to the house last night. Looking for her dealer!" I say.

"Don't fuck with me, Silver," Alex snaps. "I told you what the fuck to do and you do it. You think you're ready to leave me now?" He comes in so close to me, pushing me so tightly against the wall that I can't breathe. "You think you're too big for the show? For *my* fucking show?"

"I didn't say—" I try.

"Ain't shit else out there for you. You want to go look? You want to go out there and try it without me? You're a fucking five at best, Silver. You can't act. You're too dramatic. You're fat. You think folks in Hollywood are just dying to sign up a thirty-something-year-old black actress?"

"Alex, I can't breathe," I say, feeling my toes get numb.

"Well, that's good," he says, backing up just a little. "You remember who gives you your fucking air."

The door opens. Alex steps back from me and we watch Melanie walk in.

"I left my purse," she says apologetically. She picks up her pocketbook and looks around confused. "And my keys . . . Which are . . . ?"

"No problem," Alex says with his voice completely shifted. He kisses me on the forehead. "Just congratulating my wife on a job well done. Right, sweetie?" He winks at me and turns to walk over to Melanie. "And what's your name?"

"Melanie." She smiles at him, but looks at me.

"Nice name. Had a cat named Melanie once," Alex says. He magically produces a set of keys and drops them into Melanie's hand. "Enjoy dinner, Silver." He walks to the door and slips out.

"Oh, these *are* my keys," Melanie says, looking at the keys oddly. "How'd he . . ."

"It's an old trick," I say.

"Oh . . . You need anything?"

"Yeah. A ride to Campanile." I toss her my keys. "I'll meet you out front."

"I can't drive stick," Melanie repeats for the third time as we chug up La Brea, stopping and starting again each time she changes gears.

"You might've said that when I gave you the keys."

"I didn't know a Porsche was a stick. I'm sorry."

I roll my eyes at her. "Just get me there," I say, feeling the tires screech on the tar-topped street. People stop and look, but I can't think of driving. My mind is too knotted. I feel like maybe I shouldn't have told Alex about Juliette. I knew it would get him like that. He doesn't like it when he's not getting his way, and he'll say and do anything to change it. "And rule three, stay away from my husband," I say to Melanie.

"I didn't say anything to him. I just—"

"Just listen, because I'm only going to say this to you once. I know he seems nice. But . . . just stay away from him. Things will be easier with me if you do." I turn to her. "Easier for you."

"OK," Melanie says and the car stops again. "Gotcha."

Dressed in trucker hats and grungy T-shirts, a dozen or so paparazzi wait in small, casual-looking chatty circles outside of Campanile, LA's international-fare-serving, celeb-spotting eatery. Just years ago, the dozen would've been double and before that, they'd be in cars and trucks hiding out in front of the place and others like it—Spago, Mr. Chow, Nobu—waiting to get an eye on an unsuspecting celebrity having lunch or dinner. But the laugh has always been that no celebrity who doesn't want to be seen has a meal in any of these places. They go there for double duty: food and free publicity that doesn't make people think you're some self-aggrandizing snob, whose only goal in life is to be on the cover of a magazine. For actors, it's a necessity. Unlike musicians and athletes, even some politicians who play the same game, actors are supposed to be deep, or at least humble, not at all desiring of any attention from the public between projects or premiers. But here, that's the fastest way to die. No news is bad news. So, to play the game from both sides, we actors dress down and meet up with friends at a restaurant where we can pretend to want our privacy. But even in pretending, one can sit outside in the sun as cameras flash, leak the lunch locale, and be sure only the right outlets get a shot.

After posing for two of my favorite photographers and promising to talk to some guy from TMZ on camera after I get done eating, I find King in a quaint enough section of the restaurant to consider that maybe he's not playing into this. He's changed out of his suit and is wearing a faded T-shirt and jeans with cowboy boots. The jeans hang low and I see the top of his pelvis when he stands to hug me.

I've always hated hugging people I don't know, so I stand there with my arms at my sides, raising my hand only to pat his lower back and hoping he'll let go quickly.

But he doesn't. He wraps his arms over my shoulders and squeezes so tightly I have to force a tighter frown to stop from laughing. I can smell his cologne. It's clean. Smells green and blue. He rocks a little. Kisses me on the cheek like we're old friends or best friends. Like there's something between us, but there's nothing, and I've come only to make sure he knows it.

"Well, great," I say almost ready to push away before he finally lets me go.

"Thought for sure you'd be late, madam," he says. "I was actually surprised when your assistant called to say you were on your way."

"I make it a point to be punctual." I sit next to him at the table and take the menu from the waiter. "Thank you."

"I see. Your timing was amazing on set, too. I don't think I've seen too many actresses really commit like that."

I smile but don't respond. I know he's trying to charm me. He's trying to push his beady eyes into mine. Wait . . . did he just look at my breasts?

"What's wrong?" he asks. "You look surprised. You don't believe me?"

"Believe you about what?" I pull my shirt up a bit to cover my cleavage.

"That you're a good actress," he says.

"I'm the star of the second-highest-rated show on television. I don't have to believe you."

King laughs and eases back in his seat. "Well, I was the star of the top-rated show on television and I didn't believe any of the good things people said to me. I only heard the negative. Of course, I pretended otherwise. Funny how that works."

"Oh, please. Now you're trying to psychoanalyze me?" I ask, pulling the napkin off my lap and tossing it on the table.

"Whoa! Calm down, Ms. Lady. I'm not trying to psycho-analyze anyone—maybe myself. I was giving you a compli-ment. Care to take it?"

"Look, we can sit here and do this small talk—"

"You call *this* small talk?"

"—thing, but let's just get to the point. Alex says you're trying to come on the show."

"Yes," he looks at me straight-faced. "That's my intention."

"Well, to be honest with you," I say, "I don't know if that's a good idea. This isn't some sitcom with a laugh track. It's drama. And we don't have any teen fan clubs."

"I went to Yale School of Drama. My first acting gig was when I was sixteen. I played a cancer patient. I died on screen."

I sip my water and tell the waiter I'll only be having wine.

"Silver, I'm not here to steal your shine. I'm just trying to work. Just like every other black actor in Hollywood. It's not personal. I've been where you're at."

"And where is that?" I look him up and down.

"When you think you have everything you want, but you're afraid because you know you can lose it at any time."

"That's where you're wrong. I'm not afraid of losing any-thing," I snap.

"Really?" He folds his arms and narrows his eyes on me. "You're going to tell me you're a black actress who doesn't think about being out of work?"

"I'm going to tell you"—I stop talking to let the waiter slide my wine onto the table—"that what I think is none of your business. And what about what you've lost? About you being out of work?"

"Try me," he says, defensively tapping both sides of his chest with open palms. "I'm an open book."

"Well, if memory serves me correctly, you shot up everything you had and lost your show—"

"Sure did." He jumps in to agree before I'm done. "But I'm drug free now."

"Left Hollywood—"

"Yup."

"Shacked up with some white girl—"

"French!"

"White! And then you suddenly got deep." I finish my list and sip my wine. "How are those yoga DVDs selling?"

"You think you have me all figured out," he says.

"I wasn't the one trying to figure people out." I take one more sip of the wine and nod for the waiter to bring me the check.

"Silver, Alex called me," King says and something in me braces itself. "This was his idea. He said he knew I could pull the ratings up. I signed on just to get my face back out there. I don't need money. That yoga DVD made me enough money to produce my own show. Which I intend on doing, but I need to get my feet wet again. I hope you understand that there's no way I would've agreed to this if I'd thought you weren't onboard. I know execs spring things on actors all the time, but I would never participate if I knew . . . I just thought that since he's your husband he'd . . . tell you. But now it's obvious you had no clue."

I return the check to the waiter and pick up my purse to leave.

"There you go trying to figure people out again," I say. "Let's see how you decipher this bit of information: take your yoga DVDs and cowboy boots and go back to South Dakota to be with your cows or steers or whatever. *We* don't need you here. *I* don't want you here."

★　★　★

Self-important, wannabe shaman! I can't even think a whole sentence without "King's" fluffy smile making me nauseous. His eyes. And what kind of name is King anyway? Did he get it off some Burger King bag? I hate phonies. People who pretend they're so nice and so humble when really they just want to get ahead like everyone else. And Hollywood phonies are the worst. They're the ones who know about our lack of loyalty and try to use some kind of reverse psychology to get into your mind and "make friends." Please! They're just like the rest of them. And when guns are drawn at the corral, they're locked and loaded, ready to shoot down their so-called friends. *Calling me "Madam."* This isn't France. And talking about my acting and timing. *I don't think I've seen too many actresses really commit like that.* I'm the star on the second-rated show on television. What did he expect me to do? Stand there and look crazy when the cameras started rolling? Some routine he had. King? When I was new here, still with my bad hair dye and kitten eyes, I might've sucked that up, but I've been screwed over enough to know his act. His "I'm so perfect and pure" routine. Cowboy boots and a T-shirt on a black man? Perfect and pure doesn't get you to the top. Self-reliance does. Focus.

On the way to the studio the next day for King's read-through where Manuel decides if he has chemistry with the cast, I decide to do a little focusing of my own. If Alex can't see that King is a bad fit for the show, I'll show him. I'll send someone else with my message.

I pull in to Melanie standing in my parking space with a cup of coffee and some papers. She's dressed the same as the day before. Her fake Rolex is back, though.

"Good morning, Mrs. Stone," she says, opening my door. "Would you like me to get your bags?"

I hand her my purse.

"What's that?" I point to the paper.

"An updated version of the script. I came in early this morning and the writers were here . . . with King. I tried to call you a few times."

"I saw," I say, taking the script.

"They made changes . . . added King."

"I know, I saw it last night. It's just a reading."

"I read it, too . . . but you might want to look it over now. They changed some things."

"Changed?" I take off my shades and thumb through to the end to King's part in the script.

"Well, I noticed last night that King was just coming on as Dr. Thibodaux, Baron's college friend who's moved to Jackson Ridge. But, well, now they—"

I scan to a line where King brushes my leg and we lock eyes.

"They're making him Diamond's new love interest?" I toss the script back at Melanie.

"Seems so," she says, walking into the studio with me.

The first thing I see is King in his cowboy boots standing at the crafts breakfast table laughing with the writers.

"Give me a damn break!" I say.

"Yeah, judging from your response yesterday, I didn't think you'd be happy about it. Anything I can do?"

King turns to me and smiles.

"Good morning, madam," he calls out across the studio floor.

Everyone looks. Waits.

I nod and turn to Melanie.

"Actually, there is something you can do," I say. "It'll be your first official mission."

"Cool!"

The Black and Bourgeois
"Anger Management"
(Dummy Script)

Scene 1

INT: DR. THIBODAUX'S OFFICE - DAY
DIAMOND visits DR. THIBODAUX for her first anger management session after being arrested for choking RED.

DR. THIBODAUX
(Looking at a file on his desk.)
So, Ms. DeLoach, it says here that you're having some issues and Judge Kingston felt you would benefit from anger management workshops. Care to tell me what's bothering you?

DIAMOND
You're the doctor. You have the file. Aren't you supposed to tell me what happened?

DR. THIBODAUX
I'm not here to decide that. I'm here to help *you* decide that.

DIAMOND
For $200 an hour, you'd think you could just spell it out for me. Maybe you could give me something to control myself. Valium? Prozac?

DR. THIBODAUX
I don't think any of that will be necessary. We should just talk.

DIAMOND
About?

DR. THIBODAUX
Let's start with Red. You had a fight with her at your brother's birthday party. Got arrested. What caused the fight?

DIAMOND

Red's a lying tramp who's trying to steal my family's fortune and my brother. Wouldn't that make you angry?

DR. THIBODAUX

I'm sure it would. But why attack her? What's that going to change?

DIAMOND

As I told the judge, that was in self-defense. She hit me first.

DR. THIBODAUX

But you started the whole thing. You played the video at the party.

DIAMOND

I did what I had to do. What would you have done, clever doctor?

Dr. Thibodaux gets up and walks over to sit in a chair beside Diamond.

DR. THIBODAUX

I would've assessed the situation. Tried to figure out what bothered me so much about my enemy. Then looked inward. See, sometimes the things that bother us so much about other people are really the things that bother us about ourselves. Things we hide inside ourselves.

Dressed in his white coat and spectacles, King is really trying to give Dr. Thibodaux a run. I see what he's doing—trying to mix sexy with smart. His coat is just tight enough to show the muscles in his arms and back. The spectacles add definition to his eyebrows, intensity to his eyes. He looks like no doctor anyone has ever seen, but wishes they had.

And I guess they never will. For every piece of intensity he puts into his lines (and he does a good go of doing it—I can't lie), I pull back and steal his energy, making him fall flat. As we read, I avoid eye contact and flub a few lines. If Manuel doesn't see us connecting from his chair, he'll suggest to Alex that we send King packing. He's over.

"Cut," Manuel calls. He walks onto the set and right up to me. "Silver—I need a little more interaction," he says quickly. "Loosen up. You're somewhere between angry for being at Dr. T's office and taken by his looks."

"Taken?" I say. "I didn't read that into my lines. Diamond wouldn't go for this guy." I laugh. Point to the spectacles.

"Just go with it," he says, annoyed and backing up to his seat.

"What are you doing, Silver?" King whispers beside me.

"Come on, guys. This isn't rocket science. It's just a reading. You can play get along after we tape this for the execs," Manuel says. "Let's pick it back up from the last line." He pauses. "And . . . action!"

King moves his chair a little closer to mine and we run the last lines. He removes his glasses, nearly throwing them onto the desk.

DR. THIBODAUX
But don't worry. I can fix you.

DIAMOND
You can only fix something that's broken. You think I'm broken, Dr. Thibodaux?

King stabs me so hard with his eyes, I can't look away. I feel myself drawn into something. I see that the browns in his eyes look like roasted flecks of nutmeg. The studio gets more quiet than it usually is for a reading and I know I'm not the only one locked in.

DR. THIBODAUX

Not all of you.
(He brushes his hand against her leg.)
Just your heart.
(He locks eyes with her.)
Just your—

Melanie's voice comes barking into the silence just in time.
"I'm sorry! I'm sorry!" She apologizes again and again, coming up on the set with my cellphone held out to me as everyone looks on at her like she's a turtle in a tutu. It's almost unheard of for anyone to interrupt a scene—especially not an assistant. But this "cut" had come with my instructions. "If things get too good on set with King," I'd told her, "stop the scene with an emergency call from my mother."

"What is it?" I ask Melanie, trying to look as annoyed as everyone else.

"An emergency. It's your mother. Something's wrong," Melanie says. "I know I shouldn't interrupt, but she said it's important."

I look at Manuel and then King.

"I'm sorry, guys. I have to take this," I say. "I'll be right back."

I take the phone and dart to my dressing room.

"Was that OK?" Melanie asks when we're alone in the dressing room.

"Perfect. Exactly when I needed you," I say. I sit at my vanity and pull out a cigarette. *Anger management . . . I've got your anger management, King Colson!*"

"What do you think is going to happen?" Melanie asks.

"Nothing right now. I'm just letting him cool off a little. See, actors build on intensity in a scene. When you break it up, it's hard to get it back." I look at the clock on my phone. "Let's see . . . My emergency should fix itself in say ten minutes."

"Wow! That's an amazing plan. How do you think I did? Did I deliver my lines correctly? I mean . . . they weren't lines . . . not like what you do . . . but I had to think of them. I thought it would be hard to convince a room of professionals. How was it?"

"You did just fine."

"We were like a team . . . me and you." She smiles and walks out the door.

"King Colson . . . your time is limited," I say, looking at myself in the mirror over the vanity. "Hope you have a return ticket to your horsies. Yeeeehaw!"

The door opens again.

"What are they doing out there? Did you tell them I'm still on the phone?" I ask Melanie.

"The better question is, what are you doing in here?"

I turn toward the door and see King charging toward me.

"What does it look like?"

"Like you're having a cigarette."

"Very observant." I laugh. "Correct."

"You know what? This is ridiculous."

"Call it what you want." I pick up my phone. "Guess I'll call my mom back now."

"Don't bother to pretend," he says. He turns to walk back out.

"Who's pretending?"

He stops and walks back over to me, snatches the phone from my hand, and throws it across the room.

"What? You've gone crazy!" I say, after watching the phone burst into pieces.

"What's your deal?" he asks. "You're so fucked up in the head. So jaded. I thought people were lying about you. Maybe exaggerating."

"Exaggerating about what?"

"Oh, you don't know?" he says. "They say you're evil. A cold, angry bitch. And no one wants to work with you. Why do you think Alex came to me? I'm sure I wasn't at the top of a short list."

"Get out of my dressing room!" I shout, getting up and ready to push him out.

But he stands tall in front of me. We breathe in and out in anger together and I can see his heart beating.

"You don't need to tell me to go. I'm already gone." He leaves me standing in the middle of the dressing room. "I'll tell Alex myself." He slams the door so hard the heart-shaped glass in my vanity breaks, sliding down to the floor and cracking into two large pieces.

"Fuck! Fuck! Fuck!" I shout.

I look around the room and see that I'm alone. All alone. I'm almost never alone in my dressing room. There's always someone there. But it's quiet now. So quiet. Just like my bedroom at night. I feel like it's getting smaller. Tighter. I can't breathe.

I sit on the chaise and take deep breaths, but still I'm out of air and my throat is closing.

I look across the room at my phone in pieces. Think to call for Melanie or Oscar. I can't, though. My voice is gone.

I gasp. Suck in one long pull of oxygen and grip the sides of the chaise, feeling like I'm about to fall over. And just before I do, the door opens again, and it seems like someone's stuck a straw down my throat.

"Where's that crazy assistant of yours?" Oscar asks, coming in with an armful of dresses in big plastic bags. "I told her to meet me out back, but she—" He stops to look at me and quickly drops the dresses before rushing over. "My God, are you OK?"

"Yeah," I force. "I just kind of . . . lost my breath." I hold onto the chaise. "Felt a little dizzy."

"You look like you've seen the ghost of Natalie Wood." He fans my face and pushes my hair back behind my ears. "What's wrong with the vanity?" he asks, looking behind me at the broken glass and then turning to the phone scattered around on the floor. "And whose phone is that?"

"It's mine. It's nothing. I'll have Melanie get someone to come clean it up."

He looks at me, unnerved.

"Did something happen in here? Did Alex—"

"No, no! I'm fine!" I say, pushing his hand away.

"OK," he snarls. "If you say so. Want some water? Vodka?"

"No. It's fine."

"OK." Oscar returns to the middle of the floor where he dropped the dresses. "Julio Inglesias, you scared me. I thought you were having a heart attack, or an asthma attack . . . or maybe an anxiety attack. My little brother used to have those. He hated being alone."

"It was nothing," I say firmly. "Just lost my breath."

"Speaking of losing your breath, can you please tell Ms. Melanie to shut the hell up talking to me all the time?" Oscar goes into the closet with the dresses and continues his rant about Melanie, poking his head out the doorway every few seconds to be sure I'm still listening.

"I don't complain a bunch, but crazy is crazy and I'm not into that kind of crazy. And you know what I mean! And those eyes! Freaky!"

"Give her a break. She's new. Trying to get her foot in just like the rest of us did."

"If you say so."

I look at the pieces of broken glass on the floor. Two big pieces split jaggedly right down the middle. The heart now looks like one of those broken trinkets teenagers used to wear on their bracelets.

I get up to gather the pieces and put them on the vanity. I get one side and look at myself in the fractured glass. My eyes are red and watery. My face is pale. I look so tired. Sad. Even afraid.

"Silver, what are you doing with that glass? You'd better

put that down," Oscar says. He comes over and takes the jagged mirror from me.

"Oscar, can I ask you a question?"

"About what?" He carefully slides the glass onto the vanity.

"About me."

"Oh." His voice and body shrink a little. "Sure."

"Am I a bitch?" I stop. "What I meant was, do people say I'm a bitch?"

Oscar sits and looks at me silently.

"Well?" I push.

"Do you mean that in a rhetorical way?" he asks with a little sarcasm in his voice.

"I'm serious. Just tell me the truth."

"You know the truth."

"So, what is it?"

"Of course they do," he says finally.

"Everyone?"

"Well, not *everyone* says you're a bitch. Kind of depends on where they're from. What language they speak."

"I'm not joking."

"I'm sorry. I thought you didn't care. That's kind of what being a bitch is all about."

"But I'm not a real bitch. I'm nice to people. You? You've been here with me since the beginning."

Oscar sucks his teeth and looks up at the chandelier.

"Are we being honest?" he asks.

"That's what I want."

He looks back at me.

"There's just something that's changed in you over the years since we've been working on the show. You haven't always been the nicest person, but you have been nice. It's just that over the years . . . well . . . you've grown cold."

"I'm cold?"

"Yeah." He gets up and sort of grimaces. "You know

what . . . I don't want to talk about this." He turns and heads busily to the closet, but I follow.

"Why not? I really want to know."

"No, you don't." He slides another dress onto the rack with his back to me.

"Yes. I do. Why won't you just say it?"

"Oh, God! You're such a diva," he says under his breath. "I really don't appreciate this."

"Appreciate what?"

"You. I don't appreciate you. I mean, what is this? So, you're obviously having some kind of moment and now I have to have it with you? No, thanks. Don't try to sign me up for the rise and fall. You have a moment of weakness. I answer your questions and next week you use it to fire me. No, thanks."

"I'm not going to fire you. That's not what this is." I look into Oscar's eyes and I see something so familiar. I see that he's afraid of me. Not that he respects me. Definitely not that he thinks he's talking to a friend. But not even a boss. More like a tyrant. Someone who controls him. Someone he fears. And it's not like I'm just looking into his eyes like I do every day. They're more clear. More like a mirror. Not reflecting me. But reminding me of what my own eyes look like. What I think they look like. When I'm looking at Alex. My whole world just stops. Everything I think I know collapses into my tight space. I feel like I've been punched in the stomach. I reach to Oscar, but I know he can't see me. He walks right past.

"I have to go," Oscar says, walking out of the closet.

I follow him and stand in the frame, watching him get closer to the door, trying to think of what to say, how far I have to reach to get him. To make him stay. I don't know why, but I don't want him to leave. I don't want to be alone in the room again.

"I'm sorry," I start before he's gone. "I'm sorry if I've ever made you feel like you're less than you are. If I've ever been mean to you. Nasty to you. Made you hate me. Hate working for me." I say everything I wish Alex would say to me. Everything I want to hear each night when I'm alone in my bedroom. And just then I know I can't go back there. Not alone. Not back into the cage. I wonder how long I've been living this way. Cutting myself off from everyone. If Oscar sees me how I see Alex, how must everyone else look at me?

Oscar lets the doorknob slide through his hands.

"I do my best work here," he says to the door. "I've missed half of my son's life. Ruined two marriages to great men. All to make you a star. And sometimes I think you forget that." He looks at me. "I think you forget that we're all in this together. That we all want what's best for this show. And we all believe in you . . . well, most of us."

"Most of us?"

"You know who I'm talking about," he says and his voice gets lower. "Don't make me say it. Please don't."

We stand there and look at each other in silence until whatever's known between us is too obvious to name.

"Can I go?" Oscar asks in a near whisper.

"Sure."

Oscar's hardly out the door before my feet and something in me I can't yet name jump into my shoes and drag me back out to the set. I'm almost running. Looking desperately for one face. And I don't know what all I'm thinking. But I know I don't have time to make sense of it. I just don't want to be alone. Not anymore.

"Our plan worked! He's leaving!" Melanie says cheerfully, cornering me behind the cameras on the set. "Ding dong, the King is dead!" She laughs.

"He left?"

"Packed his stuff." She turns to Manuel, who's leading the

taping of the next scenes with the other actors. "I think Manuel's pretty peeved, but things look back to normal."

"How long ago did he leave?" I scan the room, back and forth again.

"Five minutes ago—I don't know. All that matters is that he's gone. Right?" Melanie laughs a laugh so close to mine, it's like a tape recorder playing back to me. I see myself in her eyes. "That'll teach him! He can't just come up in here and mess with Silver Stone! Not my Silver Stone!"

"Oh no," I say. "I—"

"What's wrong?"

"I think I'm going to step out for a second. I'm not taping until later. Just let Manuel know I had an emergency. Can you do that?"

"Of course I can. I'll just say it was your . . . mother . . . But that's not it. Where are you going?" Her voice almost insists on an answer.

"An emergency. Something else. Just cover for me."

I run out to the parking lot and I don't know where I'm going, but I know I need to find him. To see him. To say something.

"Mrs. Stone, can I help you?" one of the production assistants asks, coming up beside me. "Is everything OK with your mother?"

"I'm fine . . . she's fine," I say. "Have you seen King?"

"Yes," he says, pointing to the back of the lot. "I just walked him to his car."

"Thanks," I say, rushing in the direction he indicated.

I run through the maze of cars, jumping up every two rows or so to see if I can find any movement, any sign of King. I get up on my knees on the trunk of some old green wreck that looks like it has no business at the studio at all, and look out toward the back of the lot, but I don't see anyone moving. I think to call out to him, but then that sounds too crazy, especially since I don't really know what I want anyway.

"What are you doing?" I hear and I twist just a little so I don't fall off the trunk. King's standing at the open driver's side door.

"I'm . . . looking for you. Is this your car?" I look at the spotted rusty fender.

"It was my Dad's. Can you get off it?" he asks. "What do you want?"

I slide down from the trunk and stand in place until King's standing in front of me.

"So? What do you want?" he asks again, but his voice is softer.

I look up at him. Right into his eyes and I feel like I'm going to just float away. Like I need to grab onto something.

"What do you want?" he asks again and this time his voice sounds like honey.

"I— I—" I feel myself step closer to him. Him closer to me. "I—"

He grabs me by the cheeks and kisses me so hard at first, but then his hands fall to his sides, around my hips, and he's kissing me softly like he kissed my hand the first day we met. Slowly. Like a poem. I feel myself drifting away in the breeze again. I feel my hands slipping around his pelvis, into the back of his jeans.

But then a horn honks somewhere and then I snap back from floating. Realize what I'm doing. Where I'm doing it.

"No!" I say, jumping back from him and covering my lips. "Oh no! What was that?"

"A kiss," he says with his eyes still a little closed and dreaming.

"I know what a kiss is! I mean . . . why you?" I wipe my lips and look around to be sure we're alone.

"Well, I'm thinking it's because you wanted to?"

"No! I didn't kiss you. You kissed me!"

"Yes, I did kiss you," he says. "And I did it because I wanted to. Are you saying you didn't want to kiss me?"

"I—" I look into his eyes and feel afloat again. I stomp on the ground and fix my posture. What am I doing? "I just came out here to tell you that I'm sorry and . . . I didn't mean to kiss you. Well . . . I'm confused now. No one's ever said those things to me—the things you said in the dressing room. No one. And I'm just . . . I wonder how long I've been this way. You know? I'm not a bitch."

"OK," he says tediously, almost grinning. And hearing his voice sound so unaffected just annoys me. Almost embarrasses me. Suddenly, I wonder what I'm doing out in the parking lot apologizing to him for basically cursing me out in my own dressing room. Treating me like I'm some kitten new to the catwalk.

"Wait a minute," I say. "Wait . . . are you trying that whole . . . You sneaky devil!" I wipe any trace of him from my lips. "You almost got me, sir. But you need to wake up a little earlier! I'm no fool." I laugh and cross my arms over my breasts.

"A fool? What are you talking about?"

"That whole Angelina and Brad thing. You were trying to make me fall for you. Trying to make me fall for my costar. Really? Did you think that would work? Make things a little easier for you here?"

"Woman, you're crazy," he says, turning back to open his car door.

"You were just playing with me. Toying with me." I laugh, but I know it doesn't sound as easy as I want it to. "I knew it. Right?"

King gets into the green wreck and looks at me like I'm a hurt bunny.

"Right?" I ask again and I hear a soft spot in my voice that irritates me, but I can't help but to ask again. "Right?"

"Sure you're right, Silver. Sure you're right."

King starts the car and pulls out of the space with his eyes stuck on me.

He turns and waves. Drives out of my Hollywood life.

I want to hate King more than I ever have since the day he walked into my show and tried to steal my scene. I work hard at it. Frown whenever someone mentions his name. Suck my teeth whenever he crosses my mind. But then I realize that I'm sucking my teeth all the time. Like for the rest of the day. Through the rest of my scenes, meetings with the writers, running my lines, all I do is suck my teeth and relive every moment at the back of the green wreck. I suck my teeth at the way King smelled. I suck my teeth at how his lips felt on mine. I suck my teeth at his hands on my face. At me wanting them all over me.

But soon my teeth are hurting, so I have to stop sucking. And I'm stuck with just King. In my mind. I hate it. But there he is. His smell. His lips. His hands.

Back and forth in the pool doing my laps as the sun sets, I push my body so hard, making the water move between my thighs, trying not to think of him. I close my eyes, try to focus on my timing, but there he is again. Smiling and reaching. "Sure you're right." He laughs. I laugh back and kiss him so hard he falls into the car and I go down with him.

I push my hand out in front of me to make sure I don't hit the end of the pool before my turn.

In my mind, I'm reaching for King's face, for his cheeks, pulling him down to kiss me. Around his pelvis. Into his pants.

I reach for the wall.

My hand stops on something soft and hairy.

I stay beneath the water. Go down. Open my eyes and look up at it.

It's Alex's legs dangling right above my head.

I sink down farther to the bottom of the pool and watch. Look at his feet floating in the blue light.

It's dark on top of the water. I can see the moon. I wish I could stay under a little while longer. But I'm out of air again.

"Thought you were trying to drown yourself," Alex says when I get to the surface.

"Were you going to save me?"

"I might've."

I swim toward the steps.

"Getting out?" he asks.

"Yes. I'm done."

"Come on. You know I like to watch you swim in the pool. It calms me."

I stop on the bottom step to consider what he's saying, but then I keep climbing out.

"I'm cold," I say. "Wouldn't want to get sick." I grab my robe from the chair and ease into it with my back to Alex.

"King signed on."

"What?" I turn back around.

"He signed on. The execs approved it. We're writing him in immediately. His first episode is on Monday." Alex gets up from the edge of the pool.

"Really?"

"Yes. And I was a little surprised he signed on after hearing what happened in the reading." He looks at me. "How's my precious mother-in-law doing?"

"She's fine."

"Silver, I'm sorry I snapped at you. You know I don't mean those things I say," Alex says, coming over to me. "It's just that there was so much pressure behind this deal. Do you understand? I have to get things just right for you. This is all about you. My star." He holds both of my arms at my sides and kisses my forehead. "We can't lose everything we've worked so hard for. Right?"

I don't say anything.

"I don't know what I'd do if I ever lost you." He kisses me again and steps back. There's something cold in his eyes. Something I've never seen, but I know is there. "I can't ever lose you. I won't."

For the rest of the week, everyone at the studio moves as if we're expecting a baby. King is all they can talk about. Everything that makes them smile. The writers. Manuel. Alex. Even my team.

And once the news is leaked to the press, King is all the world can talk about, too. It's all over the blogs. In all of the newspapers. King's old fans start an entire Dr. Thibodaux Web site in his honor. And he's not even on the show yet. My publicist asks me for comments she can release to the press. I tell her to just share that I'm excited to have a new cast member.

But really I don't know how to feel about King coming to the show anymore. I don't know whose side he's on. What he wants from me. So, I decide to keep my distance. And when I see him on the set each day, I just smile and wave. Hope he doesn't try to talk to me or bring up what happened in the parking lot. I pose for pictures with him for the magazines. Even sit in on interviews, but I can't look at him. I won't look at him.

At night, alone in my bed, I go back to being closed in. To feeling like I'm in a cage and I can't breathe. But it's worse now, somehow. I need more Valium. More wine. Flower's tea is spiked with brandy from my nightstand. But sometimes that still won't work, and then I look at my phone and think of whom to call. Whom I can tell how lonely I feel. But there's no one. Not a soul. Not even my husband.

And then I think of King's kiss. How he seemed to make me leave all of this. Just go up into the air and look down on everything that's keeping me locked in. I remember his body. How his skin felt under my fingertips. His lips on top of mine.

I'm Diamond again in my dream. Back in Mississippi and walking that long walk down the avenue. My scarf is in the breeze. My parents are up ahead. I smile. I wave. I blow kisses. Then I see a face in the crowd. I know whom it is, but I can't make it out. The blurry face smiles back at me. Waves. Blows a kiss. The scarf blows up in my face and I have to move it to see again. And there he is. King looking at me from the sideline. He blows another kiss so softly over the breeze my bottom trembles so hard I feel it in my bed.

"You late, señora! Late!" Carmen's voice comes cracking into my bedroom.

I spring up from my Diamond dream and look around.

"What?"

She walks in, her hand extended to me, clutching my vibrating cell phone.

"You late, señora," she repeats.

"Oh shit!" I look at the window. It's so bright outside.

She hands me the phone.

"Hello?" I slide out the bed and Carmen immediately begins pulling off the sheets for the laundry.

"Good morning, Silver. It's Melanie. I'm here at the studio. . . . Standing in your parking space. Is everything OK?"

"I'm fine," I say, watching Carmen. "Just running a little behind. I overslept."

"It's still pretty early here. They're just running through the scenes. I was wondering if you need anything. I know today's your first taping with King and . . ."

When Carmen pulls at the top sheet, something hard gives way with it and falls to the floor, rolling across the room.

We both look at my vibrator as it spins and stops.

"No, I'm fine," I say, stopping Carmen from picking it up.

"Hmm," Carmen mouths.

"Don't worry about me. I'll be there in time for my shoot. I'm going for a run," I say to Melanie. I trade eyes with Carmen and put the vibrator into the drawer.

★ ★ ★

I decide to take the long way through the canyon. Up the rocky side where pebbles spray off into the air with each kick. I run hard. Try to think of what's happening to me. Why I feel so lonely. Why I keep thinking of King. Dreaming of him now. How could I let him get to me? I know it's just a game. Probably just a part of his plan. But what if it's not? There's no way. I know this place too well. Hollywood is full of shysters. Game players. King has to be one.

I lose my pacing after a group of boys with no shirts steals my thunder and passes me at one of the turns on the last stretch where you can see mansions tucked into the side of the canyon. I start walking and realize that I've been going so fast I can't feel that my feet are swollen.

"Come on; it's just a half a mile left. Pick up the pace!" I hear from behind and I already know it's King by the time he catches up to me and starts running in place beside me as I walk.

"You," I say, trying to hide any sign of excitement in my voice. "I'll take whatever pace I please."

"Suit yourself," he says. "I wouldn't go too slow, though. Let that July sun get too high and you'll go back to the studio looking like Grace Jones." He points to the sun and we both look up.

"You have a problem with Grace Jones?" I say, starting to run again. The morning heat really is on its way.

"No. That sister is bad."

"Hmm." I look ahead and dare not let even a corner of my eye peek at King in his tight tank top and shorts. Every muscle that was a secret under his shirt before is out and in the open. He looks like he belongs on a poster. "Shouldn't you be somewhere memorizing your lines for your grand debut?"

"Already know them. I wrote them myself. It's part of my contract. I get to write scenes for my character. I've had too much bad luck with writers in the past," he says. "I figured I'd spend this time connecting with my costar. Or, as you called it, pulling my 'Brad and Angelina' game." He laughs.

"Ugh," I say. "How did you even know I was out here?"

"Well, your assistant said you were going for a run, so I figured—"

"She told you where I was?" I instinctively reach for my phone, but King stops me.

"No, calm down. She just said you were running, but this is LA and you're an actress. Runyon was my best bet."

"Well, congratulations. You got me."

"God, Silver, when are you going to stop this act?" he asks as we pass through the last turn in the path.

"What act?"

"Like you don't like me. Like you hate me. When we both know what happened between us. So, kill me! I kissed a beautiful woman. But I know I wasn't alone when I did it. You wanted it, too."

"I'm married," I point out. We slow the pace and walk past the yoga park. "I just had a moment of weakness. You said something to me that made me a little sensitive and that was it."

"Look at me," he says.

I look ahead.

"Just look at me."

"What?" I turn to him and force the tightest frown I can manage.

"I like you. I wanted to hate you—just the way I know you want to hate me. But the moment I saw you up on that stage, I just fell for you. You were amazing. So beautiful. So smart. So in control. But also so delicate."

I groan and try to turn away, but he pulls me back.

"I'm not delicate—"

"And I don't want to say these things to another man's wife, but I'm not the kind of man to hold my tongue either," he says. "Alex may produce the show, but I'm my own boss."

"What do you want from me, King?"

"Look, all that other stuff aside, I just want us to get along. Forget about how I got here. Forget about what happened in the parking lot. Let's call it a truce and just be cool. What happened the other day won't happen again as long as you don't want it to."

"You sure?"

"Scout's honor." He holds up his fingers like a Boy Scout, but I think he's doing the Trekkie hand signal.

"These people are acting like Jesus is coming back," Pria says, making a long part down the middle of my scalp and smudging a little grease into my hair.

Outside the dressing room, there's nothing but racket. Alex agreed to let a crew backstage from TMZ to get an inside track on King's first day, so the cameras follow him everywhere he goes. "King isn't even this big. Not the way these people are carrying on." She focuses my head in the fixed heart-shaped mirror over the vanity, so I can see my reflection. "What about you? What do you think about him coming on the show?"

"He's a good actor. I'm sure he'll be a wonderful addition," I say.

"Come on. That's like line for line from the announcement you sent to the press. Give me the real deal."

"Well, I'm—"

"You know what, I'm sorry. I don't know what I was thinking." Pria stops me. "I know I shouldn't be in your business. That's on your list: no nosing around." She looks at me in the heart. "Sorry."

I try to let the conversation stop there with her breaks, but I do want to talk about King. To talk to someone.

"You know, Pria, about my list. Let's drop it," I say nonchalantly.

"Drop the list?" She looks like I've gone crazy.

"Not the whole list. Just that little rule . . . for right now." I smile and sit back in my seat.

"Really? Well, tell me what you think? Are you nervous?" She gushes beside me. "He's so cute. I can't imagine what it'll be like to be so close to him. I'm way past my teenage crush, but I couldn't imagine it. You know? What it would be like to kiss him? Have you thought about it?"

I want to agree with her. To gush, too, and say I've done more than think about it. But this isn't the place for that. I let her say everything I'm thinking.

"He's cute and everything, but I'm a professional," I say. "This is just work."

"Professional or not, he's more than cute. And I hear he's got more than a big ego . . . if you know what I mean."

"Really? How do you know that?"

Before I walk to the set, Pria tells me about one of her friends from college who had a fling with King for a little while when he was living in Paris. She'd told Pria he was one of the most passionate lovers she'd ever had. He'd come to her place late at night. Sweating and eager. So attentive, but also so demanding. He left her breathless every time.

When I see him sitting in his brand-new chair on the set surrounded by reporters, I imagine what he must've been like on those late nights in Paris. I try not to, but my mind skips right back to his chest heaving in and out as we ran in the park. His pelvis melting in my palms. I swallow hard and struggle for air. Try to remind myself that nothing will ever happen between us again. And that's good. Because that's what I want. Right?

He laughs at something and I think of how his lips must've felt on that girl's body in Paris. Him calling her name. Him calling mine.

He looks at me and smiles. Points to his watch.

I give a thumbs-up and sit in my chair, praying he can't see in my eyes what I was thinking. I look over to Melanie and signal for my water bottle. Cold this time.

★　★　★

The Black and Bourgeois
"Anger Management"
(EPISODE: 2015)

Scene 7

INT: DR. THIBODAUX'S OFFICE - NIGHT
DIAMOND returns to Dr. Thibodaux's office after-hours to retrieve her lost wallet.

                    DIAMOND
Oh. You're still here. I was sure I'd missed my chance.

                    DR. THIBODAUX
Hello again, Mrs. DeLoach. I'm just working late. Finishing up some paperwork. What brings you back?

                    DIAMOND
My wallet. I think I left it on the couch.

                    DR. THIBODAUX
(Searches the couch)
Well, where?

                    DIAMOND
(Eases past him and starts searching)
Maybe it's over here.

I'm reasonable, unaffected, and most professional through most of our scenes together. Dr. Thibodaux's hand on Diamond's leg. Him insisting she lay down on the couch to relax. Giving her a light massage. I focus on being Diamond and let go of the kiss on the green wreck.

But once we get to the last scene, scene seven when Diamond returns for her wallet, flashes of King sneaking into some girl's apartment in Paris ignite in my imagination and my middle trembles like I'm back in my bed alone.

I follow Diamond's stage directions, but in my eyes I'm all me. I bend over the side of the couch and arch my back like a cat's, digging under the pillow so slowly, I can see the cameraman step out from behind his lens and stare.

King comes up behind me. Puts his hands on my tight waist.

> ### DR. THIBODAUX
> I'll dig in there. I can go deeper.

I stand at the side of the couch and watch him work, his back tight from muscle to muscle.

> ### DIAMOND
> Maybe it's not down there.

> ### DR. THIBODAUX
> Well, you said it's here, so I have to dig.

DIAMOND sees the wallet on the desk.

> ### DIAMOND
> Oh, wait! Here it is, Doctor! Right on the desk.

> ### DR. THIBODAUX
> What?
> (Sees the wallet)
> Yes! There it is.

> ### DIAMOND
> (Holding the wallet)
> Now, how could you not have known it was right on your desk?
> (Flirting)

If I didn't know any better, I'd think you were hiding it from me.

DR. THIBODAUX

Oh, I'd never do that. Scout's honor.

DIAMOND

Are you sure?

DR. THIBODAUX

I wouldn't lie to you, Mrs. DeLoach. Not after digging in that couch like that—I mean, having you on my couch like that.

I remove Dr. Thibodaux's glasses and play with the tip in my mouth as I laugh. I don't remember what line I'm supposed to say next, but I drop them on the desk and run my hand up his arm slowly. King's pants tighten in the front. The cameraman's mouth opens wide. I hear someone struggle a gulp of saliva down his throat. I step toward King. Lick my top lip.

DR. THIBODAUX

Aren't you going to go now? Your car is out front.

King actually says my line back to me.

DIAMOND

Yes.

"Scene!" Manuel yells.

King and I stay looking at each other.

I turn and look at the crowd and all of the men have their mouths open.

"OK, people, now that's what we call a wrap!" Manuel says, coming up on the set.

"Whew, I thought I was about to piss in my pants! If it had

gotten any hotter in here, we wouldn't have been able to run this on the network. Good work, people!"

"What was that?" King says to me.

"Nothing. Just work," I answer. "Scout's honor." I hold up the Trekkie hand sign.

"No way you were a Girl Scout."

"And I'm sure you weren't a Boy Scout."

I walk off the set and back to my dressing room.

"Great job," Melanie says.

"Yeah, that was some chemistry." Pria pulls me into the room.

"*Muy caliente!*" Oscar pretends he's shaking maracas behind me.

"You had everyone with you. The whole room right in the palm of your hand," Melanie says.

I sit down and JimBo comes over to remove my makeup.

"How do you do it?" Melanie asks. "It was like you weren't even acting. It looked so real."

"It's just business," I say.

"Hmm." Pria trades eyes with Oscar.

"Hey, are you coming to the party?" Melanie asks.

"What party?"

"Oh, no need to tell Mrs. Diva. She doesn't party with us commoners," Oscar jumps in with the voice of an Englishman.

"Whatever, Oscar," I say. "What party are you talking about? Is everyone going?"

"Yeah. It's a cast party. Just something they're doing to welcome King aboard. Nothing big."

"Really? Where is it?" I ask and I see Pria and Oscar look at each other again.

"At the pool at the Beverly Hotel where King is staying," Melanie says. "Are you coming?"

I look at myself in the mirror.

"Yes," I say. "I'm coming."

"No way," Oscar says jokingly. "*The* Silver Stone is coming to a party?"

"Yes," I say. "Silver Stone is coming to a party."

There's always been this myth of the Hollywood star who parties all night long and crawls into bed at sunup with her bottom bare and her nose caked with white powder. And it's not always false. But most times it's so far from the truth. The ones who've made it here, the ones who want to stay at the top for more than fifteen minutes or forgo plummeting to the bottom of an early grave, party only when paid, and if at all. The days are too busy, and the nights are too short and precious to spend any time in the street amongst those salivating for just a taste of what you have. LA nightlife is like spring break on steroids. The music is loud. The people are louder. The drugs are everywhere you look. And everyone wants to make sure you're having a good time. Coke, Cognac, Cash, Cock? They'll give it to you however you want it. But the thing is, you have to be up with your trainer in a few hours. Ready to get to the studio right after that. Lines memorized. Eyes not puffy. No hangover. No crazy pictures of your firecrotch up on bossip. com. And if that's not the case, everyone makes a joke of it for a little while: you're the "bad girl." But soon, the jokes turn to warnings. And then the warnings are notices to your agent. You're uninsurable. No one believes you can escape the scene and actually do the work. Ask Lindsay Lohan.

I actually ended up going back to the studio to get one of Diamond's Stephen Burrows rainbow collection sundresses to wear to King's party. I couldn't settle on anything in my closet. Nothing seemed right. Nothing said "beautiful" to me the way that King had said it at Runyon Canyon and I wanted him to think it when he saw me. I blushed, looking at myself in the mirror. What was I doing? I'd told him I wanted this to stop. But stop what? I was finally beginning to feel like I was back in the world. A part of it. Not just watching and judging. Pria and Oscar. JimBo. They were all looking at me differently. And I was liking it. I liked how King looked at me even more.

"I can't believe you came," Pria said, meeting me in the lobby of the Beverly.

When I'd pulled up, I called her to meet me. I didn't want to walk in alone. I knew everyone would look at me. It had been so long since I'd been out at night and photogs love to get shots of what they call "unicorns."

"Yeah, I figured why not. It's a party, right?" I try to laugh a little.

"Sure, darling!" She takes a sip of the martini she's holding and links arms with me like we're sorority sisters at the frat house. "We're going to have a great time," she adds and then shouts, "Will someone get my boss a freaking drink?"

We walk to the back of the hotel along a long line of cameras and people pointing at me over a velvet rope, asking for an autograph, but Pria knows the routine. She pulls me in close to her and rushes through the throng like a linebacker, elbowing anyone who tries to block her.

When we get to the pool, I see everyone from the show scattered around the deck, laughing and smiling like I've never seen before. They all look just like real people. I mean, I've always known that they're real, but I've never seen them like this. Not away from work. Then I realize how long it's been since I've been to a party. One of any kind. Period. Even the music is different. It's like some techno mixed with reggae. It sounds awful, but I nod along and scan the crowd for King.

Pria bounces and whines beside me like she's having the time of her life. A waiter hands me a drink.

"Thanks," I say.

"You're here!" Melanie pops up. "I've been calling you."

"Yeah, I just came right over. I called Pria when I got here," I say.

"Oh." She cuts her eyes at Pria. "Well, I just thought you

should've called me. I'm your assistant. It's kind of my job to make sure you're OK."

"Whoa, I'm not blocking," Pria starts, but I stop her.

"I'm fine, Melanie," I say. "You can have a little fun. I'm just here to relax."

"You sure?" Her face saddens.

"Totally sure. It's a party, right?" I smile. "Go ahead. Have a good time."

Melanie kind of sulks and walks off reluctantly, looking back at me every few steps.

"Look at you, Mama! All loosening up," Pria teases. "First you take something off the list. Now you're at a party. And letting your assistant have a good time? Who knew?"

"Yeah, who knew." I keep looking around, but I can't see King anywhere.

"You actually came?" Oscar says, coming over with Alicia and Darrin, who are quite cozy with each other.

"Yeah, I came," I say, realizing that it'll probably be the most repeated comment I make all night. "Wait, are you two a couple?" I look at Darrin and Alicia now holding hands.

"Yes," Alicia says matter-of-factly. "We've been dating for a few months."

"I thought you knew," Darrin says. "Everyone else does."

"Yes, they're the official king and queen of *The Black and Bourgeois*," Oscar jokes.

"I guess I missed it. I read something about it online, but you know you can't trust those rags."

"Well, those rags are actually what brought us together," Darrin says. "After seeing two rumors that we were dating, I started looking at Alicia a little differently. Figured she wasn't such a bad face to be attached to."

"Oh, please," Alicia says laughing. "What about you, Silver? Where's your love interest tonight?"

The first name that comes to mind is "King" and I nearly

spit out my drink, thinking she knew what happened in the parking lot somehow.

"You OK?" Pria asks, patting my back.

"I'm fine," I say, turning back to Alicia. "You mean Alex?"

"Of course. Your husband." She looks at Darrin awkwardly.

"I don't think he's coming tonight. He's so busy and, you know, it's just not his thing."

"Well, he usually comes to the cast parties," Darrin says. He laughs and looks at Oscar. "Remember that party last week at the Sky Bar? How he got messed and went into the bathroom with those two—"

Oscar shakes his head at Darrin and he stops mid-sentence.

"Anyone want some shrimp cocktail?" Alicia asks quickly, grabbing Darrin's hand. "We're going to the bar." They walk off suddenly and bicker all the way around the pool.

For the rest of the night, everyone who walks up to me seems so surprised. They greet me like I'm a child who's been found. They insist on pouring more alcohol in my glass and a few even offer me a bump. Just like that, they pull out a vial of cocaine and spread it right out on their index finger, holding it out to me like it's an hors d'oeuvre. And that's how the party keeps going. How they all keep moving. The alcohol winds them down, but the coke picks them up. And I sit back and watch it all unravel. First Leeda falls into the pool, then Darrin and Alicia, and soon they're all hopping around the place like it's Freaknik.

"You want me to take you home?" Melanie asks, coming up to my table by the pool. "I know you need to be up early."

"I'm OK," I say, looking around. It's getting late, but I still haven't even seen King. "Have you seen King? I thought this was supposed to be his welcoming party."

"I saw him earlier. He was somewhere walking with"— she starts—"oh, there he is." She nods to King standing on the side of the pool. He's wearing white jeans and a red button up. Cowboy boots. Bopping his head to the music with a beer in his hand. "Want me to get him?"

"No." I watch him do a funny little two-step with JimBo. "Look, why don't you get me another drink."

"Sure, I can do that," Melanie says. "I'll meet you back here?"

"Yeah. I'll be here."

Once Melanie and her prodding are gone, I walk over to King and place my hand in the small of his back. I push a little.

"I'd push you in, but I wouldn't want to ruin your fancy jeans," I say when he turns around.

"Wow! Look who the cat dragged in!" He laughs so loudly I can tell he's had more than a few beers. "I'm glad you came. How long have you been here?"

"A little while. A little birdie told me they were throwing a party for you, so I figured I'd come and pay my respects, you know, to my new cast mate."

"Respects? God, woman, when was the last time you left the house? You make it sound like you're going to a funeral." King laughs and hands JimBo his beer. He steps back from the pool and takes my hand. "Shall we?" He does his odd little two-step.

"Oh, I was about to leave in a second," I say. "Not really up for dancing. I just wanted to say hello."

"Oh. Well, thanks for coming, I guess."

"Yeah, I guess I'll go now," I say and I know I sound so awkward, but standing in front of him with everyone around us, I just have no idea what to say.

"OK," he says. "Well, let me walk you to your car."

"That won't be necessary," I say. "I'll be fine."

"I insist. One cast mate to another." King takes my hand and we walk up the stairs toward the lobby.

Melanie stops us halfway, running up the steps with a drink in her hand.

"I was looking for you," she says. "Here's your drink."

"Oh, I don't need it now. I'm leaving."

"Leaving? I can walk you to your car," she says.

"I've got that covered," King says.

Melanie smiles at King, but her eyes are sharp as knives.

"It's fine," I say to her. "I'll see you in the morning."

King and I turn and continue to climb the steps, but Melanie doesn't leave. She stands there and watches.

"Kind of forceful, isn't she?" King notes.

"She's just anxious," I say, but I keep the corner of my eye on her.

King and I never quite make it to the valet to get my car. In a ridiculous and drunken plot to avoid the photographers waiting out front, King tries to lead me the long way around the hotel, but we get caught by two security guards and nearly get tasered until King convinces the second one that we're celebrities staying at the hotel.

At some point, he manages to steal a bottle of vodka from the bar and talks me into coming up to his room to see pictures of his ranch on his laptop. I resist for a little while, but the drinks and night air get to me. I just don't want the night to end. And what's waiting at home? A swimming pool and an empty bed?

"That's not a horse! That's a donkey," I say, laughing at the picture of a fat horse King opens up to show me on his laptop.

"He's a Clydesdale. My prize possession," King protests.

"Well, you need to stop feeding his ass, because he's looking a lot like a donkey right now." I hear myself slurring and wish I hadn't had the third class of vodka. But I'm still feeling so happy and laughing louder than I have in so long. Sitting in the middle of the suite floor with my shoes off, my legs out flat in front of me, I wonder why I am where I'm at. But then I think, I really don't care.

"You don't know anything about horses," King snaps playfully and snatches the laptop from me. "That's my baby. He's gonna help me start a whole stable."

"A stable of donkeys."

"No! Clydesdales! And stop making fun of him. He's just chunky."

"A chunky donkey!" I laugh so hard I fall back and hit my head on the floor. "Ouch," I groan.

King leans back and slips his hand behind my head.

"You OK?"

"Yeah. I think I had too much to drink." I stay lying flat against the floor, looking up at him.

"No way," he says, coming down to lie beside me. "You're a tough woman. A country girl. You can take it."

"Sure."

We lie there for a second and stare at the ceiling. Being next to him feels so natural. Like something I've been doing all my life.

"So how does a country girl like you end up in LA?" King asks. "Running away from a dark past?"

"No. Not at all. I'm from a small town. My parents were great. Loving. They're still together," I say. "High school sweethearts."

"Really? How do they feel about you being an actress on 'the second highest-rated show on television'?" he mocks my voice and I slap his leg.

"Don't make fun of me!" I protest.

"Come on, you know you like saying that: 'the second highest-rated show on television'!"

"It's true," I say laughing. "Anyway, they're supportive . . . as much as they can be . . . but this whole Hollywood thing just isn't for them. My father's a retired high school principal and my mother's an English teacher. I think they wanted me to do the same thing. Stay home in Tupelo and marry some frat boy from Ole Miss. Give them some grandbabies. Buy a house right down the street from them. And I'm an only child, so when I left . . . it kind of broke my daddy's heart."

"They must be happy about your success now, though," King tries.

"A little. Dad's never been here to see me. Mom came once," I say. "They don't exactly like my choice of a mate."

"Alex?"

"My mother refuses to say his name."

"Why?"

"It's a long story. Not really trying to talk about that right now."

"So what do you want to talk about?" he asks, turning on his side to look at me.

"I don't know."

"What about what happened on set today? You giving me all that rhythm . . . all 'Dr. Thibodaux . . .' " He tries to dupli- cate my voice, but he sounds more like a transvestite Playboy bunny.

"Please, that was not rhythm," I say, sitting back up. "I was working. Getting in character, you know? Diamond was sup- posed to flirt with her new doctor."

"No, that was more than acting. You were trying to get a brother worked up."

"Worked up? Please! Don't flatter yourself. I already told you that we're just going to be friends. Right?" I say, sipping the last little bit of vodka from my glass. "What you saw on set today was strictly professional."

"Well, if that was professional, what's this?"

King and I look out over our mess. The empty vodka bot- tle is tipped on its side. My purse and car keys are in the cor- ner with my shoes. My legs are wide apart and one is hanging over his.

"This is," I start, but then I forget to care. "Oh, fuck it." I throw my glass down and jump on King, kissing him wildly like I have every night in my dreams since that day at the green wreck. I sit in his lap and wrap my legs around his waist. I don't wait for him to move his hands. I grab them and put them on my breasts. We rock back and forth and soon my dress is up around my hips. I feel his jeans tighten. He slides a finger into my thong. We roll over and then he's on top of me.

"You sure you want this?" he asks, looking into my eyes.

I don't answer, because I don't know. I let the alcohol inside of me pull off his belt. Unbuckle his pants.

When the sun comes up and I can see the palm trees poking up like arrows into the sky outside the window beside the hotel room bed, I realize I haven't slept at all. I've lain in the bed beside King with my eyes closed and my body so relaxed I feel like I'm on a cloud, but I haven't slept at all. And it's not because I'm angry or upset about what's happened. That's not it at all. I just wonder why. Why now? Why King? I turn over and look at him sleeping. He looks just like the boy who had every teenage girl in the country dreaming of him.

I slip out the bed and go over to the window. Open the curtains some more so I can see the city waking with me.

"Bright lights," King growls, covering his eyes.

"Oh, I'm sorry," I say. "I was just trying to get a look outside. I'm usually up by now."

"It's fine," King says. "Just give a brother a minute to adjust. It was a late night." He laughs and rubs his eyes. Looks up at me. "You OK? Did you sleep OK?"

"Not really. I guess I was just thinking."

"Oh no. Don't tell me you regret—"

"No, that's not it. You were great. I'm just . . . well, I don't do this kind of thing."

"I understand. What do you think Alex is going to say?"

"Alex?" I laugh. "He won't even notice I'm gone."

"What do you mean?"

"Let's just say we have an arrangement," I say. "And by

arrangement, I mean he basically lives with his ex-wife. Or wherever he decides to rest his head at night. And that's never with me."

"You serious? He doesn't sleep with you?"

"He comes home a little during the week. But never stays at night. I almost never see him on weekends." I look out over the palm trees, into the smog.

"I'm sorry to hear that. I mean, I'll be honest, I knew there was trouble, but I didn't know it was that bad."

"Bad is subjective, isn't it?" I ask. "I get what I want. He gets what he wants."

"But can't you both get those things apart? Why stay married if you're not even sleeping with the guy?"

"Alex has done a lot for me."

"And you've done a lot for him."

"Yeah." I pick up my dress.

"Don't fluff that off. You can do everything you've done with Alex on your own. Don't you believe that?"

"If only it was that simple." I step into my dress and slide it up over my hips.

"Maybe it is," King says. "Maybe I can make it that simple." He climbs out the bed and walks over to me, stopping me from pulling the dress over my breasts. He kisses one of my nipples and looks into my eyes. "I told you I'm producing my own show. I'm going to shop it to some networks. You can work with me."

"You've already done enough," I say. "Let's not make any more promises we can't keep." I kiss him. "Scout's honor?"

"But, Silver!" He follows me to the door. "Silver!"

I refuse to let King walk me down to the lobby. I'm sure some paparazzi are still hiding out in the hotel and while they are sure to kick into a frenzy seeing both of us together, seeing just me could only lead to speculation and I could always pin it on the party.

When I get to the lobby, my dark shades hanging over my eyes, I offer the concierge my ticket and turn to see Melanie asleep on one of the couches.

"Melanie?" I call, walking over to her. I nudge her shoulder and she wrestles awake.

"Oh no . . . I fell asleep!" She looks around startled.

"What are you doing here?"

"I was waiting for you. I've been calling you all night." She gets up from the couch and makeup is smeared over the side of her face. "When I was about to leave, I checked with the valet to make sure your car had left and they said you hadn't. I wanted to find you. To make sure everything is OK." She looks unreasonably frazzled. Upset. Her eyes are red and puffy.

"Melanie, I'm a grown woman," I start. "I can take care of myself."

"But you told me I should always be available to you," she whines.

"Yes. I did, but that's when I call you," I say. "You don't have to avail yourself to me day and night. I know you're trying to prove yourself. I understand that, but all this isn't necessary."

"Mrs. Stone, your car's out front," the concierge calls.

"I understand," Melanie answers me. "But I was just trying to really connect with you. Let you know how much I want this job. What I'm willing to sacrifice to be here. To get to where you are. I have so many dreams. I just need someone to give me a chance. I can't go back—I just can't."

"Look, you're fine. How about this: we can have drinks sometime—at my house—private drinks. Just you and me," I say and I immediately see her face brighten. "You can tell me all about your dreams and what you want to do. How does that sound?"

"Wonderful. That's just wonderful. Thank you so much, Silver. You won't regret it," she says. "When?"

"When?"

"When can we do it?" There's a push in her voice, but I'm cool.

"I'll get back to you, kid." I wink at her before turning to walk out. "I'll see you back at the studio."

King and I are like kids on the set the next few days. I get the fever everyone else had when he started on the show and now I can't wait to get to the studio each morning. I walk in the door peeking around to see where he's at and what he's doing. My life, the show, everything seems so much brighter with him around. It's like someone went and opened a window just to let the fresh air in. He's a breeze and I'm a wish in a field of wild daisies floating away in him. I laugh at how corny that sounds but it's how I feel.

I try to hide everything, though. I keep my schedule the same. Run in the mornings. Meet Melanie at my car. Go through my meetings with the team, and then Manuel and the writers, but all I can think about all day is when it'll be time to tape and Diamond gets to connect with her love interest: Dr. Thibodaux.

And while King also tries to keep his distance, the scenes he writes get more racy with each take: Dr. Thibodaux and Diamond make out in a night club, join the mile-high club, canoodle in the pastor's quarters at Jackson Ridge Baptist. In any other place in the world, this would all seem like too much, but on our show, it's all possible in one week of taping. And everyone at the station eats it up. Alex, even. He stalks the set. Watches me. Sometimes I think he sees, but then he hears the crowd and grins with each invisible pat on his shoulder.

Everyone comes to the tapings each day and seems to do more watching than working. The cameramen stand with their mouths open. The women grin and moan. King and I put on so hard before everyone, we don't even need to sneak away to be with each other after the tapings. Our Hollywood affair is out in the open, but we're playing Diamond and Dr. Thibodaux in Jackson Ridge.

★ ★ ★

"That's some chemistry between you two," Oscar says, un-zipping my church make out dress in the dressing room after we tape the final show for the week. "Looks a whole lot like the real thing, if you ask me. But I know it's just acting."

"Well, it's a good thing no one asked you, then," I respond playfully.

"But Oscar is on to something, Silver," Pria says. "I was looking at the blogs this morning. Almost everyone says some-thing about you and King being lovers. They say that's why your chemistry is so good."

"Oh, they'll say anything. They also said I should be thrown off a cliff. And look at us now. Weren't we number one this week?"

"We sure were," JimBo says high-fiving me. "The first time ever." He pauses. "But I do think half those people tuned in to see if the rumors are true."

"So?" Pria pushes.

"So what?"

"Are they?" Oscar asks.

Everyone looks at me. Melanie twists her body around from something she's working on at my laptop to hear my re-sponse.

"Look, guys, I know I've been a little more lackadaisical around here lately and all, but there's no way I'm about to start allowing you all to grill me about my personal life," I say and they sigh collectively. "And if I did allow it, I'd tell you that there's no way I'm having an affair with any King Colson. I'm a married woman and he's my co-star. That's it."

Oh! Right there, King! Yes! Put it right there! Fuck yes! That feels good! Keep going! Oh my God! This is amazing!
I probably never should've told King that Alex hardly ever stays home at night and never comes home on the weekend.

As soon as I get in from doing my laps in the pool, I hear a pebble at my window. I go to see what the noise is and there is King standing outside wearing his medical jacket and spectacles. No shirt. Shorts and cowboy boots.

"I thought you might want to spend time with your doctor," he says.

"Are you crazy?" I answer, looking around the side of the ranch to make sure no one is out there. "If Alex catches you out here, *you're* going to need a doctor. And how did you get back here anyway?" I help pull him into the window.

"Girl, I'm from Philly. I have ways."

I lock the bedroom door.

We pretend to talk for a few seconds, but quickly the heat we've been building up all week on set turns into a full medical examination and before I know it, he is in my bed, and I am calling his name. Our lovemaking is quick and fierce. Has the kind of energy to it that only two of the wrong people having sex in the wrong place can gather. When he is inside me, I feel like the walls of my bedroom open up and fall on their sides. Like I am out in the world and just free. Not in a cage. I scream so loudly I know Carmen can hear me in the next room, but I don't care. King turns up the television, puts his finger in my mouth like a lollipop. We rock until I feel like I've drifted out into space and there are just stars all around me. We moan together, into each other, and collapse into the bed.

"What time is it?" he asks with his voice full of fog.

I look at the clock.

"A little after nine," I say.

"What? It's that early?"

"Afraid so, Doctor."

We laugh. It feels like it's after three A.M.

"Dang, woman, you stole my thunder," he says.

"Is that all?" I turn over to King.

"What do you mean?"

"Am I only stealing your thunder? I mean, I know this is probably just some random sexual affair. I'm obviously in need of sex, and well . . . *you're you.*"

"I'm what?"

"Mr. Colson. Teen Heartthrob."

"I'm a grown man. I outgrew all of that a long time ago," he says and I can see sincerity in his eyes.

"So, what is it?"

"It's definitely more than just sex. I really like you," King says. "Of course, this isn't exactly how I intended on making my big comeback to Hollywood." He looks around the room. "You know, me sleeping with the producer's wife . . . in his bed; but that's life. I'm willing to handle whatever comes my way."

"Handle?"

"Yes. What we talked about at the hotel."

"About me leaving Alex?" I say and suddenly I can smell Alex.

"Sure. If things go that way with us. Yes, I want you to leave him."

"I couldn't do that." I ease over in the bed.

"Yes, you could, Silver. Don't tell me you're still letting him get to you. His little games. You don't need him. You're a star without him."

"But we've built so much together," I say, getting out of the bed. "I can't just leave him. He was the only person who gave me a shot. He's not perfect. But he believed in me. I can't leave."

"Leave what? Leave who? Where's he right now?"

"You don't understand, King. Alex isn't what you think he is. He won't just let me go. Let us leave the show and start one." I slide on my robe and start going around the bedroom fixing things to calm myself. I move everything back into its place.

"You're afraid of him," King says.

"I think you should go." I turn off the television.

"Really? So that's it?" King gets out the bed and reaches for me, but I keep walking and picking up pillows.

"I didn't say that was it. I just need to be alone. That's all. I just need to think. This is all happening way too fast for me."

King stops and looks at me. He starts gathering his things.

"I thought you had changed. But you're still caught up in this Hollywood bullshit," he says. "You've let this place take enough from you. Don't let it take me, too."

"If you really understood, you wouldn't let that happen anyway."

I let King out the window and unlock the bedroom door.

That night in bed, I pray for a miracle. And not for anything specific. Just something. Because nothing is making sense to me anymore. My whole world that I used to be able to sum up in tight little sayings that kept me closed off from feeling was touching and warming something so cold within me. For so long I was sure there was no love anywhere for me. I'd thought I'd left it somewhere in a script and decided that the only love I could really have was Diamond. But she can't keep me from being alone. From feeling alone. She's not even real. And any dream I have of her is just fantasy. She can't look me in my eyes like King. She can't hold me. She can't go home for me. Tell my mother I haven't forgotten who I am. That I'm still alive. That I still have a heartbeat.

I hear the bedroom door open and feel Alex come into the room. I don't turn toward him. I figure he's just on one of his missions to get a tie or a pair of shoes. He'll be in and out. Back to where he really wants to be.

"You asleep, baby?" he calls.

I don't move.

He climbs into the bed and I almost feel ill. I slide closer to the open window.

"Baby," he reaches to me. Presses his palm into my back. "Wake up."

I pretend a groan. Breath deeply so he can see that I'm asleep.

He slides his hands into my panties and down my backside.

"I was just thinking about you. Wanted to come home and make you feel really good," he says. He slides his fingers between my thighs.

"Yeah, there it is," he says, rubbing me. "There's my girl."

I start crying and feel the tears rolling across my face and onto the pillow.

"Bend your bottom back toward daddy. Come on," he says.

I don't know what else to do, so I go to bend, but then a breeze just tunnels into the window. It whips up into my face and sends chills over my shoulders. I lock my legs. Tighten my middle.

"What? What's that?" Alex says after his hand is quickly pushed away from me. "What are you doing, Silver?"

"You're not going to have sex with me," I say without moving, "so stop playing."

"Sex? Come on, girl. You know the deal." He tries to push his hand back into me, but I lock my thighs tight. I jump up and turn to him.

"No! If you're not sleeping in this bed, you can't do this to me. I can't keep letting you do this to me," I say.

"Do what?"

"We haven't had sex in years, Alex. That's what."

He jumps out the bed.

"Oh, fuck this," he says. "I don't need this shit."

"Yeah, I figured as much."

"What the hell is with you? I was just trying to help you out," he says. "Fine, suit yourself. I'm out."

Act III

The Black and Bourgeois headlines the fall television show sweeps as the undisputed number-one hit. Number one! A black show! And it's not a fluke. Not a one-day maybe. We're on the air every night and each time our audience grows. It's what the show's PR team calls "viral." Everyone's talking about it, and everyone wants to know what's happening on Jackson Ridge. What will happen with Diamond and Dr. Thibodaux. They say it's the biggest love affair on soap television since Luke and Laura. Even as the other soaps were cut from the day lineups, we were kept on and run twice in the evening on cable television.

None of us expected the romance to be so big. So enormous that it took over and actually became an entity all its own. There are mugs and T-shirts. A "Diamond and Dr. T" Web site. A fan club. A viewers' prediction site where fans write clairvoyant blogs predicting what Diamond and Dr. Thibodaux's children will look like. It's all so much the writers have to struggle to keep up with the audience's whims.

Then the blogs and paparazzi turn to King and me. Pictures of us just having lunch are sold to magazines around the world. To keep things even more quiet between us, we end up doing more texting than talking and even our late-night rendezvous in my bedroom are cut when a crazy fan tries to climb in my window one night.

Alex puts bars up.

Next, he takes away the Porsche and gets me a limousine driver who reports only to him.

He says it's all for my protection, but I know he's seeing what the world is talking about. And no matter how much distance there is between me and King, we all know our connection is obvious. Alex is just sitting back and watching. Waiting.

The slug line for the last shot of the day calls for Dr. Thibodaux and Diamond to walk into a jewelry store to pick up Dr. Thibodaux's broken watch, but he surprises Diamond with an engagement ring he's already purchased.

Dr. Thibodaux is to lead me into the store. The jeweler comes out from behind the counter and hands him a ring, saying, "I believe this is it." Diamond is surprised as Dr. Thibodaux gets down on one knee and pops the question.

Lines memorized, standing outside the makeshift door to the jewelry shop, I stand hand in hand with King waiting for Manuel to yell, "Action."

"You ready for this, sweetheart?" King jokes as we wait.

"Stop playing!" I pinch his arm. "Focus. Connect with your character."

"Oh, I'm not playing. I've been for real the whole time," King says, looking into my eyes.

Every night when we text, when we can steal one moment away, he talks about his plan. About taking me away from Alex and the show. Building our own empire. Marrying me. I grin and put him off each time, but I want to believe him so badly now. Believe his plan could work. That we could be together and have it all. But what I see in Alex's eyes when he looks at me scares me. And I'm not afraid for me anymore. I'm afraid for King.

"Places!" Manuel yells and everyone rushes off the set, leaving King and me there alone.

Melanie is standing beside one of the cameras holding my script. She's dressed in her normal all black.

"And—" Manuel starts, but stops. "Wait a minute! Where's my jeweler? Hello people?" he shouts.

Everyone looks around. King tickles my waist and we laugh, but then straighten up when I see Melanie watching. She always seems so interested in what's going on between us.

Leeda runs in and whispers in Manuel's ear.

"What's going on?" King asks.

"I don't know." I look to Melanie because she's close enough to maybe hear what's happening, but she only shrugs.

"You've got to be kidding me. Left? Emergency? I don't care about her kid!" Manuel throws his clipboard to the floor. "Look, I need someone to be on set and ready to play the jeweler in like thirty seconds. I have a scene to shoot, people. Where are my extras?"

Chewing hard on the pen top in her mouth, Leeda looks around the set like it's a casting call. She sizes up the fat guy holding the camera, the intern in jeans and flip-flops, and then Melanie standing beside the camera in all black.

She whispers to Manuel and without even looking, he raises his hand in approval.

"You"—Leeda points to Melanie—"come with me!"

Melanie's face lights up so quickly, her brown cheeks burn red. She looks at me and then back at Leeda, who's already dragging her away by the wrist.

The Black and Bourgeois
"The Engagement: Dr. T and Diamond"
(EPISODE: 02101)

Scene 9

INT: JACKSON RIDGE JEWELRY SHOP - DAY

DR. THIBODAUX and DIAMOND enter the shop and are
greeted by the JEWELER.

DR. THIBODAUX
Yeah, this is the shop where I left my watch. Come on in. It'll
only take a minute.

DIAMOND
Sure, honey. We just have to make sure we get to the airport on
time. That flight to Paris waits for no one.

DR. THIBODAUX
It'll be fast. I promise.

(To JEWELER)
Excuse me, Miss. I think I left something here the other day.

When we enter the set, Melanie is standing at the counter
with her cat eyes shaking in fear. I try to get her attention, help
her snap out of it, but it's like she can't even see me. She's looking at me and King, but she's nowhere near us. She's someplace
else. And when she's supposed to follow Dr. Thibodaux's line
with, "I believe this is it," she's silent for so long, I'm sure she's
forgotten how to speak. She flashes a crooked and fearful smile
at us. And just when I feel like Manuel is about to call "cut,"
she starts to speak.

"I be—" She stops. Starts: "I be— be— be—." Stops again. Tries
to readjust her tongue, but it gets worse. "I be— be—li— be—lieve
th— th— th—"

I'm lowering my head with each syllable, anticipating its
close. I see King doing the same.

"I be— believe th—this."

Every bit of color is gone from Melanie's face. She looks
like she's dying or dead. She starts again.

"I be—" She looks so tired.

I realize I'm staring at her tongue with everyone else. Awaiting the words. Not yet wishing and hoping, but now just anxious.

"What the hell?" I hear Manuel.

Melanie stops and tries to catch her breath.

"Cut! Cut!" I yell and everyone looks from Melanie to me.

"Cut? What do you mean 'cut,' Silver? I call 'cut'!" Manuel barks. "And what's up with this stuttering? And who let her—"

Leeda goes back to chewing her pen top and backs up behind Manuel's seat.

"Look, I'm tired, Manuel. I need to get home. I'm sick," I say, trying to get his attention, but he's still looking at Melanie really crazy. "I have cramps!"

"Cramps?"

"Yes! And I was up all night and I had Melanie up helping me. I'm sure she's just tired, too. Aren't you, Melanie?"

Melanie nods, though it's a lie.

"I need to get home. And back in bed. Could we reshoot the scene with Melanie just handing the ring to King?"

"But the script says—" Manuel says.

"Manuel, I know what the script says, but I'm not feeling well. Like I said, I need to get home and I've had my assistant up all night and I know she's tired. Now, if you have a problem with that, you can speak to the producer . . . or maybe the union. You pick."

Unsurprisingly, everyone steers clear of Melanie once we finish reshooting the scene. The other assistants turn their backs to her like she's got the plague, and she follows me to the dressing room, head low.

"Hey, you guys, give us a second," I say to the team, before pulling Melanie into the room. It still stinks of the dozens of roses Alex had delivered after our fight.

Oscar rolls his eyes and stammers off. His position on Melanie hasn't changed. He thinks she's completely insane, but what I've seen from her over the months she's been working for me is someone who's so dedicated to the job, her passion can be off-putting. I know for a fact that she sleeps in her car sometimes outside the studio. Memorizes every one of my lines. And I've never once called her and not gotten an answer. Better than that, I can't ever remember seeing her talk to Alex. Not even once. And no assistant has ever worked for me this long without doing that.

I pull her to the vanity and sit her down. I know the scene on the set had to break her. It was a big chance and she just blew it. It would take a lot for Leeda to pluck her from the crowd again. Well, Leeda wouldn't do it again.

"You always ask me this question, and now I get to ask you. You OK?" I ask Melanie.

She looks up at me and I see so much pain and humiliation in her eyes.

"I messed up. I lost my shot."

"What happened? I've never heard you stutter before."

"I used to when I was a kid. But I got help and it went away. I thought it was gone . . . but with the cameras . . . and everyone looking at me . . . I was so nervous." She starts crying and sinks her face into her lap.

"We all get nervous sometimes," I offer. "Even me."

"No way," she says, peeking up. "You're never nervous."

"Nonsense! You know, every day when I tape my first scene, I still feel butterflies in my stomach."

"Really? You?"

"Sure I do. But I get over them. And you will, too. You just have to stay dedicated. Take some classes. Put yourself out there."

"You think Manuel will ever give me another shot?" she asks tearfully.

"I'll talk to him," I answer. "And when you're ready, we'll see."

"OK." She wipes her tears and smiles again. "Thank you,

L.A. CONFIDENTIAL   307

Silver. For talking to me. It really means a lot. You're like my
big sister. I love you."

"Oh," I say, but I'm not sure what else I can add. "I—"

"No," Melanie stops me. "You don't have to answer. I
know you don't love me. It's fine. I just wanted you to know
how I feel."

"Well, that's great—"

"You ready?" I hear King call from the door of the dressing
room.

"No," I say. "I still need to change out these clothes. We
were just finishing."

"Oh," King says, realizing that I'm talking to Melanie. "You
all right?" he asks her.

"Yes."

"Don't trip. It happens to the best of us," he says. "Hey, Silver, I'll meet you at your car."

"Fine," I answer. I walk to the mirror to get out my clothes
when King leaves.

"Where are you two going?" Melanie asks with her voice
so clear it's hard to know she was just crying like a baby.

"We're not going anywhere," I lie. "Just dropping him off. I
think his car is in the shop."

"I could give him a ride!"

"No, you go on home and get some rest," I say. "After the
day you've had, a few extra hours in bed are in order."

I have to look away from Melanie so she'll know the conversation is over. It's a trick I figured out with her a few weeks
ago. I pull my shirt off and head to the shower with her standing like a stone behind me.

At some point the night before, via text, King had devised
this ridiculous plot to get us together alone at the Santa Monica Pier. He'd said he wanted to ride the ferris wheel with me
and kiss me on top of the world. It was a simple request for any

two people other than us, but getting away from everyone was impossible and being somewhere in public was so risky. But more and more, I was willing to take risks. One being that I'd have to lie to my driver and say I wanted to drive to Santa Monica to get dinner at a special vegan spot on the pier. The other was that King had to go with me to make sure nothing happened to me. While I was sure the driver would report everything we did back to Alex, I was getting sick of caring. Sick of hiding. I couldn't let my world shrink back down to what it was before. I wouldn't go back into the cage.

I cover my head with a red scarf and King puts on a baseball cap and sunglasses so we can actually make it to the ferris wheel without any cameras snapping at us. The funny thing is that as famous as we are, when we cover our heads, we just look like two black people and most folks walk right past us.

Once we make it into a little blue cart and it rides the loop to the top of the ferris wheel, King and I remove our disguises. The sun is going down and his hand is on my thigh. My head is resting on his shoulder. We look out over the Pacific for what feels like forever. We don't talk in words for a long time. There's nothing to say. Our time together has been in the clouds.

King squeezes my thigh. Kisses my forehead. He'd given the guys working the machine $500 to let us float for a little while.

I look up at him. Trace the bone of his jaw, to his lips, over his nose, and up to his eyes. He's looking ahead, out over the water, but I can still see the brownest part of his eye. In there, I see myself looking at him, at myself. I feel something flicker in my gut, something like a moth brushing against my ankle or a daisy against my cheek and then I just know something. I just know.

"I love you," I say as King is saying something else and then

I realize that right at that moment he'd just said the same thing.

He looks down at me.

"I love you, baby," he repeats. "And, you know, I think I brought you here to tell you that."

The ferris wheel sits there until the sun goes down and we're so chilly we have to hold on to each other to make heat.

King and I walk along the beach. The crowd has thinned, but a few couples, teenagers, and some nighttime joggers straggle along the strand. The pier is lit up with so many colorful lights it hardly seems like a weeknight. The blue cart is back at the top of the ferris wheel with another couple hugging inside.

"What do you think is going to happen now?"

"Everything," King says. "I'm getting myself together. Ready to make a move."

"You always make it sound so simple." I laugh. "Like we can just change our lives."

"Why can't we?"

"We're the stars of the number-one show in America. That's why," I say. "And no matter how much I hate to admit it, I'm still a married woman."

King tugs my hand playfully and pulls me closer to him.

"And that's the first thing we're going to change."

"It's not that simple. You know that."

"The moment you leave him, I'm going to marry you."

I look at him.

"He won't just let me go. He'll take everything."

"Then you don't need anything." King pulls me into his arms. "I'm all you need."

"What if I don't have what it takes to do this?"

"I have enough for the both of us," King says so softly I begin to cry.

King kisses my tears and makes a loud farting sound on my cheek.

"What was that?" I laugh.

He grabs my hand and pulls me toward the boardwalk.

"Where are we going?"

"Shhh," King says as I protest his arm pulling me under the dark planks of wood. We tiptoe over damp sand. I watch my feet, afraid I'm going to step on a bottle or one of the teenagers we saw disappearing under the boardwalk before sunset.

"Where are we going?" I repeat, bending down behind King so my forehead doesn't catch one of the beams from the boardwalk.

"Shhhh," King warns again.

I laugh and grimace at the same time, afraid and excited about something I don't know.

We go along a few more feet and King stops. He pulls off his shirt and puts it on a dry patch of sand.

"What's this?"

"Just sit down," King instructs.

It's so dark, but I can see the lights from the pier. I can hear the waves from the ocean.

I sit on the shirt and King kneels in front of me.

"I love you, Mildred Gibson," he says, looking at me like we're teenagers under the boardwalk for the first time.

I giggle and pluck his shoulder.

"You think you need to say you love me to get me to make out with you under this boardwalk?"

"Oh, we're doing more than making out," King says with a serious, yet comical tone. "But I did want to make sure you knew that. That you understood that."

"Understood what?"

"That you're my greatest love," he says. "My great love."

King comes in to kiss me and I fall back into the sand with him over me.

"I love you, King Colson," I whisper in his ear.

King eases my shirt up over my head and caresses my breasts with his tongue. He kisses my nipples and I can feel him pulsating as his hips move in small circles between my thighs.

I slide my hands around to the front of his belt and try to open his buckle but I can't.

He comes up suddenly and fastens his eyes on mine as he undoes the buckle slowly.

I feel dizzy and faint. Intoxicated.

He eases his pants down and then his boxers. He comes back down to me erect and doesn't fuss to find his position. He's just there.

He bites my neck. Hard. Passionately.

I close my eyes and we escape everything together beneath the boardwalk.

The driver doesn't say anything to us when we get back to the car. We drop King at the studio and I ask the driver to go around the city for a while. I don't want to go home. I don't want the night to end.

We drive up Hollywood Boulevard and meander through the twists and turns along the hills to my home. I feel like I'm nowhere. Like I'm attached to nothing. And then I don't care about this place. These things. The car. The Hill. The Boulevard. What does any of it matter if I can't be with King?

Somehow, I stumble into the house. But I don't make it to the bedroom. I don't think I want to be there anymore. I lay out on the couch. Rock myself to sleep as I watch the shadows from the moonlight outside dance on the walls around me.

In my dreams, I hear laughing. I open my eyes and Alex is standing over me dressed in a party suit that's wrinkled from the clubs and stained with rose coloring along the collar. He looks like a demon. Like the devil over me. I don't know if I'm still asleep. I'm in a nightmare.

"You were smiling," he slurs. "What the fuck were you smiling about in your sleep?"

"Nothing," I manage, pushing up on my elbows to get from under him, but I can't and then I know I'm awake. I look around the living room. It's dark, but I can tell the sun is coming up outside.

"Nothing, my ass!" Alex laughs and stumbles. I smell weed all over him. He pulls off his jacket and drops it. "Staying out late . . . Taking niggas to Santa Monica . . . Nothing, my fucking black ass."

"Alex, stop it," I say. "You're fucked up."

"Yeah, I'm fucked up. But I ain't blind." He gets down on his knees in front of the couch. His body sways with the alcohol inside him. "I own these streets. Don't shit happen in LA without me knowing. You think I don't know? You think I'm stupid?" He pushes his face to mine and eyeballs me with a charge.

I just sit there.

"So the driver told you. That's not exactly detective work," I say.

He falls back and sits on his heels.

"You fucking him? You fucking King?"

"Do you care?"

"Don't do that, Silver. You tell me. That's the arrangement. You know it. Are you fucking him?"

"You come in here smelling of every whore you've fucked in LA and have the nerve to accuse me of something?" I say and my voice is a stabbing whisper. "What about Antoinette? Have you fucked Antoinette lately?"

"I'll take everything you have if you try to leave me," King says, trying to grab for my face. "I won't leave you with anything. You won't know who you are, bitch. And I'll kill that nigga. I swear to God, I'll kill that nigga!"

Alex mushes me back into the couch so hard I bounce

back. He wrestles me to the floor and gets his hands around my neck.

"You won't leave me," he says. "I won't let you."

"No!" I try, but I feel myself getting weak. The room is spinning.

"What!" Carmen hollers, jumping on Alex's back. She pulls him off me and I crawl away, gagging for air.

Alex falls, laughing hysterically.

"Fucking women," he says.

"You OK, Mrs. Silver?" Carmen asks, coming to me.

I get up and then I feel nauseous. Like everything in my stomach is coming out of me.

I stagger across the floor with my hand over my stomach. I feel sick.

"You OK?" Carmen reaches out.

I run to the bathroom and vomit pink all over the floor.

To celebrate *The Black and Bourgeois*'s ascension to number one, the station organized an unprecedented gala for the cast and crew in the grand ballroom at Hollywood and Highland beside Grauman's Chinese Theatre, where the Academy usually hosts the post-Oscar parties. The invitations came to the set covered in Swarovski crystals. There was to be a full sit-down dinner, a big band featuring a cabaret lineup. Jaime Foxx was hosting. And I was getting a special presentation from the station for my portrayal as Diamond. Anyone who has a name in Hollywood was invited. It was all everyone was talking about. And Oscar was the loudest. Getting my dress ready had become his mission in life.

"Mamacita, I don't know why you're getting so big," he says, standing beside me in my bedroom after pulling his final pick for me up over my waist the night of the gala. It's an emerald green Balenciaga that has so much fabric flowing behind me, he adds weights to the train to keep it down. But it's lovely and it makes me feel so special, I almost forget that Alex is in the other room waiting to take me to the ball. "You off your diet?" Oscar pushes, tapping my round belly.

"No. Just not working out as much," I lie, but I know that's not the reason for the little swelling in my stomach. "Does the dress look too tight?"

"No, it looks amazing," he says, looking as if he's going to cry.

JimBo jumps past him.

"Don't get all teary eyed. You'll make her cry, too. Ruin my masterpiece!" JimBo produces a brush and taps at my forehead. They're both dressed in tuxedos and ready to go to the gala. JimBo, of course, has managed to find the perfect matching dinky cowboy hat.

"I know," Oscar says, sniffling. "It's just that our girl has worked so hard for this. You know?"

"Oh, stop it." Pria hands Oscar a towel. "You'd think we were going to the prom."

"Wait!" Oscar stops pouting and tosses the towel back to Pria. "I almost forget my last touch."

"What is it?" I ask.

Oscar pulls a pair of fine satin white gloves from his bag like they're angel wings.

"You're not classy without gloves, Mrs. Stone," he says, bowing with the gloves held out over his head.

"You're a trip," I say, looking at all of them, standing around me in my bedroom. "All of you. Thanks."

There's a knock at the door. Alex calls me, saying he's ready to go.

"Well, that's all. Guess we'll see you at the gala," Oscar says and then whispers in my ear, "You sure you don't want to ride with us?" He looks at the door cautiously.

"That'll just bring too much attention," I say low. "Don't worry about me. I can handle it."

Oscar kisses me on the cheek.

"OK, kid."

They start getting their things together as I slip on the gloves.

"Wait," I say. "Has anyone seen my cell phone?" I look around the bedroom. I hadn't seen it in hours.

"No," they answer one by one, looking around, too.

"Where is it?" I pick up my purse.

Alex knocks again.

"Guess I'll find it when I get back."

We head to the door.

"Hey, where's Melanie?" Pria asks.

"She couldn't come tonight," I answer. "She said she wasn't feeling well."

"Thank God," Oscar says. "I didn't feel like dealing with crazy eyes anyway."

After that night in the living room with the dark shadows, Alex and I stop pretending to get along when we are alone. We don't say a word to one another unless someone else is around. One hint of trouble between us and it'll get right to the press. We agree without speaking to not let things get that far. The rumored affair between me and King is common Hollywood chatter. Everyone thinks it's cute but a real scandal could ruin us. Still, I'm not sure how much longer I can hold on. Pretend. We drive to the gala in silence. I sit in the passenger side of the black Lamborghini wishing I'd never even met Alex. I'm hardly able to look at him without feeling nauseous.

But by the time we make it to Hollywood and up the red carpet, my hand is in his and we're smiling for pictures like everything is OK. I see couple after couple around us doing the same and wonder just how many are like us. Actors in a real life horror flick.

"Alex, you look so young," one reporter calls out to get Alex's attention. "What's your secret?"

Alex smiles his smile and laughs, linking his arms around my waist for the photographer.

"What? Are you joking, man?" he says. "Look at my wife. This is my fountain of youth."

Inside the ballroom, there are so many people everywhere, I can hardly find a face I know or want to see. Everyone comes to me and Alex with well wishes. I greet and grin, but inside I'm dying. Fighting not to cave in.

The crew is sitting at tables toward the back, behind sponsors and other station big shots. I see Pria and JimBo near the bar. Oscar at a table with his new boyfriend.

Alex pulls me to the front toward our table when the lights go dim.

We sit with some of the other station producers and their wives. The wives tell me that they've got bets on Dr. Thibodaux and Diamond's wedding.

"A Christmas wedding," one jokes, winking at me for a clue.

I tell her I don't know. We don't write that far ahead.

Soon the waiters come out to serve our food.

Jamie Foxx does some impersonations of people on the show. Everyone laughs. I try to keep up. Play along. But I keep looking around to see if I can find King. I look at the table behind us where he should be sitting, but he's not there.

Alex whispers, "You think your little boyfriend will show up?"

"Oh, please," I say. "Not tonight. Let's just get through this."

Jamie does a bit about Alicia being the bad girl of the show. She surprises him by walking onstage in a red gown as he's impersonating her. They do a one-two punch routine.

The band starts again, and after Alex and the other producers stand to be recognized, a montage of my scenes as Diamond rolls on a huge screen that comes down from the ceiling. From eight years ago to present, I see Diamond change. Hair. Clothes. Makeup. Everything changes every year. Loves. Likes. Fights.

Everything. But what remains the same is this look in her eyes. This anger. A coldness. A fear from inside I know too well, because that's the only part that's not an act. That's the part that comes from me. I can hardly look at those eyes on the screen without wanting to disappear, but then I can't hardly look away.

Then there's Dr. Thibodaux in his office. Diamond walking in for her first meeting and asking for Valium or Prozac. He says she's broken and he can fix her heart. She laughs. But the cage in her eyes melts away.

The crowd hoots and then laughs at us, at the drama of the swift romance between the doctor and the diva.

I feel Alex straighten in his seat.

Last is the scene where Dr. Thibodaux proposes to Diamond in the jewelry store. Melanie hands him the ring and he gets down on one knee.

Everyone gushes. The woman next to me grabs my hand and she's shaking like it's real.

"Finally a Love for Diamond" appears on the screen as Diamond and Dr. Thibodaux kiss. The camera comes in close on Diamond's eyes and I see a change. A light. I know that's what's happened to me.

The crowd claps and from the side of the stage, out walks King in a white tuxedo. He looks amazing, shines so brightly, almost like an angel in a dream and I feel him glowing in my eyes. Everyone stands and cheers.

Alex looks annoyed, like there's fire in his eyes, but he smiles, too, when one of the other producers at the table clearly notices his discomfort.

"When I came on the show, I wasn't sure what to expect. Most shows have one diva, and everyone in Hollywood knows that Silver Stone is the diva of *The Black and Bourgeois*," King says into the microphone as we all sit and quiet down. "I must admit, though, I was pleasantly surprised by how far the rumor is from the truth. Silver is no diva. Yes, she's a star. Yes, she's demanding. But no heart could be more humble and delicate than hers. Over just a few months, she's taught me so much about sacrifice. And sticking it out. Following your map and not letting anything get in your way." King looks into the camera projecting his image on the big screen on the stage behind him. It looks like he's looking right at me. "And when you do, not being afraid to step out on faith. To take risks. To do it even when you're not sure you have what it takes. Ladies and Gentlemen, esteemed guests, I ask you all to get out of your chairs and make some noise as we recognize the incomparable work and tireless efforts of my costar, and great love, our star, Silver Stone."

The crowd roars and everyone stands up around me. I'm so full I can hardly make it to the stage. Alex, smiling like a lucky man, takes my hand and leads me through the room to the stage, tugging me so hard I'm nearly falling, but still smiling the whole way.

I'd memorized a few words, but once I'm looking out over the hundreds of faces, I have to say only what's in my heart.

"I came to Hollywood green as grass. Country. Scared. But determined. And I don't know why or when, but at some point, I thought that if I could get ungreen, grow stronger and smarter, numb, I could really win here. Really be someone. Prove everyone else wrong. And for a long time, that worked for me. I told myself a lot of lies to do it, but it worked. I climbed and climbed. And said I was doing it all alone. That I didn't care about how I did it, who I hurt along the way. What I lost. But it was all lies. All a facade. The truth is that I've never been alone here. Because all of you have been with me. I have the best team in the world. Over the years, they've made what I do look easy, but really, I'm nothing without them. They put up with my crap. With my lies. But I want them all to know that I'm so grateful that they're on this journey with me. Oscar, Pria, JimBo. They're the real Diamonds. I just play one.

I'm really still so green. Still becoming. Still country and scared. But determined to be better."

The crowd has hardly settled back into their seats from standing and clapping when I'm done speaking, before Alex is pulling me back down the steps and away from the stage.

I wave along the way, looking at the lines of faces, trying to find King in his angelic white tux.

Alex methodically snakes through the crowd and right to the back of the ballroom.

"I'm ready," he barks, leading me outside. "Let's go."

"Go? I need to say good-bye to everyone," I say.

He signals for the valet to get our car.

"You've made your speech. That's enough," he growls, tight to my face because there are people standing around. Some watching. "You fucking humiliated me. Let's go."

Alex's foot is hard on the gas sooner than the valet can close my door. The Lamborghini lurches forward and before I can look back to nod an apology for Alex nearly running over the valet's foot, we race out the circular drive and into the night. I look in the side mirror and see a single motorcycle light behind us, a white scarf flapping in the breeze behind it, but I know it isn't real. I blink and it's gone.

"Slow down," I say, pulling on my seat belt. "Why are you rushing?"

Alex keeps both hands straight on the steering wheel.

"Would it have killed you to thank me? Just to say my name?"

"What?" I ask.

"That shit was so fucking embarrassing."

"No one noticed anything."

"Everyone noticed. I was standing there looking stupid. Like a clown," he says. "I've had enough! I'll give you what you want. If you want to be with King, you can be with King!"

Alex looks nervous. His hand is shaking on the clutch. He speeds through a red light and loosens his grip on the steering wheel to turn on the radio.

Techno floods the car.

I cross my hands over my stomach and decide to be quiet. To just sit back and wait until we get to the house. Then that's it. I'm leaving. I'm calling King to tell him it's time. To tell him about the vomit on the floor. The swelling in my stomach.

We begin the climb into the hills with the car moving faster than it had in the city.

"Slow down," I try, but I know he can't hear me over the music.

When we reach the turnoff for the house, Alex keeps going straight up, back into the deep hills.

"Where are you going?" I shout, turning the music off. The wind is whipping up something awful. "You missed the turn."

"I have to get something," he says.

"Get something? From where?"

"Don't worry. I'll have you home in a few minutes, so you can call your little boyfriend," he says snidely. "I'm done with this."

"Alex, I want to go home," I say, looking at his hand shaking on the clutch.

"One stop," he says, turning off the road. "Only take a minute."

We end up stopped on a dirt path leading out onto a steep cliff where cars sometimes park in the hills to look out over the city.

Alex opens his door and jumps out.

"What is this?" I ask. "Why are we here?"

He walks around to my side, reaches for the door.

"Get out," he says, trying to open it.

"I'm not getting out." I lock the door. "What is this? Why are we here?"

Alex looks a way I've never seen. His eyes are so red. His jaw tight.

Instinct makes me fight to stay in the car, but he reaches in and pulls the door open and then me by the dress.

"I want to go home," I plead, spinning out of his clutches.

The lights from the city down the hill are bright but quiet. We're alone. Not one other car is out here. No houses anywhere.

I try to fight my way back to the car, but Alex pushes me so hard I almost fall into the dirt.

"I told you, I wouldn't let you leave me!"

"Please, Alex. Stop it! This is crazy! What are you doing?" I'm frantic. I don't know what he's planning. If he's planning.

I see lights, two white lights on the front of a car bouncing up the path toward us.

"See, someone's coming! You have to stop this," I plead with Alex. "Let's just go."

I wipe snot from my nose and cross my arms, start walking back to the car.

"No!" Alex pushes me back.

The car turns and pulls up right behind the Lamborghini.

"But they'll see," I say, not knowing what I think the other people will see, but knowing there's no good reason for Alex to be holding me out here. "The people will see—" The lights turn off. I see the green hood. The old, green and rusty car.

The door opens.

"What? King? King?" I start running to King. "What are you doing here? I have to talk to you. I have to tell you something."

"I know, baby. I got your text," he says and I can tell he can't see Alex on the other side of the car.

"Text?" I say. "I didn't send any text—"

Alex starts imitating my voice: "King, please meet me in the back of the hills as soon as you can. Turn off at the lookout sign."

We turn to Alex. He's holding my cellphone and laughing. "I see you can follow directions, doctor," he says to King.

"Alex, what are you doing here?" King asks and immediately I see worry in his face. He reaches for me but he's too late.

Alex grabs me by the neck and wrestles me into a headlock. I try to slip away, ease out, but his hold is too tight and then I feel something cold against my temple. It's a gun.

"Oh my God!" I think I'm saying, crying, screaming, but my eyes are locked on King and the sudden fear in his eyes.

"What are you doing, Alex?" King's hands go up. He inches toward us, but Alex moves back.

"Fucking lying nigga! Trying to steal from me?!?" Alex's voice is erratic. Crazy. Like he's possessed.

"Let her go," King demands. He inches toward us again, but Alex goes back some more and we're almost at the edge of the cliff. I can feel the wind from the mountainside spinning up my dress. I can't move. "This is between us."

"No can do," Alex snarls. "I wish it was just between us, but things just got a little more complicated. Right, sweetheart?" He twists the gun into my head.

"What are you talking about?" I ask.

"Oh, now you don't know what I'm talking about?" Alex snaps. "You have a little news for loverboy."

"Alex, man, this isn't right," King says, trying to put calm in his voice. "Let her go. We can handle this. You and me."

"Tell him, Silver. Tell him the news!" Alex shouts.

"I don't—"

"Tell him!" Alex jabs the gun into my head, cocks it. "Tell him!"

"I'm pregnant!" I cry, looking at King.

"Pregnant?"

"Don't worry, brother. It ain't mine," Alex says. "That's kind of impossible."

King looks back at Alex.

"We can handle this. Just you and me," King tries. "Let her go. You don't want to do this, man. Don't hurt her."

"She's not the one I'm going to hurt," Alex says, moving the gun from my head and throwing me into the dirt. He points the gun at King.

"No!" I cry.

King rushes toward him. They begin to wrestle. I hear gravel scattering and falling off the cliff.

"No!"

Alex punches King in the stomach and jumps on top of him. His back is to me, but I can see the gun again. He points it at King's head.

"Try to steal from me! Get my wife pregnant!"

I ease up. Slowly. Slowly. I can't let him take King. I can't.

I jump on Alex's back and reach for the gun.

He spins around and he's too strong. I stumble back, but keep my hands on the gun with his. King tries to get him back, to pull him off me.

And he does. But when he does, the gun is in my hand. And it's cocked. And Alex is falling on top of me.

I don't pull the trigger. But I hear the bang.

Everything stops.

A body drops.

"No!" I scream. "No!"

King is on the ground. Blood spits from his neck.

I want to reach for him, but Alex is standing beside him.

"Give me the gun," he says. "Silver, give me the fucking gun!"

"No," I cry. And it's like I'm not me. Like I'm not here. None of this is happening. It can't be.

I hold the gun out in front of me. Point it at Alex. It's all I can do.

King stops moving.

"I wasn't going to hurt you, baby," Alex pleads. "I just

couldn't let him take you. Not after everything we've worked for. Everything we've built."

Sirens are whispering far off, but getting closer. We turn to look toward the sound at the bottom of the hill.

"Why? Why?" I can't stop crying.

"Look, put the gun down and we can just go home," he says. "We can just go home. Leave here right now. Make it look like something else."

"What?"

"We can go home," he says. "You don't have to lose everything. Not with the baby."

"We?"

"We can be a family."

"Never!"

"You're not going to shoot me," Alex says. "Just give me the gun."

I see him inching toward me.

He reaches.

"Give me the gun!"

This time I do pull the trigger. Twice. *Bang. Bang.*

Alex falls.

I hear the sirens closer now.

I run to King.

"Oh, baby," I cry, falling down beside him. I lift his head up onto my lap.

His eyes are open and looking at me. But he's already cold. Already gone.

"I'm so sorry. So sorry."

I hear tires rolling on the gravel and look out to the road behind the two cars. There's one light.

It stops and I can see it's a motorcycle.

"Help!" I cry. "Help me! Over here!"

The light goes off.

"I'm over here," I call out. "Please help me!"

I hear movement in the darkness and then someone rushing toward me. I can tell it's a woman, even though she's still in her helmet. A white scarf is tied around her neck.

"I need an ambulance," I say. "Please help."

She comes and kneels down beside me. Pulls off the helmet and one long braid rolls down her chest.

"Melanie?" I say.

She doesn't look at me.

"The cops are on their way," she says.

"I need to get him to the hospital." I cry over King. His blood is all over my gloves.

Melanie gets up, looks at Alex.

"Oh my God!" she says.

"I didn't mean to do it," I try, but she's already pulling me to my feet. "What are you doing?"

"We have to go. I have to get you out of here."

"No, I can't leave! I can't leave him."

"But the police are coming. They're on their way."

We look down at the blue and red lights snaking along the winding road up the hill. The sirens are screaming now.

"I don't care," I cry. "I killed him! I killed him."

Melanie picks up the gun and wipes it off on Alex's pant leg.

"What are you doing?" I ask.

"We have to leave," she says. She puts the gun in Alex's hand, wraps his finger around the trigger.

"No! I can't leave him! I can't leave King!"

"Silver, I understand. I know you love him," she kneels beside me again. "But he's gone. And unless you intend on having"—she looks down at my stomach—"that baby in jail, you need to leave now. We can make it look like Alex lured him up here. Like he was jealous. He killed King and then he killed himself."

"I can't, Melanie. I can't leave him!"

"Do it for your baby. Get out of here now while there's still a chance!"

Epilogue

Everyone wants to be famous. Those who say they don't are lying to themselves. Those who say they do are seldom ready for what fame really is. A spotlight shining down on you that makes you think it can solve all your problems. And it can. And it might. But before it gets you there, fame can make everything in your life a problem. Create a world all its own. Turn the show you believe you perform in, to the show you live. To the show you hate. To the show you lose. I don't know why I got on the back of that motorcycle and wrapped the train of that emerald green Balenciaga around my wrist so tight. Maybe it was to protect my baby. Maybe it was to protect myself. Maybe it was to protect my fame.

I held on to Melanie, said good-bye to my great love, and rode into the black night. Into the hills.

Halfway down the back road toward my house, my head resting on Melanie's back, I wondered two things. How did she know I would be in the hills? Why did she come save me? Most of that will always be a mystery to me. I never bothered to ask. Some things in LA just must remain confidential. And others, a secret you never want to know.

Melanie helped me to my bed, wiped my tears and pulled the bloody gloves from my hands. She whispered our plot, the plan, in my ear like a witch. Alex had dropped me off and said he had an errand. I told her about the cell phone and she said it was perfect. My crew knew my phone had been missing. They could all confirm it. Alex took the phone and used it to lure King to the hills. Melanie could confirm when I got to the house. She'd been waiting there to help me out of my dress. Carmen was asleep. We just had to stay calm. Be surprised. If anyone could do it, Melanie kept saying, "you can do it."

"Where are you going?" I asked when she got up from the bed with the bloody gloves in her hand.

"I have to get rid of these."

"Don't leave me," I said. "I . . . I don't want to be alone here."

"I won't," she said. And she wasn't lying. She never left my side again.

The next season, after a flimsy L.A.-style investigation into the hillside murder was buried behind new headlines, Melanie was written into the *The Black and Bourgeois*.

Don't miss Niobia Bryant's

Mistress, Inc.

Available in stores in June 2012

Prologue

"I am standing outside the gated community of Richmond Hills, which has been shocked by tonight's fatal shooting inside one of the community's affluent homes. The police and the medical coroner are on the scene investigating the apparent self-inflicted shooting. The name of the deceased is being withheld at this time, but it's being reported that the shooting occurred in the home of his alleged mistress—just a block down from the home he once shared with his estranged wife. It seems the violence tonight was the culmination of the deceased stalking his mistress after she tried to end the affair. After being distraught by strangling her, he delivered one fatal shot to his head with a 9mm gun registered in his name. A next-door neighbor happened to be walking by when the gun was shot and rushed inside to discover the bodies. And that was an act of sheer luck for Jessa Bell, since her neighbor, who is definitely a hero, was able to perform CPR and revive her, and keep her alive until the paramedics arrived on the scene. She is now in stable condition at Fairmount Hospital. I will continue to report on this scandalous crime as details continue to unfold. This is Maria Vargas reporting for WCBL. Now back to you—"

Click.

The television set quickly faded to black. I didn't really need to watch the news report to know what happened. It was my life—or nearly the end of my life—that they speculated upon and spread the news like the clap in a whorehouse. As if almost dying wasn't enough, now my reputation would get skewered as my sins were put on front street. They might as well slap the scarlet letter on my chest and push me back into the mid-1600s.

Sighing, I turned my head on the lifeless pillow to look out through the slats of the blinds of the hospital room's window. Nothing but the moon or some light reflecting on a huge silver mechanical device on the rooftop of the shorter building next door filled my vision. Not a blessed thing to distract me from my thoughts, my reflections. My sins. My death.

I shivered and pressed my fingertips to the bruises on my throat as a vision of Eric's face filled with anger and murder flashed before me. I shook my head a bit trying to free myself of the vision, only to have it replaced by the brief memory of Eric's blood and brains seeping from his head as they rolled my weak body past him on the stretcher.

Tilting my head up on the pillow, I bit my bottom lip as tears filled my eyes. I closed my lids, but the tears still raced down my cheeks.

I almost died tonight.

That was a chilling fact . . . and I felt it to my bones. Karma is, and always will be, a bitch.

I betrayed a friend to have Eric—*her husband*—in my life. And I learned the hard way you have to be careful what you ask for. The man I fought to win at any cost became my enemy instead of the love of my life. He tried to kill me because I turned my back on *his* half-lies and part-time love.

Again, I saw his face above mine as he tried his hardest to kill me.

I knew that the three friends I turned into enemies would

probably gloat or toast with cocktails given how the tables had turned on me. How being the mistress of someone's husband had almost killed me. Tonight I'd been just a few seconds short of being able to spill all my sins directly to God—or the Devil—and that scared the shit out of me.

You have to change, Jessa Bell, I told myself, forcing my hand away from the bruises on my neck and ignoring the tenderness of my throat as I swallowed.

Releasing a heavy breath, I reached out to the side rail and pressed the button to call for the nurse.

"Yes?" someone said over the intercom after a few moments.

"Is there a chaplain on duty?" I asked, my voice slightly hoarse.

"Yes. Would you like me to call him for you?"

I paused. The end of your life was all about heaven or hell.

"Yes," I whispered, trying to ease the use of my tender vocal cords. "Tell him there is a sinner who needs his help getting saved."

Chapter One

Funerals are all about saying good-bye.

Most times they are a necessary part of seeking and receiving closure. Of course, it's the ending of a life for the deceased, but it's also the closing of a chapter—or in some cases a book—for those grieving. Closure.

And although she knew that it was quite scandalous and bold for her to be there, Jessa Bell felt like she needed to see Eric's body in that casket. Because of him that day could have also been the day people came to either wish her well into heaven or curse her straight to hell. She needed the closure.

And no one was going to stop her from getting it. No one.

Eric was dead.

No one but God or Satan could have him now. Not her and not Jaime.

Jessa released a shaky breath. When she thought about their friendship, she missed him. When she thought about their lovemaking, she could almost forgive him. When she thought about him nearly choking the life from her body with his eyes filled with rage, she wanted to see him slam-dunked straight into hell.

She still couldn't believe she never saw the craziness inside of him. He had always been the steady one. The reliable one.

Even when she couldn't depend on her husband, Marc, because he traveled frequently for business, she knew she could call on Eric.

And after Marc's sudden death from a motorcycle accident, her friend had been her rock. And that had nothing to do with sex and love. All of that came later. Unexpectedly . . . but satisfyingly. As if it was meant to be from the very beginning and they just didn't know it.

If I knew it would all end like this I would never have crossed that line. Jessa squinted her eyes as she looked at the crowded parking lot of the church and then turned her head to take in the small group of news reporters standing outside the fence with cameras rolling.

The murder-suicide attempt had rocked the small affluent town and dominated the news for the past week. Every detail. Every flawed facet. All of it. Even down to the message she'd sent to her three friends, taunting them all about running away with one of their husbands.

There was nothing the news media hadn't dug up from her Richmond Hills neighbors—and her ex-friends—and then spread like manure. Her name and image had been splattered all over the newspaper, Internet, and television.

Thank God they have a good picture of me.

With one last breath, Jessa slid on her oversized designer shades before opening the door to her cherry-red Jaguar to climb out, smoothing the severe cut of the pencil skirt she wore with a sheer black blouse with long balloon sleeves and a mandarin collar. It was the end of summer, but the temperature was still in the mideighties. She suffered the heat with the collar of her blouse to cover the bruises that had darkened to an ugly purplish color.

Pushing her jet-black hair behind her ear, Jessa made her way toward the church on her five-inch heels, tucking her clutch under her arm. She felt some fear and anxiety as she neared the small crowd of people slowly entering the church.

This was a bold and brazen move. She knew that. But there was no turning back. There was no need for shame. Everyone knew. Everyone judged. But she still had to live. There was no need to hide.

I am a victim in all this.

Still, she was thankful that everyone was focused forward and hadn't even noticed her coming upon them.

"Excuse me, Mrs. Bell. Mrs. Bell!"

Jessa stiffened as the news reporter began calling out her name.

"That's her. I know it's her," another reporter said.

A few of the churchgoers turned and spotted her coming up the steps of the church. She notched her chin higher as their faces filled with disgust, confusion, anger, or pure curiosity.

As she neared them standing in the open double doors of the church, the men and women moved back from her, opening a gap between them as if she were Moses and they made up the Red Sea. There wasn't an available seat in the entire church. Standing room only. A murmur rose through the church that was distinguishable even above the solemn organ music.

Jessa's steps faltered a bit as every head in the church turned to eye her. She was glad for the dark shades she still wore as her eyes shifted about the church until they landed on the sight of Jaime jumping up from her seat in the front pew.

Here we go, Jessa sighed inwardly as Jaime made a step but was stopped by her father reaching up to grab her arm and whisper something to her.

Jaime waved him off, pointing her finger at Jessa like it was a gun. "Are you kidding me, Jessa? Are you really this stupid or uncaring or unaware that you would show your face?"

A collective gasp went through the church at Jaime's angry words.

Jessa felt her own anger rise. The scene was uncalled for. "The last thing I am is stupid and these bruises on my neck keep me very aware of what happened *to me!*" she snapped, her eyes glittering like glass as she reached up to jerk the collar of her blouse down.

The mumblings around the church increased in sound and fervor.

"You deserve that and more!" Jaime roared. Renee and Aria came forward to wrap their arms around her.

"Ohhh, look at the besties consoling the grieving wife," Jessa taunted, wanting to hurt her. "If only she was *truly* grieving. Right, Jaime?"

Jaime lurched for her.

Jessa smirked.

Suddenly a strong male hand grabbed her arm and began dragging her out of the church. Bold, defiant, and feeling crucified, Jessa kept her eyes locked on the faces of her ex-friends even as she was escorted from the church and she felt the sweltering heat surround her like a wool blanket.

"Jessa, you knew better than to come here."

She looked up as the church doors were securely closed in her face. She was surprised to see that it was Eric's father, Eric Senior, who was the one to lead her out.

Jessa knew Eric's parents well. They had even attended social functions at her house or she'd seen them at parties at Jaime and Eric's. She'd even imagined the day she would be their daughter-in-law.

Jessa nodded as she corrected her clothing. "I'm sorry that this whole ordeal ended in Eric's death. I just wanted to say good-bye to him, Mr. Hall. I honestly had no plans to say anything to anyone."

"Call me Eric," he said.

Jessa looked up in surprise at the warmth in his voice.

She arched a brow when the tall and silver-haired version

of Eric tilted his head to the side to eye her legs. *What the hell? He's just as crazy as his son!*

"Mr. Hall," she said sharply.

He shifted his eyes up to meet hers.

"I'm sorry for the loss of your son and I apologize for the scene. Good-bye," she said, turning and walking away quickly on her heels.

Once Jessa reached her car and slid behind the wheel, she was glad to see that Eric Senior had reentered the church. She closed her eyes and breathed deeply as she fought to calm her nerves, soothe her anger, and overcome her embarrassment.

"Oh Lord, help me to forgive Jaime, Lord," she prayed, squeezing her eyes shut as she raised her hands palms forward. "Help *me* to forgive *her* and please forgive me for letting her push me to react to her, Lord. Amen, amen, amen, amen."

The chaplain at the hospital had told her to turn to God and call on him when she faced trials and tribulations. She definitely had felt the tribulations of being placed on trial as Jaime judged her.

"Ignorant ass," she muttered

"They trying me, Lord, they *trying* me," she said, pounding her fist on the steering wheel before she started her Jag and smoothly pulled out of her parking spot.

She saw the small press corps perk up as she neared the open gate. At first Jessa wished for any other way to get out, but Jaime's accusations rang in her ears.

You deserve that and more!

More? Any more beyond being strangled into unconsciousness was death. Did Jaime, or even Renee and Aria, truly believe she deserved to die? Who else felt that way?

Jaime shook her head and tightened her grasp on the steering wheel until the brown skin over her knuckles stretched thin. She slowed her vehicle to a stop just outside the gate and opened her door. A microphone was immediately stuck in her face as she exited the car.

Jessa looked into the face of Maria Vargas, the local news reporter who was building her career on the back of Jessa's shame and near death. Jessa reached up and pushed the microphone from being so close to her glossy mouth.

"Ms. Bell, I am Maria Vargas with WCBL—"

Jessa smoothly held up her hand to stop her. "Yes, Ms. Vargas, I'm very aware of who you are. I just want to make a brief statement because I believe the press—including you, Ms. Vargas—has played out the brutal attempt on my life as if it's fiction. As if my life and my feelings are not real," she said, reaching up to use one red-tipped finger to pull down the collar of her blouse. "These bruises are real. That night was real. I almost died. I made many mistakes. I am not a perfect woman, but I did nothing that was worthy of my death, and for people to say 'she brought this on herself' or 'you deserve that and more' is harsh and it's cruel. I was a mistress, not a murderer."

Jessa turned and faced the camera. "I am a victim in this whole crazy story you all are salivating over like a soap opera. For all of you out there wishing death on another person—on me—I'll pray for you. God has already forgiven me."

Jessa's heart was pounding as she turned and opened her car door.

"Has Mrs. Hall forgiven you, Ms. Bell?"

"Ms. Bell, were you hoping to attend the funeral of your ex-lover?"

"Were you turned away from the funeral, Ms. Bell?"

"Ms. Bell . . . Ms. Bell?"

Jessa ignored the rush of questions from the reporters and slammed her door shut, not caring if she took off a limb of one of the crew surrounding her car. She accelerated forward and pulled away, hating that her nerves and emotions stilled stirred inside her, until she felt unsettled and unsure.

She hated that.

Jessa was a woman used to knowing—and getting—what she wanted. But her life had spiraled out of her control ever since she made the choice to have Eric as her man by any means necessary.

She thought of one of the Bible verses the hospital's chaplain had given her to read, once she'd revealed all of her sins to him: *"If there be a controversy between men, and they come unto judgment, that the judges may judge them; then they shall justify the righteous, and condemn the wicked."*

Jessa had never been closely tied to a particular church or religion, but she knew the basics and that verse had scared her. She hadn't thought about pissing off God when she was fighting for her heart. She hadn't thought about anything but believing Eric, loving Eric, and above all, having Eric.

Be careful what you ask for.

Biting her bottom lip, Jessa released a heavy breath and steered her Jaguar toward the entrance ramp for the Garden State Parkway. She used one hand to unbutton the collar of her blouse as she steered with the other. She rode in silence, wishing she could erase the scenes replaying in her mind like an old-school record that skipped:

The first time her husband, Marc, had invited Eric over to the house when he moved into Richmond Hills. *I honestly looked at him like a brother . . . back then.*

The moment that a look shared between them had changed everything between Jaime and Eric. *When Jaime thought Eric and I weren't to be trusted she had been so wrong because that moment came years later and it surprised us both.*

That first kiss they shared in Eric and Jaime's kitchen. *Once we crossed the line there was no turning back.*

The first time they made love, said I love you, or planned to be together. *It felt like we were made to be together.*

The moment she pressed SEND on that text message to Aria, Renee, and Jaime. *They had stopped being my friends long before that. All of them.*

The moment she realized that Eric wasn't moving in with her, wasn't giving up his marriage, wasn't willing to make her his number one. *His betrayal shattered me and I thought it couldn't get worse.*

Until . . .

Eric had begun to stalk her. *I am a grown woman and his insistence didn't fool me into thinking that was love. It was pure craziness.*

And then the look in his eyes as Eric tried to kill her. Jessa shivered from that last memory as she reached up and lightly touched her neck. *Thank you, God, for letting me live.*

Jessa slowed her car as she neared the front gate of Richmond Hills. She slowed to a stop and lowered the window to enter her code into the keypad. The tall, black wrought-iron gate opened with ease and she drove forward, passing the glass-enclosed security booth and giving Lucky, the red-faced portly security guard, a brief nod before she zoomed forward around the curve leading to the clean streets lined with beautiful, stately homes that were worth a quarter of a million or more. Mostly more.

From behind her shades she ignored how the few neighbors not attending the funeral eyed her vehicle as she passed them. *Judging me,* she thought, fighting the childish urge to flip their condescending asses the bird.

Instead, she forced herself to slow down and do a slow roll through the subdivision. She refused to speed through. She refused to hide.

It takes two to tango and Eric was right there dancing with me. And once I ended the dance he tried to kill me.

Jessa's lips twisted as she eyed the large silk black wreath hanging on the front door of Jaime's house. And it was Jaime's house now. Eric's suicide left her to play the role of the grieving, suffering widow.

A bunch of bullshit. Jaime was as full as shit as a stopped-up commode. She probably had her trick, the stripper with the dick for sale, on speed dial for a "good-bye to my husband" fuck after the last guest left her house after the repast.

Jessa knew all about Pleasure. Once Eric had discovered that his perfect wife had cheated on him, he had her investigated by a private detective. He had been more than willing to lay up in Jessa's bed and share the report on Jaime. And the detective had earned every red penny of his three thousand dollars. He'd dug it all up, including Jaime's secret trips to that strip cub for years . . . and the fact that sexy Pleasure was serving up his dick at a price.

It took every trick I had to suck and fuck the anger Eric felt from his wife making a fool out of him.

Jessa sucked air between her teeth and waved her hand dismissively as she pulled her Jaguar into the driveway of her brick and stone French country styled structure. She paused a bit to see a large floral arrangement on her front doorstep. As she climbed from her car and tucked her clutch under her arm, she looked over her shoulder just as her next-door neighbor Mrs. Tuttle, Mr. Houston from across the street, and the Levys all turned away from staring at her. She felt the coldness of their shoulders even across the distance.

It was always easy to sweep at someone else's door. But the problem was there were no real secrets in Richmond Hills.

Mrs. Tuttle's gardener, Hector, was chopping down more than the bushes. Mr. Houston's wife had no clue that she couldn't get his dick as hard as could Yuri, who lived around the corner. And the Levys? Word on the street was he'd backhand his wife like a pimp did his ho if she got out of line behind closed doors.

Everyone has secrets, yet everyone judges.

Jessa shifted her eyes to Renee's spacious and pristine brick Colonial and then Aria and Kingston's beautiful Mediterranean. *Humph. Everyone.*

Turning around, she continued up onto the porch, stooping to take the card from the flowers.

Jessa,

I'm very happy you're okay and I appreciate your grati-tude for my help, but I can't accept flowers or pretend I ap-prove of your role in the entire thing.

Best,

Mrs. Livingston

The flowers she'd sent Mrs. Livingston for saving her life had been returned and her thanks thrown back in her face. The weight of their judgment bore down on her shoulders and hindered her revival. Every attempt she'd made to do better and to be better was being rebuffed.

"Fuck all of you," she said aloud in her husky voice.

With one last look around Richmond Hills, with eyes filled with just as much condemnation as her neighbors had for her, Jessa used her key to enter her home, leaving the arrangement on her porch as she closed the wooden door securely behind her.

DISCARD